'An excellent debut, and [illegible]
have a hard time putting it down'
Candis

'This book got its hooks into us and wouldn't let go.
Hypnotic, with real emotional punch'
Star

'This debut reveals a stunning writer with deep insight
into people. A beautifully crafted and compelling
story that won't disappoint'
NZ Women's Weekly

'Timeless and riveting'
Romantic Times

'The haunting tale is skilfully infused with trauma and
tragedy – and sinister suspense. [A] stirring debut'
Independent.ie

'Storytelling at its very best'
Cecilia Ekback

'[*The Other Me*] will keep you up long into the night'
Ruth Ware

'Tragic, haunting and affecting . . . a truly immersive
emotional experience and a read that you'll
want to share and discuss'
We Love This Book

'Read [*The Other Me*] and enjoy'
Independent

By Saskia Sarginson

The Twins
Without You
The Other Me
The Stranger

The Stranger

Saskia Sarginson

piatkus

PIATKUS

First published in Great Britain in 2016 by Piatkus
This paperback edcition published in 2017 by Piatkus

1 3 5 7 9 10 8 6 4 2

All characters and events in this publication, other than those clearly in the public domain, are fictitious and any resemblance to real persons, living or dead, is purely coincidental.

A CIP catalogue record for this book is available from the British Library.

ISBN 978-0-349-40336-6

London EC4Y 0DZ

An Hachette UK Company
www.hachette.co.uk

www.piatkus.co.uk

For Sara

ACKNOWLEDGEMENTS

It takes a surprising number of people to turn a manuscript into a novel. Many of my friends, family and colleagues have been a part of the process; too many to name, but I hope you all know who you are. I am grateful to everyone who has given me support and encouragement.

In particular, I must mention the following people:

I am lucky to work with Emma Beswetherick, the sharpest of editors, but also the most tactful and kind – thank you so much for your belief in me. Many thanks as well to Dominic Wakeford, Jo Wickham, and the rest of the brilliant team at Piatkus and Little, Brown, London who worked on this book behind the scenes.

To my lovely, clever agent, Eve White, I am eternally grateful. Thank you for fighting my corner and for caring so passionately about getting the manuscript right. And to Kitty Walker for all her help.

I'm grateful, as ever, to my sister, Ana Sarginson, and to Karen Jones, who took the time to read and consider drafts. My thanks also to fellow writers and good friends, Viv Graveson, Lauren Trimble, Cecilia Ekback, Laura McClelland and Mary Chamberlain for work-shopping extracts over lunches at the British Library.

My love and thanks always to Alex Marengo for believing in me while I struggled, and for talking over plots and characters late into the night. Thank you to my children, Hannah, Olivia, Sam and Gabriel, for putting up with my distraction and reading the books. And to Sara Sarre, for editorial insights, making me laugh, and all those years of friendship.

A huge thank you to the charity Walk Free for talking to me. They continue the fight against modern slavery.

www.walkfree.org @walkfree

And last, but absolutely not least, I don't think I'll ever be able to thank Maureen Kellener enough for coming to the rescue with Evie.

It seems to him there are a thousand bars; and behind the bars, no world.

'The Panther', Rainer Maria Rilke

PROLOGUE

You were born just before Christmas. After all that hate, there you were. Being you. Staking your claim. I thought I'd see him inside you. But there was no trace of his features in your small face. You were a stranger to me, a terrifying wonder. We cried all the time. You howling in earnest, and me seeping water silently without really knowing why. It was while you slept that I dared to marvel at you: your spiky lashes wet with tears, the way your toes curled in the palm of my hand, and the smell of your flaky scalp under the surprise of your thick, dark hair. As I pressed my lips to your neck, I felt the tug of my womb contracting, a pain that connected us, a reminder that you were still a part of me.

My mother came to the hospital. She sat as far away from you as she could. As if you were a disease. She kept glancing about her, pulling her scarf over her forehead. She said my father had taken it hard. That it would be best for everyone if I made a fresh start, away from home. After the adoption, my father would write me a cheque.

I watched a film once about unmarried mothers having their babies stolen from them by stern-faced nuns. And if this was a film, the next scene in our story would show how I'd pleaded to keep you; how I'd refused to sign the papers and fallen to my knees as they ripped you from my arms.

But none of this happened. You see, my darling, I was afraid: not just of my father, but of you. I'd destroyed my future by getting pregnant. That's what my father said. Except I couldn't give up on it. That shining future. I was hardly more than a child myself. I wasn't ready to be a mother. They told me a couple had been found. A nice couple. Good, respectable people. I wanted to believe that it was the best, for both of us. I know better now.

I'm sorry.

I allowed them to bear you from me with hushed movements and averted eyes. Soft steps across a floor. Inside I was screaming, but I turned my head, not letting myself make a sound.

I prayed then for you to carry the print of my lips on your cheek, the sound of my voice in your ear. To know that you were loved.

My little one.

You smelt of me, of my insides, my blood.

I didn't give you a name.

Can you forgive me?

ONE

2015

The small circle of my bicycle light makes the darkness around me deeper. I stop on the deserted road, leaning over my front wheel to click it off. Will's voice speaks in my head.

Ellie! You know how lethal these lanes are at night!

Oh, stop making a fuss, I tell him.

I'm your husband, he reminds me, resigned and patient as ever, *of course I want to keep you safe*.

William is a worrier. He's not a chest-beating male. He's the sort of man who winces barefoot over pebbles on the beach, who always drives below the speed limit, who goes back to the house to check that he really did switch the bathroom light off. I roll my eyes at the imaginary Will and he grins in his good-natured way, palms up, caught out again. Secretly, I like his fussing. It lets me be the brave one. The daredevil half of our partnership.

There's nothing to be afraid of out here. I haven't seen a car since I left the village. It's a clear night, and with the beam switched off, the world reveals its shadow-self. Strawberry fields stretch towards distant woods, an occasional farm building crouching against a starlit sky.

I've left my helmet behind; it's a relief not to have the strap yanked tight under my chin. Now tall beech hedges rise either side of me, cutting off the view, looming so high that I may as well be cycling through a tunnel. There isn't another soul on the road. I'm the only human here in the darkness. The back of my neck prickles pleasantly, all my senses snapping into brighter focus.

After I closed up The Old Dairy, turning the sign on the door and waving Kate goodbye, I hooked an apron around my neck and settled into an evening of baking in the tearoom kitchen, making a batch of chocolate cakes and flapjacks for tomorrow.

I like having the place to myself after hours. While I waited for the cakes to rise, I made a cup of tea, peeling an orange and switching from Radio Four to BBC Six Music. Some infectious Latin music came on, and I stood up and experimented with some dance steps, *one, two, three, one, two, three*, nibbling a flapjack, debating whether to be more generous with the maple syrup next time, perhaps add something tangy like apricots.

As my tyres swish along the tarmac, I can still smell the sugar and cinnamon on my skin, even with a March wind whistling past my ears. All around me, invisible life rustles and hunts and creeps. An owl hoots. I'm listening to my own breathing and the sounds of my bike – metal tinkle and air through spokes. I wonder if William's out of the study yet. I hope he's finished with work and is in bed waiting for me, glasses on the bridge of his nose as he tries not to fall asleep over a book, the cat curled at his side. I'll slip between the sheets, scooting over next to him, my cold feet finding his warm ones, settling my head in the familiar hollow of his shoulder.

I'm humming a bossa nova when a mechanical roar sears the quietness. The urgent sound of a car, shockingly loud. I brake and stop, putting my foot to the ground, listening. It's coming from behind, and it's coming too fast. Much too fast.

Instinct kicks in. I'm off the bike in moments and bracing myself at the side of the road, horribly aware of how vulnerable I am, pinned against the darkness behind a bend in the road. The car veers around the corner, wheels squealing, loose stones scattering.

I throw myself into the hedge. The vehicle accelerates past in a flash of metal, the headlights blinding me. Then it's over, and I'm left in the dark, shaking, caught up in twigs and leaves.

The driver had to be drunk. An idiot with a death wish. I frown as I listen to the revving engine fading away. But the noise turns into a sickening shriek, rubber skidding against tarmac. My insides squirm. An explosion rips the air. Then eerie silence.

'God!'

I drop the bike and run towards that empty, spinning quiet. As I round the bend, I see the bulk of the car overturned, crumpled around a tree. A monstrous shape stranded on its back. The moon sheds enough light to show the deep tracks the car has ploughed up the bank, the destroyed fence and furrows of fresh earth leading to crushed metal and splintered wood. I have to force myself to approach, heart jumping at my ribs.

My brain scrambles to understand. I fall to my knees, pushing my way through ripped-up undergrowth and mounds of dirt to look through the upside-down window. The slumped, half-hanging figure has its face turned away.

But I know him, know my husband, even broken and contorted in that dark space.

The stink of petrol is overpowering. Hot metal. Bruised rubber. There's a steady tick and hiss of something dripping. A small, removed part of me is aware of cool crushed grasses under my folded legs. My fingers are already clawing at the door handle. It's jammed tight. A wave of earth has risen and settled against the side of the car, half-covering the glass, wedging the door shut. I clench my teeth, slam my fists against the window. 'Will!'

Sobs open the tightness of my throat. I can't get at him. The front of the car has buckled, pleating as if it's made of paper; and although the windscreen's shattered, my access is blocked by a solid mess of tree and warped metal.

I remember my mobile and run, stumbling back to my abandoned bike. Falling to my knees, I scrabble through my handbag, pushing past objects until I grasp the small, hard shape of my phone. Did I charge it? I hold it up, praying that I have enough signal. With shaking fingers I jab in the emergency numbers.

'Help . . . I need help,' I gasp. 'An ambulance. My husband . . . '

The woman at the other end is calm. She's asking me questions. The authority of her voice pulls me into the world of names, addresses, directions, information.

Back beside the car, I find a stone in the dirt.

'Help's coming. Do you hear?' I hammer the rock against the passenger window, shouting to William. 'Don't you dare leave me. It's going to be OK.'

I smash with all my force, and the glass cracks, shattering

into tiny pieces. Plunging my hand through, I feel a shock of pain. But I'm inside, pushing past the buckled steering wheel and dangling fabric to touch flesh. I need to find his breath. A pulse. I move my hands across the shape of Will's face, press my fingers to his lips. Feel the gap where teeth should be. Touch something sticky. He doesn't move.

Desolation empties me out, bones and muscles sucked away.

I don't know how long I crouch on the cold earth, before my grief rises to meet the wail of the ambulance, a police car following behind. The nightmare scene around me fractures inside a pulse of blue, dancing circles of torchlight picking out details I don't want to see.

I let myself be led towards the waiting vehicles. Someone drapes a blanket around my shoulders. I stand while another person dabs at the blood on my wrists, patches up the cuts.

William was supposed to be at home. He said he had marking to do, work on his book. He said he'd be in the study all evening. Why was he driving through the night like a maniac? I drop my head, exhausted. He'll have an explanation, of course he will. My husband is predictable and steady, and he loves me.

TWO

I move from the bed to the sofa and back again, shuffling instead of walking, unsteady as an invalid. I sit for hours wrapped in a blanket. I'm always cold. My teeth chatter and clash. I can't keep warm. 'It's the shock,' Mary Sanders says, when she brings over her mushroom and chicken casserole for me to reheat for supper. People are being kind, and their kindness makes me weep. I can't tell them the truth. I imagine how their faces would change, and their gestures turn awkward and stiff; how they would pity me in a different way.

I have to feed the animals, have to collect the eggs and put the hens in their hutch at night. They are the reason that I haul myself out of bed every morning. Otherwise, I wouldn't have the strength. The Old Dairy is closed. Kate said she'd run it on her own, get her mum in to help. But it's simpler if we just turn the sign on the door.

Since the police came to see me, I've replayed my last

moments with William over and over, trying to recall any clues I missed that morning. Sunlight made the kitchen golden, blinding me at the breakfast table so I had to turn away, squinting. We sat opposite each other, not talking because he wanted to read a student's essay, something that someone had handed in late. Red ink leaked onto his fingers. When I got up to leave, he didn't look at me straight – his glance slipped over my shoulder instead of meeting my gaze. I didn't notice because I was in a hurry. Now, looking back, I can see that he'd been avoiding me. But he was definite about his plans.

'I'm going to shut myself in the study tonight,' he said. 'I've got papers to prepare and the wretched marking. Sorry. I won't be any company for you, I'm afraid.'

'Don't worry. I'll stay on at work,' I told him. 'Do the baking there.'

He knew I'd say that.

Where did you go, William, while I was mixing oats and honey with my fingertips, pouring melted butter from a pan? What were you doing while I sang along to a Latin song, alone in the tearoom?

I stand at the sitting-room window, the blanket slipping from my shoulders, and look towards the strawberry fields, towards the lane where it happened, where thousands of ruby-red fruit hang from delicate green stems, underneath the protection of glass or inside the white tent of a polytunnel. A perfect strawberry is heart-shaped, luscious, sweet. It's easily damaged. Anything but a delicate touch will bruise the fine, soft flesh, turn the surface dark and rotten. And I wonder if the impact of the crash was felt by all those plants, sleeping on their beds of compost.

The last funeral guests leave. My face aches from having to keep it from crumpling into a howl. I haven't eaten anything all day. I'm not sure if I'll ever want food again. I long to lie down in darkness and close my eyes. Stay there for ever. Instead, I wander from room to room, as if I'm looking for something.

When the doorbell rings, it startles me. I fumble with the latch, yanking it open. There's a part of me that still expects to see William there, apologetic, rumpled, full of anxious explanations.

But it's David Mallory. Owner of the strawberry fields. He has a bottle of brandy in one hand, and in the other, extravagant white blooms billowing towards me – roses, lilies.

'Sometimes it's better to have company, even if you don't want to talk.' His voice is hesitant. 'Tell me to go away if you'd rather be by yourself.'

I push my hair behind my ears, making the effort to rearrange my face into something approaching human, or at least polite. He'd been at the funeral with his grown-up son, Adam, beside him. David had shaken my hand and apologised for Henrietta's absence. 'Another of her migraines, I'm afraid,' he'd murmured. He's done his bit. He doesn't need to be here in his elegant suit, his handsome face signalling respect, proffering that ostentatious bunch of flowers. But of course, if this were the Middle Ages, David Mallory would have the title of Lord of the Manor. He plays the part, attentive towards all his people, the villagers, the common folk. He takes his duties seriously. A part of me is resentful at the intrusion, at the implication that he owes me this visit. Another is grateful for the distraction from myself.

We sit in the kitchen, the smell of flowers between us.

'Those are from Henrietta. She wanted me to bring them. She was very fond of your husband. We all were.'

I stare at the glass cradled in my hand, fiddle with the plasters on my wrists.

'How are you holding up, Ellie?'

It's the unexpected gentleness in his voice that undoes me. 'OK.' Then my face contorts, a hard sob bursting from my throat. 'Sorry . . . it's just . . . I can't believe he's really gone . . . ' I stop, swallowing.

'I just want you to know that we're here – Hettie and I – you're not alone.'

I sniff and find a hanky, blow my nose hard. 'Thanks. Sorry. I'm just . . . '

'I can only try to imagine what you're feeling.' His voice is low. 'It was a shock to hear about the accident. The lanes around here are so quiet at night. I wondered if a tyre had blown, or . . . '

'No . . . '

David says nothing but I feel his empathy; it opens a space for my confession.

'It wasn't anything like that. The autopsy . . . it showed . . . he had alcohol in his blood. A lot of alcohol.' I clasp my hands in my lap. 'He was drunk. That's why it happened. And I just don't get it, because he didn't drink. A glass of wine sometimes. A quick half after work. But he wasn't a drinker.'

I'm waiting for shock or disapproval, disgust even. But David is nodding. 'I remember. He would never accept that second glass.'

He frowns. 'Had anything upset him? Anything that might have made him want to . . . I don't know, drown his sorrows?'

'No,' I blurt the word out, then squeeze my hands. 'Nothing as far as I know. And to get into a car when he was over the limit?' I shake my head. 'He wasn't wearing his seatbelt. I don't understand. He always, always wore a seatbelt.'

I bite the edge of my nail, rip it away. A tiny pain. I'm talking too much. But it's such a relief to tell someone. I just didn't expect it to be David Mallory.

'I'm sorry.'

I raise my eyes to meet his. Steady, blue with a pale ring of yellow around the iris. His gaze invites me in.

'William was the most cautious person I know.' I blink back tears. 'None of this makes sense.'

'I wish I could help.'

I try to smile. Take a sip of my drink. It burns in my chest.

'William was a good man.' David leans closer. 'I'm sure he could clear up our questions in a moment, if he was here.'

My throat tightens. I nod. It's all I can manage.

He turns the glass in his hands. 'Do you remember when you came to supper, just after you'd moved in? Hettie said what a lovely couple you were. How refreshing it was to have new people in the village. Clever, funny, interesting people.' He fixes me with his gaze. 'You were married a long time, weren't you?'

'Twenty-two years.'

'Almost as long as me and Hettie.'

'David, you know what it's like here . . . how people like to talk . . .'

He looks at me.

I swallow. 'Don't tell anyone, will you? About him being drunk.'

'Of course not.' He clears his throat. Looks at his watch. 'I can't stay much longer. Henrietta's still in bed,' he smiles. 'She would have made the perfect Victorian with her nervous headaches.' His brow furrows. 'But she's been getting them a lot recently. I think this time it's more than nerves. I've persuaded her to see a specialist.'

Henrietta and David were the first people to invite me and Will over after we'd moved to the village. 'Just a casual supper,' Henrietta said, 'don't bring anything.' We'd pulled up outside Langshott Hall at five to eight, and turned to each other with raised eyebrows. 'They live here? Looks like something belonging to the National Trust,' I'd joked. And William had ducked his head to look up at the pale stone and shining windows, and given a low, appreciative whistle.

This is a tight-knit community, slow to welcome newcomers. It made a difference, having Henrietta and David's approval. Since then we'd always been included on their party list, even though we're not exactly their set. They go to polo matches, holiday in Venice, ski in St Moritz. But there are always connections if you look hard enough, even between the most unlikely people. It turned out Henrietta's passion is local history. William, as a historian, offered to help her when she wrote a pamphlet on the village. They wandered around the church together taking notes, spent hours poring over old maps and documents. She illustrated the pamphlet with her own photographs, which surprised me. She didn't seem the artistic sort. But William said she had a good eye for composition.

It's easy to misjudge people. And I remember how Will and I had thought David part of the establishment. An Old Etonian, we'd guessed. Completely charming but a bit dense about real life. Not someone you could ever be close to.

David puts his empty glass on the table. 'I'd better get back.' He reaches for his jacket hanging on the back of the chair. 'If you need anything, Ellie, anything at all. You know where I am.'

We stand up at the same time, and I stumble against my chair as I move to shake hands. But his arms are around me. After the first shock, my chin comes to rest against his chest. He smells of freshly laundered cotton, the subtle spice of his cologne. He's taller and leaner than William, his body unfamiliar, but warm and alive. The loneliness of my future washes over me like a cold wave. He gives a supportive squeeze and steps away. I feel unbalanced on my own, as if I'll topple over.

Next morning, daylight falls on dusty carpets, unwashed cups and the pile of unopened mail on the hall table. I can't give in to lethargy any longer, can't ignore life. The tearoom has been shut for too long. I need to get on with living, however hard it is. I'll start with the mail, I think. Fuelled by a strong coffee, I scoop up envelopes and take them into the kitchen to open at the table. It's bills mostly. Some more cards of condolence. I leave the bank statement till last. It was William that dealt with our personal finances, even though I was better at maths. I had my hands full with running The Old Dairy.

The end balance is much lower than I had expected. There must be a mistake. I frown, tracing the figures with my finger, money out and money in. Nothing seems to be amiss, except that the start balance is also very low. Upstairs in William's study, I haul the bank folders out from under the desk. I find my answer in the first statement. Last month there was a withdrawal of five thousand pounds. Cash.

I sit back in the chair and rub my forehead. I don't understand. I dial the number of the bank, and eventually I'm put through to one of the staff who assures me that, no, there is no mistake. The money was taken out by William in person.

I put the receiver down and sit staring at the phone, as if the dead mouthpiece is going to leap up and speak, giving me answers. I switch on his computer and tap in his password. It works. He's had the same one for years. I trawl through endless messages. It's all academic business and run-of-the-mill stuff. Nothing about finances. I don't get it. What did he need the money for? Why cash, for heaven's sake?

His wallet is on the chest of drawers in our room, familiar, battered leather, stained with age. He'd had it in his pocket the night he died. I open it, half expecting wads of notes to fall out. There's only a grubby tenner tucked inside. I empty the wallet, checking through a couple of bank cards, library card, coins, pulling out a few crumpled receipts. Nothing but small purchases. Books. Cinema seats. Petrol.

No new gadgets have appeared in the house. There are no plane tickets falling onto the doormat. Something stirs in my gut. I place my hands over my belly, pressing hard as if I can stop the anger that's growing inside me.

What were you playing at, William? What were you thinking?

I find his battered mobile phone and charge it up. It was given back to me sticky with his blood. Now I wonder if it holds answers. When a bar of battery shows, I scroll through his recent calls and text messages. Nothing unusual jumps out. Messages telling me *Coming home now, W X.* Asking *Anything to eat? Starving.* His familiar shorthand making my throat ache.

Frustrated, I abandon the phone and root around inside the drawers of the dresser, yanking them open, tossing clothes aside, checking right to the back and in all the corners. Rolled up socks. A ball of string. A marble. I open the wardrobe, smelling the warm, musty scent of my husband as I lean into his old tweed jackets and corduroy trousers, slipping my hand into pockets. I find a couple of clean cotton hankies, a button, stubs of pencils, a stone with a hole in.

I don't know what I'm expecting to come across. A diamond ring? An order for a new roof?

I stand on tip-toes to pull down the stacks of old shoe boxes from the shelf inside the wardrobe, ripping lids off, scattering contents over the floor. Old photographs. Unworn shoes stuffed with tissue. Letters from his parents, long since dead, the envelopes fading with age. Academic magazines. I rifle through everything, my heart beating. Nothing. I lie flat on the floor to look under the bed, sneezing at the dust that rises from an old cricket bat, a disused fan heater, a pair of musty walking shoes still encrusted with dried mud.

I stare around me, noticing a water stain on the ceiling, a line of green mould tracing the window sill, a cobweb with a fly trapped in the middle. Things have been rotting around me, disintegrating. I ball my hands into fists. Why did he get into the car roaring drunk? A problem at work? The appearance of a disreputable old friend? Or was he in trouble, and hadn't told me?

Wrenching open the deep drawer at the bottom of the wardrobe containing Will's sports clothes, I pull out trunks and goggles untouched by chlorine. William had never been one for exercise, although his New Year resolution each year had been the same – to take up swimming or running or tennis – and sometimes he'd actually managed it for a day or two before he gave it up, never to be mentioned again. The drawer was really a terrible waste of space. Behind a crumpled, clean pair of track-suit bottoms, there's a bag I don't recognise – a soft weekend bag.

When I pull the zipper its contents spill into my hands like guts. Women's clothes: cream trousers and knickers spewing out of the stuffed interior. I pinch the edges of a cashmere sweater with my fingertips, holding it away from me; a lacy nightdress insinuates itself across my knees, its folds silken and clinging. I push it off with panicky shoves. There's an unfamiliar perfume – roses, amber – as if another woman is leaning close, her breath against my cheek. I've begun to tremble as I poke inside a striped wash-bag, amongst pots of face creams and a toothbrush. I find a hairbrush. Long hairs caught in the bristles. Not mine. None of this is mine. I throw the brush from me with a cry, and it falls with a clatter in the corner of the room. I put my hand to my face, lurching to my feet. Bile rises, filling my throat.

In the bathroom, I grip the rim of the sink, staring at the small dark mouth of the plug hole. I can smell sewers, the foul stench of drains. My forehead is clammy. I didn't expect this. Not William. How could he? I turn the cold tap and lean into the rush of water, splashing my face, slurping from my cupped palms. I feel as though I'm hallucinating, as if everything I've ever known is made of paper and is blowing away in the wind.

THREE

When did Will and I last have sex? Had there been a clue inside that intimacy, inside the way he'd touched me, something different that would have told me that he was seeing someone else? And then I realise. The clue is that I can't remember.

We'd stopped having regular sex. We were comfortable, cosy. We cuddled. We switched off the light and yawned. He'd held my hand under the covers, murmuring goodnight before he turned over and went to sleep. I hadn't worried about it. We'd been married for years. We were content. Our relationship hadn't been based on passion, not even at the beginning. We loved each other. We were friends.

But it was a lie. Our contentment. Our friendship. William had been bored with our life – with me.

The aroma of coffee and freshly baked cakes fills the room. Sunlight slips through the big glass windows, catching the steam rising from cups of tea. The Old Dairy smells and looks as it always has, a friendly, cheerful place to relax and eat delicious carbohydrates. Standing here at the counter, watching my customers sipping their drinks and chatting, it's as if nothing has changed.

'Good to have the place open again,' John Hadley calls over to me, taking his hat off as he pulls out a chair at the window table.

Mary Sanders and Barbara Ackermann are sitting together, having an animated discussion. One fleshy and square, solid in her sense of self, the other tiny, narrow boned, nervous. Mary waves in my direction. 'Two more cappuccinos over here, Ellie.'

I pour cold milk into a jug, zapping it with steam. The liquid sucks and froths. Milk has to get to 140 to 160 degrees for a perfect cappuccino. I texture the top of the drink, and bang the jug to get rid of any bubbles. Then I make two espressos, pouring the milk into them, sprinkling chocolate over the top, swirling it into two hearts.

William is dead.

My husband was having an affair.

The thoughts are inside my head, clashing like cymbals. Irene Morris is hovering by the counter, frowning through her glasses, trying to decide whether to buy a flapjack to take home with her. I'm not listening. I'm staring at Kate instead, as she sashays over to Mary and Barbara's table, bending to place the cups before them. I watch her reach a hand behind to tug at the hemline of her very short, short skirt. She has the slim, muscular legs of a girl who once played in netball teams, and now spends Thursday nights dancing jive.

It couldn't be Kate, could it? She wears purple shadow on her lids and heavy black eyeliner winging out in Cleopatra flicks. Her sartorial style and her frightening make-up habits would have been incomprehensible to William.

Kate turns and catches me staring. She gives me a cheerful grin. Red lipstick glinting. I'm ashamed. Of course Kate wasn't the other woman. She'd never do that to me. Besides, there'd been no sparkly tops or micro skirts amongst the clothes.

I'd thrown the bag and its contents away. Tipped the lot into a bin liner and flung it deep into the dustbin. I'd felt sick letting the fabrics touch my skin. They'd clung and caught at my fingers, leaving a faint scent of perfume and leather. The clothes disgusted me, horrified me. As I slammed the lid, a thought occurred, paralysing me for a second: had these clothes belonged to *him*? Had William been a cross-dresser? I'd laughed out loud. A shaky laugh. The idea was even more ludicrous than my husband having an affair. None of the clothes would have fitted him. They were all size eight.

I close my eyes. Whoever she is, knowing her identity won't help. I have to move on. Such a slick cliché. I have no idea how to put it into action. Why was the bag in our house? Did he bring her there, sleep with her in our bed? The idea is impossible. I can't move on with all these unanswered questions. But without William, I'll never have answers.

The bell above the door trembles, and I glance up to see Brigadier Bagley come in, except this isn't the ex-army man I know, the man with *The Times* under his arm, striding with confidence, immaculate in his tweed suit. This new brigadier stumbles over the threshold and sinks into the nearest chair, hands feeling before him as if he's gone blind. His skin is waxy. I hurry over, crouching beside him. 'Are you all right?'

He closes his colourless eyes and shakes his head.

'Shall I call Doctor Waller?' Kate bends close to the brigadier. 'Have you got a pain in your chest? Are your fingers tingling?'

He stares up blankly.

'What is it?' I touch his arm.

'I've just come from the Mallorys'.'

I can sense Mary and Barbara behind me falling silent, honing in on the drama. Kate goes away and comes back, places a glass of water on the table. The brigadier raises it to his lips, takes a couple of gulps.

Kate gives me an anxious look over his head.

'It's Henrietta . . . ' He rubs his temples. 'I can't take it in. I've known her since she was a baby. Watched her being christened.'

'Has something happened?' Mary's voice is sharp.

She and Barbara have abandoned their coffees to cluster around.

'Cancer,' he says, his voice so low I can hardly hear him.

'How awful.' Kate puts her hands over her mouth.

'It doesn't have to be the end of the world. Is she in hospital?' Barbara is a cancer survivor herself. 'Can they operate . . . give treatment?'

I'm shrinking from the reality of it. I can't deal with any more horror. Brigadier Bagley's chin concertinas into his neck. His fingers tremble on the table. 'They didn't catch it in time. She's being cared for at home. There's nothing to be done.'

Those headaches. I remember David telling me that he was

going to insist that she see a specialist. I caught a glimpse of her about a week before William's accident; she'd been driving past the duck pond on the village green. She'd waved to me, huge sunglasses in place, her profile framed with a sweep of immaculate hair, like a latter-day Jackie Onassis.

I can't believe that this has happened. Henrietta seemed so blessed, so protected inside her gilded world; I'd thought of her as someone who couldn't be touched by ordinary tragedies, by the ugly, cruel things in life.

I make a madeira cake and pick a bunch of flowers from my garden. Outside the entrance to Langshott Hall, I lean out of my window to press a buzzer; tall metal gates swing open and my tyres crunch over gravel up the winding drive to the Georgian house. I've only been here on social occasions when the place was brightly lit and David stood on the doorstep to welcome his guests, a clink of glasses and murmur of polite conversation drifting into the night. Now it's strangely deserted. I stand by the solid front door and rap the brass knocker. The peonies I picked this morning spill over my hands; the touch of their cool, satiny petals is reassuring. I realise I'm nervous.

A dark-haired girl opens the door and accepts my gifts with a nod of thanks. She doesn't introduce herself. 'Mr Mallory. He's not in.'

I feel a disconcerting mix of relief and disappointment. Standing here on the threshold, the cavernous interior of the house is silent. Over the aroma of beeswax and dog, I can smell illness, the sour tang of it, rotting flowers, disinfectant, airless rooms.

On the drive home, I remember how I threw handfuls of dirt onto my husband's coffin, and now I'm afraid David will be doing the same for his wife. Yet only a little while ago none of us had any idea of the disaster lurking in the shadows, waiting to spring like a hungry wolf.

News of Henrietta's death comes just three weeks later. The village is in shock. Tragedy creates a ravenous appetite for comfort food, and the tearoom is packed every day; I can't keep up with the demand for chocolate cake and custard tarts.

The Mallory family have a small, private funeral. A cremation. Henrietta's ashes scattered on the land she'd loved. But when her memorial is held a few days later, there are crowds of mourners. Everyone from the village is there, crammed into the church. Those who can't squeeze into the building stand in the graveyard. I spot one familiar face after another. Barbara sits next to me, weeping into her hanky. 'She was an inspiration to me.' She grabs my fingers and squeezes painfully. 'She reminded me of Princess Di. The beautiful people always seem to die young, don't they?'

Brigadier Bagley reads Psalm 23, his normal parade-ground voice weak with grief; *He makes me lie down in green pastures.* Barbara whispers that the brigadier was close friends with Henrietta's parents, that he'd known her all her life. *Even though I walk through the valley of the shadow of death, I will fear no evil.*

As we leave the church, Barbara clutches my elbow for support. 'At least she was happy – loved. David was always so protective. Do you remember when she fractured her wrist? He fussed around so much you would have thought she was made of china.' She sighs wistfully. 'It must be nice to have someone to care for you like that.' Her hand flies to her mouth, face a mask of horror. 'Oh! Listen to me! When you've just lost your husband.'

I pat her arm. 'It's all right.'

Surrounded by people keeping a respectful distance, David and Adam stand together. Rachel, David's daughter, is dressed in an elegant black suit, eyes hidden behind dark glasses. She leans against her husband for support. I can't see their little girl, Pip. She must have stayed at home. Adam stares at the ground, shoulders hunched. But David faces the crowd, his face tight and pale. His jaw hard against the emotion that he must be fighting to contain. David isn't the sort of man to cry in public. I want to comfort him, as he comforted me. I know how much he must be hurting inside.

Afterwards, I nearly ring a couple of times – but hang up at the last minute, not wanting to seem too familiar. Unlike me, he has his children, his family to turn to. There's no reason why he'd want to talk to me. I didn't know Henrietta as a friend. We were only ever acquaintances.

Over the following months I serve him at the tearoom, and we make meaningless small talk across the counter. The summer season at The Old Dairy is busy, and I'm grateful for the work, and for my exhaustion. Autumn comes, turning the beech hedges gold, my garden damp and misty, rotten apples dropping from the trees in the abandoned orchard. I glimpse David at a distance, in the village, driving past, once or twice with Pip, his grandchild. But we are never alone, and after a while it becomes harder to remember that hug in my kitchen, how close I felt to him.

I spend my first Christmas without William. Kate invites me to have lunch with her family, but I know that spending time in that small house packed with relatives will make me feel even more isolated when I go home. I wonder if this is how it's always going to be, and I try not to cry, not to sink into self-pity. I hardly think about David at all now. He's retreated into being David Mallory again, his veneer of wealth and charm in place, bright and impenetrable as glass.

FOUR

Then after the daffodils have opened and the raw edge of winter has gone, he rings.

'I've been thinking about you,' he says.

I nearly drop the receiver.

'It's been a difficult time. I was wondering . . . well, you've always been so kind to Pip whenever I've brought her into the tearoom . . . I thought perhaps you might like to come with us to the circus?'

'The circus?'

'To be honest,' he's saying, 'you'd be doing me a favour. It was always Henrietta who knew how to do these things. And I think . . . ' he falters. 'It would make it seem more . . . normal if there were two of us there with Pip.'

He sounds nervous. I didn't think David Mallory could be nervous. I hate circuses. I would pay good money not to go to one.

'Of course,' I find myself saying. 'Of course I'd love to come.'

*

And so here I am, oohing and aahing with the rest of the audience as I gaze up to watch a man arching through space, arms extended to link hands with a woman swinging to meet him in mid-air. My stomach contracts as the spangled woman lets go, looping into a shining somersault, turning inside the suspended breaths of upturned faces.

I glance over at David. He's watching me with a serious expression. I swallow, suddenly shy. But then he's bending down to talk to Pip, his hand ruffling her hair.

The noise of children's voices under the Big Top is like a flock of squabbling starlings. Clowns come cavorting into the ring. With a sigh of pleasure, Pip slips her small hand into my own. The childish fingers, sticky with candyfloss, tighten as a clown stops in front of us and aims a hose in our direction. We have ringside seats, and I brace myself for a soaking. The clown's painted smile stretches as coloured paper streamers come shooting out. Pip squeals in delight. David gives me a conspiratorial wink across her head.

And that's it. The moment that gives me hope I could have a life again. I smile back at him. And gratitude, mixed with something that feels like joy, unfurls in my chest.

As the clowns posture and joke around the edges of the ring, men in overalls are busy in the background erecting a large round cage with high sides. The last of the clowns has left, tripping over his big, flapping feet, and the tent darkens, a spotlight hitting the interior of the cage. A man with a blond plait steps into the ring, clutching a whip. A woman skips in after him, one arm raised in a salute. Both of them stand together and take a brief bow. The audience stops clapping, laughter fades. A drumbeat begins.

Pip gasps, bouncing in her seat as a lion prowls into the ring. He's a big male with a shaggy mane growing halfway down his spine. The creature's ribs show through its dusty coat. Pip is transfixed, her thumb in her mouth.

'I didn't think they allowed animal acts like this nowadays?' I whisper to David.

'This is one of the last big cat shows,' David whispers back. 'The whole tradition is on its way out.'

'Good. I hate seeing animals in cages.'

'Me too.' David grimaces.

The lion-tamer cracks his whip, and with a snarl, the lion takes a lazy spring onto one of the stools arranged around the outside of the cage. Four more male lions enter the ring.

All five sit back on their haunches and paw the air, like gigantic kittens playing with dangling ribbons. The audience claps. I glance at Pip, watching with round eyes. Another snap of the whip and the biggest lion gets down into the sawdust and springs through a glittering hoop. The nearest one is twitching the end of its tail, jerking the tufted plume back and forth, its ears laid flat. In a domestic cat, these would be warning signs.

Even though I've been watching, I hardly register when it happens. Substance is transformed into shadow, powering through dust particles, a flight of claws and teeth. The lion has launched itself with a gigantic spring towards the top-most height of the cage. It's landed on the back of the female trainer, all four hundred pounds of it, pinning her to the ground. There is a second where the whole tent is silent. And then, like a wounded child catching its breath, the screaming begins.

The lion-tamer spins around. He lashes out with his whip. The beast crouches low over the body of the woman, and opens its mouth in a roar. The sound is deep and savage; more than a warning; it's a cry of pain, of endless enduring, the cry of something held captive for too long. The whip slices across its back. It doesn't flinch. The other lions on their stools are restless, weaving from side to side. One's jumped down and is prowling backwards and forwards behind the lion-tamer. Outside the cage, dark figures gather around a huge hose; a water jet spurts onto one of the lions, startling him, but the stream of water catches the tamer too, and he slips and falls to his knees.

Most of the audience has got to their feet; some have scrambled over rows of chairs to get further back from the ring. Parents hold younger children in their arms. Yet nobody can leave, nobody can take their eyes off the spectacle unfolding before them. The woman isn't moving. She's a limp rag flung to the ground, blonde hair tangled around her head, one hand flung up as if in submission.

I don't remember seeing another man getting into the cage, but there he is. Tall, with thick grey-streaked hair, a weathered face. He isn't dressed to perform. There's no braid, or gold buttons, or bright capes. The man slips through the fraught atmosphere. He ignores the hysterical tamer, the rushing water and prowling creatures, and moves softly towards the fallen woman and her captor, keeping his body sideways, not making eye contact with the animal. The lion roars. I imagine the hot gale of its breath, the meaty stink of its throat. The quiet man turns slowly to face the lion. He holds out his hand, as you do to a strange dog. The man seems to be steadying the moment, halting the fall into catastrophe. I hold my breath. The lion has its lips curled in a snarl; it slinks forward, ears pricking. I wait for it to spring.

The creature crumples to the ground. I blink, not understanding. It rolls over at the man's feet, showing the softness of its stomach, eyes staring blindly, mane darkened and soaked by puddles. The woman and the lion lie apart, both completely still. With an intake of breath, I see that she's been clawed: angry colour seeps through her jacket, the fabric ripped and stained with blood. The tall man bends close to the fallen lion, his hand brushing the lolling head regretfully, and then he's kneeling over the woman. My view is blocked as others crowd around them, and I notice someone holding a tranquilliser gun over their shoulder.

'Let's get out of here.' David is standing, Pip clasped against his hip, her arms around his neck. She's taken her thumb out, a wet, pink curl by her open mouth.

'Did the lion want to eat the lady?'

David touches her cheek. 'Of course he didn't want to eat her, sweetheart. He was playing a game. That's all.'

David's already muscling his way through the crowd with Pip in his arms. I glance back at the cage, my eyes scanning the people inside, but I can't see the tall man any more. What kind of person dares to approach an angry lion? I follow David, stumbling over an empty drink can, suddenly tired. The shock of what's just happened has drained me of energy. I see the same effect on the faces around me.

David bobs ahead, Pip over his shoulder. I struggle through

the milling bodies and find them outside waiting. An ambulance draws up, lights flashing.

'Will the lady die?' Pip is asking. 'Was the lion dead?' She presses her hands around David's head, flattening her palms over his ears.

'No,' David reassures her. 'The lady will go to hospital to be mended. And the lion was just sleeping. See,' he glances around at me for confirmation. 'It'll be all right, darling. Nothing to be scared of. Just a silly lion playing a silly game.'

I nod.

'Silly lion,' Pip repeats uncertainly.

After settling Pip on the back seat and strapping her in, David opens the door for me. I sink into the plump leather, reaching for my seatbelt.

'I'm sorry.' He hesitates beside me. 'The evening didn't turn out quite as planned. I hope that poor woman will be all right.'

When he's at the wheel, manoeuvring the car to join the jam for the exit, he speaks while looking straight ahead. 'I'd like to see you again, Ellie.'

I'm not sure that I've heard him correctly. I swallow.

He turns to glance at me. 'If you'd like to?'

'That would be ...' I'm fumbling, not knowing how to explain. 'Yes. Thank you. Except. I'm not ...'

'You're not ready. You don't want to rush anything.' He nods. 'I know.' He gives me a steady look. 'But you're a beautiful woman. You shouldn't be sitting alone at home. I'd like to take you out for dinner some time. It doesn't have to be any more than that.'

William and I used to joke that David and Henrietta made us feel as though we should tug our forelocks when they drove past in their Range Rover. I want to rush home and tell Will. '*Guess what . . . ?*'

Tears prick the back of my eyes. Will isn't there. And I'm ashamed, because I know David better than that now. I don't trust myself to speak. I nod instead.

It's like a kind of homesickness. It waits for me here, sliding forward the minute I turn the key in the lock and shut the front door, leaning against it, listening to the emptiness. The cat comes winding down the stairs, her tail caressing every spindle, blinking out of the shadows. I bend to scoop her warm body into my arms and bury my face in her fur. She wriggles, annoyed, wanting to get down, hungry for supper. She opens the small pink cavern of her mouth in a meow, needle teeth glinting, and I remember the dark man moving towards the lion, the woman like a puppet on the ground.

David called me 'beautiful'. I put my hand to my cheeks. My face catches me out in the bedroom mirror. A frown creasing my forehead. Large, slanting bones, freckled, sun-burnished skin. I don't think I'm David's type. I'm not well-groomed; not like Henrietta. I forget to pluck my eyebrows. I almost never go to the hairdresser. My tawny hair falls in tendrils and curls to below my shoulders. Perhaps I should do the sensible thing, get a bob or cut it short. I don't have a daughter to tell me these things.

If we'd had children our lives might have been different. Sometimes one person isn't enough. I wasn't enough. But Will never seemed to want more. He revelled in the peace and quiet of our life; he always pulled a face if we had to go out in the evening. Dinners were his idea of torture. 'Can't we just stay at home?' he used to ask.

I remember one night when we were going to a party, pausing to finger a necklace that Kate had just given me. 'Do you like it?'

'Lovely blouse. Is it new?' he'd offered, mild panic on his face.

He didn't see the necklace. And the blouse was something I'd worn countless times. Compliments didn't come easily to him. I could have been wearing rags and he wouldn't have noticed. It was the person inside he cared about. That's what he always said. He didn't seem to have a flirtatious bone in his body.

I never found out who the other woman was. It must have been a work colleague, maybe even a student. I spent nights awake until sly streaks of dawn crept through the curtains, torturing myself with images of someone who was prettier, cleverer, kinder than me. Then I made myself stop. I took pills. Little white pills that knocked me out as efficiently as a hammer, leaving me groggy and sour-mouthed the next day.

Knowing her name won't alter anything. I've taken down our wedding photograph from the mantelpiece. I've packed every picture, every reminder of him away in the chest at the bottom of our bed: his framed degrees and doctorate, the picture of him in his gown and mortar, the one of us on holiday in the Lake District at the top of a mountain waving into the camera. His lies have given me permission to think about what it would be like to have another man touch me. I'm not ready to be a widow, alone with her cat.

In bed, William's side is a cold slab of empty sheet. I roll into the middle of the mattress, claiming the space, and press my hands over the soft cushion of my stomach. For years I've turned away from mirrors, scrubbed my skin with soap and water, worn practical clothes that cover me up. I was an academic's wife. When Will walked into the pub where I was working, it wasn't love at first sight, but it did seem like fate. He came back, night after night, until I'd agreed to go on a date with him. He was in his last year at Christ's College. Listening to him talk about Medieval Europe, I'd admired his passion. Something about him reminded me of the book about King Arthur I'd read as a child. Not that William would ever swing a sword; it was his sense of chivalry and need to see justice done that was Lancelot-like.

I should have known that nobody is really that noble. Nobody is immune to temptation. I run my hands over the curve of my hips, wondering how they would feel to someone else, exploring with fingers different from William's sturdy ink-stained ones. The thought is strange, frightening. It's only been William for such a long time – and over the years my body has changed. I'm not eighteen any more.

FIVE

1990

Twenty-five years earlier

The twist of tiny balls, coloured in red, yellow, blue and grey look like a muddle of worry beads, or perhaps a complicated game to test a player's IQ. I trace my finger over the photograph of the DNA molecule. A double helix. I close my eyes and begin to recite, 'Hydrogen, oxygen, nitrogen, carbon—'

'Eleanor.'

I open my eyes. Stiffen. My mother's voice comes from the bottom of the stairs. Faint through the door. But I know that wavering, sweetened tone.

'Eleanor, come down and say hello to everyone!'

With a sigh, I close the textbook.

Opening the door of my bedroom, the clamour of voices and laughter in the living room grows louder. My mother's voice rising above it: 'Don't make me come up and get you!'

Mum's face is a pale oval at the bottom of the stairs. When she sees my reluctant fingers trailing the curve of banister, she pouts, moving one hand to her hip. In her other, she holds up a cocktail glass. Shaken not stirred. An olive on a stick. A 007 joke that my father frequently resorts to.

As I reach the bottom, Mum touches my hair, pats with manicured nails at the wild, tawny strands as if they are a disobedient pet.

'My goodness, you do look a fright, darling.'

I smell the hit of gin on her breath, and duck away. 'I'm revising, Mum.'

'Your father wants you to make an appearance,' she says, leaning close. 'Don't be selfish.'

We enter the bright heat of the living room, Mum flinging open an arm, flicking blonde curls back from her forehead. 'Look everyone, here she is . . . dragged out of her stuffy old room to say hello.'

Faces turn, mouths obediently opening in greeting, or caught swallowing crumbs of canapé. The men are all in suits. Their wives, lipsticked smiles drawn on, hovering at manly elbows. It's like being stuck in the Fifties.

'Hello, Mr and Mrs Nicholls.'

'You get bigger every time I see you,' Mrs Nicholls says, as if this is both an accusation and unexpected phenomenon.

'I may have stopped growing, actually. I'm seventeen now.'

Mrs Nicholls laughs, rolls her eyes and takes a nervous sip of wine. The adults, losing interest, have turned back to their conversations. Mum tilts her head flirtatiously, fluttering her hands at something Mr Nicholls says. I wander into the dining room next door. Everything is exactly as it always is: the table glittering with polished glasses, silver tableware, white plates on a crisp white tablecloth; wine bottles open and waiting. It's like a time warp in this house. Nobody would believe it was the 1990s. My parents have dinner parties every week. My father says they're necessary for making contacts and social standing – he works for a big pharmaceutical company. A girl from Impington comes over on her bicycle and helps serve and clear away. Mrs Oaks, our daily, doubles as cook on dinner-party days. But Mum always makes the puddings herself. A trifle and a Black Forest gateau sit on a shelf in the fridge. I know, because I dipped my finger into the cream on top of the trifle, licked and dipped several times, before I patted down the evidence and shut the door.

'Ah, so here's the belle of the ball. Hiding away, as usual.'

I turn to find Les Ashton standing behind me. Tall and broad shouldered, he doesn't have a paunch like most of the others. Les is perhaps my favourite of my parents' friends. He seems to take a genuine interest in me, even if his jokes are embarrassingly risqué.

He pinches my cheek. 'How's the revising going?'

'OK, thanks.'

'And what's it all for, all this work? Got a career in mind?'

I blush. 'I'd like to be a doctor. A children's doctor.'

Les is our local GP. He nods. 'Excellent choice. Aim high. Why not? I know you'd be a wonderful paediatrician. Clever girl like you.'

I clasp my hands tightly, my heart doing little back-flips of happiness.

His eyes move to the doorway and he smiles. 'Jason, there you are. Just telling this daughter of yours that I approve of her career choice.'

My father bends his head; his glasses shine in the candle-light so that I can't see his expression. 'You'll get nowhere if you skulk around down here,' he says. 'Go and get on with your work, Eleanor. This is no time for socialising.'

I open my mouth to protest, and close it again. Les gives me a knowing wink. I turn away to hide my smile. He makes me feel grown up.

In the living room, my mother's voice rises above the clattering conversations. 'Time to eat, everyone. If you'd like to come through—'

I escape, taking the stairs two at a time, sure-footed in the dark. We've lived in the house since I was little. I know every corner. Have spent solitary hours playing dolls' tea parties, making dens in the airing cupboard and boats out of the chest on the landing. The noise of the adults below becomes a murmur, a swelling rhythm like the sea.

I wish my parents could understand that I'm not a child any more. Les Ashton sees me properly. It was he who first inspired me to want to be a doctor. One day I plan to tell him that. Perhaps when I'm in my first year at medical school I'll drop it into the conversation casually, and he'll ask me details about the course, one adult to another, one medic to another.

I was seven years old when I fell off the swing in the garden. I hit the ground shoulder first. The world lit up like a fireworks display, the fizzing pain inside me exploding in a long scream that brought my mother running. We ended up in the local surgery. I couldn't see clearly, couldn't focus on anything except the red agony inside. But the doctor's calm voice became something to cling to.

'You've dislocated your shoulder, Eleanor,' he said. 'The bone has popped out of the socket. Like a ball out of a net. It's nothing to be scared of. Breathe slowly for me, there's a good girl. I'm going to put the bone back into place.'

His hands were steady. By then I was sobbing quietly, trying to breathe like he'd told me to, listening to his voice, his directions. My mother was hysterical. She'd had to leave the room, pressing a hanky to her mouth. It was Les Ashton who kept me calm, who made my shoulder better with one swift twisting wrench, slotting one part of me back into another.

SIX

2015

The hens come clucking as I walk over the grass. They gather by the gate, heads bobbing in anticipation. The latest addition, a brown hen I've named Clover, has shabby tufts of feathers sticking up in clumps; her thin neck is rubbed bare. Clover is an ex-battery chicken. All my girls are, sold off because their laying wasn't good enough. It felt exhilarating when I released them into their new open-air home. They huddled together at first, not understanding they were free, unfamiliar with grass as a substance to walk on. The others have had time to fatten up, for their damaged beaks to repair. Now they cluster at my feet, reckless and squabbling, pecking at my shoes as I scatter grain.

It was Will who helped me bang in the posts for their pen, bruising his thumb with his enthusiastic, inept hammering, who kept me company on the trip to collect them, and poured me coffee from a thermos flask to celebrate.

Walking over to the far side of the paddock, I see there's a rotten maple that needs to come down, and the fence beyond is swamped in brambles. Nutmeg the donkey puts her head over the gate. The pale hair of her muzzle trembles as I rub between her eyes with my knuckles. She sighs as I give her a carrot, crunching thoughtfully. Gilbert, a goose with a crossed beak, hovers nearby, keeping a jealous eye on her. Gilbert was destined to be someone's Christmas dinner. He's not at all grateful for being saved. He's besotted with Nutmeg, follows her around the field like a misguided, reproachful suitor, nibbling on her legs when she lets him, hissing at anyone who dares to try to get close to his girl. I'm allowed to lean over the gate, but if I want to go into the field, I have to tiptoe around the edges or he'll make staccato rushes at me, neck outstretched and wings flapping.

We moved here five years ago, after spending our married life in rented places, travelling from one university town to the next as Will climbed the academic ladder. This cottage with its two and a half acres of land, outbuildings, vegetable patch and orchard of apple trees was the home I'd always wanted, but never thought I'd own. The cottage isn't big. It has low beamed ceilings, and plaster walls that bulge in places. Upstairs, the floors list like a wallowing ship. The bedrooms are tucked under the eaves. But outside there's space. We're miles from the village and there are no houses between us and the horizon.

It was an evening in July when the removal van finally trundled away down the lane, and Will and I were left with the packing cases. We ran through the cottage, whooping like children, until Will cracked his head on a beam. While he sat with a wet cloth clasped to his skull, I poured wine into some mugs unearthed from one of the cases, and we wandered into the overgrown garden, the sky still bright at eight o'clock. We stood together, sipping our drinks and surveying our property. Mosquitoes and gnats flitted around us. In the distance, arcs of white gave off a pale glow, like the reflection of water.

'What's that?' I squinted, shading my eyes from the sun.

'Polytunnels,' Will said. 'Good for profit. But they don't do much for the landscape, do they?'

I frowned. 'Let's just pretend we're near a lake or something.' I turned and examined the friendly, low-slung lines of our cottage, a warm feeling in the pit of my stomach. 'I hope you'll be able to manage the car journey to Canterbury and back every day.'

'Too late to think of that.' He squeezed my shoulder. 'I've had years of being able to walk to work. I've been spoilt. I'd travel three times, ten times as far, to come home to this. And you.'

I probably made some joke then. William was rarely romantic. I always thought I wanted him to say things like that – sweet, sentimental things. But when he did, I found I couldn't respond properly. I must have disappointed him, undermined his confidence.

Had he paid *her* extravagant compliments? Had he given her presents – presents bought with our money? Perhaps she drew another kind of behaviour from him because she was more feminine, less bossy, more admiring. She would never have teased him for being a wimp.

Had he been seeing her then, as we stood in our brand new home? I rub my eyes, frustrated at the never-ending questions, angry that I've let myself fall into that trap again. I've started to wean myself off the sleeping pills. I have to focus on 'now'. Life without William. I have my animals, and the tearoom. I'm due there in fifteen minutes. Kate will already have taken in the delivery of milk and bread, and be setting out cakes under the glass cabinet, cleaning the coffee machine.

As I walk towards the house, something on the ground catches my eye, making me stop. An apple core, caught in long grass. Not from my orchard. The apples aren't ripe yet. I stoop to pick it up. I don't eat raw apples. I prefer them cooked, preferably in a cake. The flesh of this one is still crisp and pale. I can see teeth marks.

I think of the migrant workers that come to Kent for the fruit-picking. There used to be break-ins and thefts, people sleeping rough in doorways and sheds. But David is the biggest farmer around here, and since he's provided accommodation and food for his workers on a caravan site, migrants are hardly seen in the village, and the problems have stopped.

My neck prickles as if I'm standing in a cold draught. Nothing moves, except Nutmeg and Gilbert grazing in the paddock, and the hens clucking gently, scratching at the dirt. Birds wing overhead. I hesitate, glancing at my watch, and walk towards the rough area at the back of our property. I stand at the broken five-bar gate, staring into overgrown thickets in the old orchard. I can't see anything inside the tangles. Then I force myself to open the doors of the outhouses and, risking Gilbert's fury, I move quietly over the paddock to look inside the stable. My heart stutters each time. But the dusty interiors contain nothing except cobwebs and old tools and an empty hay net.

It's only an apple core. It could have been dropped by a bird or a fox. And now I'm late. I'll have to cycle fast.

Kate smiles at me from behind the counter, a cloth in her hand.

'You didn't really need to come in.' She glances over at three customers, lowering her voice to a whisper. 'Think I can manage. I did a couple of takeaway coffees earlier,' she adds. 'David and Adam.' She gives a secretive smile. 'There's something about that man.'

'Which man?' I keep my voice casual.

'Well, both are regular charmers, aren't they? You'd never know David was a grandfather.' She sighs. 'But it's Adam I was thinking of. He's so handsome. And it's romantic, too. You know, him being adopted.'

I stare at her. David and Henrietta had talked about their children and their grandchild many times, in the way that people do, slipping in little bits of information, occasional light-hearted complaints and barely suppressed boasts about their various achievements. Henrietta's eyes always lit up when she talked about her son. I'm surprised that adoption was never mentioned. But then, why should it be? It was a private matter. I remember David carrying Pip from the Big Top, how he'd held her with tender, protective arms.

'Is their daughter adopted too? Rachel – Pip's mother.'

Kate bites her lip. 'I think so.' She blinks at me. 'I wasn't really supposed to say anything. Adam told me ages ago, when we were just kids, teenagers drunk on cider at a party, but he doesn't like people to know. Probably thinks it's disloyal to David and

Henrietta. Don't tell anyone, will you? I hardly know him any more, and I wouldn't want him to be annoyed.'

I shake my head.

Kate smiles. 'We all fancied him. All the girls at my school. When he came back from boarding school, he was a real tearaway. Got in trouble with the police a few times in the holidays. Now he's back at home, a single man. And he'll be inheriting the farm someday.'

'Sounds like you've got plans, Kate.'

She blushes and looks down at her nails. 'God, no. He'd never look at someone like me.'

'Never say never.' I watch her scooping butter out of a large container into dishes. 'You're pretty and clever and funny. What man wouldn't be interested?'

I see the idea slide through her, making her eyes dreamy. But then she straightens her shoulders, tucking bleached hair behind her multi-pierced ears.

'Nah. I've got my man. Pete may be a bit of a football bore. But he can dance, and he's all mine. By the way, David said to say hello. I think he was hoping to see you,' she adds.

I feel my cheeks redden and go over to a table where Mary and Barbara are sitting together over their cups of tea. I pour fresh boiling water into the pot. They hardly acknowledge me.

'Geraniums? Again?' Barbara is saying. 'I think we can do better than that. A bit municipal and predictable.'

Mary sits up straighter. 'No dear, I can't agree. Carnations are municipal. Geraniums are robust, joyful.'

'Really? I've always thought they were common things.

And don't you dislike their smell? Musty, I've always thought. Reminds me of cat pee.'

The two women sound polite, but they don't fool me. Underneath their civilised exteriors they're heaving with rage. All the locals ever seem to talk about is the approaching Best Kept Village in Kent competition. We lost out last year to Bidborough, and this year the community is united in their determination to win back the award. Signs on the village notice board order *Don't Forget Edges and Hedges!* and *Pick It Up! No Litter Here!* There are endless meetings to discuss the pros and cons of hanging baskets, the positioning of benches, and which verges need white stones placed upon them to prevent tractors ripping up the turf.

Mary would keel over in shock if she saw the wild grasses and piles of dead wood on my land, the tangle of brambles and rampant mare's tail in the orchard. It's lucky that I'm too far out of the village to risk offending any of the visiting judges.

I console myself with the thought of all the bugs and butterflies that thrive here. There's nowhere for an insect to hide in the village's immaculate gardens.

I'm refilling the water trough in the paddock when I hear a sudden rush of feathers and frightened squawking coming from the far hedge, and know that the cat is after the pigeon's nest in the fir trees. I run in the direction of the noise, wading through long grass towards the disused orchard and the tall, dark trees beside the hedge. The noise has fallen into silence and when I call her name, Tilly comes trotting out of the undergrowth, tail fluffed up and eyes half closed in desire. No feathers in her mouth. 'You leave them alone.' I bend to stroke her. Something catches my attention. A hunched shape at the foot of the rotten maple. I go closer. It's a rucksack, stranded on its back like a giant beetle. I press my hands over my mouth. Someone *is* here. I stare around me, eyes swivelling left and right, flicking across familiar territory.

I don't have my mobile on me. It's sitting on the kitchen table. Or it's in my bag. Probably out of battery. I take some deep breaths. Who would I call, anyway? If a migrant worker or a passing tramp has decided to spend a night under one of my trees, it's not a matter of life or death. He or she will move on. I'm lucky enough to have a home, a bed. I've read about the migrant and refugee crisis in the papers, the arguments for keeping them out, and the arguments for letting them in. When I see the photographs of weary faces staring through wire, I always think it could have been me – it's only by chance that I was born in the right place, in a safe country. This is all true, but it doesn't stop my heart from pounding.

Darkness moves, and the shape of a man materialises out of the shadows on the other side of the field. Adrenaline kicks in my veins. He's tall, wide-shouldered. I step behind the tree out of sight. My heart rate has increased to a frantic battering. After a moment of holding my breath, I dare to peer around the edge of the bark. He's too far away. The sun is behind him. I can't see his features.

He bends and then straightens. He has something in his hands. White flowers from my lime tree. His hair flops over his face as he looks down at his haul. He prowls rather than walks, with a slight lurching gait, bear-like. He passes by close enough for me to see more of his craggy face, and then disappears through the five-bar gate, into the tangled wilderness of the orchard.

I look down at the rucksack. It must belong to him. Worn canvas sides strain around its contents, misshapen and swollen, stuffed too full. There's a darned patch, the colour of the thread a darker green. Neatly done. The outer flap is fastened with twine. I finger the leather strap, slipping my hand into an outer pocket.

A rough cough sounds behind my shoulder. I yelp, twisting my head to stare up. His face looms close to mine. The trespasser. I smell sap and earth. The sweet scent of lime. His eyes hold mine in an accusing stare, brows scrunched into a frown.

He steps back. 'I'm not going to hurt you. That's my bag.'

I stand on shaky legs, folding my arms. 'You need to leave. Now. Or I'll call the police.'

'There's no need.' He's still holding the flowers. 'I just want to get my things.'

But he doesn't move. He stares at me, as if considering some difficult question. I wish I hadn't left my mobile in the house. I don't think I could outrun this man. He's lean, with sunburnt skin tight over his bones. A nose that must have been broken at least once. Dark hair that's streaked with grey, thick and grizzled, covering the collar of his weathered leather jacket. Workmanlike clothes. Sturdy boots with mismatched laces, and a Swiss Army knife in a sheath on the belt of his jeans. I have an odd feeling that I've seen him before.

'For tea,' he says, offering the lime petals. 'Have you had linden tea?'

I frown. 'They come from my tree. You're trespassing and stealing.'

'I didn't think anyone was here,' he says. 'No car in the drive, and the place was locked up. Thought it might belong to weekenders. I was going to spend the night in the rough, over there.' He jerks his head behind him.

'But you must have known it was private.'

'I figured I wouldn't be hurting anyone.'

'And the animals. Who did you think they belonged to? It's obvious the place isn't deserted.'

He sighs. 'I didn't say it was deserted. The animals could belong to anyone. Someone with this much land might rent some out to other people who need it. Look,' he rubs his forehead, 'I'm sorry for trespassing. It was just for one night. I'll be on my way.'

His English is faultless. The slight accent hard to place. A mix of Eastern European and American. He bends down, and as he stoops to retrieve the bag I have a better look at his profile.

'You were at the circus the other night!' I exclaim. 'In the ring. With the lions. You saved her – the woman on the ground.'

'Maria.' He settles the rucksack on his shoulder.

'For a moment I thought Maria was going to get eaten.'

'He wasn't going to eat her. He was frustrated.'

'Well, it was pretty terrifying.'

Knowing that this was the man in the cage, the one who saved the day and quite possibly Maria's life, it's a bit like meeting an actor from a favourite film. Suddenly, I feel more relaxed. There's a connection.

'Aren't you with the circus any more?'

He shrugs. 'The lions have gone.'

'You looked after them? That's why you were there?'

He nods.

'And now?'

'I'll look for some work. I can turn my hand to most things. Then,' he gives a lopsided smile, 'I'll move on again.'

Questions form on my tongue. But something tells me not to ask. He wears his privacy like a badge. 'Try the Mallory fruit farm,' I offer instead. 'It's worth asking there. They might be taking on extra pickers around now.'

He narrows his eyes. 'I will.'

I begin to turn away, and stop. 'You can stay in the orchard tonight. If you need to. Just for one night.'

'Thank you.'

I hesitate. 'How did you know,' I ask, 'how did you know I was here, behind the tree?'

'I saw you come out of the house, watched you find my bag.' He gives me a sidelong look. 'Thought I'd better keep an eye on my stuff.'

'I would never—' I stop, remembering my intention to examine the contents of the rucksack, my hand in the pocket.

I walk towards the house, aware of him behind me. I straighten my shoulders. I realise that he must have been observing me as I went about my chores, turning the tap and filling the trough, talking to the hens, scattering corn, scratching my head. How long had he been watching me? I falter. And why was he so sure that the place was locked? Had he tried the doors? I'm isolated here. I don't like the idea of strangers testing my doors, peering through my windows.

I hope I've done the right thing. Letting him stay. I don't even know his name. I turn and glance back, needing another look, some reassurance, a smile or wave. But there's nobody there. He's disappeared. And I think of a wild creature, how you can see them standing on the edge of a forest or jungle, but one blink and they are gone.

SEVEN

Standing at my bedroom window, I stare into folds of impenetrable darkness, waiting for moonlight to pick out shapes, even though I know I won't be able to see him from here. The orchard is hidden behind the stable roof. From across the fields comes the eerie high-pitched scream of a vixen. I wonder if he's lonely, frightened. Then I shake myself. He's a giant of a man, well into his forties, maybe older. He's out-stared a lion. He isn't going to be afraid of the dark. He's obviously used to sleeping rough: that backpack spoke of long journeys.

I've checked all the locks on windows and doors, just to be on the safe side. I'm not a complete idiot. I might have been impressed by my wild camper's ability to calm angry lions, but that doesn't mean I'm going to make myself vulnerable to a stranger – because that's what he is. My initial flush of familiarity has worn off, leaving me feeling the first doubts. He had a knife on his belt.

He'll be gone by tomorrow, I reassure myself. I've always followed my instincts about people. But I was wrong about William, the other voice reminds me, and there was another mistake a long time ago. I screw up my eyes – I can't think about that.

I reach out to take a pill; my thoughts are churned up, my nerves raw, and I don't want all those unanswered questions about William invading my head. But what if I need to be alert in the middle of the night? I can't take a sleeping pill while there's a strange man sleeping in my garden.

I wake, thick tongued, heavy limbed. I think I drifted off in the early hours of the morning. It feels as though I've been bashed over the head with the cricket bat I keep under the bed. I raise myself onto my elbows, rubbing my eyes. Through half-drawn curtains I see the splatter of rain drops on glass. Then, with a small shock, I remember what happened yesterday, and struggle free of the covers. Standing at the bedroom window again, this time I find myself looking out into watery daylight at a bedraggled garden, sodden lawn, and puddles forming in the paddock. Nutmeg standing with her rump to the wind. No sign of my visitor. He'll be drenched. Maybe I should offer him a place to get dry. Even a coffee?

I pull on my wellingtons and coat and splash outside. I make my way through long, wet grass, slowing as I enter the brambly depths of the overgrown orchard. It's muddy underfoot, and I push my way gingerly through bushes, holding back trailing creepers, avoiding sharp thorns.

'Hello?'

There's no answer, just the flutter of wings and the sound of rain on leaves. A thrush on a branch ruffles her feathers against the wet and trills loudly. I edge my way between trees, looking for signs of someone having slept here. There's nothing. No ashes in a cold circle, no beaten area of grass. I wonder how he could have spent a night and not left a trace.

Maybe the rain drove him away. Maybe he hasn't been here at all. I need to feed the hens, let them out and collect the eggs. Outside their hutch is a neat nest of damp moss, and placed in its soft interior are six eggs. He must have collected them earlier this morning. I bend down and touch the smooth shells, wondering if he took one for himself.

The rain has stopped, and someone in yellow oilskins and a matching sou'wester is painting swatches of colour onto the lamppost newly erected in front of the village shop. When I get closer, the figure turns her head and I recognise Mary's determined face. She was in charge of the committee that lobbied the council to have the lampposts changed, and I have to admit they are much prettier than the stark modern ones we had before. Mary has dabbed patchwork squares of black, green and grey onto the metal.

'We'll be taking a vote on the final colour at the meeting tonight,' she tells me. 'Time is running out. We really have to get our skates on if we're going to be ready for the judging.'

I squint at the swatches. 'I like the black best.'

'Really?' Her expression is unconvinced.

I smile to myself as I push open the shop door. Somehow I don't think she'll be passing on my vote.

It's Sally-Ann at the till. She's usually more interested in filing her nails and gossiping than serving customers and I'm in a hurry. I need to get the extra milk supply back to the tea-room. By the time I've grabbed the things I need, she's ringing up another shopper's items. They are chatting in low voices, but as I wait in the queue with my wire basket heavy on my arm, they fall silent. I recognise the back of John's balding head, his tweed jacket.

'Oh, hello Ellie. Have you seen this?' Sally-Ann asks me as she jabs her finger at a newspaper spread out on the counter.

The photograph appears to have been taken from a helicopter. It shows a line of bumper-to-bumper lorries. Miles of miserable traffic. Stick-figure people seem to be running alongside the vehicles. There's a close-up shot of a man trying to open the doors of a lorry.

'Terrible, isn't it?' she says.

'I know.' I shift the basket to my other arm. 'All those poor, desperate people.'

'The migrants?' Sally-Ann raises her eyebrows. 'It's the lorry drivers I feel sorry for. It says here that this lot are out of control, marauding. They carry knives. Bang on the drivers' windows. Try to climb inside, underneath, even on top of the cab. I'd be freaking out. Can you imagine? All those drivers want is to get the job done, so they can have their dinner, get back to their families.'

'Well, yes,' I say carefully. 'But we don't know what awful things the migrants have had to go through. Some of them are refugees running from war, horrible atrocities, poverty. Nobody leaves their home if they don't have to.'

John is shaking his head. 'The thing you have to ask yourself is this: why is it our government's fault that these people only want asylum in England? I mean, why isn't Hungary or Albania good enough for them?'

Sally-Ann frowns. 'They know they'll have an easy life if they can get into England. With our welfare system and the National Health and everything.'

I clear my throat. 'Sorry, I'm in a bit of a hurry. Do you think you could ring these up for me, Sally-Ann?'

She begins to scan in my shopping slowly, her eyes sliding back to the photographs in the paper.

John clears his throat and turns to me. 'I wouldn't be fooled by sob stories if I were you.' He adjusts his hat. 'Ask yourself this – how many Islamic fanatics do you think are hiding amongst that lot?'

He leaves the shop, the bell jangling behind him.

Sally-Ann gives me a horrified look. 'Blimey. He's got a point there. That's a scary thought.'

I can't let myself get upset. What did I expect? William always said that this was one of the drawbacks of living deep in the country, inside a small community of mostly retired people. They all feel they've worked hard for the privileged life they lead. They don't want it upset or threatened by people they view as 'foreigners'. Will and I agreed to stay clear of the quagmire of politics, never to discuss it with our new neighbours.

'We moved for the space and the peace,' Will said. 'Let's keep the peace by keeping our heads down and enjoy all our lovely space.'

We had acres of our own, and we were surrounded by beautiful countryside. The village itself is marked in all the guide books as a destination: narrow streets are lined with timbered buildings; mullioned windows overlook a pretty square where pansies sprout from cattle troughs. There's a duck pond on the green. There's even a castle. And Thomas Becket's bones once rested at the Norman church. We couldn't believe our luck. We weren't going to let a few suspect political opinions spoil our joy.

But my upset is turning to anger with myself as I walk along the pavement towards the tearoom. Cartons of milk in two heavy bags swing against my calves, pointy edges jabbing at me. I held myself back from speaking out for my own selfish reasons. I didn't want the hassle of going through an argument I knew I wouldn't win. And I need these people. They are my neighbours, my customers. I can't afford to antagonise them.

Up ahead of me I see a familiar figure. He's walking away from me with that loping gait, his battered rucksack on his shoulders. I hurry to catch up with him, the bags banging onto my legs, the plastic cutting into my fingers.

'Hi,' I call out, breathlessly.

He stops and turns.

'How did it go at the fruit farm?'

He shrugs. 'No work.'

'Oh, I'm sorry.'

I see that he has dark rings under his eyes. It feels as though his lack of a job is somehow my fault. I put a finger between my teeth, thinking. 'I have some clearing that needs doing.'

'Clearing?'

'Brambles, mostly. A couple of fences want repairing. There's a tree that needs to be chopped down, too.'

Out of the corner of my eye I notice two people on the pavement opposite, standing still, their gaze turned towards us.

He nods. 'Sure.'

'But I'm out today. I won't be home till around six.'

'I'll come tomorrow morning then.'

His direct manner is unsettling. I incline my head in agreement. 'Where will you go now? Tonight?'

'You don't have to worry. I'll be there tomorrow. Eight o'clock?'

'It's quite a walk ...' I begin, before another look at his well-worn boots and rucksack reminds me that this man is used to covering distances.

'Ellie. Ellie Rathmell.' I introduce myself, wondering if we should shake hands.

'Luca,' he says, giving me a long stare. He places his hand on his heart.

As I turn back towards the tearoom, I see that the watchers on the opposite side of the street are Irene and Barbara. I call out a greeting, but they duck their heads as if they can't hear me.

EIGHT

At five to eight the next morning, Luca is waiting outside my door. I stumble down the stairs, dishevelled, barefoot in jeans, my hair unbrushed. Tilly purrs at my feet, curling herself around my legs as I turn the handle, nearly tripping me up as I step forward. A light rain is falling in a silent mizzle. His hair is silvered with misty wet. He's hunched over, collar up, a hand cupped around a cigarette. I usher him inside, wondering where he spent the night.

He licks his fingers and carefully pinches the cigarette out, slips it into his pocket as he crosses the threshold. He has to stoop under the beams. I lead him into the kitchen and put the kettle on, taking down two cups. I presume he's had no breakfast. But he shakes his head.

'I'll get on, if you show me where to start.'

At the door I fumble with the zip of my coat, then I'm at the ungainly disadvantage of having to hunch over, bottom in the air, hair flopping into my face as I shove my feet into wellingtons. I catch the smell of him: nicotine on his breath, earth and mulch, and damp, smoky fabric.

We walk over to the field together, and I'm aware that he has a slight limp, the drag of his left leg. That explains his odd movement.

'Tools are kept in the shed next to the stable,' I tell him. 'There's a ladder in the garage. If you can't find what you're looking for, just ask.'

He unlatches the gate to the paddock. I open my mouth to warn him about Gilbert. But the goose comes flapping around the corner before I get a chance. His crossed beak is snapping and hissing, wings spread wide, beady eyes alight with indignation and rage.

Luca doesn't flinch. He walks on calmly. But as Gilbert goes to attack his legs, Luca bends down and grabs the outstretched neck in one hand, fingers clamping like manacles. Immediately, the goose goes slack, soft bellied, limp. For one terrible moment, I think Luca is going to snap Gilbert's snowy neck. Instead, he pins the bird's wings to his side with his other arm, scoops him up and deposits him in the stable, shutting the door.

I suppose a goose is easy to deal with after facing a lion. I open the shed door, and watch as he picks out secateurs, a saw and a scythe.

'Did you work with the lions for long?'

He tests the edge of the saw with his thumb. 'I'm not a lion-tamer. I looked after them.'

'You must have been upset when they were taken away.'

He's rummaging inside a wooden box on a shelf. 'Do you have a knife sharpener?'

I scratch my head. 'Not sure.'

He begins to hunt through the rest of the untidy shelf. 'The lions went to a safari park. They'll have a better life there. They should never have been taken by the circus in the first place. Animals aren't here for our amusement.'

I feel a prickle of injustice. 'I know that.'

'But you still came to see them.'

'I came with a friend and his child because I was invited. I didn't even know the lions would be there. I . . . '

His mouth remains tight. He continues to rummage amongst the old, rusty tools. I'm not sure if it's the state of the tools or me attending the circus that's offending him. I take a steadying breath. I don't have to justify myself to this man. But I want to prove to myself as much as everyone else that I've done the right thing in employing him.

'And that's why you left?' I ask in a tone that I hope suggests friendly interest. 'Because your job ended?'

He shrugs. 'My job ended when I fell from a trapeze years ago. I damaged my leg. I stayed because of the lions.'

'Oh . . . I'm sorry.'

'Don't be. I'm lucky to be alive.'

I hesitate for a moment, but he doesn't elaborate. Under the beaten-up leather jacket, the broad lines of his body are visible. I remember those trapeze artists that had impressed me in the Big Top. The fearless way they'd sliced the air, turning somersaults above my head.

I can ask him to leave any time I like, I remind myself. I go back to the house, pausing to scratch Nutmeg's rump. From behind the stable door I hear Gilbert's subdued honking.

I'm a baker that likes to get her hands dirty, the kind that ends up with dabs of sugar on my forehead, chocolate on my chin, pale handprints on the pockets of my jeans. I love the soft rub of flour between my fingers, the crumbling texture of dough, the grit and shine of demerara sugar, the way that marzipan gives as I roll it, thick and gleaming on the board. Even when I'm cooking in big batches, I'm still caught up in the pleasure of how the alchemy works to transform simple ingredients into something else, something divine, dense with flavour and complex layers of taste.

I can lose myself inside the process of baking – cakes, muffins, biscuits, macaroons, gooey, crunchy, light, sticky – I'm constantly refining my recipes, trying out new ones, reinventing classics. There's a science to it that appeals to me. I'm making Victoria sponges today. They're a favourite with customers. You can't do anything too clever with them; it's the way the tang of jam and richness of cream complements the mellow, light sponge that makes them work. The cake is the backdrop. Ingredients have to be the best.

I'm beating butter and caster sugar, whizzing it in the machine, when Luca's face appears at the window. Startled, my hand opens. The egg I'm holding falls. It splatters at my feet, fragments of shell, brilliant yolk, and gooey albumen splayed across my shoes and the tiles.

He's apologetic when I open the door. 'I did knock . . . '

I wave my hands. 'My fault. It was too noisy to hear you.'

He's got rid of his jacket and rolled up his shirt sleeves. His forehead is damp, and I catch a sour whiff of perspiration. He offers me back the empty plate and stained mug from the cheese sandwich and cup of tea I'd taken him at lunch.

'Do you want to see what I've done so far, let me know if it's what you wanted?'

I dust flour from my fingers, wiping them on my jeans, and take off my apron. 'By the way,' I pause, shrugging on my coat. 'I was wondering if you'd heard anything about the injured woman. Maria – is she OK?'

He pulls his eyebrows together, shakes his head.

'Oh, I thought you would have heard something by now.'

'We weren't friends. We had very different opinions.'

He's cut back nearly all the brambles and hauled them into a pile, and made a start on the tree, cutting down the top-most branches and hacking them into rounds. The stable door stands open. Gilbert is shadowing Nutmeg at the other side of the field as she grazes. I'm not sure if it's my imagination, but the goose seems embarrassed. Luca follows my gaze and his mouth twists in a smile.

'We know where we stand now. Him and me.'

Relief lifts my heart like a sail in the wind. Luca is a hard worker. He's done more in one day than I could have achieved in a week. I want to seize his hand and squeeze it in gratitude. It will take another day to finish the job, though.

I think of the empty garage.

'Would you consider staying for a night or two? To finish the job?' I hurry on, 'My garage is empty. I could rig up a camp bed, get you some bedding. There's running water. A sink. And there's an old outhouse behind the cottage. It used to be the privy before we put in the indoor bathroom. I can include your meals in the payment if you like.'

He takes out a cigarette and cups his hands around the strike of flame, dips his head and inhales. He lets out a stream of smoke, and nods.

I fetch clean bedding from the airing cupboard. He helps me drag the camp bed down from the attic. There's an old electric fire that will take the chill out of the stale air in the garage. I flip the switch on the wall and one bar of crackling fluorescent glare ignites in the rafters; it's not exactly homely, so I find a spare side light, and with the help of an extension lead, I plug it in next to his bed.

We stand back to admire the finished room.

'Well, it's not the Ritz,' I say, uncertain now that I'm doing the right thing. Who wants to sleep in a garage? And once he's installed, will I ever be able to get him to leave?

I'm surprised by the sound of laughter. A deep belly guffaw. I gaze up into his face, seeing the lines of it soften, his eyes glistening. The laugh becomes a cough, and he shakes his head, covering his mouth with a hand.

'If you've ever slept rough, this is as good as the Ritz. Believe me.'

I bring over a tray of soup and bread, a glass for water, a packet of biscuits and a banana, and he receives it from me with careful hands, a cigarette jammed in the corner of his mouth.

'Goodnight,' I say.

He sets the tray down on the floor by the camp bed. The side light is on. It throws long, leaping shadows across the big, draughty space. The floor is cold concrete. I should have brought a rug out. I think of his cough.

But he's closing the door. 'I'll start early,' he says. 'Don't worry about breakfast. I don't eat it.'

I move from room to room in the lit-up cottage pulling curtains and blinds. With no neighbours for miles, I've never been in the habit of shutting out the night. But I'm aware that Luca might be wandering about in the darkness. Every time I pass blank panes of glass, I catch the blur of my own reflection and give a start. Getting ready for bed, I turn off the overhead light in my bedroom and stand in the shadows peering down at the one small window in the garage. I can't see anything. I draw my curtains with brisk tugs.

I wonder what he's doing, if he's comfortable, what he's thinking. I've never met anyone with a more inscrutable face. He's like one of those old-fashioned anti-heroes in a Hollywood film – a James Dean or Marlon Brando with a cigarette dangling from a sneering mouth, too macho to string a sentence together or show his feelings.

Before I get into bed, I tiptoe downstairs in my pyjamas, my bare feet soundless, and slide the bolt shut on the back door, turn the key in the lock. Tilly meows, making me start. I find myself whispering to her. I don't even know his nationality, if he has a family, a prison record.

I can picture Will's expression, his concern, his impatience with my impulsiveness.

Luca risked his life to rescue someone he didn't even like. He's a hero. I pull the covers up and push my face into the pillow, shutting my eyes, screwing my fists into them until sparks jump.

I can't sleep. I have some pills left, but I don't want to take them. I start to name all the collective nouns I can think of, something that used to work for me instead of counting sheep: a mischief of mice; a murmuration of starlings; a pomp of Pekingese.

I fumble in my bedside drawer, finding the packet, placing two little tablets on my tongue.

NINE

1990

The party is full of drunken couples swaying to the sound of Elton John singing 'Sacrifice'. My face is pressed into Ed's shoulder, his arms around me. It takes me a moment to register the hard swell prodding my leg. I jerk away, face flaming.

'Bloody hell,' I say to Julia later in the girls' loo. 'He had this huge hard-on. It was such a shock.'

Julia is admiring her new bleached Madonna haircut. She leans across the wash basin to roll Kissing Potion onto her lips. 'Yeah, right,' she drawls. 'Such a shock.'

I ball some tissue and throw it at her. 'Oh, shut up! You know what I mean!'

I don't know if he'll want to spend any more of the evening with me now. But Ed is waiting outside the powder-room door.

'Let's get out of here,' he says.

We stumble outside, laughing. Standing next to each other

in the cool spring air, his laugher ends in a snort. Our earlier embarrassment hangs between us. I wipe my eyes. Ed leans against the wall and rolls a joint. My heart skids through a couple of beats.

'Want to go for a walk?' he asks, striking a match and dipping his head towards the flame.

My chest tightens, and I nod, accepting the joint from him, breathing it in carefully so that I don't cough.

I'm preparing myself for his kiss, when Julia and Mark turn up. We gather together in a huddle behind the church hall. Ed passes the joint, and we take it in turns to inhale. I feel sick from the sweet muggy scent, the smoke a dizzy swirl in my lungs.

'There's a rowing boat tied up. I noticed it earlier,' Mark says.

Just along the lane, the meadows of Grantchester dip gently to the banks of the river Cam, the slow slide of dark water that runs through fields of cows until it reaches Cambridge, where it drifts on under the ancient stone of college bridges.

Laughing and shushing each other, the four of us walk through damp grass to the water's edge. Ed keeps the joint clamped between his lips as he unties the rowing boat. Mark helps us girls in, the boat tipping and trembling under our lurching weight. Julia sits down hard in the stern, and I squeeze beside her, tugging at my hem to try to cover some thigh.

Mark crouches in the prow, while Ed takes the oars. He's obviously rowed before, and the boat moves off downriver smoothly, nudging through treacle-dark water. The row-locks clank, wood creaks.

'Is it very deep?' Julia asks, looking over the side.

'Deep as an ocean. And the fish are man-eaters,' Mark replies.

I roll my eyes. 'Very funny. Don't worry, Jules, you can stand up, honestly.'

The rhythmic splish of the oars is mesmerising. Ed's shoulders strain as he pulls, swearing when he misses a stroke. Mysterious shapes slip by. Trees and bushes. The huge silhouette of a cow ducks away from the bank as we pass, making Julia scream. I tilt my chin and look at the moon, a yellowy orb hanging inside its own misty halo. I can feel Ed's eyes on me. I push a tendril of hair away from my eyes, run my tongue over my lips. I hope the moonlight is flattering.

When we reach the city, the river widens, and backs of colleges rise up out of the night. Going under an arched bridge, we hear running footsteps over our heads. The clattering of heels on cobbles. Reflections of walls and spires ripple across the water, and the ghostly shapes of three swans drift past.

Some of the windows are lit up and uncurtained, and we catch sight of students moving behind the glass. Watch as one couple embrace under a single bulb. Mark and Ed cheer.

'Look over there. Carrot-top alert!' Mark says. 'What a swot! Perfect for you, Eleanor.'

I follow his pointing finger and find the boy, framed in a window. He's lit by an angle-poise lamp, tousled red hair falling over his face as he concentrates on a book. He must have heard voices, because he looks up. He has a nice face, plain but kind, and he looks slightly dazed. Mark and Ed give snorts of derision; Ed wolf-whistles.

Ed turns the boat with one oar, swirling the prow around. 'Getting late, folks. Think we'll head back.'

'Wait,' I say. 'This is dull. I thought we were going to do something exciting.'

'Like what?' Julia asks.

I look around, and then down at the river. 'Swimming.'

'You're kidding! It's April. It'll be freezing,' Mark says.

But I've spoken the words, and I'm gripped by a desire to distance myself from the others, from the mean edge in Ed's voice, the braying laughter, from the way the evening has unravelled and become disappointing and sour. I want to scare myself. I begin to pull off my shoes, unbutton my cardigan.

'You can't!' Julia cries. 'It smells.'

I stand up in my underwear. Ed reaches out and touches my goosepimply thigh. I hold my nose, and jump.

I hit blackness and gasp. The water is cold, bone-jarringly cold. My limbs tangle in weed. I kick out, swallowing a mouthful of rank-tasting river. The part of my brain that hasn't frozen remembers that there are diseases in water like this; rats swim and urinate in it. I imagine I see the scurrying of a creature at the water's edge, hear the small splash of its long-tailed body. The water is implacable. It crushes me. I close my mouth and eyes and flail towards the boat. The others haul me in as if I'm a slippery outsized fish.

Julia wraps the cardigan around my wet shoulders. 'Jesus! You idiot!'

I can't speak. My lips and tongue are numb. Hair clings to my cheeks. But I feel elated, as if I've done something extraordinary. The triumph of it lights a fire in my belly. I manage a smile, looking up into Ed's surprised face. And suddenly I can see the kind of man he's going to grow into, dull and conventional, thick-set.

I don't want a man like that, or the red-haired student tethered to his books. I'll get away from here, find real love, a wild, true thing that will set me free.

I begin to laugh, a hiccupping sound, broken by my shivering.

Julia rubs my back. 'God. She's hysterical. Can't you row any faster, Ed?'

I bare my chattering teeth, throw back my head like a wolf and laugh at the moon. I can't move my fingers; my body's clenched around the cold in my bones. I know the others are making *she's loco* faces at each other over my head. But the feeling is still blazing in my belly. I have choices, a future. I'll meet someone brave and wonderful. I'm going to have a life that matters, be a doctor, save lives, make a difference.

TEN

2015

Staring out into the wet garden, a figure catches my eye, and my heart gives a tiny skip. There's a man in the field. Then I realise it's Luca. He's already hard at work.

After collecting the eggs, I go over to see him. He stops for a moment, wiping his forehead with the back of his forearm. The maple tree's fresh stump gleams, pale and raw. I can smell sap, the last living breath of the wood. I nudge it with my toe. There's something poignant about a fallen tree. I look away from the brutal jagged edges.

'Were you comfortable last night?'

He nods.

'You're getting on so fast.' I look over to the old orchard, the riot of undergrowth, the mass of choking thickets growing up around a handful of ancient fruit trees. We always meant to tackle it, when we had time. 'Would you consider staying on for a bit longer to clear the orchard?'

He shrugs. 'Those trees need rescuing. I'd be happy to do it.'

'Where are you from? I can't place your accent.'

'Originally? Romania.' He scratches the back of his neck.

'I suppose you've travelled a lot?'

'Yes. Europe. America.' He waves a hand. 'All over the place.'

It sounds as though he was born into the circus life. I'm not going to ask. His reticence makes me feel as if I'm interrogating him.

'I'll be out all day, at the tearoom,' I say.

Luca raises a puzzled eyebrow.

'My cafe,' I explain. 'The Old Dairy.' I swallow, feeling uncertain. 'Will you be all right for food and things?'

We've agreed a price, cash in hand, and his lodgings included, but I haven't given him any money yet.

'Yes. Thanks.'

He doesn't eat anything. No wonder he's so lean. He must live off fresh air. Not like William. When we'd met he'd been a skinny student, a man-boy, but he'd fattened up as he'd aged, gaining a comfortable padding of flesh. He had a sweet tooth – loved cakes – could never resist sampling anything I was making. I was forever slapping his hand away as he dipped a finger into bowls. He used to pat his stomach ruefully. 'My penalty for marrying a baker.'

I liked his roundness. There was more to hold in my arms at night. I miss him. Despite everything. My body yearns for his warmth in bed, his familiar breathing next to me. I'm lonely. I think that's part of the reason I've asked Luca to stay on. Just to know there's another human nearby. Although he's not exactly good company. I miss the easy flow of my conversations with Will, the comfort of daily updates, snatches of village and university gossip.

Kate calls for me, giving a polite beep on her horn as she pulls into the drive. We load the boot of her car with cake tins. She notices the shape of Luca in the distance.

'Who's that?'

'Luca. He's doing some manual work for me. Used to be a trapeze artist in the circus.'

'That's exotic.' She's chewing gum, and smacks it between her teeth, taking one last lingering look at Luca. She climbs into the driving seat. 'Kind of sexy, isn't he? But you're OK with that? Leaving him alone at your place?'

'I've locked up of course,' I say briskly. 'But he's trustworthy. I feel it in my gut.'

'Oh well, in that case!' she grins. 'Can't argue with your gut.'

I am tempted to tell her about William, to prove a point, to show that trusting people isn't such a black and white matter. But I don't want the whole village gossiping about me. And Kate does like to chat. As the car rumbles around country lanes, Kate tells me about her Sunday, how Pete the boyfriend watched football on telly, wouldn't take her out to the pub until the game was over, and then ignored her and spent the night rehashing details of the game with his mates.

'The lads around here, they're so . . . ' she bites her lip, thinking, 'so unsophisticated. Uncool. There's nobody with any style. Nobody who knows how to give a girl a good time.'

She jerks the wheel to the left as a lorry rounds the bend. It towers over us, the menacing width of its bumper taking up the entire road. I brace myself against the passenger window. Massive wheels roll past. These are the same lanes that Will was on when he had the accident. The broken fence has been mended, trailing barbed wire replaced. The tracks gouged into the bank where he spun out of control are softened by weather and time, new grass spouting inside dirt wounds.

A steady trickle of customers comes in, a few regulars and some tourists, eating cake and drinking tea, ordering hot chocolates and bottles of Coke, munching sandwiches and packets of crisps. The place is filled with the low murmuring of conversation, the whirr of the coffee machine and clink of china.

The bell jangles above the door. Kate nudges me, and I turn to find David and Adam standing in front of the counter. I smooth dry palms over my apron. I'm convinced that David has forgotten – he's never going to ask me to dinner.

'We'd like a cake, Ellie.' David gazes down at the display. 'Maybe that one? I've got Rachel and Pip coming to tea.'

'Of course.' I'm leaning inside the glass, sliding the plate out.

I want Kate to fold a cardboard container for me, but she's gazing up at Adam under her lashes. I can see why. He's grown into a handsome young man, lean-boned and hungry-looking. He slumps against the counter, hands in his pockets. Even though he's slouching, he towers over his father. How old is he now? Must be in his early twenties. When we moved here, he was away at boarding school in the sixth form. He's been working on the farm for the last few years, but I don't know him well. I remember him at his mother's funeral and wonder how he's coping. His dark eyes watch me with interest.

'Hello, Adam,' I smile. 'How are things at the farm?'

'Hard work,' he says. 'Dad uses me as slave labour!'

'Very funny.' David gives his arm a little push and turns to me. 'By the way, I haven't forgotten,' he says in a low, teasing voice, as I hand over the white box, tied with a red ribbon.

I move towards the till, waiting for payment, feigning an air of unconcern.

He grins as he gives me a ten-pound note. 'How does this Saturday suit you?'

I tilt my head, as if I'm considering an invisible diary. 'I think I'm free. That would be . . . nice.'

I'm certain he knows very well that every Saturday night is a blank space on my calendar, and I'm embarrassed now that I couldn't admit it.

'You're going out with David Mallory?' Kate stares at me, as the door shuts behind them.

I put my fingers to my lips. 'Not in that sense,' I explain in a hushed voice. 'He's just being friendly. It's just dinner. Not a date.'

I watch the back of their heads as they climb into the Range Rover. One blond, one dark. Now that I know that Adam is adopted, I wonder that I didn't guess before. Neither of his parents looks anything like him. I remember Henrietta's delicate bone structure and pale skin. How she used to touch Adam with her long fingers, holding his arm, rearranging his hair.

Kate drops me off at home with a cheerful wave. I follow the path around to the back, and I can't stop my eyes flitting from one window to another checking that everything's as I left it.

Nutmeg comes to the gate, pressing her warm nose into my palm. I reach up and stroke one of her long ears. She's getting fat, I think, looking at her low-slung belly. When she arrived from the donkey sanctuary, I could count every rib.

Something catches at my senses. I work it out after a moment. It's the gap where the maple used to be. Funny how the shapes of missing things imprint themselves onto our subconscious as a sense of wrongness. I gaze around the field. I can't see Luca. Then a figure unfolds itself, and I realise that he's been kneeling the other side of the fence. He's holding a hammer, and he raises it in greeting when he sees me.

I switch the radio on and twiddle the knob, finding a music channel. A pop song. I don't recognise it, but the catchy rhythm makes me swing my hips. I haven't danced properly since I was a teenager. Will wasn't a party person. He always had so much studying to do for his PhD, then students' work to mark, writing his books. He couldn't concentrate if there was noise. I danced alone in the kitchen with the radio turned down low, tiptoed past the study door, went to bed on my own with a book.

I turn the cold tap and wash the earth off a couple of carrots, dry my hands and peel an onion: burnished strips of parchment flake from the hard-packed flesh. I wipe away a stinging tear, allowing myself to think about David, his exact words when he came into the tearoom and how he said them. Analysing doesn't help. I have no idea if he actually likes me. All I know is that he makes me feel tongue-tied. That's my own insecurity talking. Nothing to do with him. He can't help it if he inhabits his clothes with ease, if his skin has the glow of someone who's just stepped out of a hot shower, or that his eyes are the colour of a June sky.

I take a knife to the carrot, chopping it into precise rounds of brilliant orange. The blade makes a satisfying rat-a-tat-tat on the board. Glancing up, I see Luca appear around the corner, whistling. He disappears into the garage. He seems to have settled in. He hasn't asked me for anything since he arrived. It was the right thing to do to offer him work and a place to stay.

I tip some oil into the pan, turn up the flame. The onions sizzle and begin to soften and colour. I'm cooking for two. It's a habit I can't break. But that's OK, because I have Luca to feed.

I stir carrots into the pan, my mind not ready to relinquish the image of sitting across a restaurant table with David, candles perhaps, a simple vase with one rose. *You're a beautiful woman.* I tip a bag of mince into the vegetables, watch as the pink begins to brown. I never looked at another man while I was married to Will. I always believed that he felt the same about me.

ELEVEN

David will notice everything, from the colour of my eye-shadow to my taste in jewellery. With a small intake of breath, I put up a hand to pat at the messy strands, remembering how my scalp itched with irritation when my mother did the same thing to me. It's too late to worry about my hair now.

When I hear the low pulse of the Range Rover outside, the slam of a heavy car door, I'm in my room, fastening dangling Moroccan silver into my ears. I've tried on nearly everything in my wardrobe. Discarded clothes are draped over the bed in a jumble-sale pile. I'm wearing a floral maxi dress that I found in Oxfam and purple tights. I slip a long silver necklace over my head and take one more look at myself in the full-length mirror on the back of the door. I'd like to think I've nailed boho chic. But in David's eyes, it'll probably translate as scruffy eccentric.

The bell goes and I hurry downstairs, scooping my coat off the hook in the hall. Standing on the mat, I steady myself, hoping he won't be able to tell how nervous I am. Despite what I said to Kate, this feels like a date. It's been so long. I'm afraid that I won't know what to do or say. I moisten my lips and open the door. David leans in to brush my cheek with a kiss; he's wearing a navy suit, shirt and silk tie.

Will's only suit was mustard corduroy. I could never persuade him to spend money on something more up-to-date. He'd wear it with one of his soft checked shirts, his tie skew-whiff, top button undone.

David gives me his wide, white smile.

'Just a minute.' I clear my throat. 'I'll be with you in a sec. I'd better tell Luca I'm going out.'

I catch a look of surprise on his face, but I've already turned, making my way through the kitchen and out of the back door to the garage. Luca opens up immediately. I smell nicotine, earth, glimpse the neatly made camp bed behind him. Shadows leaping across the bare wall.

'I'm going out for the evening. With a friend.' I shift from one foot to the other. 'In case you needed anything before I go?'

His silence unnerves me. I nod. 'Well then, goodnight.'

I feel him looking at me. The intensity of his interest is scalding. My skin prickles with it. I hold my coat in front of me. His mouth lifts in a crooked smile, as if I've said something amusing.

I can't imagine what he'll do for the whole evening. I don't even know if he reads. What does he do for entertainment? His rucksack didn't seem big enough for anything but the bare necessities.

David is waiting in the car. 'Who's Luca?' he asks.

'He's helping me. Clearing the land. Mending fences. That sort of thing.'

'Oh, I don't know him, do I?' David turns the wheel. The car glides around corners, nosing through the dark. A speckle of insects gathers in the headlights.

'He isn't local. He was with the circus. We saw him, actually. That night. When the lion attacked the woman. He went into the ring.'

David raises his eyebrows, then frowns. 'I don't remember anyone going into the ring. I couldn't take my eyes off that lion.'

'Well, Luca's left the circus now.'

'But if he's not local, where's he staying?' David's voice is curious.

'He's sleeping in the garage.'

David shoots me a glance. 'Really?'

I set my shoulders and stare through the windscreen.

David brakes as a creature rushes across the road, low to the ground, long tail dragging. He glances away from the road to fix me with his gaze. 'Just be careful, won't you?'

I make a noise in the back of my throat. A noncommittal gargle. I can't let other people's opinions shake my confidence in myself. Trust is a better part of being human; if I slide that door shut, I'll be sealed up inside myself, crippled by the betrayals of life, damaged goods.

David has a table booked in a French restaurant in Canterbury. Cocooned inside the buttery leather interior of the car, the drive passes quickly. The restaurant is exactly as I'd imagined: intimate, candle-lit, with waiters scurrying in the shadows, presenting bottles of wine for inspection, darting forward to refill glasses and pick up dropped napkins.

David leans across the pristine table. 'I'm sorry it's taken me so long to do this.' I shake my head, but he's continuing. 'I wanted to ask you before, but somehow it didn't seem right. For a long time, I was just getting through the days.'

We sit back while the waiter places our starters before us.

'How are you?' He picks up the salt cellar.

'Fine,' I say quickly, not wanting him to ask me about William.

'You must ask me if you need anything. Remember I said so before? I could have found someone to help on your land.' He sprinkles salt onto his soup. 'You didn't have to ask a stranger. '

'Luca,' I say. 'He's called Luca. Thank you. I suppose I'm not used to asking for things. I've always been self-reliant. Maybe I'm too proud.'

I prod a piece of fig onto my fork. Place it in my mouth, sweet, granular against my tongue.

He's smiling. 'That's nothing to be ashamed of. I admire a woman who can fend for herself.' He looks down at his plate. 'Hettie wasn't like that.'

'Really?' I thought of the slender, self-possessed woman I'd known. Always busy with some charity or other. Never too busy to have her nails painted, her hair done.

'But then,' he tips his head to one side, 'I suppose that was one of the things I loved about her. Her vulnerability. And of course she was a wonderful mother, like a tiger where her children were concerned. I'm contradicting myself.' He smiles. 'What complicated creatures we are.'

'I wish I'd known her better.'

'She went downhill so fast.' His voice is low. 'She'd had those wretched headaches for a long time. But the diagnosis was a shock. I blame myself. I should have forced her to go to a specialist sooner.'

'You couldn't have known.' I play with the stem of my glass, twisting it round and round.

'Sorry.' He blinks. His eyes are bright. 'I didn't want to talk about sad things. Not tonight.'

'I don't mind. I'm happy to listen.'

He reaches across and touches my hand. 'Remember how delicate she was?'

I nod. She'd had skin so thin it was almost translucent and narrow, elegant bones. I remember her in a plaster cast on at least two occasions. Fragile. Not like me.

'But she was health conscious,' David's saying. 'She hardly drank. A glass of champagne occasionally. Didn't smoke. She was a vegetarian, for Christ's sake! She cared about her figure, never ate puddings or cake.' He raises his shoulders. 'I suppose I thought she was immune to illness.'

I remember how I'd thought her immune too, for different reasons – being beautiful and rich. How stupid. None of us is ever truly safe.

'Now,' he says, straightening his shoulders. 'Let's make a pact. For the rest of the evening we're going to talk about other things. About us.'

And we do. We discuss our musical preferences, our favourite books, and laugh about the Best Kept Village competition and the upheaval it's causing. By the time our plates are cleared away and we've shared a chocolate mousse, I've drunk too much. The edges of the room blur, David's features swim in and out of focus. I excuse myself and go to the Ladies' where I look at myself in the mirror, steadying myself under unforgiving lights, gripping the cold curve of basin. My mascara has smudged. I do my best to repair the damage.

David's already paid the bill. He stands with my coat ready for me.

In the car on the way home, he puts on some music. Classical piano. 'This is beautiful,' I say. 'What is it?'

'Schumann's *Fantasie in* C. The third movement.' He turns up the volume. 'This bit moves me to tears.' He glances over at me. 'We should go to a concert one day.'

I look out at the vague shapes of hedges and trees. The cloudy night sky. Music fills the car. The sound quality is extraordinary, not like the CD machine we had in our Renault, where discs used to jump and stick. Was William listening to music the night he crashed? His favourite Bob Dylan, or Leonard Cohen? I close my eyes, absorbing the flow and fall of piano notes. It's too warm inside the air-conditioned interior.

David is doing all he can to make this evening perfect. I don't want to complain about feeling stuffy. 'Do you think Adam will stay on at the farm with you? Or does he have other career ideas?'

'I'm lucky. Rachel and Adam both want to stay in the family business. Adam loves the farm. He always was a bright boy, turns out he's got a good business head on him. He's a great asset.'

David never mentions that Adam is adopted. He treats him

and Rachel exactly as if they're his own. That shows huge love. I feel guilty that I'd let his glossy surface blind me to who he really is.

It seems natural to invite him in for a coffee, or brandy. I still have the remains of the bottle he brought over a year ago. He laughs when I tell him.

'Just for a moment,' he says.

So here we are again, sitting at my kitchen table drinking cognac. But I don't say it aloud. I don't want to remind him of those last weeks of Henrietta's life. We share so much, he and I. We've both lost our partners. I gave my son away. He adopted his. He's a better person than me. The brief hug we gave each other that night feels possible again. I slide my hand across the table and he takes it at once. His skin is warm.

We sit for a moment, not speaking. Then he's standing up, and my fingers are still in his. He's leading me towards the door, towards the hall. I follow, up the inky stairs. It feels comforting to be led, to follow blindly behind, not thinking. David pauses on the landing, and I realise that he doesn't know which door leads to my bedroom.

I don't switch any lights on. It's better like this, moving in and out of moonlight; a sense of unreality and the loosening effects of alcohol make it feel as though I'm floating. He pulls me close, and the weight of his body is against me, solid and human. The smell of his cologne in my throat. He cups the back of my head with his hand, presses soft lips over my mouth, and his tongue is moving between my lips. My body contracts with desire. But the shock of the unfamiliar hits me like a blow. He's not William. I jerk my head away. There's an intake of breath as he releases me.

'I can't,' I whisper, burying my face in my hands.

I can feel him standing close, not touching me. I hunch my shoulders. I'm weeping, tears sliding around my nose.

'It's my fault. I got carried away . . . ' His voice breaks.

I make the effort to steady my breathing. 'It's not you. Not your fault.'

He puts a gentle hand on my arm. I let his fingers rest there, and he squeezes and takes them away.

'I need a moment.' My nose is leaking. Snot and saliva on my skin.

I close the bathroom door behind me. Slide the bolt across. I sit on the loo and pull out a roll of paper, tear off several strips and blow my nose. I blame myself for letting him lead me up the stairs. David is used to being in charge; he has a natural authority. I'd felt the force of it as he'd towed me behind him. He'd been hard to resist. But I shouldn't have been so weak. I splash my eyes, leaning over the basin. When I dare to face my dripping reflection, my eyes are bloodshot, the skin puffy and blotchy. I wipe away a smudge of eye-shadow, run a finger over my eyebrows, remembering, with a small jolt, the night of the school disco when I thought I'd ruined everything with Ed.

I hurry back to my bedroom. The light is on, but David's not here. I gaze around me, taking in the open wardrobe, the chest of drawers cluttered with ornaments and spilt face-powder, all exactly as I left it. I feel a stab of panic. Has he gone? I didn't hear his car engine or a door shutting. Puzzled, I go onto the landing. There's a light coming from under the door of William's study.

David is standing at Will's desk, looking down at the mess of papers and books, the blank computer screen.

He meets my questioning stare. 'You haven't been able to clear anything away, have you?' he asks in a low voice.

I shake my head.

'Me neither. Henrietta's things are all over the house. Even her clothes in the wardrobe. Is that macabre?'

'It's hard to . . . ' my voice trembles, 'lose those last links . . . '

He straightens his crumpled tie. 'Can we try again? Or have I spoilt everything?'

'No – I'd like that,' I say quietly.

'Thank you.' His voice twists. 'I miss her. But I want you to know that I didn't kiss you because . . . because I was lonely. You're so beautiful. And I don't think you realise it.'

He moves across the room, passing me softly, 'Goodnight, Ellie. I'll see myself out.'

Without turning. I hear him pause on the threshold. 'It's a process, grieving.' I hear the scratch of his soles against the carpet. 'Call me whenever you want.'

I put a finger to my lips. I can taste David's kiss. The first time I've kissed another man in over twenty years. I look over my shoulder. I thought I heard the sound of William breathing, the rustle as he turned the pages of a book. He's all around me – his books and work spilling out of shelves and across surfaces; the study is untouched. I've hardly been in here since Will died, not since I went through the bank statements. Not since I checked the computer.

One of the desk drawers is half open. It's crammed with papers, notebooks, broken pencils, chocolate wrappers, cheque-book stubs, loose pages from notebooks. A mint covered in dust sits on the desk. My husband was a slob. But I knew that already. So did he. We used to joke about it.

I pick up the mint and drop it in the bin. Something catches my eye: a crumpled piece of paper tucked into the corner. I'm certain that the bin was empty the last time I was here. I'd checked. Not carefully enough, obviously. I reach down and pick it up, smooth it out. Will's handwriting. And then I see my name, and my heart jumps. It's a letter, for me. My fingers are shaking as I place the paper directly under the lamp on the desk, so that I can make out the words, the familiar scrawl.

My dearest,

I've been a lucky man, because I was in the right place at the right time when I met you. But I'm not sure that I've been able to love you in the way you need to be loved. I try my best, Eleanor, but I can't help feeling that you've always held something back from me. If I was someone else, perhaps things would be different.

This isn't an excuse for my behaviour, for what I've done. None of this is your fault. And I've found it very hard to keep from telling you. Guilt is a terrible burden. But I hope that when I can explain properly, you will understand and even forgive me. I've never thought of myself as a knight in shining armour before. Perhaps I've been deluded or weak, but we all want to be needed, Eleanor, it's just human nature, so I hope you won't blame me because when she . . .

The sentence is unfinished. There's a page missing. I hunt around in the drawer, turning the whole thing out onto the floor and searching through the mess. I gaze around the study, at the stuffed bookshelves, the filing cabinets, the box files piled on top of each other, the sprawl of papers and books sliding across the desk, and rub my eyes with my fists.

I walk unsteadily into the bedroom. Sitting on the edge of the bed, I crumple the letter in my hands, squashing it back into a ball. My heart closes. The words repeat in my head.

A knight in shining armour . . . We all want to be needed, Eleanor, it's just human nature, so I hope you won't blame me because when she . . .

Nausea rises into my throat. I was right. He'd wanted someone more feminine than me, somebody who allowed him to be the strong one. He must have been with her the night he died. The last person he saw in this world was her. She got drunk with him and watched him climb into the car, let him drive away.

I am furious at her stupidity for letting him. At my own stupidity for not knowing. And most of all – I'm angry with William. I wish David was here to put his arms around me. I wish I'd kissed him back.

TWELVE

1990

I put my hands over my ears to block the sounds coming from downstairs. A summer cocktail party spilling out of the house onto the patio. Mrs Oaks has spent the afternoon making tiny rolls of cucumber and white bread, sticking pineapple and cheddar onto sticks, sprinkling heaps of cod's roe over cream cheese. The girl from Impington will be passing plates of these delicacies around on trays. Voices below blend into a low roar, rising and falling; when sharp bursts of laughter come, they make me jump.

My bedroom is like a prison. I pull at the opening of my blouse, undoing a couple of buttons. There isn't enough air. My skin feels clammy. I go to the window and throw it as wide as the sash will go, leaning out into the violet evening. But there's no breeze. Stale August heat rises from the baked lawn, from the tarmac and gravel of the drive. A man's voice exclaims loudly; I hear the forced trill of my mother's answering laugh, and bring my head in sharply, knocking it against the frame.

I pace my bedroom floor. Up and down. Then I lunge forward and push at the pile of exercise books on my desk, sweeping them off in an arc. They slide over the edge, flipping open, scattering onto the floor.

I collected my results from school yesterday, and was summoned into the living room as soon as I got home. My father stood over me as I sat on the edge of the sofa, feet together, head bowed.

'This is such a disappointment,' he said. 'Such a disappointment. Do you have anything to say for yourself?'

I stared at the texture of the rug under my feet, the weave of rust, red and orange, delicate patterns made in India by children's fingers. Bile rose into my mouth.

'Are you ill? It's terribly hot,' Mother asked, crossing one leg over another, and fanning herself. 'Shall I fetch you some water?'

I shook my head. If I didn't say anything, they'd have to let me go, let me escape back to my room. A drop of sweat ran down my neck, unbearably ticklish.

My father shoved his hands into his jacket pockets. His fingers curled into fists. His temper revealed itself in details: a stiffened expression, a vein beating at his temple, his angry, restrained hands. I watched him out of the corners of my eyes.

Since then, I'd been persona non grata. My mother nervous and tentative around me, my father coldly ignoring. And then this party, taking up Mum's time, focusing the energy of the house around it. I know that I've failed to perform. I was supposed to be paraded around as a party piece: the successful Grade A student, the perfect daughter. I doubt that I'll be called down tonight. If I am, I'll refuse.

I go to the window again, concealed by the fall of curtain. More adults have come onto the patio, cigarettes and drinks in hands, laughing and chatting. I smell nicotine, the ashy drift of it. Someone is standing under the oak tree smoking. I see the glimmer of red moving, a tiny glow in the shadows. He tosses the sparking remains, grinds it underfoot and steps forward, strolling towards the house. It's Les Ashton. His tall figure is unmistakable. He glances up towards my room.

I sit on the bed, slumping over, dirty hair falling into my eyes. I wonder what the others are doing – Ed, Mark, Julia – whether they're out celebrating. Ed has a new girlfriend now. A pretty girl from the Lower Sixth with a freckled nose and large breasts. When the phone rang earlier, I'd half hoped it might be him. I'd hidden upstairs, listening to my mother talking. 'Well done, Julia. That is good news.' Mum's voice sounded stiff. 'I'll just call her, dear.' But I'd refused to come. I couldn't listen to someone else's life going on as normal. Couldn't listen to Julia's excited plans.

I put my hands over the rounded curve of my belly, feeling the extended rise of flesh. When I sit down, it presses over my thighs in a doughy fold. I've been wearing loose clothes, fastening my waistbands with safety pins. Nobody has noticed. But I can't pretend any more. There is a foetus curled inside me: soft nails forming, heart smaller than a bud, a blind creature sucking at my blood.

I pull back my arm and make a fist, take a quick breath, and smash into the tight swell of my stomach. The pain jolts through to my spine. I imagine the tiny skull broken and crushed, fingers startling wide as starfish. And I ball up my hand and punch again.

THIRTEEN

2015

Since the day I lost him, I've imagined how my baby would change and grow, getting plumper, taller, his gums sprouting milk teeth, changing from a toddler to a child, and then a gawky adolescent with a croaking voice and too-big features. By now he'll have got past teenage horrors like acne and braces. He'll be a young man. Twenty-four.

My parents arranged a closed adoption. For eighteen years I had no way of contacting him. But when he reached his eighteenth birthday, I sent a letter to the agency to be passed onto him with my details, explaining why I'd given him up, asking him to contact me. Every time the phone rang or there was someone at the door, every time I opened my email or a letter fell onto the mat, I held my breath, hoped it was him. It's been years now and still no word.

I never told William about my son. At first, it was too raw, and then as the years went by, it would have seemed cruel to tell my husband that I'd kept something so important from him: that I'd had a child and given him away. When I wrote the letter, I nearly confided in Will. But somehow the moment was never right. I told myself I'd tell him when my son made contact. But that never happened. Now I know that Will always sensed that I was holding a part of myself back. That's what drove him to find someone else – someone who gave him everything, told him everything.

Oh, William, why didn't you just ask me?

I pad about the kitchen in bare feet, making myself a cup of tea, a slice of toast. I eat standing up. I should do some baking and cooking today. Stocks of frozen soup are running low in the freezer at the tearoom. I've got the radio on for company. Time is a healer, my mother said. She was wrong. I silence the radio with a click, run upstairs to find some clean socks, and back down to pull on my boots. The day outside the window is bright and windy.

Luca is in the orchard. He's using an electric strimmer. He has ear-muffs and goggles on, and he's staring down at the blade slicing through undergrowth. The roar of the engine blots out the noises around him.

He's completely focused on what he's doing. He must have needed this kind of concentration when he was a trapeze artist. He switches off the engine, pushing the goggles up onto his forehead. I wander over to him, suddenly self-conscious. His boots and ankles are flecked with bits of cut grass, the smell is pungent and green. He smiles that lopsided smile.

'Want to help?'

He has a muddy smear on his cheek, and the rubber grip around the glasses has left indented marks on his cheeks.

I open my mouth to say no. But the sun is warm on my shoulders and the idea of going back into the empty kitchen isn't attractive. He passes me a rake, repositions his goggles and turns back to work. The noise of the machine cuts out any possibility of conversation. There's something comforting about working alongside him, the simple chore of raking, our companionable silence.

Cutting back the undergrowth has uncovered a large, muddy pond. Its shallow, stagnant water is a perfect breeding ground for mosquitoes. We decide that it should be filled in. He's going to use the turned earth from the other side of the field. He begins to trundle over wheelbarrows of freshly dug soil. We work for another couple of hours. I've forgotten to put my watch on, but my stomach is telling me it's lunchtime. As he tips out the latest load, I put the rake to one side.

'Shall I make us some sandwiches?'

He nods, picks up the handles of the barrow, arms and back straight.

The kitchen is reproachful. The oven standing cold. I ignore my pangs of guilt. I have all evening to catch up with the baking. I can work into the night if necessary. It's good to be warm from physical exertion, a skim of sweat on my skin. I imagine all those happy endorphins buzzing around in my brain. I open the fridge, pulling out jars and packets. I sing as I hack chunks of mature cheddar, cut generous slices of fresh bread and spread them with butter. For some reason I'm belting out a number from *The Sound of Music*. I stop to pick at a crust. I'm hungrier than usual.

I return with cheese and pickle sandwiches and two mugs

of coffee. To my surprise, Luca is walking towards me, a riot of green in his hands, and he's smiling.

'Look what I found under all the brambles. Mint. Rosemary. Sage. Smell.'

I bend towards the bouquet.

'Close your eyes.'

Startled, I do as I'm told. I inhale the sweetness of mint, the sharper tang of rosemary, the musky piquancy of sage. The smells are intense. And so is my awareness of him. I can hear him breathing, swallowing.

I open my eyes.

'Closing off one sense makes the others work harder.' He steps back. 'If you like, I'll plant cuttings from these outside the kitchen. Make you a herb garden.'

We sit together, leaning against the fence, the sun on our faces. I position myself on my outspread coat; Luca settles himself with crossed legs, at ease on the damp grass.

'You said you had an accident at the circus?'

He bites into his sandwich. He chews steadily and swallows. 'I missed a catch. My timing was off. We were performing without a net, so—' he shrugs.

'You could have broken your back!'

'I was lucky. But it was the end of my career.'

'Did you like being a trapeze artist?'

He sips his coffee and smiles down into the mug. 'The word "like" doesn't cover it. It's a passion. To fly as a human, it's something else. A kind of magic. Trapeze artists are different from any other performer. You have to be a bit mad. A bit . . . ' He seems to be searching for a word. 'Extreme,' he finishes.

I've never heard him say so much at one time. 'Did you learn any other circus skills?'

'Knife throwing.'

I look at the blade on his belt doubtfully. 'Really?'

'No.' He gives a short laugh. 'I'm joking. But I can juggle.'

'I've always admired people who can do that. I'm all fingers and thumbs. Can't even catch properly.'

'I'll teach you one day,' he says. 'If you like.'

My cheeks are suddenly hot. I glance down at my hands. 'It sounds as though you were passionate about the lions, too. Not just the trapeze.'

He blinks. His smile wiped away. 'You can't feel passion for a caged animal. Only sorrow.'

'I know.'

We are silent for a moment. He looks at me, narrowing his eyes. 'You have a . . . ' he taps his cheek. 'Just here.'

Startled, I put my hand to my face and rub. He shakes his head, and leans across, brushes my skin with the tips of his weathered fingers. I inhale crushed herbs. 'It's gone. A bit of mud I think.'

Our faces are close. I see that his dark eyes have flecks of green inside them. I swallow and pull back. 'Thanks.'

He's taken a packet of cigarettes from his top pocket; he shakes one out and puts it in his mouth without using his fingers, strikes a match and inhales.

I turn away to collect the plates and mugs, pile them onto the tray.

'I was wondering why you chose this place,' he asks. 'It's a large plot of land for one person to manage.'

I hesitate, not knowing how much to tell him.

'I've upset you.' He frowns.

I shake my head. 'No. It's OK. My husband and I bought it together. It was our dream to have some land. But he . . . he died . . .'

To my horror, hot tears well up, and I scrub at my eyes with my fist. When I look up, Luca's forehead wrinkles as though he's going to say something, but we both hear a voice shouting my name.

David is striding across the lawn to the orchard. He waves. His familiar green jacket and greying blond hair make me feel relieved, on safe ground again.

'Hello, I was just passing,' he says as he approaches. 'Thought you might like to have lunch.' He looks at the tray. The pair of mugs and plates. 'I see I'm too late.'

I feel caught out.

'This is Luca.' I gesture behind me. 'Luca, this is David. David Mallory.'

David steps forward. I expect them to shake hands, but Luca thrusts his hands in his pockets. The air tightens. David looks at Luca's mud-streaked face, his bare, muscular forearms, scruffy jeans and battered workman's boots. Luca seems to empty himself. His gaze is blank. His expression gives nothing away.

'Well, don't let me keep you,' David says.

Luca walks away, towards the remaining undergrowth. I hear the roar of the strimmer.

David takes the tray from me, one eyebrow raised. 'Did I say something?'

'He's not a big talker. But he works hard.'

At the door to the cottage, he hands me back the tray. 'I wanted to make sure you were all right . . . after I left?' His voice is soft.

'Yes.' I blush at the memory of my lips breaking away from his. 'I'm sorry . . . about . . .'

He waves his hand. 'Come to lunch this weekend. Rachel and her husband and Pip will be there. And Adam of course. A family affair.'

'Are you sure?'

He nods. 'Sunday. One o'clock.'

Mist lies across the valley, so thick that I can't see to the other side of the field. Gilbert and Nutmeg emerge out of clouds, Nutmeg's eyelashes glinting with moisture. By mid-morning, the mist has begun to burn off, but not enough for me to think that risking the road on my bike is a good idea. I'll walk to David's cross-country. I can cut through Martha's Woods. Luca is nowhere in sight. I leave a note pinned to the garage door. I'm presuming that he's taken Sunday off. I hope so. Our agreement is very vague, I realise.

The way to the beech woods winds steeply uphill, the track worn away into ruts; slashes of chalk show through like glimpses of bone. In the field off to my right, I can just make out sheep grazing on the far slope. Soon I'm hot and panting.

Martha's Woods are mostly beech and ash; their close-packed trunks twist towards the sky, curving and forking, searching for light. The mist is deeper amongst the mesh of branches. Water drips from leaves. At first, I thought it was raining. I pull my coat tighter, doing up buttons. I feel like Little Red Riding Hood.

When the creature appears, it's as if it has materialised out of the mist: a nightmare hound blocking my path. The kind of dog that has sharp ears and docked tail. The hair on its back bristles in a ridge, and its top lip trembles and curls. I catch a glimpse of teeth, wet pink gums. This is no ghost-hound.

William was terrified of dogs. He'd been bitten as a child. He'd showed me the scars on his wrist. Maybe his fear has leaked into me, because my mouth is dry, and my heart leaps erratically.

'There. Good dog,' I manage. And I hold out my hand. My fingers tremble.

The animal lets out a low growl.

I can't run. I look at the dense muscle pushing up under its skin. The long, strong legs. This is a dog bred to be territorial, to take down intruders, outrun thieves.

'Oh, God,' I whisper.

Somewhere further on in the woods, there is the sound of a whistle. The creature hears it too. It quivers. The whistle comes again. Loud, sharp. The dog puts its head on one side.

Go on, I urge it silently, go to your master.

It wheels round and runs off, galloping towards the shrill call. I let out my breath, putting a shaky hand to my heart. After a moment, when I'm sure that it's gone, I gather myself and continue along the path, stumbling on a root. I glimpse something through the trees. A figure bending over. The dog is there too, watching the figure. I pause, staring through the tangle of branches and mist, not able to make sense of what I'm seeing. I walk slowly, getting brief snatches of the scene through the trees. Then, as I'm nearly on top of them, the shapes come together like a finished puzzle. There are two dogs. One is waiting nearby, sitting to attention, and the other is sprawled on its side, lying flat underneath a man who's kneeling on the dog's shoulder.

The man turns his head. It's Adam. I see a fleeting glimpse of something defensive, confrontational. His face changes when he recognises me, a smile spreading. He gives the dog's head an almost affectionate shove into the ground, then gets up slowly. The dog doesn't move. Adam snaps his fingers, and the creature staggers to its feet. The other dog moves forward to stand beside it. They make a matching pair.

'He ran off. Can't have dogs like these getting away with tricks.'

'But . . . what were you doing?'

'Just reminding him who's master. It didn't hurt. But he has to know that I can dominate him when I want.' He places a hand on the dog's head. 'People are too sentimental with animals. If you let a dog think it's pack leader, you'll make it unhappy, because it'll think it's in charge. It stresses them out. I have to be pack leader. Then he can relax.'

'Oh,' I dare to move a little nearer to the dogs, both watching Adam intently. 'What are they?'

'Dobermanns. We use them as guard dogs on the farm.'

He attaches leads to the dogs' collars, and looks at me over his shoulder. 'You're coming to lunch, aren't you?'

Looping the leads around one wrist, he gets a packet of cigarettes out of his pocket and offers it to me. I shake my head.

He inhales and gestures along the path. 'Shall we walk together? I'm going back now.'

We fall into step. The dogs trot by his heels, docile, calm. It's hard to believe that one of them is the same animal that had me trapped, teeth bared as if it was going to spring at my throat.

'What are their names?'

'This one's Max. And that's Moro.'

'They're beautiful. Well, now they are.'

'I'm sorry if we gave you a shock,' he says cheerfully. 'Did you meet Max back there?'

'Yes – I have to admit he gave me a nasty moment.'

'He wouldn't hurt you.' He clamps the cigarette in the side of his mouth, looking down at the animal with a fond glance. 'Dad got Max for my birthday when I was sixteen. He's eight now, which is old for this breed.'

'You're . . . twenty-four?' I can't keep the unsteadiness out of my voice.

He gives me a quizzical look through drifting smoke.

'Sorry. Nothing.'

He stops. 'No. You were going to say something?'

'It's just that . . . well . . . my son would be twenty-four.' I swallow. It feels extraordinary to say those words aloud. I have a floaty sensation in my stomach.

'I didn't know you had a son.' He drops the cigarette and twists his toe over the glowing end. He looks confused. 'Did he . . . die?'

'No.' I take a deep breath. 'He was adopted. When he was a baby.'

'Oh.' He doesn't break stride. I have to hurry to keep up with him. I glance across at him, trying to assess his expression. He almost looks angry, his brows drawn together, his mouth turned down.

'I hope . . . I hope that he's as happy as you.' My words come tumbling out. 'I hope he's as loved as you, wherever he is.'

I want to tell Adam that I've never spoken about my child before. I want him to know that he's special, because I chose to tell him. But Adam is silent, head down. I've embarrassed him.

'I know you're adopted,' I say softly. 'I hope you don't mind me saying it. I'd never mention it to anyone else.'

There's a beat of silence. Our feet move soundlessly over the path. I wasn't supposed to know about the adoption.

'I don't usually talk about it,' he says. 'People make judgements.' He seems suddenly shy. All his bravado gone. 'Ellie? Can I call you Ellie?'

'Of course!' I clear my throat, relieved.

'Do you miss your son?'

I can't speak for a moment. 'Yes,' I manage. 'Every day.'

'Then why did you give him away?'

It's as if I've been slapped. I realise that I don't talk about this for exactly the same reason as Adam doesn't. People make judgements.

'I was very young. Eighteen. My parents were upset and disapproving. They weren't going to help me. I was alone. And I was scared.'

'But you're sorry now.'

He doesn't know how cruel he's being, I tell myself. He can't possibly understand. He's just being curious.

'Yes.' My voice is tight. 'I haven't had any more children. But even if I had, I'd regret giving him up.'

He turns and give me a serious look. 'I'm sure your son is fine. Look at me. I'm doing all right, aren't I?.'

I smile.

'I can't talk to anyone about being adopted.' He walks on, kicking a stone out of the way. 'When I was at boarding school some kids found out and I got bullied. So I got into the habit of keeping it secret. Anyway, I don't want Dad to think I'm not grateful. That I'm unhappy. Because I'm not. We have a tight family. I know where I belong. You can't stop being curious though, feeling ... I don't know ... like a hole inside. And sometimes I wonder how different my life would be ... if she'd kept me.' His cheeks flush.

My words rush out. 'You can talk to me, if you ever want to.'

He nods, then glances away, swallowing.

'So ... are there any other guests for lunch besides me? Anyone I don't know?'

He turns back to me, rearranging his face. I see his relief that we've changed the subject.

Langshott Hall is like an oversized doll's house, perfectly square, with big sash windows, a porch over the grand front door held up with Doric pillars. It sits in a big walled garden with sweeping trees and landscaped lawns. Once through the wrought iron gate that marks the entrance, a winding drive arrives at the front of the house. The drive continues on past it and becomes a track that leads to the farm. I've never been there, but you can glimpse the roofs of buildings, stables and barns where the soft fruit is sorted and packed. Lorries come and go through the night at the height of the season, but they don't go through the village, so people don't complain.

Adam and I crunch over the gravel, and he leaves me at the

front door with a wave. 'I'll go and sort the dogs out. See you later.'

I watch him from the porch. He walks with a swinging grace, with the limber, confident stride of a young, healthy creature. As he leans down, murmuring to the animals, his hair wavy with damp, I can see the boy in him. The child in shorts with a cricket bat.

David answers my ring and ushers me inside; he's beaming, a glass of red wine in one hand, hair flopping over his forehead, cheeks flushed. He seems different in his own home, more casual and happier than I've seen him before. Pip comes barrelling out of the room behind and crashes into her grandfather's legs with a cry of delight; she presses her face into the backs of his knees. David bends down and sweeps her up into his arms. She wriggles and laughs.

'And you know this little monster, of course.' He blows a raspberry into her stomach, setting off her giggling again. He puts her back on her feet carefully, and touches my shoulder. 'Come on, let's get you a drink.' Pip runs ahead of us. 'Here, let me take your coat,' he adds, holding out his arm.

The house is full of mouth-watering smells. In the long, blue living room, a pretty blonde woman lifts her head and smiles at me, and I recognise Rachel, David's daughter. A man with a moustache is bending over Pip, tickling her chin.

'You know Rachel, of course.' David puts his arm around her proudly.

She brushes her cheek against mine. 'Hello Ellie, I'm so sorry about William. I haven't seen you properly since the funeral.' She's as polite and composed as her mother. 'Have you been introduced to my husband, Paul?'

I shake hands with the moustached man. We've met before at a Mallory party. I'm not sure if he remembers.

'They've just moved house to Canterbury,' David says. 'But I'm glad to say that Rachel still does my paperwork. Still works for her old man.' He winks at me. 'We need her to keep the rest of us in order.'

The high-ceilinged room has big windows draped with floral curtains. Furniture gleams with age and polish. Over the mantelpiece is a portrait of a woman, framed in gold. It's a large oil painting, full of lush colour. The woman's skin is luminous; her grey eyes regard the room steadily. One elegant hand rests on the back of a chair, the other touches the long coil of brown hair that falls over her shoulder.

David says, 'I had that commissioned soon after our wedding.'

I'm aware of my own straggly hair plastered to my forehead, and my jeans, muddy from the walk over. David hands me a glass of white. A dry Chablis. He's remembered.

'Now then, I believe we can go in. Lunch is served.'

'You walked here?' David exclaims, as he carves the beef.

'She did. We met in the woods.' Adam is nodding at the other end of the table. 'She had a run-in with Max.' He winks at me.

Rachel turns to me, her eyes wide. 'Are you all right? I know it's hard to believe, but their bark really is worse than their bite.'

I shake my head, embarrassed. 'It's OK really. I'm fine. And it was good to walk over.'

'But you haven't replaced your car?' David looks horrified. He piles slivers of pink meat onto a plate. 'How do you manage? You're miles from the village.'

'I was reluctant to get another after . . . the accident. But I think I'm ready now.'

'I have a friend in the business. He could get you a good deal.'

'Dad always has a useful friend,' Rachel whispers to me, mouth twitching in amusement. 'It doesn't matter what the occasion is, he'll have a contact up his sleeve.'

A dark-haired girl hovers behind our chairs, and I recognise her as the girl who'd answered the door when I brought flowers and cake. She places a gravy jug on the tablecloth, pouring water into our glasses. Adam sees me looking at her.

'Anca is from Romania. She actually came to work on the farm. But she's a talented cook.' He smiles at the girl. 'As soon as we realised, we didn't want to waste her skills on picking fruit.'

'Just taste this beef,' David says.

I take a mouthful. 'Yes, it's delicious.' I aim my remark at Anca. But she's already disappeared into the kitchen.

I put my knife and fork together on my plate, and turn to Rachel. 'I keep spotting beautiful family photographs. Some gorgeous ones of you as children. And local landscapes. Is someone in the family a photographer?'

'That's Mum,' she smiles. 'She was always snapping away.'

'Did she take that one on the wall?' I point to a picture of David with a couple of children in wheelchairs.

'Yes. It's a photo from a day Dad and Mum spent at Action Kids,' Rachel explains. 'A charity that raises money for disabled children. Dad gave them a big cheque. He's such a hero, honestly.'

'Rachel!' David leans forward. 'Sorry, Ellie. My daughter can't see her old man's faults. I taped rose-tinted glasses to her nose when she was a baby.'

I laugh. So does Rachel. She nudges me and whispers, 'Don't let him fool you. He ran the marathon last year to raise money.'

I look at the photograph on the wall again. It's a black and white shot. David crouches between two children in wheelchairs. They're all holding hands and grinning into the camera.

I don't want to leave David's home, the warmth and laughter of others. The thought of going back to my quiet cottage makes me feel like I'm sliding backwards. It's been a relief to get away from my own thoughts, from thinking about William. But I'm aware that I'm the only non-family guest, the odd one out. When I stand up and ask for my coat, David has it in his arms almost immediately, is putting it over my shoulders, his hand on my back, steering me out of the door so fast that I nearly stumble. I have to shout my goodbyes over my shoulder.

I glance at him as he opens the car door.

'Sorry. Bit obvious, wasn't it?' he grins. 'I couldn't wait to get you on your own. I've missed you.'

'I thought you just wanted to get rid of me!'

I'm laughing, but as I clamber into the leather interior, his hand brushes mine, and my mouth is suddenly dry. We drive in silence. Hedges and fields pass in a green blur. It's as if we're sealed off from the rest of the world. I'm aware of his muscles moving under his forearm as he changes gear, a tendon in his neck rising as he turns his head, my own shallow breathing.

When David pulls up outside the cottage, he switches off the engine and turns to me. We look at each other, and he doesn't make a joke, doesn't say a thing. It's me that leans across the gear stick to press my mouth over his. This time I have no guilt, no doubt.

He strokes the side of my face. 'Lovely Ellie,' he whispers.

I'm trembling as I get out and shut the door.

'I'll call you,' he says.

The car slides away and I don't move, except to raise my arm and wave goodbye, my face split into a huge smile. The sound of the engine fades into the stillness of the evening air. When I turn to the house, I'm startled to find Luca standing by the side gate. He's watching me with a stern expression, a huge roll of wire in his arms.

'I hitched to Canterbury.' His voice is a growl. 'Now I can get on with mending the broken fencing.'

I nod, unable to speak. Probing my mouth gingerly with one finger, I discover that I've bitten my tongue.

FOURTEEN

I open my eyes to find David standing above me in his dressing gown, holding a tray. Steam drifts from the spout of a teapot. I can smell warm toast, fried bacon.

'I didn't know what you wanted. So I brought everything.'

He places the tray on the bedside table and I wriggle into a sitting position, clasping the sheet to me. Last night I'd been tearfully grateful for the pleasure of skin on skin, his fingers in my hair, his tongue on my body. But in the bright light of morning, I'm aware of the comparisons between me and Henrietta. She was a woman who didn't eat cake. She was a woman who had waxes and manicures.

He bends and kisses me. 'Come on. Dig in. There's all kinds of goodies here.'

'I like this hotel.' I reach out to take a cup of tea, not letting go of the sheet.

'Good.' He crunches on a piece of toast.

It was just two days after the family lunch that he asked me to dinner again. This time, we ended up in his room, ripping off each other's clothes, falling onto the bed in a tangle of limbs. He talked to me as he covered my body with kisses. He asked questions too – *like this? Harder? Softer?* My cheeks flushed. This wasn't the kind of sex I was used to. I couldn't answer. Embarrassment made me mute. But he was a man who knew how to touch a woman. And at some point in the early hours, I fell asleep in his arms. I thought of William only briefly, as if the memory of him was already fading. I drifted into dreamless, blissful nothingness, with no need of pills.

'Listen, I've got to get up. Work, I'm afraid. But no rush. You can languish here as long as you like. Have a shower.' He gestures towards the door to the en-suite. 'Plenty of clean towels.'

I nod. 'Thanks, but I'd better get going too. I have to feed the animals before I go to the tearoom.'

'At least eat your breakfast.'

He strides around the room pulling clothes off the back of a chair, finding a fresh shirt in the wardrobe. Unlike me, he is completely at ease with his nudity. His body is slim and strong, the body of a man who runs marathons, his buttocks paler than his tanned back. I'm not used to watching a naked man while I eat my breakfast. A breakfast delivered on a tray by my lover. A sudden bubble of hilarity catches in my throat. My moment of joy is followed by anxiety. I've been with the same man for over twenty years. I'm a novice at this. Does he really want to see me again?

He comes over and drops a kiss on my head. 'Let's talk later.'

I smile. He's so much more intuitive than I'd realised. I'd

thought the privileged elite were emotionally stunted from being beaten at boarding school and brought up by nannies.

When the door shuts behind him I allow myself a luxurious stretch, staring around me properly, admiring the glossy wood of the huge four-poster bed. The wallpaper is a William Morris design with curving branches and exotic birds. Sunlight falls across the intricate weaving of Turkish rugs, picking out sumptuous colours, red, gold, midnight blue. A vase of red roses stands on the dresser. I force myself out of bed. I'll shower at home. The poor hens are still shut up in their hutch. I search for my clothes from last night, finding them scattered around the floor. The only untidy note in the room.

Without David filling up the space, I'm aware that this bedroom was once Henrietta's. I presume that she chose the wallpaper, the Egyptian cotton sheets and the raw silk curtains. I find my tights, pick up my bra and hook it on with difficulty. As I dress, my eyes dart around, looking for signs of her, for Henrietta's things – jewellery, ornaments, photographs – I'm curious and afraid at the same time. But I can't see anything that would have belonged to her. Puzzled, I open a wardrobe door, and I'm confronted with David's suits covered in plastic wrapping. Racks of ties line the back of the door, slithering colour and pattern. I touch them briefly. I can smell David's cologne, that musky, leathery scent.

Neither of the wardrobes contain her clothes. There are lots of David's shirts. His coats and sports jackets. I look around, frowning. It wasn't long ago that David told me he hadn't been able to move her things. I imagine him coming back that night, pulling her dresses and skirts from hangers, bundling them into bags or boxes. Packing away the evidence of his life with Henrietta, all those memories.

Then I realise, he must have made the effort to clear the room because he knew we were going to sleep together. He was sensitive to how I'd feel. He'd understood that it would be difficult for me to see her things. He cares about me. The knowledge is like a hug.

Downstairs, I pass rooms that I've never been in, glance through doorways, seeing hunting prints, oil paintings, antiques, more flowers. The scent of them is heady in the house. I'm tiptoeing, holding my breath; I don't want to run into anyone. If Adam appears in a doorway and demands to know what I'm doing here, what will I say? Should I tell him that I just spent the night with his father?

I get to the kitchen without an encounter. It's a huge room, stone-flagged, with an impressive Dutch dresser that covers one wall, and a pine table that would seat an army. Langshott Hall is resonant with old money. There's nothing new or flashy here. As I place the tray on the side, I sense someone behind me, and turn with a start. It's Anca, neat in an apron. I'd forgotten that she worked as the cook. She moves forward without speaking and begins to stack the dirty dishes in the dishwasher.

'Thank you.'

She doesn't look at me. 'Mr Mallory. He left something for you.' She jerks her head towards the table. A white envelope.

I pick it up, feeling something lumpy and hard through the paper. I tip the contents out and a keyring and fob fall into my hand.

There's a note. *Now you don't have to walk to my place.*

*

Outside in the drive is a red Fiat hatchback. I click the fob; the lights flash. I pull out my mobile and dial his number.

'You like it?' He answers at once.

'I don't know what to say . . . '

'Thank you?'

'Of course. But I have to pay you back! How much was it?'

'We can talk about money later. It's two years old. It comes with a warranty. It's a good little car. I've taken the liberty of sorting out some insurance. Try it and if you like it, we can discuss the price.'

'How did you get it so quickly?'

'My friend in the business. I called him on Sunday after I dropped you off.'

I stare at the Fiat. 'It's perfect . . . but I'd be happier if we could sort the money out now . . . '

'Relax. I'm not trying to be a sugar-daddy.' He laughs. 'I'm too young anyway.' There's a beat of silence. 'That was your line, by the way.'

I haven't got behind a wheel since William's accident. Despite a moment's trepidation as the engine starts, I feel a sense of empowerment; I press my foot on the accelerator and pull away down the drive. The journey from his place to mine is ridiculously easy after walking and cycling, even though I get stuck behind a truckload of migrant workers, men and women crammed onto an open-top trailer as they're transported between fields. Faces stare at the Kent countryside with blank expressions. These are the lucky ones, I remind myself. They've got a job and a roof over their heads, unlike those people stuck at Calais and on beaches and at railway stations across Eastern Europe, people who are risking their lives and those of their children to cross the Mediterranean in tiny boats, or by hiding themselves in airless lorries.

I park in front of the cottage and slip through the side gate, hurrying towards the hen hutch. But the hens have already been let out and are happily clucking in their run, pecking at scattered corn. At the side of the hutch there's another nest of moss, exactly where he left the last one. This time there are eight eggs. I stare over towards the orchard, spotting him in the distance, head down, digging. I want to thank him, but I'm aware of how I look in my clothes from last night, my bedraggled hair and the smell of sex on my skin. I shout his name instead and wave. But he doesn't hear.

One look at me is enough to make Kate suspicious.

'Something's happened,' she says accusingly, with her head on one side. 'You seem different. Happy.'

I blush and busy myself unpacking fresh scones.

'Well?' She's leaning on the glass counter scrutinising me.

'God, Kate. Does nothing get past you?'

'Nothing. And I'm guessing this might have something to do with that date you went on? David Mallory?'

'Shhh,' I put my finger to my lips, glancing around.

The tearoom is a touch-paper for gossip. I don't know if David wants our relationship to be common knowledge yet.

'Come for a drink tonight,' she says. 'This deserves celebrating.'

I laugh. 'OK. A quick drink. And now you'd better get on

with your job. Remember that? What I pay you for? Customers? Coffee?'

I gesture over towards a table where John sits, his expression one of exaggerated patience.

Everyone in the village seems to know that Luca is staying in my garage.

'A circus? He's a gypsy?' Margaret Briscoe raises her eyebrows as I put her pot of tea down on the table. 'Really, my dear, you should have asked me. Alf has been doing my garden for years. I could have spared him for a week or two.'

'He's not a gypsy.' I am patient, buoyed up by my shiny new happiness. 'He saved a woman from a lion.'

Mary is buying a muffin at the counter. She purses her mouth. 'The day we built the Channel Tunnel was the beginning of all this madness. It's a mistake, allowing these foreigners to invade.'

'People were arriving in England to make it their home long before the Channel Tunnel was built.' I keep my smile fixed. 'And Luca isn't invading. In fact, he's planning to leave soon.'

After locking up for the night, I see Mary's big blue Volvo parked outside the village phone kiosk. There's a steady roar coming from it. When I get closer I find her vacuuming the inside of the box, the nozzle clattering around corners. A bottle of disinfectant stands on the grass. She looks up, her face flushed.

'You'll be putting a vase of flowers in there next!' I say.

She switches off the vacuum cleaner. 'What?'

'I said, you'll be putting a vase of flowers in there next.'

'Not a vase, no.' She wipes the perspiration from her lip. 'A nice pot of hyacinths, I thought.'

She switches on the machine again and bends to her task.

'Right,' I say to her floral bottom. 'Silly me.'

I'm glad she can't see the grin on my face.

I'm unlocking my car, the corners of my mouth still twitching, when a muddy Land Rover pulls up and James Greenwell leans out of the window. 'I wanted to have a word.'

I step closer.

'I hear you've got an itinerant staying in your garage?'

'Sorry?'

'We don't like foreigners around here.'

Three black Labradors scrabble in the boot. Wet noses pressed to the glass, white teeth. I notice a rifle propped up. A bundle of dead rabbits is slumped on the passenger seat. Speckled fur. Limp, lifeless bellies and dangling legs.

I look away. I can't get used to the casual slaughter of live creatures.

I raise my eyebrows and sigh heavily. 'How many times do I have to say this? He's not an itinerant. Or a gypsy or an illegal migrant. He's working for me.'

He scowls. 'This isn't a joke. Someone's been taking pheasants. Those birds are valuable. Coming from the city, I don't expect you to understand.'

I open my mouth to reply, something scathing and final, but he's already driving off in a cloud of diesel fumes.

I stare after him in disbelief. I'd wanted to tell him that I'm proud to be a city person if it means holding to the rule that someone is innocent until proven guilty. Here it's all upside down: Luca is guilty just because he's foreign, a stranger. Where's the empathy, the humanity?

I wonder how many other villages are like this one, how many people are reading the paper and watching the news with horror on their faces, not at the plight of others, but at the inconvenience it creates for them.

FIFTEEN

I'm struggling out of my new car, both arms full of empty cake tins, when my mobile rings in my bag. I drop the tins and fumble with the clasp, rooting around amongst papers and pens and keys. Any second it's going to go to voicemail. I crouch down, tipping half of the contents onto the drive, and grasp the phone.

'I can't stop being relentlessly cheerful. I've even started whistling,' David's voice says. 'Adam's desperate to know what's going on.'

'You haven't told him?' I stand up, breathless.

'I'm going to do it tonight. I need to tell him before you stay again, to avoid any embarrassment over breakfast.'

'But do you think he'll be upset? I don't want to hurt him.'

David sighs. 'Adam was Henrietta's favourite. They were very close. I know parents aren't supposed to have favourites. But you can't control feelings, can you?'

'I don't want him to think I'm muscling in. I'd never dream of trying to . . . to take her place.'

'I know that. Don't worry. He's a generous kid, really. And I know he likes you.'

Warmth spreads through me. When we met in the woods and had that unexpected, intimate exchange, I was worried that afterwards he might regret his confidences.

'So what are you up to tonight?' David's asking.

'I'm going out with Kate. We'll probably go to the pub.'

'Have a good time.'

'I'm sure I will.'

'How's the car, by the way?'

'I love it. Thanks for sorting it out. Don't forget to let me know how much I owe you.'

'I will. And Ellie . . . thank you.'

'For what?'

'For being you.'

The connection goes dead. I stare at the mobile. *For being you.* I don't know what he sees in me. But I have to keep on doing it, being *me*. A smile spreads across my face. And none of it matters any more – the petty comments, James's rudeness – it all fades away.

I tell Luca that I'm going to be out for the evening. He's hunkered down on his camp bed in the garage listening to a tiny transistor radio. The news. A deadpan voice is talking about migrants again, listing a tally of drownings. Luca hardly bothers to glance up at me, and I shut the door quietly, feeling guilty that I don't want to listen, that I'd rather be off somewhere else, with a friend, drinking wine, talking of frivolous things, talking of love.

I find Kate at a table in the corner, already halfway through her Chardonnay.

She leans across the table. 'Come on then, tell me what's going on with you and David?'

'I don't know.' I look down at my hands. 'I stayed at his place last night. And he seems to want to see me again.'

She squeals and grabs my fingers. 'You slept with him!'

I duck my head and look around. 'Not so loud . . . '

'He's gorgeous. What was he like in bed?'

'Kate!'

'On a scale of nought to ten?'

'You know I'm not going to answer that!'

She stands up. 'I'll get some more drinks in. We'll see how talkative you become after a few more of these . . . '

'I'm driving!' I call after her.

I watch her chatting with the bar staff. She knows everyone, it seems. But then, it's a small place, and she grew up here, and so did her parents before her. It's that kind of village.

She comes back clutching our glasses and some packets of crisps. 'So I guess if you start hanging out at the Hall, you'll be seeing more of Adam.' She puts the drinks on the table and rips open a packet of salt and vinegar. She grins as she crunches on a crisp. 'I'll want details if you see him without his shirt on. Bet he has a six pack. Definitely report back if he's seeing someone. I'll need her name and address. I happen to know a good hit man.'

'You said you were happy with Pete.'

'I don't think I used the word *happy*!" She takes a large gulp of her drink. 'Anyway, there's no law against fantasising, is there? Come on, Ellie. Drink up.'

I infuriate her by sipping my wine slowly, but the chattering warmth of the pub and her company has an effect. I feel relaxed, full of positive thoughts about the future. I look around and realise that this is what normal people do – go out after work, have a drink with friends, laugh, share problems and joys.

'But seriously, I'm glad you're seeing David,' Kate is saying. 'I know how horrible it's been for you since . . . since William died. But you're young. You shouldn't be on your own for ever.'

'He was having an affair.'

The words are out of my mouth before I can stop them. She's the first person I've told.

'What?' She stares at me. 'William was unfaithful? *William*?'

I nod. 'You must promise not to tell anyone. It's . . . I don't know . . . it feels so degrading. I think he must have been seeing her the night of the accident. They got drunk together. I found a bag with her clothes in my house.'

Kate's mouth is open.

'He left me a note telling me he was being unfaithful. He said that he was this woman's "knight in shining armour".'

'Knight in shining armour!' she repeats. 'Well, I suppose that's the kind of thing a history professor would be into. Medieval outfits. Chainmail and leather.' She sees my face. 'Sorry. Sick sense of humour.'

I grimace. 'It's so stupid it's almost funny. Except it's not. This is my life. He was my husband.' I stare down at smears of grease on the table. 'He took five grand out of our account without telling me. For all I know he was planning to run away with her.'

Her voice softens. 'He seemed to adore you. I know he wasn't demonstrative or anything. But I could see it in his eyes.'

I can't look at her. I rub a finger through a drop of spilt wine.

'And you don't know who she is?'

'Nobody in the village. It must be someone he met through the university. I hope it wasn't one of his students. Hope he didn't sink that low.'

Kate's looking at me with a bemused expression. 'Ellie, he didn't need to know this woman first, not with internet dating. If he joined a website, he'd have his pick of women from all over the country. It could literally be anyone.'

'Internet dating?' I frown. Of course. The old William wouldn't have heard of internet dating. But there's a whole other William that I never knew.

'I looked at his computer,' I remember. 'Nothing like that came up.'

'He has a computer at work though, doesn't he? And he wouldn't have used an account or password that you had access to.'

I tip my head back and drain my glass. 'It doesn't matter. I've realised there's no point in me knowing her identity. I need to move on with my life.'

Kate grins. 'I think you just have.'

The garage is dark. Luca must be asleep. I try not to make any noise as I crunch over the gravel and open the front door. I slip off my coat, standing at the foot of the stairs looking up towards the landing. A faint glow is coming from upstairs. I must have left a light on by mistake. I begin to mount the stairs. A floorboard creaks under my foot as I reach the top. The light clicks off.

I'm in darkness, the hair on my arms prickling, my ears full of the thunder of my own heartbeat. I slip into my bedroom and shut the door, dragging a chair over and jamming it under the handle.

Someone is here. In William's study. I need to call the police. Then I go cold as I realise that my mobile is in my handbag, which is hanging on the banister in the hall. There's no extension to the landline in the bedroom. I go to the window. It's a long drop to the path below.

My head roars with concentration as I listen, but whoever it is must be standing completely still, or else they can move as quietly as a cat. My mouth is dry. I remember the cricket bat under the bed and get down onto all fours, pulling it out. I weigh it in one hand, gripping it tight. Then I slide the chair away and turn the handle quietly. The resulting click seems loud as a gunshot.

I peer out into the unlit length of the landing. My heart stops. A figure stands at the top of the stairs. A fractured silhouette is all I can make out. Something pushes up against my legs, and I let out a choking scream. Tilly goes rushing past.

The figure disappears down the stairs: loud footsteps, careless pounding. The slam of a door. Gone. I wait, listening carefully. He's gone. My shaking fingers search for the light switch. The landing is flooded with brightness. There's the stick of rubber soles on the wood of the hall. The softness of quick shoes mounting step by step on stair carpet. He's coming back for me. I stagger into my bedroom, slamming the door.

I grab the chair again and ram it back under the handle, and stand panicky, unbelieving, staring at the blank of my door. Fists knock. Sharp knuckles on wood. I catch my breath, pushing my palm over my mouth.

'Ellie? Ellie, are you all right? What's happening?'

Luca's voice. Thank God. I pull the chair to one side and open up. Luca fills the frame, his dark features lit from the back by the hall light, so that shadows lengthen his nose, cast hollows under his cheeks. I can't see his eyes properly. He's breathing hard.

'What's happened?' He leans closer. 'You screamed.'

'Someone was here.' My voice trembles.

He puts both his hands on my arms, fingers curling around my biceps, and squeezes hard. A shiver runs through me. 'Look at me, Ellie. You're all right now.' I manage to nod. 'I'm going to make sure they've gone.' He lets go and disappears down the stairs.

I rub my arms where his fingers were. I don't want to be alone. I follow him. Stepping into the hall, I flick the switch, snapping on the glare of overhead light.

Luca appears from the kitchen. 'The window in the pantry. A pane smashed. They must have put their hand through to open the catch.' He looks at me. 'Should you check that nothing is missing?'

My teeth are chattering. I don't want to be alone, but obediently I go back into the rest of the house, turning on more lights. I remember my handbag. I find it hanging on the banister post and rifle through the untidy contents, checking my purse.

Nothing has been touched. I glance into the sitting room. And then go back upstairs and open the door to Will's study. The same mess confronts me as before.

When I get back to the kitchen, Luca gives me a mug of hot tea. I take it gratefully. A scratch runs across the back of his hand, beaded red. I glance up at his face. He regards me steadily with an expression of concern. I look at the scratch again. 'You've hurt yourself,' I say quietly.

He starts and seems to notice his hand for the first time. 'A bramble,' he says. He wipes his skin on his trousers, a tiny smear of blood.

I watch him, calculating the distance from here to the back door, how many steps to get to the Fiat, how many seconds to start the engine. I move to the other side of the table.

'Did you discover what they took?' he asks.

I shake my head.

'Do you want to phone the police?' He begins to walk towards the phone on the sideboard. 'A friend?'

I take a deep breath. I'm being an idiot. I let go of suspicion and in its place exhaustion enters me like a drug, making my eyelids heavy. I hold onto the heat of the mug. 'No – I'll deal with it tomorrow.'

'I've secured the pantry window. I can replace the glass tomorrow. But they won't be coming back,' he says. 'I'll make sure of that. Try to get some sleep.'

Daylight helps to scrub my fear away, so that when I call David I manage to tell him calmly without my voice shaking. He says he's coming straight over.

'Why didn't you call me sooner? Last night?' he says as soon as he arrives, his face crumpling. 'You must have been terrified.'

'Luca was here. I didn't want to wake you.'

Under his tan his skin has gone grey. He paces my kitchen, frowning. He turns to look at me. 'You didn't get a look at the intruder?'

I shake my head. 'It was dark.'

'Nothing's been taken? You're sure?' David stares out of the window towards the garage. 'Obviously it wasn't a professional job.'

I nod.

'Maybe it was local teenagers? Or travellers. I noticed there's a new lot camping outside Martha's Woods,' he says.

I close my eyes, seeing the figure at the top of the stairs. Not a teenager. An adult. There'd been cash in my purse, an envelope of money in the drawer of the kitchen table, a silver clock on the mantelpiece, other bits and pieces a thief could easily have pocketed. But nothing has gone.

Luca walks past the kitchen window eating an apple.

'Didn't you say he was leaving?' David leans over the sink to stare after him.

'Yes. Tonight.'

'I'm glad he was here for you, but we don't know anything about him, do we?' He paces the floor, rubbing his chin. 'You should get some chains on your door. Security lights. You need to be more safety conscious. You're very isolated here.'

I nod again.

'If you like, I'll have a word with Ian Brooks. The chief inspector at the local station. He's a friend of mine. Don't worry about filing a report. He'll deal with the whole thing discreetly, make inquiries without bothering you.'

'Thanks.' I feel exhausted. I'm relieved not to have to make phone calls, to go into town to fill in forms and be interrogated.

David pulls me against his chest. I can hear his steady heart beat through his shirt. He drops his lips onto my head, kissing my hair.

'Promise me you'll phone if anything like this ever happens again,' he says. 'And you can come to me if you feel frightened. In fact, why not come back with me now?'

'Adam . . . '

'I've told him. He's happy for us.'

'Thank goodness.' I pull away from him gently. 'I'd love to come. But I have some baking to do. So I need to stay here for a bit. Anyway, it's like getting on a horse after you've fallen off, isn't it? I mustn't run away. I can't let this drive me out of my own home.'

He touches my chin. 'I always knew you had guts, Ellie.'

As soon as David's car has left the drive, Luca puts his head around the kitchen door. His tall frame blocks the light.

'I've found some work at another fruit farm. In Little Billing. Would it be OK if I stayed on for a while? If I could base myself here for the season, I'd repay you by doing chores, keeping the land up.' He waits, watching my face carefully. 'Maybe you want to think about it?'

At his words, my muscles unclench. 'You can stay.' I try to keep my voice nonchalant. 'There's always something that needs doing.'

I turn my back on him so that he can't see my face. I force myself to get on with measuring out self-raising flour, sieving it into a bowl, cutting butter into squares, until I hear the click of the door closing.

I sink into a chair, putting my head in my hands. I'm more shaken about the break-in than I admitted to David, or even myself. It wasn't a robbery. Nothing had been taken. It was almost as if whoever it was in my house had been looking for something in particular. But if that's the case, I feel a shiver of fear, will they try again? Knowing that Luca will be within shouting distance makes me feel better. He was capable and sensible last night.

I put my finger against my chin where David touched me. It felt good to be admired by him. It gave me a reason for believing in his attraction to me. I'm not Henrietta. I'm not beautiful, whatever he says. I like him thinking I'm brave, that I have guts. I don't want to shatter his illusion.

SIXTEEN

1990

I wake up feeling hot and shivery. My bones ache. I hope it isn't Weil's disease.

'Flu,' Mum says, putting a hand on my forehead. 'You'd better spend the day in bed. Mrs Oaks will be here if you need anything. I'm going up to town to meet Lulu. Afraid I can't get out of it, darling.'

I lie sweating, headachy. I stretch my limbs, letting my leg dangle out of the covers. I didn't think you could catch flu from getting chilled. I remember the sharp slap of water as I'd entered it, the black lip of river closing over me.

I sneeze.

Mrs Oaks brings me up a bowl of tomato soup and some toast. She plumps the pillows behind my head, wheezing. Her skin smells of onions. I don't want the soup. My head hurts when I move it. I close my eyes, thinking of Ed, wondering if I should see him again. Something has changed since the evening in the rowing boat. A kind of falling away. A disappointment. I lie flat, looking at the ceiling, bored. I want to read – I've just started *The Magic Toyshop*; but when I try, the print blurs and my head thumps.

I must have drifted off. The light has changed. The sun has moved to the other side of the house, and the room is dusky with shadows. I can hear wood pigeons on the roof, their soft cooing reminding me of Sunday mornings and the smell of cut grass.

When the door clicks open, I think it's Mrs Oaks come to take the tray.

'How's the invalid?'

I start, pulling the cover tighter over my chest and struggle to sit up. Les Ashton strolls across the carpet towards me. 'I just thought I'd see if there was anything you wanted.'

He stands by my bedside, hands on his hips, athletic chest out. And I look right up the black triangles of his nostrils. I have an urge to laugh. He sits down, the bed springs creaking under his weight.

'I'm between house calls. Forgot my cigarette lighter last time I was here. Mrs Oaks told me you were poorly.'

'I don't need anything. I'm fine. Thank you.'

His mouth curves into a half-smile. 'Want me to take a look at you?'

'It's just flu.' I sneeze, and he passes me the box of tissues from the floor. I blow my nose, balling the tissue, not knowing what to do with it. He offers up the bin silently, and I drop the damp screwed-up thing into it, feeling ashamed. I lie back, the room swimming. I hate him seeing me ill, red eyed and snotty. It seems odd to be alone with him in my room, even if he is a doctor. I know my mother would be shocked, but Les isn't a stuffed shirt like my parents. He treats me like an equal.

He reaches forward and lays the back of his hand on my forehead, takes my wrist and feels the bump of my blood. Shakes his head. 'Your pulse is racing.' Then he pushes his thumb into my palm, stroking in little circles. I let out a gasp. He looks at me.

I hold my breath. My body suddenly rigid. I try to slide my fingers away. But Les has imprisoned my hand in his. 'I've always wondered what your skin would feel like.' He runs a finger along the curve of my hot cheek. 'Soft. Like a baby's.'

My heart thumps.

'You know how much I want to touch you, don't you? I think you've known it all the time.' His voice has lowered to a confiding whisper. He's taken hold of the covers, folding them down neatly. 'Let me listen to your chest, child.'

My mouth is making the sound for 'no'. A strange rasping noise comes out.

He laughs. 'Don't be silly. I'm a doctor.'

I keep still as he carefully undoes the fiddly buttons of my nightdress and opens it. The corners of his mouth twitch. I know he's staring at my breasts, but my gaze has drifted beyond him, towards the far wall. I look at the curving pattern in the wallpaper, the golden blur of the Klimt poster. Then he lays his head down, one ear tight against my skin. His stubble scratches, his cheekbone digs into me. I raise my chin, so that my mouth is further from the oiled strands of his hair. I hold my breath. I just have to wait for him to remove his head, to leave my room. This is Les Ashton. My father's friend. A doctor.

When he sits up, his mouth sags open, moist and stupid-looking.

His breathing has quickened, and his eyes looked odd, unfocused. 'Eleanor,' he whispers, with a pleading catch to his voice. His mouth comes close, hovers above, so that I see the push of his tongue, its wet, slug texture, the gold glint where a tooth should be. His breath hits me, brown and sour.

It's very fast then. His fingers beneath the covers, pushing my nightdress, everything rucked up and wrong. His weight crushing my ribs. I am limp. I shrink back inside myself, flattening the sharp details of the moment, shutting out the room, the man, his hands. Under my skin, I am scrabbling to get into the deep pit at the centre, curling up there, leaving my body on the sheet.

SEVENTEEN

2015

David hands me a small blue box tied with a white ribbon. When I open it, I find a pair of gold and pearl earrings cushioned on silk. The pearls each have three diamonds next to them, positioned like hearts. They're nothing like the things I usually wear. He encourages me to try them on, and as I slide the tiny posts through my lobes I look at the box again and see the name *Tiffany & Co* engraved on it.

He touches my cheek. 'They suit you.'

'It's not my birthday.' I press my lips together to stop myself saying anything else stupid.

'I thought they might cheer you up.'

I remember how I'd wanted William to surprise me with romantic gifts and how it hadn't been part of his character. At least, not with me. I don't want to drive David away with my lack of response.

'Thank you.' I hug him, nearly knocking him off balance.

He laughs. 'Seeing you smile like that . . . it's all the thanks I need.'

We lie together warm and satiated, my muscles relaxed, the salty skin of his arm under my lips. The sex gets better each time. The running commentary doesn't seem so strange any more; I'm even finding it a turn-on, although I can't join in, can't reply. His bedroom is familiar now. I feel safe inside his arms, inside the solid confines of the four-poster bed.

As I'm drifting off, the sudden sound of Max and Moro barking in their kennels wakes me, and I think I can hear Adam's footsteps on the landing. A door closes. There's the muffled sound of voices on a radio, or perhaps a real girl's voice, Adam replying. David has fallen asleep and I settle myself against his shoulder, close my eyes again.

The next morning, David brings me a cup of tea and home-made muffin.

I bite into the airy texture, tasting walnuts, bitter-sweet cranberries, crunchy sugar on top. 'This is delicious. Did Anca make it?'

He nods, doing up the buttons on his shirt.

'Watch out,' I smile. 'I might steal her from you.'

He sits down, crossing one bare foot over the other and reaches for a pair of socks. Amazing, I think. The man even looks sexy when he's putting on socks.

I slip out of bed, grabbing his discarded dressing gown to wrap round me. I still don't feel confident about revealing my body. 'I'm going to make the most of your luxurious shower this morning.'

'Good. Not rushing home for the hens?'

'I don't have to,' I tell him as I brush past on my way to the bathroom. 'Luca's staying for a bit longer. He can look after the animals when I'm not there, and keep an eye on the place. To be honest, it's a relief.'

Rain batters the windows, distorting the view of the castle gates, blurring the Elizabethan houses across the square into white and black abstracts. I take a jug of boiling water over to Irene. She spoons sugar into her tea and takes a sip. Her face changes, mouth turning down and she puts the cup down abruptly, liquid slopping over the sides.

'Salt!'

'I'm sorry?'

'It's salt, not sugar.'

I taste a few granules. She's right. 'I'm so sorry. I'm not sure how that happened. I'll get you a fresh cup of tea and some actual sugar. Of course, we won't charge you today. Have a muffin too, on the house.'

When I bring her a new pot, her Yorkshire terrier is on her lap. She feeds him crumbs. Lets him lick the butter off her teaspoon. I pretend not to notice.

'How's Baxter?'

'He's such a good boy.' She tweaks the bow between the dog's ears. 'Did you see the poster outside the village hall? Mary is arranging a collection for those people in Calais – donations of coats and blankets. That kind of thing. And there's to be a raffle as well. For the refugees from . . . where is it now?' She frowns. 'Syria. That's it.'

I try not to show my surprise. 'Both of those things sound like great ideas. When I get half a minute I'll look out some clothes.'

'It must be a comfort to have this place to keep you busy. It's difficult being a widow.' She pauses. 'I lost my Peter ten years ago today.'

'I didn't know. I'm sorry.'

She blinks rapidly. 'Your husband was a kind man, reminded me of Peter. Always the first to open a door, give directions. A gentleman.'

'Yes,' I move away. 'Yes. He was.'

'He wouldn't be happy about you having a strange man about the place, would he?'

The smile freezes on my face. At first I think, stupidly, of David. But of course she means Luca.

'I'm not one to make judgements about people – but others will. There's a lot of talk in the village. I'm only thinking of you, dear. Of what's best. Your new . . . lodger . . . he's not English, is he?'

'Irene, I'm sorry, but I have to get on,' I say firmly. 'I have things to do.'

My hands tremble around the empty jug. I can imagine her shocked expression if I told her the truth. *My husband was having an affair. And I'm having amazing sex with David Mallory.*

Kate isn't working today. She's doing a part-time course at the local college. She wants to be a beautician. The days she's not in always seem to be our busiest. I hurry over with John's pot of tea.

'I hear you had lunch at the Hall,' he says.

Sometimes I think there's a spy network in this village. I can't get used to everyone knowing everyone else's business.

'How they must miss Henrietta. She was a saint,' he says. 'The work she did for charity and for this village.' He shakes his head. 'Irreplaceable. And of course,' he looks at me with rheumy eyes, 'she was a devoted mother.'

I try not to take his comments personally. I know that nobody would describe me as a saint. Not even if I were dead. I help Irene into her coat. Outside, a car drives past, windscreen wipers on. I glimpse Adam at the wheel. I have a fleeting look at his passenger, a pretty girl with auburn hair.

I hold the door for Irene as she steps outside, Baxter tucked into her coat, her umbrella up. Adam has parked his car on the village square and is dashing from the shop, head down, back to the car. He must have nipped in for a paper or cigarettes. Through the rain, I see him turn to the girl in the front seat and cup her face in his hands; they kiss. Her head is thrown back, pressed against the steamy window.

I shut the door quickly, aware suddenly that he might look over and see me watching. It's lucky Kate isn't here.

Soon after, the door clangs and David comes in with Dr Waller, struggling to get his umbrella down. I clear my throat, uncertain of how to react to seeing David in public. I have a flashback to him naked above me, his hands pressing mine down into the pillow. The two men are in the middle of a conversation; Dr Waller laughs at something David says, and David claps him on the shoulder and strides over to the counter. I can't meet his gaze. I'm grateful for the distraction of the doctor waving at me as he sits down, motioning drinking from a cup. 'Coming up,' I call out to him. 'Your usual.'

In the corner, the brigadier makes a disapproving noise in his throat and shakes out his damp copy of *The Times*. David stands at the counter, his waxed jacket dripping, his hair stuck to his forehead. I have to resist the urge to reach across and wipe away the wet from his face.

'I was passing,' he says, 'and I wanted to let you know that we've been invited to a dinner party this Friday. Will you come?'

'I'm invited too?' I ask in a hushed voice, glancing behind David. I can see heads turning in our direction, and I know they will all be straining to hear our conversation.

'Originally it was just me. But I rang to tell them about you. They want to meet you,' he smiles.

I swallow my pleasure. 'I'd better take the brigadier his morning scone. He doesn't like to be kept waiting,' I whisper.

As I slide past David with a plate in my hand, I feel the languid brush of his fingers against my spine, and I shiver, wanting him again.

'I'll pick you up,' he says, with no effort to be subtle. 'Eight o'clock.'

I approach the brigadier's table with my cheeks burning. The whole village will know of my relationship with David. And I'm glad.

I kick off my shoes and flex sore toes. Groaning, I rub my back where it aches. It was a long day without Kate. There wasn't a moment to take a rest. Maybe I should find a second waitress, an extra pair of hands and someone to replace Kate when she's absent, especially now it's the busy season?

I go upstairs into Will's study, mulling it over, because I'm not sure I can justify the expense, but I could at least begin by roughing out an advert. Then I can send it to the local paper if necessary, maybe get a flyer printed up and put it in the tearoom window – the shop and the pub would be good places, too. But as I settle myself at the desk I remember Kate in the pub, her comments about internet dating. I switch on the computer, frowning, and set my fingers to the keyboard. I Google 'dating sites'. I am instantly overwhelmed by the choice that pops up on the screen, all of them cheerfully enticing me to sign up now for my free dating trial and singles nights; hundreds of possible matches; find love with eHarmony. Kate was right: anyone anywhere could arrange a new lover – it would take a few clicks of a button. I switch off. I don't want to imagine William in this room, his eyes roving across the profiles of different women.

I'm at the oven in the kitchen, heating milk for a hot chocolate when I get the feeling I'm being watched. I turn with a start. Luca stands on the threshold.

'Ellie, can I talk to you?'

I gesture for him to come in, and whip round just in time to rescue the milk before it boils over.

'A couple of policemen came today,' he says.

'Police?' I startle, spilling milk as I pour it into my mug. 'What did they want?'

'To talk to me. They said they'd come to ask questions about the break-in. But,' he pushes his fingers through his hair, 'they just wanted to check my papers, to see if I was legal. I got the feeling they wanted to make trouble for me.'

'You are, though. Legal, I mean?'

'Yes.'

'I'm sorry they bothered you.'

'They didn't get what they wanted.' Luca looks grim. 'They were looking for a reason to take me to the station for more questioning.'

'I didn't know . . . I didn't expect you to have to go through that.'

He comes closer, looking into my face. 'I wondered if you'd asked them to come – if you had doubts about me.'

'Why would I have doubts?'

'You'd be foolish if you didn't,' he says quietly.

There is something in his eyes, something dead. He's used to distrust. He's hovering by the door. Neither of us speaks. I can hear the clock ticking on the wall. I fight the impulse to grab his arm, hold him steady, like he did with me that night. He'd squeezed my biceps hard enough to hurt, but the pinch of pain had centred me.

'I'm not from around here,' I say. 'I was born in Cambridgeshire. My husband and I, we lived in lots of places at the beginning of his career. University towns. Edinburgh. Liverpool. The people in this village exist in a small world. A lot of them are retired. To be honest, it can feel a bit claustrophobic sometimes.'

'I said hello to a woman yesterday, and she hurried away as if I was going to mug her.'

I laugh. 'You will get a bit of that, I'm afraid.'

'It's OK. People are suspicious of strangers. I never stay in one place long enough for it to change.'

'Margaret Briscoe thought you were a gypsy, just because you worked at the circus.' I smile, thinking he might find it amusing.

'I am descended from gypsies.'

'Really?' I look at him carefully to see if he's joking.

'My mother came from the Roma. They get a tough time of it in Romania. Her family were persecuted. But she never wanted to leave – it was her home.'

'But you left.'

'I didn't have much choice at the time.' He sticks his hands in his pockets. 'But I would have anyway. Itchy feet. Maybe it's my gypsy blood.'

I'm encouraged to press on with another question. 'Were you born into the circus?'

'No.'

His dark gaze pins me into stillness. The memory of Adam kissing his girlfriend flashes into my head. My heart falters, and I look away, mouth dry.

'Your parents weren't circus people, then?'

He stands up so abruptly that he kicks the chair, his movements stiff, eyes glazed. As if he has become someone else. I don't understand what I've done wrong, what I've said to upset him.

I watch him through the window. His broad shoulders and straight back, the slight drag of his leg. Of course. He doesn't believe me. He thinks I lied and that it was me that called the police.

I bring up David's number on my mobile. 'The police were here, questioning Luca. Was that anything to do with your friend . . . '

'Ian? Yes. When you said that Luca was staying on I thought it was sensible to get him checked out. Make sure he didn't have a criminal record.'

'You didn't ask first – you didn't tell me.'

'Yes. I did. We talked about it.'

'I don't remember.'

'Look, does it really matter who said what? I thought the important thing was to get a check on Luca. And you'll be glad to know that there's no criminal record. Not that we know of. He's not an illegal migrant either. But the officers said that he seemed shifty.'

'Shifty? He's just jumpy around authority. The police don't treat people like him with any respect. You can't blame him.'

I stop, realising that this is the first time I've raised my voice to David, and that we're on the brink of having an argument. I grip the phone, listening to a rush of silence.

'Darling, I only want to make sure that you're safe,' he says quietly.

My stomach does a tiny flip. It's as if he's touched the back of my neck with his lips.

'Sorry,' I whisper.

My fingers go to my earlobes, to the delicate, neat gold and pearl rings, twisting them round and round.

EIGHTEEN

One little word, *darling*, that's all it took. When I click off my phone, my annoyance about David calling the police has completely disappeared. I don't know why I got so defensive over Luca. David is right, it's reassuring to know that Luca has no convictions, no record. David is trying to look after me, protect me. I want to rush over to his place and apologise for my mood, go straight to bed with him.

But he hasn't invited me. Maybe it's a bit early in the relationship to just turn up on his doorstep? I can't sleep, though. Feelings bubble inside me. The cottage is too small. I want to dance, to run, to lose myself inside the passion of two bodies together. I want to feel David's skin under mine. But I'm alone. So I begin to spring-clean. It's just a way to channel all that energy, except as I go through the house I know it's a way of marking a turning point in my life. I need to do it thoroughly, digging underneath the history of me and Will. I want to make everything new. To get rid of the ghost of William, make room for the future, for hope.

I wake amongst chaos. There are mounds of dusty curtains ripped down from poles, heaps of William's clothes, his jackets and coats bundled up ready for the Calais collection. I was moving furniture in the early hours of the morning, and the wardrobe is still marooned in the middle of the bedroom floor. I remember that I'd stripped the covers off the sofa and armchair and found a green stain under one of the cushions. One of William's pens must have leaked and he'd covered it up, neglected to tell me. A small deceit to add to the big ones.

I stretch, aware of sore muscles in my neck and shoulders. The wardrobe was a beast; I had to dig my shoulder in and heave with all my strength, but I was determined to get at the layers of dust hiding behind it. The morning sun shows up cracks in the ceiling, filthy window panes, the sorry state of the carpets. I stare about me in horror. The whole place needs redecorating, not just spring-cleaning. What have I done? I don't have the time to finish what I've started. Kate's not in again today. There's baking to be done. As I grab my car keys, ready to leave, the phone rings.

It's Mary. 'I wanted to ask you a couple of things, dear. First of all, if you'll contribute some things to our little collection for the refugees at Calais. Blankets, tents, shoes, tinned food, bags of rice. That kind of thing. We'll be taking offerings at the village hall this Sunday.'

'I heard. Great idea. I've already got some things ready.'

'Good. The other thing is a favour: would you be able to commit to making the food for the raffle evening?'

'The raffle evening?'

'For the Syrian orphans. This coming weekend. All sorts of people are contributing prizes.'

'Oh, yes.' I can't refuse. 'Yes . . . of course.'

'That is a relief. It's a bit last minute, I know. But I told the others you wouldn't let us down. We're not expecting anything proper – just nibbles. You know the kind of thing.'

'How many people are you expecting?'

'At least fifty. More, I hope.'

'Right.' My voice is pale.

Driving home from the tearoom, I hope the chaos will have magically disappeared. But of course it's waiting for me as soon as I open the front door. I have no idea how I'm going to get the extra cooking done. I scrape cat food into a bowl for Tilly, roll up my sleeves, stare around me. David will be here at eight o'clock, and I have to get ready for the dinner party and clear up before then. I look at my watch. It's an impossible task. I haul the vacuum cleaner out from under the stairs, begin to shake cushions, push piles of magazines under surfaces.

Luca knocks on the kitchen door. He steps inside, looking amused. 'What happened? Looks like a tornado's been through.'

I put my hands on my hips. 'Sorry. Can't stop. I've got to get this place sorted, and then I'm going out . . . '

He takes four oranges out of the fruit bowl. He begins to toss them up with lazy swoops of his hands; and the oranges fly through the air, backwards and forwards, spinning and falling.

I watch him, startled and impressed. But I don't have time for this. I bite my lip. 'I've got a lot to do . . . '

'You said you wanted to try it.'

'Juggling?' I push my hand through my hair. 'Now?'

'Have a go.' He stops and offers me an orange.

'No. I—'

'It'll be good for you.'

'Good for me?'

'You look anxious. You can't be anxious when you're juggling.'

He's implacable. His expression determined.

I sigh. 'Just for a moment then.'

He stands behind me. 'Keep your elbows in. Feet should be about hip width apart.'

His fingers are gentle on my elbows, guiding them into position. I can feel his breath on my neck, smell the sweet tang of the fruit.

'Practise throwing just one ball from one hand to the other.'

I throw it up.

'Not too high. Keep it at eye level to start with.'

I'm watching the arc of orange, feeling the weight in my palm as it lands, calculating the length of time it takes to go from one hand to the other.

'It looks fast, but it's a slow art.' His voice comes from behind me. 'Keep your elbows in, remember. Relax.' He moves to the front of me, stands watching with his hands on his hips. 'Juggling only works when you're relaxed, balanced. Control your energy. Now. Try two.'

He tosses me the second orange. I manage to keep both fruit in the air for a couple of throws, and then I've missed a catch and the oranges are rolling under a chair.

I'm laughing and so is he. He kneels down and retrieves the fruit. 'Not too bruised I hope.'

Over his head, I catch sight of the kitchen clock. 'Damn. I've got to get ready. David will be here in a minute.'

It's as if a light's been switched off. Luca puts the oranges back in the bowl, his back straight, suddenly business-like again. He's at the door, nodding goodbye, and I watch him disappear towards the garage. After a moment, I can hear the muffled noise of his whistling.

When David arrives, I haven't even begun to tackle the muddle spreading from one room to the next. I've been too busy rifling through my wardrobe, panicking about what to wear. In my head, the portrait of Henrietta looms over me, with her elegant, understated clothes, her effortless beauty. Nothing is really perfect. Of course there were cracks in the Mallorys' marriage, just like everyone else's. I remember once catching them in the middle of a row, and being shocked at the naked emotions on their faces: her mouth tight, his fists curled at his sides in frustration. As soon as they'd seen me, they'd both slipped back into their usual united front, her smile in place, his hand on the small of her back.

David kisses me and then notices the state of the cottage. He gives a low whistle. 'What's going on?'

'I'm spring-cleaning.' I wave an arm. 'Only now I've got all the food to make for the raffle evening. Did you know about that, by the way? Mary has suddenly become some sort of charity powerhouse just when I thought she had her hands full with the Best Kept Village thing.' I rub my forehead, looking around me. 'The problem is Kate's away . . . I don't know how I'm going to get it all done—' I break off and stare at him. 'Could you spare Anca for a day? She'd be the perfect person to help me cook. I'd pay her.'

David rubs his chin. 'Don't worry about money. She has a salary from me anyway. Look, maybe she should come for two or three days. She could help you with this, too.' He gestures around him.

I remember the immaculate state of his house. Nothing out of place. Each object an exquisite work of art.

'That would be amazing. Thanks.' I tap my chin, smelling orange zest. 'I'd need her for a day at the tearoom. Friday would be good – if you think she'd be happy to do it.'

'I know she will. I'll get someone to drop her off tomorrow morning then, to get started with all this,' he says. 'Then she can do a day at the tearoom on Friday, and another day here to finish the spring-cleaning.'

I notice that he's looking at my outfit. Velvet trousers and a peasant blouse.

'You don't like it?' I smooth a nervous palm over my hips.

'It's not that,' he says. 'But I want you to feel comfortable. And I know it'll be a formal evening. Women in little black dresses.' He shrugs. 'There's time to change, if you like. Up to you.'

I feel prickling under my arms. I clear my throat. 'I'll see if I can find something more . . . suitable then. If you don't mind—'

He gives an encouraging smile.

I have nothing remotely suitable. In the end, I drag out the navy dress I wore to William and Henrietta's funerals. It's stiff wool with scratchy lace panels. I bought it in a mist of grief, not caring what I was doing. But David nods in approval. He steps close, tucks a strand of my hair behind my ear. 'Are you going to put some lipstick on?'

I touch my naked mouth in surprise. 'I don't usually wear it. But I can do.'

I find a Clinique lipstick in my bag, a stub of red left in the tube, and draw it on, using a hand mirror. My mouth looks suddenly enormous and lush.

The minute the host opens the door and ushers us inside, I'm glad I changed. David was right. All the women are in dark dresses with the lustre of pearls at their necks, diamonds glinting at fingers and ears; the men are like David, in well-cut suits and ties. As I'm introduced in a blur of smiles, handshakes and curious glances, I have a moment's vertigo, thinking myself catapulted back in time to one of my parents' parties. Someone puts a glass of champagne in my hand. I recognise a couple from one of David and Henrietta's dinners. The woman smiles but can't remember my name. James Greenwell is here. I don't want to talk to him; his gaze slides across me as if I'm something unpleasant, faintly embarrassing. I knock back the champagne in a couple of gulps, bubbles fizzing in my nose. David moves forward, and I'm towed behind as he says his hellos to everyone in the room, patting a back, making a swift joke, moving on until we've covered the whole room.

'You're good at this,' I whisper to him.

I gaze around me, wishing that I'd read the newspapers, that I had some intelligent conversation to contribute, as I'm sure Henrietta would have, but I've been in my own world for too long. Suddenly I'm homesick, wanting to be back in my kitchen, trying to juggle with two oranges, Luca laughing beside me. I reach out and take another flute of champagne from a passing waiter. My mouth leaves a red smudge on the rim.

There are ten guests sitting down to dinner. Candles flicker from candelabras, the silverware shines, I half expect to hear my mother's voice telling everyone there's a choice of beef consommé or prawn cocktail. I'm relieved that James is at the other end of the table. When I turn to the man on my left, I'm happy to find that it's Dr Waller. I relax, beginning to feel more at ease. I can hear David talking politics across the table.

'I hope you don't mind,' Dr Waller says, 'but David is a good friend of mine. He told me about you two. It couldn't have happened to nicer people.'

I get up to find the bathroom, feeling a new sense of optimism. When I go back to the table, David looks up and gives me a conspiratorial smile. I slip into my seat and finish the last of my wine, my confidence returning.

A woman leans across an empty chair towards me. I've never met her before. She pats her ash-blonde hair. 'Hello, so you're David's new girl?'

She doesn't wait for me to reply.

'We've all been dying to know who snared him. There's been quite a queue of hopefuls, as you can imagine. By this age there are so many of us going around again, aren't there?' She gives me a bright smile, her eyes taking in my hair, my dress. 'Well, I must say, I wasn't expecting you to pop out of the woodwork. But then, David has always been a dark horse. And who could hope to replace Henrietta anyway? I think it's charming that he's found someone so very . . . different from her.'

I fold my napkin up, smaller and smaller, pressing the creases, wanting to fling it onto the table, push my chair back and leave.

'They all liked you,' David says on the way home. He's playing another classical track on the CD. I'd been grateful for it, hoping I wouldn't have to speak. My head is spinning, and I'm longing to get into bed.

I failed a test tonight. The only person I relaxed with was Dr Waller, a man who's kind to everyone. I couldn't be sparkling and sophisticated, but I couldn't be myself either. I drank too much, probably made a fool of myself. I can imagine the gossiping as soon as David and I left. *What on earth is he doing with her?*

David parks outside the cottage, and we sit in silence for a moment, just the clicking of the engine cooling. Darkness presses against the sealed windows. I'm too warm. I put my hand to my throat.

'Ellie.' David takes my fingers and folds them inside his own. 'What's the matter?'

I stare out of the windscreen. 'You could go out with any woman in the county. I don't belong in your world – I'm not like the others—'

'Thank God!' He takes my hand and presses it to his lips. 'I don't want you to be like them. I have no respect for people who have everything handed to them on a plate. I love that you are natural, that you are strong and independent. I don't want you to change.'

I see the woman pushing her ash-blonde hair back from her face, her critical gaze: *who could hope to replace Henrietta?*

I blink the image away. I don't want to replace her. I take David's hand and squeeze. 'Do you want to come in?'

Seeing David here at night makes me think of the embarrassment of that first kiss. Everything feels different. I can't believe that I rejected him, that I ever had a moment's uncertainty about it.

He seems too big for the place; he walks bending his head to avoid the low ceilings and odd angles. He laughs as he has to squeeze around the wardrobe in the centre of the floor, stepping over piles of clothes and old papers to get to the bathroom. 'It's an obstacle course.'

He comes back smelling of toothpaste, and takes my face in his hands.

'You're insane. Have you even made a start on the study? You've got a ton of books and papers in there.'

'I'm leaving that room to last,' I tell him. 'But when I've finished, *World of Interiors* is going to be begging me to let them do a feature.'

'We should spend more time here,' he says. 'We always seem to be at my place. This is your home. I want to get to know it better.'

It's after we make love and are lying together, drifting off, that David's voice sounds above my head, pulling me back from the brink of unconsciousness.

'Ellie, I need to tell you something.'

'Hmm?' I shift so that I can hear him better.

'I can't let you go on thinking the kind of crazy thoughts you had tonight . . . ' He breaks off and sighs.

I'm awake now. I turn to face him. 'What do you mean?'

'I hate it that you think you're not good enough, that you don't fit in.' He clears his throat. 'It's not right.'

I swallow, and my hand rests on his chest.

'I'm not—' his voice is tight. 'I'm not who you think I am.'

I raise myself onto my elbows and look down at him, wishing the room wasn't so dark. I want to see his face.

'I don't understand.'

'You probably think I went to some boarding school, that I've always lived in a house like Langshott.'

'Well. Yes . . .'

'Listen, the truth is, I come from Merton. I went to the local grammar. My father was a sewage inspector. We lived in a little semi off a main road. I was hungry to make something of myself. I went into the army and became an officer. Did a tour in Afghanistan. After that I worked in the City. In both those places I mixed with the kind of people that had been given wealth and privilege as their birthright.'

I hold my breath.

'It wasn't that I was ashamed of my background. I just knew it didn't belong to me. I felt as though there'd been a mistake. I was like a fish out of water at home. A different species from my parents and brother. When I met Henrietta at a party, she had it all: looks, education, wealth, class, brains. I fell in love. To my surprise, she returned my feelings.' He pauses and I can hear the click of his tongue. 'I'd reinvented myself by then. I'd made it my business to study my contemporaries, to read the right books, discover how to tell a good wine, which knives and forks to use for what. I even had elocution lessons. She didn't have a clue that I wasn't really part of her world. I explained my background after the first couple of dates. To my amazement she still wanted me. Her parents weren't so understanding. Her father made it clear that he didn't approve. I was too common for his daughter. But Henrietta wouldn't give me up.'

I move further away from him. 'I had no idea.'

'Does it matter? Do you mind that I'm from Merton?'

I burst into giggles. 'Of course I don't mind!' I roll back into the warmth of him. 'Why would I care where you went to school? I'm not like that. You know I'm not.'

'I know.' He hugs me hard. 'I love that about you.'

'What about the village? Does anyone know?'

'I'm not going to lie about my background. If people want to dig a bit deeper – ask me which school I went to, if I'm related to so-and-so – they pretty soon work out that I'm not from their tight little society.'

'It shouldn't matter where you come from.'

'I don't think it does – not to most people. But a few react like Hettie's father. The brigadier, for one. He's stuck in the past. He wasn't happy about me marrying into the family. He made unpleasant comments when I took over the business after her father died. Didn't approve of the Aiken-Brown farm becoming the Mallory farm. He thought I'd make a mess of fruit farming. I've proved him wrong, and anyone else with the same view. I think the old man has some respect for me now, even if it's grudging.'

'I'm glad you've told me,' I say.

He rolls me onto my back and looks into my face. In the dim light, his eyes shine, and I stare up at him before he dips his mouth to mine.

We lie together, holding each other, and I stroke his chest sleepily. I can understand why he wanted to reinvent himself. There's nothing wrong with having aspirations, dreams. I understand that very well. The important thing is that he's been honest. I feel his body slacken into sleep, his breathing changing. I realise that I'm completely relaxed too. I'm not listening for footsteps on the landing, the sound of glass shattering downstairs. Even if Luca is nearby, it's not the same as having David here in bed with me.

I'm woken by the sound of a ringtone. Blearily, I turn over, hugging the pillow. I can hear David talking in a hushed voice. He sounds annoyed. He leans over me.

'I have to get back,' he whispers. 'Farm business.'

'Is everything OK?' I rub my eyes. 'It's still the middle of the night.'

He kisses my shoulder. 'Nothing for you to worry about. Go back to sleep.'

I wake alone, and stretch my hand into the empty space. There's an impression in the pillow where David's head has been. The faint scent of his cologne. I've slept in my marital bed with another man, had sex in sheets I once shared with William. It feels like a kind of ritual, a spell to break with the past, one much more powerful than spring-cleaning.

My mobile beeps as a message flashes up. I pick it up and squint at the screen. *Morning, gorgeous. I miss you.*

I laugh. I miss you too, I think.

It's a beautiful day and I'm grateful that I've had an extra half hour to lie in bed, safe in the knowledge that Luca will have fed the animals. I remember that Anca will be arriving this morning. What a relief to know I'll have some help to clear up this mess and get the food done for the raffle.

I smile at the memory of David walking around like the Hunchback of Notre Dame, head at a zombie angle to avoid the sloping ceilings. He's much too tall for the place. His Georgian house has long windows, big doorways, lofty ceilings, everything scaled up for aristocratic inhabitants. I would never have guessed about his background if he hadn't told me. I hug the knowledge to me, and the warm feeling that comes from his trust.

Swinging my legs over the edge of the mattress, I pad downstairs to feed the cat and make breakfast. I unlock the back door, turn the handle to let in the sunshine that's failing to get through the grubby windows.

The open doorway is a bright slice of light. I blink, dazzled. Something sags against wood. I step forward, not understanding. There's a bag hanging from the outside of the kitchen door. And then I gasp. It's not a bag. A dead chicken hangs from a nail. The body droops, head dangling, wings falling open, feathers catching the sun. Someone has hammered through its feet.

The world slows and drags like a film reel running down. A lazy bluebottle buzzes and settles on a dull eye. A splash of blood drips, dark and wet, onto the doorstep.

NINETEEN

A scream tears the air. A loud noise that goes on and on and doesn't seem to be coming from me.

Luca is there, holding my shoulders, shaking me until I stop. I can't speak. I point towards the thing and hear his intake of breath. Out of the corner of my vision, between my fingers, I watch him pull the nail out, gripping the creature by the neck, its head flopping uselessly. He drops it on the ground, where it lies in a pathetic heap. And I see her properly then. Her broken body suddenly familiar.

'Clover!' I kneel beside her. 'Oh my God. Clover.'

I stroke her small head, the bloodied feet curled into brittle claws. One eye stares up at me blankly. I begin to wail, my tears darkening brown feathers.

'There's nothing you can do.' His voice is gentle. 'Leave her.'

Luca gets me up, steers me inside and sits me down at the

table. He moves about, switching on the kettle, finding a teabag, spooning sugar into the mug. I slump over, shivering.

'Her neck is broken,' he says. 'I don't think she suffered.'

'Why?' My chest hurts. 'Why would anyone do that?'

'A warning,' he says, as he pours water.

I gaze at his broad back, not understanding.

'Does anyone bear you a grudge?' He places an A5 piece of lined paper on the table. It looks as though it's been torn from an exercise book. Someone has scrawled in shaky capitals: NOBODY WANTS YOU HERE. 'It was attached to the nail.'

I gasp and push the paper away. There's a smear of blood on it. I can't stop staring at the scribbled words. He puts a mug in front of me.

'Drink,' he orders.

My mind is spinning. A warning? The woman at the party. Her face swims before me, mouth turned down in obvious fury that I'd bagged David ahead of her. She had a grudge. But she didn't look like the type to wring a bird's neck and nail its feet to my door. Then I remember all the recent snide comments from the locals about the migrant crisis – John and Sally-Ann in the shop – and there had been those remarks about me giving Luca a job, hints that he was untrustworthy, an illegal migrant. But these are friends and neighbours, people I've known for years. It feels as though I've fallen down a hole in the ground like Alice in Wonderland. Nothing makes sense.

'You must have been in the garage when they came.' I clasp the hot mug. 'Didn't you hear anything?'

'I was out last night,' he says, turning to face me.

It's only then that I look at him properly. His right eye is swollen shut, the skin stretched tight, purple as a plum. He squints out of it. I glimpse a slit of bloodshot white. And there's a scratch across his cheek, as if someone has raked him with their nails.

'Your face!'

'It's nothing. I walked into a branch in the dark.'

'You should put something on it . . . '

'I told you.' He looks irritated. 'It's nothing.'

'I'd better phone the police. David. Let them know about this.'

Luca is crouching before me, his fingers tight on my wrists. 'No.'

He's gripping too hard. It hurts. I lean back with a gasp. He seems to realise what he's doing, and lets go.

'I have to tell someone . . . ' I swallow.

'You've told me.' He puts one of his large hands over mine. As big as a bear's paw. 'Take a moment to think about this. How will the police protect you? But I live in your garage. Nobody will hurt you while I'm here. There will be no more dead things. I promise.'

Luca is right. David would be on the phone to his inspector friend immediately. The police would consider Luca a suspect, especially after the break-in.

I bite my lip. 'But . . . there was the break-in and now this . . . do you think I'm in danger?'

He shakes his head. 'Whoever did this is a coward.' His mouth is hard. 'And I'll be here, just in case, waiting.'

'I . . . I don't know.'

'If you tell anyone, I'll have to go,' he says in a low voice.

'Because they'll make sure I take the blame. And I don't want to leave you alone, not after this.'

We both glance towards the open doorway and the clump of feathers that is Clover's poor bedraggled body.

'I'll bury her,' he says. 'I'll show you her grave later. You don't want to . . . '

'Eat her? No.' I shudder. I rub my face. 'What time is it? There's someone coming over this morning to help me tidy the house.'

We both hear wheels crunching into the drive and Luca uncoils himself from his crouching position, moving to the other side of the kitchen.

I take a deep breath, steadying myself. 'That will be her.' My stomach lurches. 'I hope David hasn't come too.' I stand up, straightening my shoulders, tidying my hair. 'Her name's . . . damn . . . I've forgotten.' My head is still fuzzy with shock. And then it comes to me. 'Anca.' I glance down. 'God, I'm in my pyjamas . . . '

I look round, wanting Luca to get the door for me. But he's already disappeared.

There's a polite ring on the bell.

Anca is waiting on the doorstep. She gives me a swift, assessing glance – bare feet and rumpled night clothes – before resuming her examination of her shoes. Practical white trainers. She's plumper than I remember under her shapeless top. Thick dark hair falls against pale skin.

I hold the door open and she slips through, taking off her jacket. She's wearing a housecoat with buttons down the front and a pair of yellow rubber gloves. She stands like a surgeon waiting for her patient.

'Did David drop you off?'

'No. Bill. From the farm.'

I'm relieved. David would have seen that I've been crying. He would have known that something was wrong, and I couldn't lie to him.

I explain that I'd like her to concentrate on cleaning the house today, hoping that my voice isn't as shaky as it feels. I lead the way to the sitting room and show her the chaos. Rolled up rugs. Ornaments piled on the floor. Dust motes flicker and turn inside morning light. I look at her doubtfully. Is it too much to ask? Anca doesn't flinch.

'I'm afraid it's like this in every room. It would be great if you could go through the whole place trying to get some order back. Except the study upstairs. Don't bother with that. I need to sort it out myself.' I gesture towards the kitchen. 'Cleaning things are all under the sink or in the pantry. Is there anything you'd like to ask?'

She shakes her head.

'If you get time, could you wash the windows?'

She looks at me blankly. Maybe she hasn't understood. But then she nods. 'Which product for this?'

She obviously doesn't want to chat or waste time. Like Luca, I think, remembering that they are both from Romania.

I can't get the image of Clover out of my mind, her open beak with the tiny grey tongue pushing behind. Spots of dark blood dripping onto the doorstep. Her delicate neck snapped. Just when she'd been given her freedom. What have I done to make someone do something so cruel? But perhaps this isn't to do with me. I think of the five thousand pounds and how it's disappeared into thin air. Maybe William was being blackmailed, and now the blackmailer is back, only this time it's me they're targeting. I frown. The note was very clear. *Nobody wants you here.*

I go into the study. There must be something that would give me an answer. A clue. I stare at the crammed bookshelves and piles of magazines and academic manuscripts. It could be anything. And I have no idea how I'll find it inside this mess. I don't even know what I'm looking for. I take some books out of the first shelf and flip through them. My hands are trembling. I clasp my fingers tightly, remembering Luca's words. He's right. He's the only one who can help me. The police would ask questions and then go away. I don't think a dead chicken will be a priority for them. David has his farm to run. He can't live here all the time. I don't want to be alone.

I can't let this destroy everything I've worked for. I need to carry on as normal, keep going with my everyday routine – which, right now, is sorting the study. I need a box to put books in once I've finished checking them. Get some order, a system. There's a couple of cardboard boxes in the attic, left over from moving. I go to the bedroom to fetch the hook for the trapdoor.

As I'm searching for the hook, which isn't where I'd thought, I'm aware of low voices below the window. I cross to the glass. Anca and Luca are together outside the kitchen. Anca has her sleeves rolled up, cloth in hand, a bucket of soapy water by her feet. Luca is standing close, talking in an urgent tone. I don't understand the words. He must be speaking Romanian. She's shaking her head. He puts a hand on her arm, and she steps away, shrugging him off. I watch his face closing in disappointment or annoyance. He tries again, and this time she hisses at him, angry shoulders raised. I step back from the window, puzzled. If I was in a strange country, I'd be happy to meet someone who spoke my language.

When I go downstairs, Anca is busy washing the windows outside the living room. Her face is free of any signs of her recent exchange with Luca. I watch for a moment, looking through the slow trail of soap suds and water. Her cloth moving across the glass. She seems unruffled so I decide not to say anything; I don't want to embarrass her or make a big deal of it. Perhaps I misunderstood.

I look at my watch. I need to open the tearoom. I tell Anca that I'm going, scribbling down my mobile number in case she has any questions. As I'm getting into the Fiat, I remember the missing part of the letter. I should keep searching for that, too. It might tell me the identity of William's lover. Maybe I do need to know who she is after all, in case there's a link to the note.

I'm at the door of The Old Dairy, writing on the outside blackboard, chalk on my fingers – *Cream teas. Fresh local strawberries* – when Adam drives past. The pretty redhead is with him again. She turns to look out of the passenger window. She reminds me of someone.

I'll have to tell Kate that Adam has a girlfriend. I'm not looking forward to it. She gets a dreamy look on her face whenever Adam's name is mentioned. In fact, she seems to be in a daydream all the time. We've had more mistakes like the salt in the sugar canister. All of our milk cartons got left out of the fridge and were soured by morning. I had to compensate several customers with free cups of tea and coffee before I realised. Then Kate managed to switch the freezer off at the wall, and I lost weeks worth of home-made food. I've never known her to be so absent-minded.

When I get home, there's no trace of Clover's body. Not even a feather remains on the doorstep. I wonder where Luca has buried her. I knock on the garage door, but he must still be at work. Anca isn't here either. She said she'd be leaving at five. The cottage looks almost normal. She's worked hard. Surfaces are shiny. There's a smell of beeswax and disinfectant and the windows gleam. I go into Will's study and begin my search again for the second page of the letter, for something that the intruder might have wanted, or something to do with blackmail. I'm confused by what it could be; we have nothing of any real value, and Will wasn't a scientist or spy. He was a historian. I've never seen so many books and files and bits of paper in one small space. If anything, the mess seems to be worse than it was this morning. The piles of books seem taller.

I start at his desk, throwing some things away, filing others. I don't find the missing part of the letter, but I find several books that belong to the university. I suppose I'll have to post them back to his department.

Since the break-in, I always double check the windows and doors before I go to bed. As I pull the kitchen blinds, I see someone leaning against the garage and my heart bumps, before I realise that it's Luca. He stares up at the cottage, the red glow of a lighted cigarette in his hand.

I raise my arm in greeting. But he doesn't answer. I don't think he can see me here in the dark.

The next morning, Anca comes to the tearoom, and I set her up in the kitchen to do some baking. She's got her hair done up in a tight bun, a huge apron covering her clothes. She even wears thin gloves. David told me not to worry about the cost. But it makes me feel guilty not to give her anything for all her hard work, so at the end of the day I try to press a twenty-pound note into her hand. It's only supposed to be a gesture. She reacts as if I'm forcing her to take stolen property. When she sees that I'm not going to change my mind, she snatches it from me and slips it into the pocket of the big apron, a strange, closed expression on her face.

TWENTY

I've found my old trainers and some exercise clothes. I've decided that I should try to go for a jog. It's hard to fit anything extra in with all the baking I'm doing at the moment, but if I get up an hour earlier I can manage, or even at night when I get back from the tearoom. I'm aware of David's sleek runner's physique, his lack of fat. When I was living with William my waistline wasn't an issue.

I set off at a run down the track at the side of the garden. The ground is rough with mud dried into hard ridges, clumps of long grass. I stare down to see where I'm putting my feet. I don't want a sprained ankle. It's only a few minutes before I'm struggling. My calves are burning. How did I get so unfit? I stumble to a walk, hands on my sides. I have a stitch under my ribs.

I stop, hands on my knees, panting. Around me deserted fields stretch towards blue-black woods. Anyone could be watching me from behind those trees or the hedges that dissect the fields.

A flock of crows rises in the distance, wings beating at thin air, harsh voices circling the landscape. I stumble into a jog and force myself to keep going, heading for home.

I stand by the paddock gate and take deep breaths, telling myself not to be stupid. Whoever it is that dislikes me, they haven't threatened me physically. Nutmeg and Gilbert wander over to say hello, and they stay and watch me do some stretching. I clasp my hands above my head, leaning to the left and then to the right, then hook my foot up behind me, pulling to ease tight quads. But when a figure appears from behind the stable, my nerves kick in and I wobble and yelp.

It's Luca. He pats Nutmeg's neck and gives me a steady look.

I'm aware of my red face, my saggy sweat pants and stained T-shirt. I pull at my ponytail, tightening the elastic band.

'I've found something in your shed,' he says.

'What?'

'A small visitor. Do you want to see?'

I follow him over the lawn and he opens the shed door slowly. Inside the dim interior, behind the lawnmower and plant pots, is a heap of sacking. I can hear a strange low noise, almost like snoring. Luca leans down and twitches a corner of the material. There's a hedgehog there, fast asleep.

I gasp. 'How did it get in here?' I crouch down to get a better look, and Luca does the same. Our knees touch.

'The door must have been ajar,' he whispers. 'We need to remember to prop it open now, so he can get out again.'

'Should we feed it?'

He shakes his head. 'I'll leave some water. But he's wild. He'll find his own food when he wants.'

There's something about the small creature curled into a ball that makes me feel better. Life going on, nature taking care of its own. I realise that it's getting late and I still need to take a shower. 'I'd better go. I have to drop some things off at the village hall.'

Luca stands and puts out his hand. He hauls me up, his palm warm and calloused. We stand very close for a moment. I breathe in earthy, woody scents, the faint tang of manure in the shed.

There's a buzz of activity and conversation. Trestle tables wait to be filled. Large notices stuck to the walls proclaim different drop-off points for different items. The floor is covered with piles of coats and blankets. There is an odour of old fabric, mothballs, dusty attics. I spot Mary and Barbara stalking about with clipboards and pens, both of them with the same preoccupied, important air. John comes panting in with a huge old-fashioned tent bag spilling from his arms. There's a hole in the bottom and metal pegs drop through, clattering behind. I crouch to pick them up. He grabs them from me, flustered.

I spot James and his wife handing over a stack of tinned foods. He catches my eye and holds my gaze for just a moment too long, his expression cold. My pulse bumps under my skin. Then I hear my name, and there's Dr Waller waving to me across a crowd of bobbing heads, and the tension in my shoulders relaxes. The next time I look at James, he's laughing with his wife. She sees me and raises her hand in greeting, nudging him, and he smiles over. Did I imagine his first reaction? It's so busy. Hard to focus on any one person properly.

I've brought William's clothes. They've been neatly folded by Anca, and packed into boxes. His shoes are in a bin bag. I find Barbara and hand them over to her, mumbling what the contents are, before I hurry away, not wanting to see her pity or embarrassment when she realises I'm donating my dead husband's wardrobe.

As I make my way to the exit, people smile and say hello. A blur of familiar faces. I feel dizzy. Fear rushing in. Does someone in this room hate me? Perhaps whoever killed Clover broke into the house, too. Perhaps that was a warning. Not a real robbery. Because nothing was actually taken, was it?

But would anyone really want to scare me because I didn't agree with their views on migrants? Because I've offered Luca a job? It seems ridiculous. And as I gaze around me at beaming faces and full hands, at the gifts that are piling up, I remember what William used to say about actions speaking louder than words. All of this generosity erases the negative things these people said about refugees. Maybe the person who bears me a grudge isn't local after all; it's someone else, someone I don't know, a stranger.

I drive over to David straight after closing up the tearoom. Adam opens the front door to me, jangling a set of car keys. He looks preoccupied.

'Are you going out?'

'Work's twenty-four seven at the moment. There's chilling and packing to oversee. Could be an all-nighter.' He puts his hand over his mouth, suppressing a yawn. 'On the bright side, Dad's paying me overtime.'

'I hope you've had supper? You can't work through the night without eating proper food. I've brought some flapjacks over. Do you want to take one with you?'

He dips his hand into the Tupperware box. 'Can I take two?'

'Of course.'

He crams in a big mouthful and chews, nodding in appreciation.

I turn and watch him walk over to the Defender. He climbs in and starts the engine. He's such a handsome boy. He's still chewing. I feel pleasure that he's treating me as if I'm part of the family. I remember how proud Henrietta was of him, how she couldn't stop touching him, tidying his hair, holding his arm.

'I've got pizzas in for supper,' David says, ushering me into the kitchen. 'Anca's not cooking tonight. I've told her to take time off while she's working for you,' he explains.

'Oh, I didn't think.' I feel guilty. 'I could have made us something.'

He kisses my cheek. 'Not after a day on your feet. A bottle of wine and a pizza is my idea of heaven anyway.'

He pours me a generous glass and I perch on a chair and watch him pulling out knives and forks, rooting around in the fridge for some extra parmesan.

'We could have spent the night at your place again,' he says. 'I meant it when I suggested it last time. I like your cottage. It's cosy.'

I shake my head. 'It wouldn't be fair on you while you're so busy here. Don't forget, I've got Luca to do the animals now. I don't need to be at home.' I take a sip of my chilled Chablis.

'Does Anca live in the house? I don't even know how many bedrooms you have.'

'Eight.' He slides two bubbling pizzas out of the oven. 'But Anca doesn't sleep here. She has one of the caravans on the field. I have fifteen vans there for the people who come for the fruit-picking. It's like a little village in itself. We've built facilities for washing and things on site. There's a dining area too. I'll show you round one day. Anyway, I think she's happier in her own space. It makes the line between work and leisure clearer for everyone.'

My mouth is watering as David puts my plate in front of me. The smell of melting cheese reminds me that I forgot to eat lunch. It was another busy day at The Old Dairy. Anca stayed in the kitchen getting on with the baking for the raffle quietly and efficiently. I'll be sorry to see her go. Tomorrow is her last day with me, and I've asked her to spend it at the cottage, doing a final clear up.

As we finish the wine, David stacks the dishwasher. He says over his shoulder, 'You know what I'd like to do?' He turns with an apologetic shrug. 'Just collapse and watch a film in bed.'

I'm relieved. I don't feel like sex so much as just being held.

He wipes his hands on a tea towel. 'At this time of year it's non-stop. But the great thing is,' he yawns, 'I can relax with you.'

I stand up and go into his arms. It's better than sex, I think, the fact that he wants me in his bed to watch films, to hold each other, for familiarity and comfort. In a way, it's more intimate. He presses his chin to my head. We stay like that for a long time.

'Darling,' I whisper under my breath, not quite loud enough for him to hear.

We settle together against the pillows of the four-poster, lights off, just the flickering screen of the TV throwing shadows onto our faces. David leans away to rummage in his bedside cabinet and pulls out a package. He drops it in my lap.

'Another present?' I'm embarrassed and pleased.

'Couldn't resist.'

I open the shiny silver paper and find a long, slim box. I lift the lid, and inside folds of white tissue I find something slinky and black. It's a pair of knickers. Not the kind I wear. These are delicate silk thongs trimmed with lace.

'Wow.' I can't imagine wearing them. I'd feel ridiculous.

He grins. 'I had this idea of you in them, with nothing else on except your apron.'

'You're luring me to the dark side, aren't you?' I try to match his rakish tone.

'Certainly hope so.' He picks up my hand and kisses it. 'You know, I worry about you.'

'Why?'

'You work so hard. You don't get any time for yourself. And it must be hard to be surrounded by all those tempting cakes. I think you need to, I don't know, maybe take up a sport ... go jogging or swimming.'

I flush. 'You mean, you want me to lose weight?'

'Not for me!' He shakes his head. 'I love your curves. Just for you. For your health.'

'I did go for a jog ... '

'Great. Listen, I know how hard it is. The secret is discipline. You go for that jog come hell or high water. Make it your priority.'

'I was going to say, and I hated every minute of it! And I swore I'd never do it again.' I give a shrug. 'Maybe I'll think about swimming or something. But I really don't have much free time.'

He pats my hand and turns back to the TV, presses 'play'. The opening for *North by Northwest* begins. 'I love old movies,' he says. 'Can't beat a classic Hitchcock.'

I lie beside him, wooden. Does he think I'm overweight? Henrietta was practically skin and bone. A hot sense of humiliation prickles at me. I don't want to feel like this. Since he told me about his background, our relationship has changed, deepened. I can't let something petty like this spoil things.

By the time the climax of the film comes, and Eva Marie Saint and Cary Grant are clambering over the stony faces of Mount Rushmore, hanging onto a president's nose by their fingertips, I've got over it. I press myself into David's side, and his hand tightens on my shoulder. I wonder then, as the credits roll, whether we will make love after all, but David pushes back the covers and gets out of bed. He stoops and tugs on his jeans.

'I've got to work,' he explains. 'It's good for Adam to have the responsibility. But he's still learning. Stay and sleep. I'll climb back in in a few hours' time.' Doing up his shirt, he leans over to kiss me. 'I'll try not to wake you.'

After I've listened to a distant slam of a door, David's footsteps crunching on gravel below, I'm wide awake. I lie alone in the big expanse of bed, alert, surrounded by the unfamiliar silence of the house. Eight bedrooms. All of them empty. Without my sleeping pills I know I'm destined for a wakeful night. Eventually, I slip out of bed and pad to the window, looking into the dark garden. The moon paints a pale sheen over the lawn. I can just make out the roofs of the farm buildings behind the tops of trees. A glow illuminates the area. Several electric lights are on, turning the sky a dirty yellow.

I think about getting dressed and finding my way to that light, hoping it will lead me to David. But he's working. I pull on his dressing gown, wrapping it close for comfort, and the thought occurs that I could explore a bit, have a nose into parts of the house I've never been into. David won't mind.

The corridor is unlit. For some reason I walk softly, like a thief. Cautiously, I push open doors looking into different rooms, snapping on light switches, finding everything as neat and formal as a hotel. There's no evidence of anyone living in them. I worry that I'll stumble into Adam's room by mistake. He might have come back early. I can imagine how confused he'd be by the intrusion. So I knock gently before I twist handles. The next door opens into a lovely room, decorated in dusky pink and gold, with a big double bed and an antique French wardrobe. I realise with a small shock that there are personal belongings in here – a perfume bottle and a jewellery box on the dresser – and I'm about to exit hastily when I recognise something, a green suede coat hanging over a tall mirror. I've seen it before. I have a flashback to the last time I saw Henrietta driving past. She'd been wearing green. I go into the room and feel the buttery softness of the sleeve.

I open the wardrobe. It's full of women's clothes. Some

swathed in plastic. Handbags and scarves dangle from hangers amongst the dresses and jackets. David hadn't got rid of her things after all – he'd just moved them into a spare bedroom. I feel sick. I'd been so certain that David had got over her death, had been able to deal with his grief. But this room tells a different story.

A fragrance comes from the fabrics. I lean closer, inhaling. The scent is familiar. Rose, amber. I frown, remembering the bag of clothes in William's drawer. I'd smelt the same perfume. And now that I think of it, all those clothes had been Henrietta's style, classic, elegant, expensive. The long hairs caught in the brush I'd hurled across the room, they'd been brown. Long and brown, like her hair. My fingers move to the perfume bottle on the dresser. I squeeze, spraying a fine mist into the air, and it's as if Henrietta's in the room with me.

I sink onto the ornate bedspread, my hand over my mouth.

Henrietta. William. Their names repeat in my head, going round and round, not making sense. My husband in his tatty suit, his spectacles sliding down his nose. Henrietta, holding herself aloof, her immaculate jeans, perfect white shirt. She couldn't be the woman he was having an affair with.

Impossible. The whole idea is impossible.

A creak comes from the dark corridor outside, a floorboard moving slowly as if someone is transferring their weight. I stand up, my face flushing hot and then cold.

'Is someone there?'

Nobody answers and I hurry over to the door and open it wide.

'Anca?' I call into the emptiness. 'Adam?'

The only answer is the sharp bark of a dog. It comes from outside, from the kennels. Max and Moro. Then there's a clamour of angry snapping and snarling. They must have seen a fox, smelt a badger.

I shut the wardrobe door and hurry back to David's room, my heart fluttering, bare feet soundless on the long stretch of carpet.

TWENTY-ONE

The bedroom door creaks open and David's hushed steps approach. I pretend to be asleep. The mattress dips as he slides in next to me, his hand finding my hip under the covers. He muffles a cough. I can smell the outside on him, a hint of grass and earth. Soon his breathing slows and deepens, and his fingers twitch and slacken against me. I keep my back turned, unable to relax, watching as dawn brightens the fabric of the curtains, and all the objects in the room swim out of darkness into visibility. Wood pigeons on the roof make a soft, throaty cooing. At any moment the alarm will go off and David will wake, and I'll have to pretend that everything is all right.

He mustn't find out that I've been snooping. I can't tell him that I know he's keeping a room in his house as a shrine to his dead wife. I can't tell him that she was having an affair with my husband. Panic kicks under my ribs. I've already concealed Clover's death from him. It feels as though our relationship is tarnished, spoilt before it's properly begun. How can we build something good and true over a lie? I should have told William about my child. The untruth was there, all those years.

David's alarm is the sound of waves on a shore, hypnotic and gentle. I can sense him stretching and yawning behind me. I behave as if I'm finding it hard to wake up, mumbling and turning my head on the pillow, eyes shut. He switches on the radio. A newscaster's voice spills into the room. *The Former Yugoslav Republic of Macedonia has declared a state of emergency, restricting its borders as 2,000 refugees enter the country daily.* A woman's voice now. She's angry. She's saying that London is far too slow to separate the issue of conflict refugees from economic migrants. David changes channel. A blast of classical music. Vivaldi's Four Seasons. He moves across the room. I hear a swish as he opens the curtains. I keep my eyes closed while I wait for him to go into the shower. The weather forecast. *Hot today, reaching temperatures of thirty degrees.* As soon as I hear the roar of water, I get up and dress quickly, furtively, tripping over as I hurry to slip my feet into sandals. I stand at the bathroom door and call out that I have to run, will see him later.

'What?' he yells.

'I have to go,' I shout back.

'No kiss goodbye?' His voice comes through the noise of the power shower. A rain storm in a jungle.

I approach the steamy cubicle slowly, watching his blurry form wiping his face and fumbling for the handle. He turns off the flow of water and opens the glass door leaning towards me, dripping and naked. I reach up to press my mouth against his, feeling his teeth through the softness of his lips.

'I'd get out of here fast, if I were you,' he says. 'Otherwise I'll be forced to grab you.'

His damp hand print is on my arm. It dries as I hurry down the curving staircase into the hall. I can smell frying bacon. It must be Adam in the kitchen because Anca is going to be at my house today – her last day of cleaning. I could take her with me, I realise, but I have no idea exactly where the caravans are; in a field behind the farm buildings, I guess. But I don't want to have to go tramping through grass and negotiate the bustle of the fruit-picking and packing that must be going on over there at the farm. And anyway, she's expecting to get a lift with Bill. As I open the front door, Adam appears out of the kitchen, a sandwich in hand. He's mid-chew. He stops abruptly when he sees me, hesitating, and I have the feeling he wants to retreat the way he came. Instead, he gives a careless wave in my direction and hurries past, disappearing up the stairs.

I aim the fob at my car parked in the drive. The Fiat's lights flash, winking orange. As I get behind the wheel, I'm trying not to feel snubbed. He probably has a hangover.

Kate bounces into The Old Dairy, five shades of blue on her eyes. I'm so relieved to see her that I give her a hug. She laughs and pulls away.

'You missed me then?' She rubs my shoulder. 'Wow, your neck muscles are tight as a nut. I learnt how to give a lymphatic drainage massage,' she tells me. 'You should let me practise on you.'

'Sounds great, but . . .'

I point to the Japanese tourists descending from their

air-conditioned bus parked on the market square, cameras around their necks, sunglasses on, caps sporting the British flag or Burberry check, mobile phones busily recording as they wander amongst the cattle troughs. A few of them are already making for the tearoom.

'Another time.'

As I make cappuccinos and pots of tea, write out bills, slip coins into the till and wipe tables, I try to push the image of William and Henrietta out of my mind. But I can't stop seeing my husband touching her hair as he used to touch mine, holding her face in his hands. Opposites attract. That's what they say. When I'm alone, I screw up my face and bite my lip until it stings to stop myself from screaming. How could William and Henrietta do that to me and David? And the risk had been huge – having an affair in a place where everyone knows everyone else – someone must have seen them. Is the whole village talking about it behind my back? Heat flares through my face.

Kate whistles as she works, an exotic creature amongst the tourists and pensioners, her lips coloured brilliant fuchsia, silver hoops dangling from her ears. 'Didn't I tell you? I finished with boring Pete ages ago,' she confides as we pass each other in the kitchen. 'No more Saturday nights spent watching football on telly. Life's a lot more exciting now.'

I'm not going to mention Adam and the pretty redhead. Kate's clearly got over her crush. I'm guessing that some new man has got her attention. But she laughs when I ask her who it is.

'I'm a single girl. I can have my pick of anyone now. I'm not going to tie myself down to some shmuck.'

A tourist sitting at the window table with her two children lets out a shriek. She pushes the children's plates away and stands up, her face red.

'Is anything the matter?' I hurry over.

'Look at this.' The woman holds up a shard of glass. 'It was in the jam. They could have eaten it!'

I take the piece of glass from her, sticky with strawberry conserve.

'I'm so sorry. I have no idea how—'

'We're leaving,' she interrupts. 'You're lucky I don't report you. We won't be paying.' She hurries the children out of their chairs, swinging her handbag over her shoulder. 'Come along,' she's saying. 'This place is disgusting. I'll be leaving a review on TripAdvisor!'

I show the glass fragment to Kate. She shakes her head, eyes suddenly brimming with tears. 'I'm sorry . . . I don't know . . . maybe it's my fault.'

'Kate, you're doing your course as well as working at the tea-room at the moment, and on top of that you seem to be burning the candle at both ends. No wonder you're making mistakes.' I take a deep breath. 'This mustn't ever happen again. Not ever. Someone might have got hurt.'

She nods, not meeting my eyes.

'I was thinking of looking for someone else – another waitress – maybe just for the summer season . . . '

'Oh, no, don't do that,' she says quickly. 'I know you can't really afford it. We don't need anyone else. And the season is nearly over. I promise to do better.'

*

The brigadier is the last customer of the day. I'm thankful that he wasn't here when the glass was found. He's sitting over a copy of *The Times* as usual, his empty tea cup by his elbow. I glance at my watch.

'Can I get you anything else? Only we're closing in five minutes.'

He stands up slowly, as if his back is stiff, and folds the paper, tucking it under his arm. He's dressed in an immaculate tweed jacket, pale blue shirt and deeper blue tie. His brogues shine like conkers. I've never seen him look anything but elegant.

'I'd be careful if I were you,' he says, picking up his hat.

I frown, not understanding.

'Be careful of David Mallory.'

'David?'

'The man's a fraud. He's not all he seems.'

I flush, trying to control my anger. 'I know exactly who David is, thank you. Maybe you should just leave him alone.'

'Well,' he makes a noise in his throat, stepping around me. 'You've been warned.'

My hands grip the steering wheel, white knuckles locked. I drive badly, crashing the gears. My throat is tight. There's a pricking at the back of my eyes. I've kept my emotions in check all day. Now tears run down my cheeks, and I'm sobbing in big, messy gulps.

Damn it. I thump my fist on the wheel and hit the horn, sending an angry blast of sound into the country lane. I'm angry at the whole world. David warned me about the brigadier. But hearing his arrogant words stops my breath. I'm sick and tired of people's judgemental attitudes, of the gossiping. It makes me want to run away.

I get stuck behind one of the tractors towing a trailer transporting workers to another field, and I'm forced to idle along. Men and women packed onto benches on the back. One of them catches my eye, a man with curly brown hair. He notices my gaping mouth and tear-streaked face, but he doesn't react, just looks impassively. I drag my arm across my cheeks, wiping with my sleeve. The workers jolt and sway with the movement of the vehicle until the tractor turns off into a field, and I can change gear, accelerating forward in relief.

Anca made most of the food for the raffle evening yesterday, but I need to bake and prepare sandwich fillings for tomorrow at The Old Dairy.

The cymbals are back in my head. The clashes repeat *William and Henrietta. William and Henrietta.* And I don't know how to shake the noise out. I trudge upstairs to change into a T-shirt and denim shorts, screw my hair into a messy top-knot. As I go through the house I notice that Anca has worked her magic. There are clean curtains hanging at the windows. The carpet is fluffy under my feet. The air smells of lemon. I glance into the study. In contrast to the rest of the house, this room looks even worse. I blink. I can't face the mess. It seems to be growing like bindweed. I don't have time, anyway. Not now.

In the kitchen I play loud music, singing along to lyrics filled with pulsing optimism: Al Green, Aretha Franklin, Marvin Gaye. I *will* survive, I think, as Gloria Gaynor belts out her classic anthem. I can't let this beat me. I won't be a victim. Not again.

I tip glistening sugar into a bowl and switch on the mixer,

whisking eggs, grating nutmeg, slicing chocolate. The fan I've brought down from the attic stirs my damp T-shirt, flips the strands of hair glued to my neck. I run a spatula around the edges of a baking tray, and the brigadier's face comes back to me, his nasty words and cold eyes.

The air is pungent with the buttery scent of warm sponge. The draining board piled with washed cake tins and upside-down bowls. I wipe my forehead with the back of my wrist. I won't be able to sleep yet; there's too much adrenaline inside me, and I've got a crashing headache. I turn off the music, untie my apron and go into the garden.

Smells tangle around my ankles – lavender and rosemary, burnt earth, parched grass. The night has its own dark and elusive scent, an invitation to walk across the lawn, moving away from the lights of the cottage into the shadows. I'm guided by starlight and moonlight, and the whisper of the river in the distance. I haven't walked its banks since last summer when Will packed up a picnic for us. It rained, and we ended up huddled under an umbrella, munching soggy sandwiches and drinking tea out of a flask. Henrietta wouldn't have liked getting muddy and wet. Her suede coat would have got ruined. What did they do together? Where did they go? I remember her bag of clothes in our house, and blink away the thought of her in my bed.

I blunder on over uneven ground, picking my way over the ridges of the field – David's field – climbing over a barbed wire fence and scrambling down a ditch and up the other side. Too late I feel the slap and sting of nettles, cursing and leaning down to rub my calves.

The curve of river is dark under fringes of motionless trees.

I'm already slipping off my shoes, wondering how deep it gets in the middle. I shrug off my shorts and pull my top over my head, feeling a shiver of exhilaration, aware of odd, ticklish sensations playing across my bare skin.

Mud squelches between my toes, and I'm gasping as the water deepens and gets colder. It swirls around my waist, invisible weeds stroking my limbs. I lie back, letting my feet rise, abandoning myself to the weightlessness of the water, its cold, velvety rub. Above me, through the opening of branches and leaves, a silver eye looks down, brightening my flesh where it emerges, chilled and exposed, toes, knees and breasts rising towards the pull of the moon.

I think of my leap into the river Cam. I'd felt brave then, euphoric with possibilities. But after my son was adopted, my promised future eluded me. Without the right exam results I couldn't be a doctor. Depression swallowed me whole. I existed on a diet of anti-depressants. I couldn't manage my retakes. My life seemed to be over before it started. William saved me.

David's shown me that I'm still desirable, attractive. These last few weeks with him have been a new beginning. I don't want it to end now, to give up being part of his family, the chance to know Adam properly, perhaps to play a maternal role in his life. Can I tell David that Henrietta and Will were lovers? How will he react? Could we even continue to see each other, knowing our partners betrayed us with each other?

The cold of the river has set my teeth chattering and I climb out onto the bank, moving about trying to get warm. It's difficult pulling fabric over damp skin. The zip on my shorts snags. My toe is stinging where I stubbed it. When I squat to investigate, my fingers touch a flap, something sticky. A noise makes me stare around blindly, my heart racing.

It's a bird inside a tangle of branches, wings struggling, then the release of feathers and indignant squawking. There are other sounds in the undergrowth, the stealthy cracklings and rustlings of animals, paws scratching. I hurry through trees, pushing through sharp twigs. Shadows move. Behind the clamour of my blood, I imagine that I can hear someone else breathing. I stumble into a run, seeing, with relief, the lights of the cottage.

A branch snaps. There's a low exclamation. No animal made that sound. I bite my lip to stop myself screaming. Hurry. Hurry. I was mad to come out here in the dark alone. I remember Clover hanging upside down, the nail through her thin feet. A sob breaks in my throat. As I'm leaving the cover of the trees, a hand closes around my arm. I scream. Try to jerk away. A figure towers over me.

'Ellie?'

My legs are weak. He lets go of my arm, and I nearly fall.

'You frightened me,' I say in a shaky voice. 'What are you doing?'

He takes a cigarette out of his pocket and lights it. The small flame casts his eyes into hollows, accentuates the downward turn of his mouth. He exhales. 'I like the peace at night.'

A few minutes earlier and he would have caught me naked. I'm shivering. He takes off his leather jacket and hangs it over my shoulders. He limps by my side towards the house, holding barbed wire up for me to climb through, pulling back branches. At the door of the cottage, I pause and slip off the jacket, giving it back to him.

'Goodnight.' He's already turning away.

'Luca.' My voice squeaks. I falter, pushing damp hair behind my ear, stupidly shy. 'Would you come in, have a quick drink with me?'

I feel his resistance, so I add quickly, 'I could do with the company.'

He nods.

I take the stairs at a run, calling out that I'll be down in a minute, for him to get the wine and glasses out, help himself. I scramble to grab a towel and jumper, and I'm back in the kitchen before he's finished locating a bottle of red wine in the cupboard.

'Do you often go for night walks?' I pour two glasses, smiling at him. I want the other Luca to come back: the one who tried to teach me to juggle, who showed me the hedgehog.

'I like to be on the move.' He scratches his head. 'I've slept out under the stars more nights than I can count. Being confined makes me claustrophobic.'

'We're different then. I love being surrounded by countryside. But my home is important to me. Bricks and mortar. I need security.'

'Home isn't land or bricks though, is it?' he says. 'It's people.'

The way he looks at me, his intense eyes unblinking, it's as if he can see right through me. I swallow, and put my hand to my throat. It's tight and painful.

'I suppose you *have* to think that if you're forced to leave everything behind,' I say slowly. 'When I see the refugees and imagine how they must be feeling.' I shake my head. 'I hope this crisis ends soon.'

'This isn't something that will be over and forgotten about,' he says, his eyebrows drawing together. 'This is the way it is now.'

'What do you mean?' I wrap my arms around myself. I can't seem to get warm.

'Just that displaced people are part of the future.'

'But people will go back to their own countries when they can, won't they?'

'They probably would if they could. But the way the world is changing, I don't think many people will have that option.'

I stare at him in horror. His words make sense. What would it be like to be driven away from my home? To never return. Could I do it? Start all over again, with nothing? I wonder what Anca's story is – why she left her country and family. I haven't even asked. I will next time.

'Did you see Anca?' I sneeze, and my eyes water. 'She left before I got back. I wanted to thank her for doing such a good job.'

He shrugs. 'I was at work.'

I can't stop shivering. My shoulders convulse. My teeth chatter.

He frowns. 'Looks like you've caught a chill.'

'I'm fine.' I jerk my head up, watching him. He's at the kitchen surfaces rummaging around in my cupboards. There's the clatter of metal. Lids rattling.

'What are you doing?'

'Have you got any carrots, onions, some paprika?'

'Yes, but—'

'I'm going to make you some soup,' he says. 'You need it.'

'I'll help . . . ' I stand beside him watching him chop an onion.

His skin is darker than mine, rougher, more weathered. Big muscular hands and strong, splayed fingers. I notice a red graze over his knuckles.

'Go away,' he tells me. 'Sit down.'

I do as he orders and he strides over and flings his jacket around my shoulders, rubbing my arms briskly through the leather sleeves. Friction heats my skin. He doesn't wear after-shave or cologne. He smells of the earth. There's a salty tang of sweat. I have a yearning to lean closer, to touch the skin under his shirt.

I clear my throat, embarrassed. I feel disorientated. But he's already moved away, and he's singing as he chops and slices. The knife moving quickly in his skilful fingers. I can't understand the words of his song. It must be Romanian. It has a gypsy lilt.

'My mother used to make this soup,' he calls over his shoulder. 'Garlic and paprika will drive out the devil and make you well. That's what she used to say.'

He looks in the fruit bowl and takes a lemon, chops it in half and squeezes it over the pan. Adds a grinding of pepper. I'd never thought of him as domestic.

The soup bubbles, steam rising, aromatic smells making me hungry. I slump at the table watching him, noticing how at home he is in my kitchen. His jacket presses down on my shoulders, heavy and warm, weighty as if a live animal is wrapped around me, pinning me down.

TWENTY-TWO

Despite windows flung wide, the bedroom is stifling, heat trapped under low ceilings. I thrash about in crumpled sheets, fighting off images of William and Henrietta. Should I tell David? I can't think straight. I can't shake off my feelings about Luca.

The urge to touch him was powerful, a yearning. After we finished the soup and he was saying goodnight, I had to stop myself from grabbing his hand and asking him to stay. Drug addicts must feel something similar when they want their next fix, because this is a blind, aching need, beyond reason.

I must be delirious.

I'll do better today. I'll be polite, but keep my distance. And later, when I go over to the Hall, I'll somehow find the courage to tell David about Henrietta and William.

There are letters on the doormat. I stoop to pick them up. A couple of bills. And a package addressed to me. It doesn't have a stamp. Someone has hand-delivered it. I rub my finger along the seal. The package is thick and heavy, as if there's a book inside. I rip it open. Twenty-pound notes. Fifty-pound notes. Lots of them. I sit at the bottom of the stairs and pull out wads of cash, neatly fastened with elastic bands. I begin to count the money. But I know before I reach the final number, that it will add up to five thousand pounds.

I start up from the step and snatch open the front door, peering into an empty drive. A bird flutters from the hedge. Of course they haven't waited on the doorstep for me to find them. I scratch my head, staring at the package. A blackmailer doesn't return money to the victim. Not unless they have a sudden guilty conscience. I need to find somewhere safe to put it. The filing cabinet in William's study has a key.

The room is a riot of scattered books; drawers gape and files lie open, their contents ripped out. I frown, standing in the middle of it all clutching the package of money. Did I really leave the study in such a state? I prod a spreading pile of papers with my toe and catch a glimpse of yellow. I squat to investigate. It's rubbery to the touch. Empty fingers flopping. Anca's cleaning glove.

I told her not to come in here. But she wasn't cleaning or tidying. From the look of the place, she'd been delving into drawers, throwing papers, rooting into files as if she was a thief searching for valuables. Either that, or she was very angry about something. I lock the money in the cabinet and take the glove with me. When I get to David's this evening, I need to ask her exactly what the hell she's been doing.

*

I leave The Old Dairy early to set up the refreshments in the village hall for the raffle evening. Mary and Barbara have transformed the room with decorations, flowers, chairs, brightly coloured posters with pictures of the prizes. I lay out the tiny sandwiches, the slices of lemon cake, the miniature profiteroles and cheese straws that Anca helped prepare. My mother would have approved – fiddly finger food was the height of sophistication in her book. I would have preferred something more casual, perhaps chunks of banana and date loaf, humus and pitta bread, a herby salad. But Mary has the same idea about food as my mother.

'I can't thank you enough,' she says, leaning over the table approvingly. 'We'll get a photo taken before the crowd demolish it.' She motions to a photographer standing by and he points his camera at the spread.

'We're documenting the whole evening. You'll read about it in the local paper tomorrow. There's a journalist here somewhere. And we'll have lots of snaps of the occasion up on the noticeboard in here too. I'm going to caption them myself. We'll keep the Syrian pictures in the hall, to remind people what we're collecting money for.' She gestures to the gallery arranged on one wall.

I walk across to look at sobering images: destroyed buildings, a crying child, a group of women in headscarves wailing behind a roll of razor wire. I fold my arms and stare at this other world. Poverty and fear and desolation look back at me.

People are beginning to come in, anxious to get a good seat. The room is filled with chatter. There's a party atmosphere. James is running a bar from a trestle table, and people are clutching plastic cups of wine or beer, juggling paper plates piled with nibbles.

'Delicious food, dear!' Irene says, popping a cheese straw into her mouth.

I sneeze. My forehead is hot. Flu. I must have been coming down with it when I swam in the river. I smile at Irene, but I'm thinking of the money locked away in the filing cabinet. Whoever's been persecuting me, getting the money back is a positive message. It has to be. A sign that it's over.

John, the host for the evening, is up on the stage with a microphone. He introduces a school choir. A bunch of self-conscious teenagers troop onto the stage. They arrange themselves in a semi-circle and open their mouths, and unexpectedly pure, childish voices launch into a version of 'Hallelujah'. I blink a tear away.

Mary has organised a slide show and takes her audience through the history of how the crisis has happened, pointing to graphs and charts of statistics, explaining what the chosen charity will do for the refugees. There is polite murmured approval and a round of clapping when she's finished.

I notice David slipping in at the back, shaking hands and nodding as people greet him. He said it would be a struggle to get here. I'm glad he's managed it. I know he's donated a big prize. A night at a five-star hotel in Canterbury. John asks one of the choir to come up and hold the bucket. He dips into it and begins to call out numbers.

I work my way past people to David, and he curls his arm around my shoulder. 'Look at Mary Sanders; she's like the cat that got the cream,' he murmurs.

Mary has returned to her chair on the stage behind John. She has a spectacular blue rinse for the occasion, and a matching dress. She beams at the individuals coming up to offer their winning tickets in exchange for their prizes.

'I know she can be bossy. And this Best Kept Village competition has sent her over the brink,' I say. 'But I'm full of admiration for her now. Restores my faith in human nature, in fact.'

He laughs and puts a hand into my hair, ruffles it. 'You're coming home with me tonight, aren't you? You look very sexy with your cheeks flushed.'

I put my hands to my blazing face. I should probably go home, take some aspirin. But I remember, 'I need to talk to Anca.'

'Anca? Why?'

'She left something at my house.'

He grimaces. 'You might find it difficult.'

'Why?'

'I'll tell you at my place. Let's get out of here.'

I take the Fiat, following behind David in the Range Rover. He drives fast through dusky lanes, his brake lights flashing at corners. On either side, the Mallory fields stretch towards the horizon, each one filled with polytunnels. In this half-light, they look like spines of huge creatures, a clan of pale dragons. I keep the rear beams of the Range Rover in sight, concentrating on changing gears, staying at a safe distance from David. An oast house looms up, its three chimneys silhouetted. Then we've reached the curve of tall garden wall, and the gates swing open.

In the house, David goes straight into the kitchen and opens a bottle of wine, pours me some. He clinks his glass against mine.

'Well done. The food was a triumph. Mary Sanders owes you.'

'Anca made most of it. Is she here?'

'She's left.'

'What do you mean?'

'I mean, she's gone. Packed up and disappeared.'

'That was sudden – where?'

David shrugs. 'I don't know. She wasn't clear about her plans. The thing is, she was pregnant.'

The shapeless housecoat. Her rounded contours. I hadn't noticed her properly, hadn't been paying attention. I feel guilty. I'd been more interested in how useful she could be to me.

David takes a large sip of his drink. 'She only told me about the pregnancy when I asked outright. I was concerned. She's pretty far on and shouldn't be working so hard.'

'Is she with someone? Who's the father?'

'She was very cagey about it. Eventually I managed to get some details out of her. He's Romanian apparently, another migrant I expect, and he'd got rough. She never used the word "rape", but . . . I'm suspicious.'

I catch my breath. 'Poor Anca.' My guilt is increasing.

'I think the father, whoever he is, has come back into her life recently. She implied that she'd been frightened by someone. That she couldn't stay in the area any longer.'

I frown. 'And you have no idea where she's gone?'

He purses his mouth and shakes his head. 'I feel as though I've let her down. I told her we could protect her. I didn't expect her to run off. I hope she's on a flight home. She's taken everything from her caravan.'

'She wasn't too far along in her pregnancy to fly, then?'

His brow crumples. 'I hadn't thought of that. I hope not.' He looks at me. 'What was it you wanted to give back to her?'

I startle. 'Nothing. It doesn't matter.'

When David's back is turned, I take the rubber glove out of my bag and shove it deep into the bin. The idea that Anca might have been raped makes me cold, makes my insides squirm and grow small and tight. I wish she'd talked to me. I hope that she's all right. I hope that she's safe, wherever she is.

David is lying with his arm flung back, snoring gently. I can't sleep. My throat hurts. The pink and gold room is just a few feet away. It seems like a dream now. A hallucination. Henrietta was untouchable. An ice queen. But I always felt she was hiding something. While we made small talk standing in the street, or I served her in the tearoom, she knew she was having an affair with my husband. Everything she said to me was a lie. The thought takes my breath away. Who was she really? I slip out of bed, moving slowly, grabbing David's gown to wrap around me. I sneak out of the room, down the corridor, counting the doors on my right. At the fourth, I hold the handle and turn softly. But it doesn't give. I push harder. It's locked.

I put my ear to the wood and listen. I can't hear anything except the muted sound of the grandfather clock ticking in the hall below. The loose floorboard under my feet creaks and I shift away, walking back to David's room through shafts of moonlight.

David mutters as I slide in beside him and I hold my breath, suppressing a sneeze, but he doesn't surface. His arm loops around my waist and I rest my fingers on his warm forearm. How often does he go to the gold and pink room to be alone amongst her things, her scent, his memories? Is it a daily pilgrimage? I imagine him burying his face in her clothes, breathing in the last fragments of her. It's private. That's why he locked the room. Jealousy pricks. I'm a horrible person. I can't be jealous of a dead woman.

I press my hand over my burning forehead. If I told him that Henrietta had been having an affair with William, she wouldn't be so perfect any more. He'd feel differently about her. But what proof do I have? A letter with no name. I threw the bag away. Her things. They were taken by the bin men weeks ago. Even if I wanted to break his heart, I don't have anything to make him believe me. And I don't want to do that, he doesn't deserve it. I can't tell him after all. I was wrong. It will be worse for him to know.

TWENTY-THREE

Two people stand on the market square chatting to Mary Sanders. The strangers are dressed like tourists. One has a camera around his neck. I can hear Mary's high-pitched laugh from here. The sun glints on the shining windows of the Elizabethan houses behind, picks out the brilliant reds and pinks of geraniums spilling out of cattle troughs. Above the little group, the new street lamps curve prettily.

Kate watches them through the window. 'That woman can spot judges in a heartbeat, although she'll be pretending that she's just being helpful. Did you see the judge last week disguised as a boiler man from British Gas? They're supposed to be anonymous. It's a joke.' She nods towards the square. 'She'll be bringing them in here soon.' She bunches the tea towel in her hand. 'Can't wait to hear her bang on about last night. What a triumph it was. How much they raised for the poor refugees. It's a real feather in her cap.'

'That's a bit cynical, Kate.'

'Is it?'

She looks pale and tired. Her bleached hair is showing its dark roots. We only have one customer at the moment. Irene is eating a scone slowly, crumb by crumb, feeding morsels to Baxter, and making her tea last by topping it up with boiling water every fifteen minutes. Through the glass, I see Mary waving in our direction, and as if choreographed, all three of the figures on the square begin to cross the street towards The Old Dairy.

At that moment, Baxter jumps down and strains at his leash, yapping in excitement. Irene is bending over him, trying to shush him. But the dog dances on the spot, mouth open. He seems to be trying to escape towards the corner of the room. Puzzled, I glance over.

'Kate. Lock the door. Quick,' I hiss.

'What?'

I point to the corner.

She opens her mouth in horror, but runs to the door and slides the lock across just as Mary arrives, the two strangers behind. Mary's face contorts in surprise and then fury as Kate turns the sign on the door to 'closed'. I watch Mary collect herself, turning to the undercover judges. I see her lips forming some quip or explanation. Then she's ushering them away towards the village hall.

There's a dead thing in the corner of the room. A long thin tail, a dark slack body. Irene has her back to it, oblivious. She's busy with the yapping Baxter in her arms.

I approach the creature cautiously. A faint smell of rot hits me. It's been dead for a while. I gasp and look into Kate's face. She's blank, but I can see panic in her eyes.

'Kate, you were the last one yesterday. You locked up.'

'But it wasn't here when I left.'

'Did you lock up properly? Set the alarm?'

She nods.

I was the first to come in this morning. I unlocked the door, turned off the beeping alarm. She's telling the truth. I missed seeing the rat because it's in the far corner. I stare at the carcass. 'If anyone noticed this . . . '

She makes a strangled sound, half sob, half gasp.

' . . . we would have been shut down. The Food and Hygiene people would have been all over us.'

'Everything all right?' Irene has swivelled around in her chair. 'Can I have the bill, dear? I don't know what's wrong with Baxter today. He's being a naughty boy.'

The little dog is wriggling in her arms, his nose twitching.

I stand up. 'Of course. Just a minute.'

'I have no idea how it got here . . . honestly.' Kate's mouth trembles as if she's about to cry. 'And what that woman said about putting a bad review on TripAdvisor . . . ' she swallows. 'One of the customers yesterday mentioned that she was pleasantly surprised by the food here. I thought it was a weird thing to say, so I looked on TripAdvisor. And there are negative comments. Complaints.'

My chest feels tight. 'Get Irene her bill and keep her talking while I take it through to the back.'

I pick it up in a plastic bag and throw it into the industrial bin in the alley behind the tearoom, wiping my hands on my apron with a grimace. I remember the salt in the sugar. The sour milk. The broken plates. The shard of glass in the jam. And now, bad reviews. I stand with my hands pressed over my eyes. Energy drains from my body. It's not over. It's a vendetta. Someone wants me to leave, wants to drive me away from my home, my business, from David.

TWENTY-FOUR

The photo has gone viral, his image circling the globe. I stare down at the newspaper. The little boy looks as though he's sleeping. He lies on the wet sand, head turned to the side, plump babyish limbs relaxed. He is three years old. The beach is in Turkey. He drowned trying to cross the Mediterranean with his family. His older brother is dead, too.

I trace the child's body with my finger. A large tear splashes onto the newsprint, making it soggy. I'm crying for him, and for the others who have no names, no images in papers like this one, whose pictures don't flash up on TV screens and Twitter pages and Facebook walls. And I'm crying for my little boy, who was once this age, and whose sweet tender hands I never kissed. I'm crying for the babies I couldn't conceive with William. All those months that brought my period when I was praying for it not to come. My eggs washing away in a bloody swill. Pain cramping my gut.

I put my head down on the table. It's all mixed up. This one small child. The senseless deaths of hundreds. All the misery in the world. Corruption and stupidity. The loss of William. His affair with Henrietta. The fact that someone, somewhere, hates me enough to persecute me. I struggle upright, wiping my eyes, trying to catch my breath.

When I handed over William's pint in that Cambridge pub, I knew I'd seen his freckled face somewhere before. I remembered his earnest features framed in a window, his red hair lit by a lamp, before I'd taken that leap into the dark waters of the Cam.

After months of old-fashioned courting, William asked me to marry him. I'd begun to train as a midwife when I moved out of my parents' home. It wasn't my dream of being a doctor, but it was still a career that I could be proud of. Except I couldn't do it. Being near pregnant women and newborn babies was unendurable. After that, I didn't have the qualifications or the heart for anything more than working as a barmaid or waitress. Then there was William. I was happy to help support my clever husband through his PhD. I knew I could never again be that girl shivering in a boat. Her convictions and her optimistic dreams were lost.

When Will got his first research post, we agreed that it was the right time to have a child. It didn't happen. Years slipped by. I'd asked him if he wanted to go to a doctor, have tests, to see if we could have IVF.

William shook his head, a sheepish look on his face. He took my hand. 'Dearest, perhaps it's selfish of me, but I like having you to myself.' He removed his glasses, pale eyes blinking. 'Do we really want all that fuss? We're happy together aren't we, Ellie? Maybe we should just accept that this is the way it's supposed to be.'

Guilt made me hold my tongue. I didn't insist. Now I know that all this time I resented it.

I stand up and walk away from the photograph. I can't look at it any more. I can't pull air inside my lungs. I half run, half stumble out into the garden, mouth gasping, hands at my neck, ripping my shirt wide. I am surprised by the light, by the brilliance of the sun. Birds swoop above me in a clear basin of blue. I stop at the boundary hedge and gaze towards the polytunnels and the woods beyond. It was exactly here that Will and I stood together with our glasses of wine, toasting each other and our new home, our new life.

'Ellie?'

I start at the sound of Luca's voice.

He limps over the grass with narrowed eyes, his usual intensity honing in. He sees everything. I turn back to the view, blocking him out, hunching my shoulders. He's behind me, and my senses gather, prickling and alert, feeling the physical force of him. I can hear him standing there, considering me.

'I'm going to the orchard,' he says quietly. 'There are apples ready to pick. I could do with your help.'

I know he's gone because the air around me feels cooler, somehow emptier.

Luca is reaching up to test an apple, to see if it's ready to pick. I watch him for a few moments and then I join him, cupping my hand around a fruit, giving it a gentle twist to see if it comes away from the branch. It does, releasing with a gentle snap. I close my fingers around the waxy globe, bring it to my face and inhale. The howl inside me threatens to break free again, and I push it down.

Luca and I work together without speaking. The physical routine calms me as I twist and pull the stalks, stretching to reach into the tree and bending to place apples amongst the others, pausing only to rub the ache at the base of my spine. Luca's sleeves are rolled up and I notice the thick, gleaming skin on his forearms, his strong wrists and nimble fingers. I want to put out my hand and press it over the bulk of his shoulders, feel his muscles slacken under me. I long for that human connection.

We work at the same tree so that we can use the same tub, but we never collide, never as much as brush arms or hands.

I stop, wiping my brow, and look around at the summer landscape, needing to centre myself. When I turn, Luca is watching me. And I glimpse something in his expression that makes my mouth go dry. Immediately he irons it out, makes himself blank. But it's too late.

'Have I done something wrong?' The words are out before I can stop them.

He straightens up and regards me gravely. 'I don't know. Have you?'

'What? No.' I stare at him. 'What do you mean?'

He takes a step forward, and another, so that he's close enough to touch me. I feel the roughened tip of his finger brushing my skin just under my eye.

'Why were you crying?'

My heart is stuttering. 'Because . . . ' I can't explain. I hang my head. 'It's complicated.'

He moves away from me. 'Funny isn't it, we've been living within a few feet of each other for weeks.' He narrows his eyes. 'I'm grateful. You gave me a job, invited me into your home when it would have been easy not to. But we haven't got much further, have we?' He folds his arms. 'Neither of us knows the other.'

'You weren't exactly forthcoming when you first arrived.' I tilt my chin; my heart is thumping now with a sense of injustice. 'I always got the feeling you were keeping secrets. I still do.'

'We both have our secrets, Ellie.' He picks up the tub. 'I guess it's the way we humans are: suspicious, afraid.'

He walks towards the cottage, carting the tub as if it was filled with feathers instead of solid, fat apples. The smell of the fruit is on my fingers. The scent of freshly picked apples making me think of damp mornings and turned earth, summer days getting shorter, the nights drawing in.

TWENTY-FIVE

I'm in the study, tidying up the mess that Anca made. It's too hot to hurry, so I go slowly, painstakingly checking through the pages of every single book, every single file. The missing bit of the letter doesn't turn up, and neither does anything else that a thief or blackmailer would want. The only thing of value in the room is the five thousand pounds safely locked in the filing cabinet. I wonder if Anca was looking for money. I remember how she snatched the twenty-pound note from me.

I don't want to go to bed alone. I know I won't sleep. Luca's words keep going round and round in my head. Why did he ask me if I'd done anything wrong? It could have been a rhetorical question, a defensive comment. But I got the feeling he was serious.

He is outside somewhere. Close enough to run and find. This madness has to stop. I walk over to the door and shut it firmly, to keep myself from doing something I'll regret. I sit in Will's chair at the computer, switching it on, and go onto Google. I type in *knight in shining armour.*

An idealised or chivalrous man who comes to the rescue of a woman in a difficult situation.

My fingers move across the keys. *Grudge.*

A feeling of resentment harboured because of some real or fancied wrong. The desire to harm someone; ill will.

I tap in *Romanian gypsy* next and find an article written for the *Telegraph* in February 2013. It's about a group of Roma who've been evicted from their homes and forced to live outside the city on a rubbish dump. The oppression they're facing in their own country means that right-wing politicians over here fear there will be a mass migration of Romanian gypsies into the UK.

I stare at the article, and I can taste bitterness in my mouth. The current mass migration has swept up far more than Romanian gypsies.

The light outside has faded now; the room is shadowy. The screen before me is the only bright thing in the room. I press the 'off' button and I'm plunged into darkness. I stand up, not wanting to be in William's chair, where he must have sat composing his letter to me. Had it been a Dear Jane letter? If I'd found the missing page, would I have discovered that he'd been planning to leave me?

It's hot in the study, airless, oppressive. An owl calls outside. I go to the window and push it wide open, looking out into the garden at the crouching shape of the garage. There's no light, but Luca might still be awake. I can't go on with this churned-up anxiety inside me, not knowing if it's in my head or real. I'm going to go and talk to him, to explain what I'm feeling. To ask him if he feels the same.

I hurry through the house, switching lights on as I go, blinking in the sudden, disorientating brilliance. My bare feet are soft on the stairs. Outside, the path to the garage is warm under my feet, the concrete holding the heat of the day.

I hesitate for only a moment before I knock. An urgent need to see him consumes every part of me. I knock again, louder. But there's no reply.

I push at the door and put my head around, calling quietly, 'Luca?'

He's not there. The garage is empty.

I go without breakfast but Tilly comes crying for hers, and I hush her meows, tipping hard food into her bowl so quickly that it spills and I have to scrabble on the floor, picking it up. I flit past the kitchen window like a ghost, not daring to look, just in case Luca is there. Thank God he was out yesterday. It saved us both from an embarrassing disaster. Luca must know that I'm seeing David. He would have been horrified by my behaviour, disgusted too.

I don't want to be like William.

My phone beeps in my pocket. I pull it out to look at the text.

Coming over tonight?

Yes.

I press 'send'.

I put my finger on the entrance buzzer and speak into the microphone. The big electronic gates swing apart. I park next to the

Range Rover and mud-splattered Defender and knock on the front door. I need to reassure myself that my feelings for Luca aren't real, to remind myself how lucky I am to have David.

The door opens. A girl stands at the threshold. A pretty redhead.

'You're Adam's girlfriend!' I smile. 'I'm Ellie.'

I put out my hand. She doesn't move, staring at my outstretched fingers with a puzzled expression. But then she's touching me. Palm to palm. Her grip is non-existent: limp and cool.

'Constanta.'

I recognise her accent. She's Eastern European. 'Is David here? He's expecting me.'

'In the sitting room.'

Her eyes slide away from mine. She tucks her hair behind one ear. Even without a smile, she's very beautiful. She turns and goes in the direction of the kitchen.

The sitting-room door is shut, but I can hear raised voices before I reach it. David and Adam are arguing. Their voices are hot and angry. I falter, embarrassed, outside the door.

'Why do you persist in keeping it up?' David's voice.

'What if I want to?' Adam sounds sulky. 'Anyway, it was you who got us into this. You made the deal. You can't break it now.'

'Deals are made to be broken. Like rules.' There's a dull thump, as if something has fallen onto the carpet.

'I can't believe you're talking like this . . . '

'Stop being so soft. Think of the farm. Your future.' I've never heard David sound so hard. 'She'll drag you down.'

'I'm going to meet her tomorrow. And you can't stop me.'

'I don't like it being such a regular thing. It's too easy for someone to notice – Jesus. What time is it?' There's a pause when I imagine David's looking at his watch. 'Ellie's coming over after work . . . '

I can hear movement, the rustle of something being put down, a body in motion, and Adam says something else but I don't catch it, because I'm back-tracking rapidly up the dark hall towards the front door.

As David steps out of the sitting room I've reached the entrance mat, where I stand motionless with my hands clasped behind me, as if I'm marooned on a small island.

'You're here!' He's striding towards me with open arms. 'I didn't know. Did someone let you in?'

His broad smile confuses me. He's switched moods so quickly. I blink at him stupidly before I manage to reply. 'Adam's girlfriend.'

'Constanta.' David is by my side, his lips on mine. 'Did you have a chat?'

'I think she was in the middle of something.'

'Well. You're here now.'

'She's lovely. She's not English?'

'Constanta? She's Romanian.' He puts his arm around my shoulder. 'Have you eaten? There's chicken salad if you—'

'No,' I say quickly. 'I've had supper.'

I couldn't force any food down, not at the moment. I feel slightly sick. There was something about the row, hearing their private anger, and the underhand, voyeuristic way I stood there in the hall eavesdropping. It's given me an empty, grubby feel.

I sit in the kitchen while David eats, and I have to look away as he forks mouthfuls of rocket and tomato into his mouth. Snatches of their row come back to me – I can't ignore it, can't pretend it didn't happen.

'I couldn't help overhearing,' I say. 'You and Adam. You were . . . arguing. Is everything OK?'

David stops eating. He frowns briefly. 'Oh, that.' He takes a sip of wine. 'Adam's strong-willed and so am I. We clash occasionally.' He smiles. 'We always sort out our differences quickly, though. I hate atmospheres, don't you?'

'So Adam's all right?'

'He's fine. It's better to get problems out into the open. A bit of shouting never hurt anyone.'

'I suppose Will and I never really shouted much.'

He grins, forks up another mouthful. 'Didn't think you did. He seemed a gentle sort. I know it's frowned on to lose the English stiff upper lip. But I think the Italians have it right – don't let things fester.' He raises his glass to me before he drinks. 'Losing your temper isn't a sin.'

As I watch him talking I feel distant, as if I've floated out of my body and am hovering far away, outside the room, outside the house. I don't want to have sex with David. Not tonight. Panic rises in my throat. I begin to sweat.

David puts his knife and fork down. 'What's the matter? You're pale.'

'Sorry. I still don't feel well,' I say. 'I might have to go home.'

He leans across and lays the back of his hand against my forehead. 'You are a bit hot. Shall I drive you?'

I shake my head. 'I'll be fine.'

'Let me have a word with Adam before he goes out. I'll be back in a minute. I want to say goodbye to you properly.'

He leaves the kitchen and I hear him calling for Adam. I'm startled by the ping of an iPhone. A message coming through. David has left it on the counter charging.

I stand, hovering by my chair. It's quiet outside the room, but I edge over to the threshold and peer into the gloomy hall to make sure he's gone. I catch my breath. David's just there, talking to Constanta. Her head is bowed submissively. I stay hidden as Adam bounds down the stairs. He cuts between his father and Constanta, and his arm flies up angrily. Constanta scurries away, and the two men disappear into the sitting room. I hear their raised voices. Clearly the row isn't over.

I peer down at the iPhone. The screen flashes. *11 a.m tomorrow. Let him come.*

There's the sound of footfalls echoing closer and I lurch into my seat, with my back to the phone. I didn't catch the name of the sender. I'm not sure there was one. I saw the letter 'X', that was all, as if it was code.

'Right, are you sure you're OK to drive?' David's face is creased with anxiety.

I nod.

He pulls me close, hugging me to his broad chest. I stiffen in his arms. How can something that felt right yesterday feel so awkward now? I breathe deeply, telling myself to relax, to stop being stupid. I pat his back. It's the best I can do. He holds my arms and looks into my face. It takes all my willpower to hold his gaze. His eyes are blue, with a yellow circle around the pupil – they invite me in, just like they did that first night when he came to visit after William's funeral. Except there's something else there now, something sharper.

'Hope it's nothing serious,' he says.

'It's just the end of the flu I caught the other day.'

Outside on the drive, he holds the driver's door open for me and shuts it carefully when I'm sitting down.

'Fasten your seatbelt,' he says.

My fingers fumble with the clasp, slotting it in. He watches as I push the ignition and turn the wheel, reversing the car. My heart kicks when he leans down and raps on my window. I wind it down.

'Call me later. Let me know how you are.'

I hold up my hand in a salute as I drive away, wheels crunching through gravel, and I watch him in the wing-mirror, how upright he is, staring after me. The evening folds itself around him, and I suddenly feel guilty. He looks lonely. But as I turn the corner and the big gates swing open, I feel nothing but relief.

TWENTY-SIX

The clock on the wall of The Old Dairy says it's ten o'clock. We have no customers at the moment. Kate is browsing through a glossy magazine, her chin in her hands, a black coffee by her elbow. If I'm going to go then it has to be now. My car is parked on the other side of the market square. It will take ten minutes to drive to David's house.

I grab my bag and car keys. 'Just popping out, Kate. Won't be long. I've got my mobile if we suddenly get busy.'

Kate glances up. 'No problem.'

She came in today with dark brown hair. No blue tips or peroxide streaks. It's the first time I've glimpsed something close to her natural colour in all the time I've known her. She's been wearing jeans and baggy tops, as if she can't be bothered to think about her clothes any more. I've asked her several times if she's OK. She always nods. But there's something distant in her eyes, and I hope that she'll change her mind and decide to tell me, whatever it is.

Driving over to Langshott Hall, my hands tremble. I know I shouldn't be doing this. But I couldn't get their words out of my head. It just seemed such an odd argument. I couldn't make sense of it. My foot relaxes against the accelerator. The car slows. Maybe it's a bit extreme to play detective, to try to find out who the person is that Adam has to meet. It's none of my business. But I'm here now, in sight of the gates.

I park the car on the verge, a little way back from the entrance. I tap my fingers against the gear stick in a jumpy rhythm. Curiosity killed the cat, a small voice in my head tells me. Of course, I have no idea how long it will take Adam to drive to his mysterious eleven o'clock meeting. He might have left at the crack of dawn. As I'm thinking this, the gates swing open and the Defender turns into the road, driving away from me at speed. With an intake of breath, I spin the wheel and bump off the grass to follow him.

Tailing a moving car is more difficult than I could have imagined. I hang back, hoping he won't notice me. But if I misjudge it, suddenly he's disappeared. Once or twice, I think I've lost him. Gradually, I realise that he's heading into Canterbury.

It's both easier and harder to follow the Defender in the city. The busy traffic helps to give me cover, but there are traffic lights and pedestrian crossings to negotiate, and sometimes a bus or lorry will block my view. Then a woman pushing a pram steps out in front of me and I have to brake; the traffic light up ahead is changing to orange and I watch helplessly as Adam drives through. By the time I get there, it's red. A crowd of pedestrians saunter across. I catch sight of the Defender through bobbing heads before he disappears behind a lorry. What am I doing? This is hopeless. I should get back to The Old Dairy.

But as the light changes to green and I cross the junction, I glimpse his bumper at the end of the road. He's got caught in a jam. I hurry to catch up, crashing the gears, exceeding the speed limit. I'm going to get fined for this. He's heading down backstreets into the student area of town. It's easier to keep him in my sights in these quieter roads. He parks under a plane tree and gets out. I pull into a space a few cars down from him. He glances over his shoulder and I sink low in my seat, and then he's walking towards a small, run-down cafe.

Out of the car, I hesitate on the pavement, feeling exposed. I don't dare follow him into the cafe. It's a tiny place and there'll be nowhere to hide. The windows have Indian fabric draped over the lower halves, making it impossible to look through. Disappointed, I go back to the car and get in. I wait for forty-five minutes, glancing up every time anyone goes in or out. Eventually, Adam reappears. He's on his own. He hurries to the Defender and gets in, slamming the door. The car swings into the empty road and disappears, spewing out diesel exhaust.

I give it another moment. The next person to leave is a woman. I lean over the steering wheel, trying to see who it is, but there's a post box in the way, and a couple of teenage boys saunter past, skateboards under their arms. I glimpse short cropped blonde hair. She's wearing sunglasses. She's thin, dressed in plain black jeans and a top. She turns away from me and is hidden behind the skater boys. Frustrated, I get out of the car, but by the time I have, she's gone. I hear an engine starting and a cream Mini pulls out from behind a parked camper van and disappears.

I get back into the driver's seat, puzzled. I haven't been able to get a proper look at her. But it was clear that they didn't want to be seen together. I don't know for certain that she was the woman he'd been meeting, except I have a feeling, a kind of sixth sense that it was her. Both she and Adam had the same furtive look about them. I glance at the name of the cafe as I drive past. The Tarot Pack is written in untidy, hand-painted purple letters.

Back at the tearoom, there are several people in for lunch. Kate is behind the counter, efficiently making up a sandwich; she glances at me, obviously relieved that I'm back. Barbara and Mary are at their normal table, with their coffees between them. They are laughing about something. Mary wipes her eyes and waves at me.

'You look happy,' I say.

'I think we might be getting some good news soon,' Mary says, looking almost flirtatious as she arches one eyebrow.

'About the competition,' Barbara explains. 'The award ceremony is tomorrow.' Then she seems to notice something about me, and she sits up straighter. 'Beautiful earrings.'

I touch my lobes. The pearls. I'd forgotten that I was still wearing them.

'Thanks.'

'They're from Tiffany's, aren't they?'

'Yes,' I raise my eyebrows. 'How did you know?'

'Henrietta had exactly the same pair. She showed them to me. She knew how much I love fine jewellery.'

'Henrietta?'

'David was always giving her beautiful things.'

'Are you sure these are the same?'

She peers at my ears again and nods. 'Exactly the same. Those little diamonds in a heart are a giveaway. Were they a present, or did you spoil yourself? Nothing wrong with that. I once bought myself an emerald ring. Although I wear it on my right hand, of course,' she adds, going pink.

I manage to smile and hurry away, finding my way to the safety of the kitchen. Kate is gesturing at me through the door – someone wants a coffee. But they'll have to wait. I lean against the sink with my back to the tearoom and grip the steel surface, the cold rim under my palms. I close my eyes. Then slowly and carefully, I remove the pearls and put them on the surface.

I remember him dropping the blue package in my lap. The white ribbon. The tiny box. I'd never owned anything as delicate, as extravagant. I bite the end of my thumb, thinking of the pink and gold room, all her things lying there unused. I picture him rifling through her jewellery box and selecting them, putting them into their original package. Henrietta was the sort of woman who kept her jewels and clothes in the state they came in. There had been rows of shoe boxes in the wardrobe. Huge hat boxes on the shelf above.

The gold had pierced her flesh, the pearls had sat snugly against her lobes. I'd had sex with David wearing them. His mouth on my neck, his lips whispering those words – the ones that made me blush – as he'd explored my ear with his tongue.

TWENTY-SEVEN

There are five missed calls from David on my mobile. He's left four voicemails. I listen to them, my heart fluttering. The messages become gradually more and more anxious. In the last one he just says: *Call me. I'm worried.*

I don't know what to say. Giving me Henrietta's earrings was a cheap trick. Maybe I'm just a replacement, a second best, a body to sleep with because he's lonely. I don't know why he picked me, and not one of those other women in their little black dresses, with their knowing glances and blow-dried hair. Perhaps because I'm so different from Henrietta, he'd hoped it would be less painful, that I wouldn't remind him of her so much.

Something has died inside me. I don't want to see him. I couldn't go to bed with him or pretend that everything is as it was before. It's not. And I know it never can be again.

My fingers move to the buttons on my phone. It's tempting

to send him a message. But that's a coward's way out. I have to talk to him, face to face. I'll go over after work.

Sorry. Didn't mean to make you worry. But we need to talk. I'll come over at 6 p.m.

I press 'send'.

I look up at the stone quoins and shining windows. Nothing stirs in the early evening light. Nobody comes when I ring the bell. It's before six. I closed early because we had no customers. The summer season is coming to an end. But it's not just that – I think those bad reviews are having an effect. I gaze up at the house. Someone buzzed the gate to let me in.

I wonder if I can find David at the farm. I walk past a block of empty stables, remembering that Henrietta once kept horses. A faint smell of manure lingers. Nothing stirs except a ginger cat sitting outside a barn washing its back leg with conviction, all its attention on its delicate ablutions. It doesn't glance up. I could be invisible.

There's something I take to be an old sports car inside the barn, its shape camouflaged under tarpaulin. Behind that, a stack of straw bales looms in the dim interior. Everything is clean and orderly. My footsteps sound on the hard surface. Swallows swoop from the eaves of the barn; one dives low enough to set a breeze across my head. They'll be leaving soon, flying back to somewhere hotter, skimming across oceans and cities.

The concrete surface gives way to a hard, rutted track. There are big brick buildings ahead. I see people in dungarees moving about, some of them carrying boxes. A couple of men in black jackets are chatting together and smoking. To my right I glimpse caravans through gaps in bushes and trees and the mesh of a fence. A volley of barks makes me start, spinning around. Two Dobermanns are charging towards me, mouths open, wolfish fangs glinting.

The dogs come to a halt and crouch at my feet, lips curled back in silent snarls. I remember a name. 'Max,' I try, my voice shaking. 'Good boy, Max. Good dog.'

Adam appears around the corner; he clicks his fingers and both dogs turn, slick as eels, and rush to his side, stubby tails wagging, tongues lolloping, cartoonish and benign.

'You've come to see Dad?'

'I'm a bit early. Nobody answered at the house.'

'Maybe he's still on the phone. He was when I left. Troubles with one of our supermarkets.' He stoops to pick up a stick and hurls it away, both dogs bound after it, gangly legs skidding playfully. 'How about you, Ellie? Everything OK?' He turns to look at me. 'How's it going at the tearoom?'

I'm happy he's back to his old self. He seems pleased to see me. 'Good, thanks. Well, a bit quiet at the moment.'

He gives me a questioning look, and I notice that he has dark circles under his eyes. 'Don't worry,' I smile. 'It'll pick up later.'

He puts his hands in his pockets. 'You and Dad . . . you seem to be getting along.'

Guilt tightens my throat. Once I've told David that it's over, Adam won't be in my life in the same way. Just when we're beginning to develop a relationship. I hurry to keep up with his long strides. He stops abruptly and I nearly walk into him.

'Ellie . . . ' He glances behind us. 'I wanted to talk to you—'

'Hello!'

I start at the sound of a loud, cheerful voice. It's Rachel. She's tottering towards us in high heels, hand in hand with Pip. 'Nice to see you again, Ellie,' she says as she comes to a stop in front of us. She tugs at her child's hand. 'Say hello, darling.'

Pip is wearing a pink leotard and tutu with wellington boots. She looks up under her fringe and smiles shyly. I crouch next to her. 'You look like a princess! Are you going dancing?' She nods and giggles.

'Have you been in the packing barns?' Adam scowls at his sister. 'You shouldn't take Pip in there. You know there's lots of dangerous machinery. It's no place for a kid.'

Rachel rolls her eyes. 'Relax. I'm not going to let her run off. Anyway, it was just a quick visit. I had to check on some production issues and go over paperwork with Dad.' She tucks a strand of gleaming hair behind her ear. 'And now Pip has her ballet lesson in Canterbury, and we can't be late. Are you coming to say goodbye to us?'

She begins to pick her way along the track towards the house, Pip bobbing by her side. 'Uncle Adam!' she calls, beckoning over her shoulder.

Adam sighs. 'Let's go.'

We wait outside the house while Rachel drives off, Pip in her child seat in the back of the car. Adam waves to his niece. 'My sister is a nightmare. But Pip's a good kid.'

'What were you going to say,' I ask him, 'before?'

He bends to pat one of the dogs. 'I can't remember.'

Adam shows me into the kitchen, where David's on the phone, talking and gesticulating. He ends the call as soon as he sees me and his face relaxes into a smile. He strides over and leans down to kiss my mouth, but I move my head and we bump noses.

'Still here?' He turns to Adam. 'Don't you have anything useful to do?'

Adam scowls. 'Don't worry. I'm leaving.' He turns to me. 'Goodbye, Ellie.'

'Didn't you sort your disagreement out?' I ask after Adam's left.

David sighs. 'Kids. You think it'll get easier when they grow up. But it doesn't.' He opens the fridge. 'I think we both need a drink.' He's already busy uncorking a bottle of Chablis.

I accept the glass and take a gulp, choking when it goes down the wrong way.

David pats me on the back. 'Steady. There's plenty more. I've got a whole wine cellar downstairs!' He gives my shoulders a squeeze. 'What's all this about needing to talk?'

I step away from him. 'I'm sorry.' I put my drink down on the counter. 'I think we've rushed things. I'm feeling . . . different . . . about us. Having doubts.'

'Doubts?'

'I'm sorry.'

'What are you saying – that we should take things more slowly?'

'That we should . . . I don't know.' I lose confidence, and take another swig of wine. 'I think it's over. Between us.'

David sinks into the nearest chair. 'I see. This is very sudden.'

'I'm sorry.'

He gets up and comes towards me. 'Stop saying sorry all

the time, Ellie.' His face is dark. Then he touches my cheek. 'I just wish I could understand why you've changed. Have I done anything wrong?'

'No,' I shake my head.

I remember asking Luca the same question.

David is pacing up and down beside the sink. 'I can be too pushy, too brash. I don't mean to upset people. It's hard to shake off the past. Where you come from.' He stops and rubs his forehead.

'It wasn't anything like that.'

'Then why are you leaving?' He reaches out, holding me above the elbow, fingers pinching. I don't think he realises how tightly he's gripping.

I wince. 'David, you're hurting me.'

His mouth trembles. I remember the locked room with Henrietta's things, the earrings I've been wearing for weeks, thinking they were new, a gift just for me. Henrietta's ghost has always been here – waiting in the shadows. The idea of William and Henrietta having sex, whispering together, sharing secrets and intimacies, makes me sick. Sleeping with David almost feels incestuous now.

'David!' I yank away, and his fingers unfurl.

I rub my arm. I have an urge to walk out, run to my car and start the engine. The house feels suffocating, a heavy weight filled with gleaming furniture and huge paintings, family history stretching back for generations. Henrietta's family. A past that has nothing to do with me. It makes me breathless.

'I can give you time, if you need it.' He's holding himself upright.

This must be hard for him. He's not used to being refused. I shake my head.

'And just like that, you're going to walk out on me?'

'I hope we can be friends.' I slip the Tiffany box out of my pocket and place it on the counter.

'Keep them,' he says. 'They belong to you.'

'No,' I say. 'No, they don't.'

He looks at me then, and there's a glimmer of understanding.

'I don't want her things,' I say. 'I'm not her. I'm not Henrietta.'

TWENTY-EIGHT

David rang almost as soon as I left his house yesterday. I didn't pick up. I've turned my phone to silent. I know there are messages from him on my mobile. But I'm ignoring them. There's nothing more to say.

I've always used baking as a therapy. So I'm making a lemon and cardamom cake. It's an experiment. If it works I'll try it out at the tearoom, see what people think. I'm crushing the cardamom pods with a mortar and pestle, and the scent is exotic, making me imagine countries I've never been to. Somewhere far away from here. India, perhaps. The Cardamom Hills.

Tilly trots in, meowing for food and attention, and with a quick knock as he opens the door, Luca follows behind. I turn back to my cake, busying myself, adding the crushed spice. I can't look at him – I don't want him to read my expression. He'll know what I'm feeling.

‘I wanted to tell you that I’ll be leaving soon,’ he says. ‘The season’s finishing. Workers are being laid off.’

Disappointment falls through me. I force myself to keep a steady voice. ‘Oh, when?’

‘In a week.’

‘You’ll go back to Romania?’ I ladle the cake mix into a tin. Slide it into the oven. ‘Whereabouts are you from?’

‘Maramureş, in the Carpathians. It’s rough, mountainous land covered in forest. My family had a small farm.’

I gaze out of the window, across the flat expanse of my garden and paddock, towards the strawberry fields and the woods beyond. This must all seem so tame in comparison.

‘Do you have brothers or sisters?’

‘A sister. Marisca.’

‘She must miss you.’

‘We write sometimes.’ He leans against the kitchen table, fumbles in his pocket and brings out his cigarette packet.

‘You’ve . . . you’ve never talked about your family before.’

He tilts his head and looks at me. ‘Haven’t heard you talk about yours either.’

‘No.’ I flush. ‘I’m an only child. I had a falling-out with my parents.’ I look at him. ‘Then I got married young. And William became my family.’

‘Well then, you’ll understand.’ He takes out a cigarette, rolls it between his fingers. ‘I’ve left my family, too – left my past behind. My mother was a wonderful woman. But my father was a bully and a drunk.’ He looks away. ‘We spent our lives trying to avoid him.’

‘Oh . . . I’m . . . I’m sorry.’

He goes to the open doorway and lights up, blows his smoke

into the garden. 'There were animals in the forest. Bears and wolves.' He stares into the distance. 'Once my father trapped a wolf. He kept her in a cage in our yard. She was dying. Pining for her freedom. I slipped her scraps, brought stones and pine branches from the forest, pushed them through the bars to remind her of home. I begged him to open the cage. But my father wouldn't let her go. He liked having power over a wild thing.'

I don't know why he's telling me this, but I've been holding my breath at his flow of conversation, at the idea of the wolf in the cage and Luca as a boy, watching the creature through the bars.

'Do your family know you're coming?'

He picks the cat up, holds her in his big hands, the cigarette jammed in his mouth. She crawls onto his shoulder, drapes herself around his neck. 'My mother is dead and my sister's married. There's no family to go back to. I'll travel – find work – Germany, maybe.' He reaches up and tickles Tilly under her chin. 'Have you seen Anca?' he asks, looking at the cat.

'No.' I stand up straighter. 'Why?'

He exhales a stream of smoke. 'Nothing.'

'She's gone,' I tell him. 'David thinks she went home, to Romania. She's pregnant.'

He turns to me, and there's no surprise in his face. His eyes harden, darkness concealing his thoughts. He pulls the cat off his shoulder and she springs to the floor as he disappears into the garden. I watch him walk past the window.

I remember Anca below my room with a bucket of soapy water, and how she stepped away from Luca as if his touch scalded her, and I feel a shiver of uncertainty.

*

I wake up panting. I've kicked off the top sheet and lie across my rumpled bed, caught in a strip of moonlight, breathing hard. My skin is slick with sweat. I heard a scream. It pulled me up out of a nightmare. A scream, faint and far away.

The moment when Les Ashton pushed himself on top of me is there in my head, panic in my body again. His damp hand clamped over my mouth. Was Anca raped, too? I get out of bed and creep towards the window, peering into the blank night. The smudged impression of a woman's face looks back at me. I hardly recognise myself – eyes anxious pits, my mouth gaping – I hold my breath, listening hard. And I know that it was me that screamed. My heart is beating like a trapped creature. A prickle runs down my spine, as though I'm being watched, as if there are wolves in my bedroom, padding behind me.

I knock once. There's no answer. He's out again. What's he doing, night after night? Where does he go? I remember him promising to protect me. How can he protect me if he's never here? I push at the rough surface of the door. The garage is cold inside. Thick concrete repels any heat. I shiver, rubbing my arms. Moonlight comes filtering through the small window set high up. I blink, adjusting my eyes, staring into the shadows until I can make out shapes of things. 'Luca?'

It smells of apples, their sweet-sharp tang. He's stored the crates against one wall. I go over to the neatly made camp bed. His rucksack leans against the wall. There are two books and an empty cup on the floor next to the bed. A pair of jeans folded on the end. I crouch down, brushing my hand across the worn denim, pulling away with a gasp, as though it's his flesh under my fingers. I click on the light on my mobile, pick up the first book and flick through, settling on a page.

A poem. Rainer Maria Rilke. I know this. It's about a panther. I turn the well-thumbed pages. I didn't expect him to read poetry. My idea of him shifts with another unsettling jolt. The second book is a novel, but it's in German and I don't speak German. I squint at the title, but can't make sense of it.

I go over to the rucksack, push my arm inside and feel around the worn canvas interior. Clothes, a tin mug, a leather sheath. I pull the knife out of it and test it gingerly against the fleshy pad of one finger. Long and sharp, the blade clean. My heart jumps. There's another book. A notebook, covered in dense, sloping writing. It's in a foreign language, one I don't recognise. I'm guessing Romanian. The words look urgent somehow; the pen has pressed hard, the letters spilling out in a hurry. At the back he's drawn a rough map. I recognise the cottage, the fields between here and the village, David's house and the farm, with the river marked along one side.

I think I hear a noise and quickly push everything back where it belongs. I stand still, listening. A solitary beam of moonlight slides from the rectangle of the window.

Sunday. I wake late, a scratchy headache pressing behind my eyes. I put the kettle on to make myself a strong cup of tea and stand at the open kitchen window waiting for it to boil. Although the sun is bright, there's an autumnal feel in the air, as if hidden frosts are already turning gold into silver. The sound of running water makes me look up. Luca is at the outside tap. He is bare-chested. He's splashing himself with cold water, rubbing vigorously with a flannel, bending and turning. His jeans and boots are soaking. The summer has tanned him. He's like something carved out of mahogany, but his torso is paler than his arms. I shouldn't be watching him like this. I am about to turn away when I notice mottled purple marks across his ribs. He has bruises as if he's fallen down a flight of stairs.

I leave my tea, ignoring the singing kettle, and go into the garden.

When he hears me, he turns quickly, grabbing at his shirt and pulling it on over wet skin. 'I thought you were out.' He does up his buttons, his fingers moving quickly.

'Do you know Anca?' I ask. 'I mean, did you know her before you came here?'

His expression changes, closing in the way it always does. He shakes his head. I expect him to turn, to walk away. But his thick dark brows move up his forehead and his mouth twitches.

'I met her for the first time when she was washing the windows. We spoke then. She's a brave woman. Coming here to a foreign country, trying to survive.'

I wonder what he said to her that day. I'm sure he made her angry or afraid.

'Nobody has any idea where she is. David's only guessing she went home.' I watch his face. There's no flicker of remorse. 'I'm worried about her,' I finish.

'So am I,' he says.

Damp shows through his shirt, darker patches. He didn't dry himself because he didn't want me to see his bruises. I gesture towards his ribs. 'How did you hurt yourself?'

'I fell off the shed roof. I wasn't concentrating.' He pushes his hair away from his eyes. 'I need to ask you something,' he says, 'about David Mallory.'

My heart slows.

'Do you love him?'

He's staring at me intently. It makes my stomach clench.

'David?' My gaze moves to his feet. His battered boots. 'We're friends. That's all.'

He reaches out to touch my chin, and I start. But he raises my head so that we're looking into each other's eyes. His gaze is narrowed. I should tell him that it's none of his business. Instead I do nothing but stare back, my mouth dry. He drops his hand and I turn to go.

'One more thing,' he's saying.

'Yes?'

'You've got a woodpecker. I saw it a couple of mornings ago.'

'Oh,' I falter. 'Is that bad?'

'Could be. For the apple trees. So I rigged something up.'

He's already limping over to the orchard. I follow. I'm confused at first. Light bounces and spins among leaves. There is the flutter of ribbons, a tinkle of wind chimes, a turning brilliance in reflected slices of blue sky. All of the trees are garlanded with objects, hung with tiny mirrors, bits of cloth, fraying rope, stones and tin cans.

I gasp. 'This must have taken ages!'

'Recycled rubbish, most of it. I worked at night. I told you I don't sleep much.' He smiles. 'It is a kind of art, I think. My present to you.'

'A present?'

'A goodbye present.'

I stare at the trees. As the branches move in the wind, they give out a soft metallic whisper, a dry rustling. The assortment of objects and rainbow colours are like another kind of harvest, a crop of rare fruit. I can't look at him. I'm afraid of what he'll see.

TWENTY-NINE

I hurry into the corner shop with my list ready.

Sally-Ann glances at me and a strange expression flits across her features. 'Morning, Ellie.'

I smile at her and dump the heavy basket next to the till.

'Shocking news,' she says in a hushed tone. 'You can't trust them, though, can you? People like him.'

'I'm sorry?'

'That man,' Sally-Ann says. 'The foreign one staying in your garage.'

'Luca?'

'Terrible.' She moves chewing gum around her mouth. 'He deserves to be put away.'

'What are you talking about?'

'You must be relieved nothing happened to you. I wouldn't like to be so isolated. I wouldn't be able to sleep nights, knowing someone like him was just outside my door.'

'What's happened?' My voice is shrill.

She stares at me, mouth open. 'That girl at the farm. She's pregnant. Everyone's talking about it. You must know. He raped her.'

My dream from last night flares into life. My stomach churns. 'Who told you?'

'John.' Sally-Ann sweeps her long sandy hair behind her ear. 'Apparently the girl's run off, so they can't press charges against him.'

'Press charges?'

'I expect the police will want to question him anyway.' She picks up a loaf of bread and scans it. 'Nobody wants him here. People are angry. Upset.'

'He's not staying at my place anymore,' I say quickly. 'He's gone.'

She widens her eyes. 'Gone?'

'He's left the country.'

She purses her lips, disappointed. 'Sure sign he's guilty then.'

'No,' I say. 'This is all a mistake.'

I have to wait while Sally-Ann rings up my shopping, picking over my things with her long, silver nails, packing teabags, cat food, bread, milk and tins of tomatoes into a bag.

'This isn't the first attack in the village,' she's saying. 'But last time it was a local girl that got raped. One of the workers on the Greenwells' farm. Rough sort. Foreigner. He got caught and did time. But she never got over it. Committed suicide a few months later. That's why James Greenwell only uses English workers now.'

I put my hands in my pockets to stop them trembling. 'I didn't know.'

'Happened before you got here. Years ago.'

I don't trust my voice, so I nod instead, sweeping the bag onto my shoulder and fishing for the Fiat's keys in my pocket. I feel Sally-Ann's eyes on my back as I make my way between the aisles towards the door. In the street, I notice John and Irene chatting to each other. They turn and stare while I fumble with the car door. I throw my bag onto the passenger seat, tins of tomatoes spilling out, rolling onto the floor.

THIRTY

1990

I turn side-on to the mirror, examining the shape of the bump, pulling my blouse tighter against its outlines, against the new, full shape of my breasts. Then I let the fabric drop, rearranging it in fluffed-out folds. Even wearing a voluminous top and standing with my shoulders forward, there's no hiding my belly any longer.

Les Ashton continues to be a constant visitor at our house. He arrives for evenings of bridge, drinking cocktails, making my mother laugh; he comes to every party, every dinner, as if nothing has happened. I scurry upstairs as soon as the doorbell jangles or his confident voice booms from the hall. If I can't escape in time, I stand with my eyes fixed on a spot near his feet, while he chats and makes jokes. Once, when he found me on my own, he got hold of my arm. 'You're not angry with me,' he asked, 'are you?' I'd shaken my head. 'So stop behaving like a spoilt brat,' he said.

Staring at my distorted reflection, my throat thickens at the memory. I hate him. I hate the child he's put inside me. I keep thinking that I'll wake up one morning and it will be gone. That it's all a mistake.

My mother has suggested that I give up cakes, that my sweet tooth has got a little out of control. I wanted her to guess the truth so that she can solve the problem. But she can't see what's right in front of her.

Outside, there are wood pigeons cooing in the oak tree, bees blundering through late-blooming roses, the honeyed light of evening touching everything with gold. Inside, the house is shuttered and dark. My father is in his study. I knock on the door and wait for his reluctant voice. 'Enter.'

He looks up, pushing his glasses up his nose with one finger and sighs impatiently. 'Yes, Eleanor? I have a lot of work to do.'

Since my bad results, he's hardly talked to me, hardly acknowledged my existence. I know he'd been bitterly disappointed that I hadn't been a boy. But at least I'd been a clever girl.

'I have to tell you something.' I stand before his desk as if he's a headmaster.

'Well?' He makes a flicking motion with his hand.

There's no easy option, no way of softening it. 'I'm pregnant.'

He takes his glasses off. His mouth tightens, the skin around it growing yellow. 'What?' His voice quiet.

I'm unable to meet his eyes.

'Who was it?' His voice shakes. 'Which boy?'

I run my tongue around the inside of my teeth, trying to

find some moisture. I gaze at the carpet, my feet planted there under me. Blood rushes around my skull.

'It wasn't . . . not a boy . . . '

He's taken off his glasses and is rubbing his eyes. He goes to the door and yanks it open, yells into the dark hall. 'Miranda!'

My mother comes in looking frightened.

'Eleanor is . . . pregnant.' He stumbles over the word. 'One of those boys she goes around with. You've been too soft with her. And now . . . ' He gazes at me as if I'm a cracked crystal vase. 'She's ruined.'

'Darling . . . is this true?' my mother whispers.

I nod.

'Who did it? How pregnant are you? We'll have to get you to a doctor. Les Ashton. He can help.' She bites her lip. 'We can rely on him to be discreet.'

'No!'

They both stare at me.

'Les Ashton. He . . . he came into my room. I tried . . . but he was stronger—'

My father rises from his chair, spine straight, his face working in strange contortions, mouth opening and closing. 'Stop this,' he hisses. 'Stop these lies.'

'I'm not lying!' My voice quavers. 'He . . . he forced me.'

Saying the words breaks something inside. Sobs come out in a choking, barking mess. The weight of them fills my chest. I can't draw breath. Snot leaks from my nose. My father leans away from me, his mouth turning down. 'Les Ashton is a friend. A doctor.'

'No.' I shake my head. 'No. He did it.'

'Stop lying.'

'He came into my room when I was sick. Mummy was in London—'

My father slams his hand onto the desk. 'Enough!' he barks.

I bite the inside of my lip. 'Please . . .' I whisper.

'Just tell us how many months you think you are,' my mother says quickly. 'We need to get rid of it. An abortion.'

'I don't know . . . maybe nearly seven months,' I murmur.

'Oh God.' My mother is pale. 'I think it's too late.'

My father shakes his head. 'You've ruined your life. You know that, don't you?'

The breath leaves my body.

I see my mother's frightened look, and in her eyes I see that she believes me. It's there. Then it's gone. Sheeted. She looks at me with a blank expression. Her bright mouth wobbles. 'Why didn't you come to us before?'

'I thought I was ill at first . . . I didn't . . . I thought it would go away.' I rub my eyes. 'I don't know what to do.'

'Too late,' my father says. 'Too late to think about that.'

'I'll make some calls,' my mother says. 'There are places you can go. Agencies who deal with this kind of thing. Plenty of people want to adopt.'

'Mum,' I breathe.

She steps around me, nervous fingers plucking her blouse, and stands by my father, not meeting my eyes. The floor tips, sliding from under me, the world rearranging itself, throwing me out of my old life into a cold new place.

And as the weeks go past, I begin to think that I brought it on myself by wanting Les Ashton to like me, by wanting his approval. I let him pinch my cheek and give me secret smiles behind my father's back. I let him come into my room and sit on my bed.

THIRTY-ONE

2015

I run into the house, dumping the bags on the table, shopping falling to the floor, and hurry into the garden. Luca's not there. I put my head round the garage door and see him sitting in the shadows, writing in his notebook. He looks up when he hears me, pushing the book away, waiting for me to speak.

'Everyone in the village is talking—' I take a deep breath. 'They're saying . . .'

He stands up and comes towards me. 'What are they saying?'

'That it was you . . . that you raped Anca.'

He stands completely still; just his fingers move, clenching into fists.

My lungs are struggling to pull in enough air. I want to ask the question. I can't. The words gather inside my throat, choking me.

'I know what you're thinking.' He takes a step so that we are only inches apart and reaches out, places his hand over my heart. 'Listen,' he says. 'Listen hard. In here. Inside yourself. You know the answer.'

Neither of us moves. My chest rises and falls under the swell of my breath, his fingers rising and falling with it. Then he walks away. His limp is more pronounced and he looks suddenly smaller, somehow shrunken. I wish that I'd got hold of his hand and clung on, squeezing tight. I feel as though I'm sinking. The space between us expands as if an ocean is rushing in.

'She didn't seem to like you.' I swallow. 'I saw you together.'

He stops, and turns to face me. 'Anca wouldn't answer my questions. She's afraid.'

My heart is thumping hard. 'What's she afraid of?'

'I don't know.' His brow furrows, then he shakes his head. 'It's an instinct I have, about the fruit farm. The Mallory place.'

'David's farm?'

'When I went over there to ask for work. It was the way they turned me away. All the security. They're hiding something.'

'You could be right.' I put my thumb nail between my teeth. 'I overheard a row between David and Adam. I didn't understand it. But it felt wrong. Adam is meeting some woman in secret, and David doesn't like it. I don't know . . . it's odd.'

'A woman?' He frowns. 'A girlfriend, perhaps?'

I shake my head. 'I don't think so. He said it was part of a deal. It doesn't make sense.'

'No.' Luca agrees. 'But I've been trying to get to the truth for months. Nobody knows anything – or they won't talk. The place is like a fortress.' He sounds tired. 'I was going to leave, anyway. And me being here now – it'll be difficult for you.'

'No.' I say it before I can stop myself. 'It's not difficult. I don't want you to go.'

'I don't like to leave you alone – not until we know who did that to Clover.' He narrows his eyes. 'But if I'm going to be accused . . . it will get unpleasant.'

'Anca's left the village. No one's accusing you. It's just a rumour. And there's something else.' I turn away, hiding my pink cheeks. 'I told Sally-Ann you'd gone back to Romania. The whole village will have heard the story by now. I thought it was for the best. To give you time. Stop them from talking and prying.'

He rubs his neck. 'I'm not going to hide. I haven't done anything wrong.'

'You don't know what they're like. This will turn into a witch-hunt. But if they think you're not here, it will blow over. They'll find something else to gossip about.'

He frowns. 'I suppose if David thinks I've gone . . . maybe it'll be easier to get onto his land.' He walks a couple of paces. Stops and looks at me. 'I can look for Anca. Ask around among the migrants on other fruit farms. See if someone knows anything.'

'But you'll have to be discreet. And we should be careful here too, in case someone comes to check.'

'I can sleep in the orchard. The stable.'

'I have a spare room,' I say carefully. 'And there's Will's study. You can sleep in the house. I have no neighbours – you can stay hidden.'

He shifts from one foot to another, looking doubtful.

'Why don't you put your things in the spare room to keep them dry and safe. Then you can sleep there, or not.' I persuade him as I would a child. 'It's up to you. But we should clear this place.' I look around, wondering how to help.

He nods, and then he picks up his books and drops them in the rucksack. He strips the sheet off the camp bed in one lunging movement, and stands with bent knees to roll his sleeping bag with efficient twists of his large hands. I watch him padding silently around the space, sweeping the garage clean of himself, of any evidence that he was here. It takes him moments. He knows how to disappear.

THIRTY-TWO

He's in the spare room and I'm in my bedroom. I think I hear him breathing, hear creaks and rustles every time he moves. I can almost see him through the thin plaster walls. Can he sense me, too? After a moment, I take a furtive look down the corridor. The door of the spare room is shut.

I slip off my jeans and knickers, pull off my jumper, unhook my bra and stand before the full-length mirror. My skin feels peeled back, tender. I run my fingers over broken veins across my calves, cellulite dimples on my thighs. Since turning forty my body seems to be grounded differently, as if I've grown closer to the earth, as if my body has relaxed and let itself out a little, like a woman taking off a corset. I pinch the fold of flesh around my middle. I wasn't brave enough to let David see me naked in daylight.

There is a sudden hush in the house. A kind of absence. Luca's gone to sleep. I mustn't think about him, mustn't imagine what it would be like to unbutton his shirt, push my hands across his chest, lay my cheek against the warm aliveness of him.

He's gone in the morning. The kitchen shines, surfaces cleared. He always skips breakfast. I have a sudden fear that he's left for good, and run upstairs, throwing open the door to the spare room. The bed is immaculate. It doesn't look as though it's been slept in. But when I go to the other side, there is his rucksack, neatly packed, his sleeping bag rolled up. I let out a sigh of relief. I'd got used to Will's untidy, male presence, his clattering footsteps and fumbling attempts to cook, the spreading mess of dirty cups and papers and books and odd socks that appeared as a kind of trail around the cottage. There's nothing of Luca's anywhere in the house. He hasn't even left his toothbrush in the bathroom.

I ring Kate and ask her if she can manage on her own at the tearoom today. She can call if she needs me to come in.

'We're not busy at the moment,' I tell her. 'I can catch up on paperwork at home.'

The day has become grey, heavy with the threat of rain. I'm sitting in the living room, checking through the tearoom's accounts, when I hear the crunch of tyres on gravel. I get up to peer out of the window and my heart stops. The gleaming hulk of David's Range Rover is parked outside.

Luca is somewhere out in the field. It's too late to warn him. The doorbell rings. I press my hand to my mouth, unable to move. The bell rings again. I'm afraid that David will look in through the window and see me here, hiding. So I go to the door and open it.

'Ellie.' He's holding a bunch of brilliantly coloured flowers. And I remember the night after Will's funeral, how he came with those extravagant lilies and a bottle of brandy. 'I was worried when Kate said you were at home. It's not like you.'

The wind catches his hair and ruffles it. He puts a hand to his collar. 'Aren't you going to invite me in?'

Maybe Luca will hear David's voice. He'll see the car. Surely he'll notice the Range Rover. I wish we'd thought of a secret sign – some signal that would alert the other one to danger, like hanging a tea towel out of the window.

I stand back and David comes in, handing the bouquet to me, wiping his feet on the mat. I put the flowers down on the sideboard. The cellophane crackles.

'You've been ignoring my calls. I wanted to make sure you're all right.' He glances out of the window towards the closed double doors of the garage. 'So, Luca's gone this time?'

'Yes. Who told you?'

'Mary, I think.'

'Someone's started a rumour . . . they're saying that Luca raped Anca. It's not true, is it?'

'Isn't it?' He frowns. 'She told me the father was Romanian, and that he'd come back to the village recently. Later, I thought it was strange, because she was reluctant to go to your house again after that first visit. She seemed afraid.'

'Afraid?' Doubt presses at me. I push it away. 'Well, he's gone now. So we'll never know.'

'Ellie, listen, I wanted to explain about the earrings.' He turns to me, his brow furrowed.

'There's nothing to say.'

'I wasn't thinking straight.' He rubs his eyes. 'I'm sorry. I didn't want to upset you. The thing is . . . they weren't being used. It seemed such a waste. '

'It made me feel second best,' I say quietly. 'Cheap.'

'But that's the opposite of how it is.' He reaches a hand towards me. 'You have to understand, I come from a background where we counted every penny.'

I cross my arms.

'Ellie, I can't stand this – we're like strangers.'

I sigh. 'David, it all happened so fast. You swept me off my feet.' I push my hand across my eyes. 'We needed each other. We were both lonely. But that's not enough, is it?'

'There was something between us. I felt it.' He sits down abruptly and rubs his cheek.

'Yes,' I admit, 'there was a moment when I felt something too, when I thought we could have a relationship. Then I realised I was wrong.'

He looks at me and his face is full of need. 'I miss my wife. You're the only person who can understand what it's like.' Emotion tightens his voice. 'I didn't let you know how desperate I felt. It wasn't fair on you.'

There's a tug of empathy in my chest. My husband seduced his sick wife. Somehow that makes me guilty, too. I approach slowly, and sit beside him. He makes a strange strangled sound in the back of his throat. I put my hand over his. His fingers twitch and he curls them around mine, clasping tightly.

'Is there really no hope?' He struggles to get his words out.

Horror travels through my limbs, turning my skin cold. I want to pull my hand back from his hot grasp.

'I know it's not my business . . . but I have to ask,' his mouth crumples. 'Is there anyone else?'

Colour burns my cheeks, and I fight the instinct to put my hands over my face. 'No.'

He sighs and he's so close that I can see the tiny broken veins in his cheeks. 'Are you sure?'

I fold my lips together.

'You can tell me,' he says.

'David,' I say as firmly as I can. 'There's nobody else.'

I glance up at the window, half hoping and half fearing that I will see Luca in the garden. It's begun to rain, drops of water speckle the panes and the sky is sullen. The house is silent, folding a hush around us as we sit, linked by our joined hands.

'Aren't you lonely, out here all on your own?' he asks. 'Wouldn't you like to belong to somebody again?'

'I didn't *belong* to Will.' I drag my fingers free. 'We were committed to each other. That's different.'

There's a low roll of thunder. I glance out of the window. If only I knew where Luca was, I'd feel better, less nervous. The rainy garden is empty. I catch a brief movement in the field that must be the donkey disappearing behind the shed. Trees are swaying, gusts of wind shaking leaves free from branches.

David unfolds himself slowly. I feel that I should hug him, comfort him, but I don't want to give him any encouragement. He straightens his jacket.

'You can't blame me for not giving up.' He touches my cheek softly. He pauses on the threshold, gazing up the stairs. 'I don't regret a moment of it.' He looks at the rain through the open door and turns. 'I'm still here for you. If you change your mind.'

I notice a silhouette in the passenger seat of his car. With a small jolt, I realise someone is there. A heavy man with a bald head. I seem to recognise him. Then I remember, it's the man who used to drop Anca off and pick her up.

'Didn't your . . . friend . . . want to come in?'

David steps outside, wincing at the rain, falling heavily now. 'What? Bill? No. We're going on to a meeting together. Farm business.' He puts his collar up. 'Don't feel sorry for him. He's getting paid for sitting there.'

THIRTY-THREE

As soon as the Range Rover disappears, I hear the click of the back door closing softly.

'You just missed David,' I say, without turning.

Luca stands beside me; the storm has got worse. We look at the empty drive in silence, trees tossing and rearing; a branch breaks free, falling onto the gravel, white severed edges like tossed bones.

'What did he say?' Luca asks. 'Did he talk about me?'

'He's suspicious. He wanted to check that you weren't here.'

Luca moves away from the window.

'We need to be careful,' I tell him. 'He's convinced that . . . that you're the father of Anca's child.'

My hands are cold and I rub them together. Pigeon-grey clouds swarm together, winging across the sky, blurring into a dark inky mass. The rain has become a deluge. Water crashes onto surfaces, hammers against windows, batters trees and bushes.

‘You still trust me,’ he steps close, ‘don’t you?’

I’ve put all my eggs in this basket, I think. And I remember how carefully he arranged the real just-laid eggs in the nests of moss.

I nod.

It’s too wet even for Luca to go outside. I’m glad. I make us tomato soup, and we eat it with hunks of bread and butter. The kitchen windows are steamed up, and it feels as though we are hidden by sheets of rain, sealed in by water.

He mops up his soup with a crust and puts it in his mouth.

I stretch out to collect his plate and our hands touch. My skin tingles. The sensation runs up my arm, making me shiver.

He pulls away, puts his hands under the table.

I pile the plates into the sink. The attraction is all in my head; I’m like a child, imagining that because I feel it, he must too. A plate slides out of my grip, clattering into the bowl.

‘Tell me again why you think there’s something wrong at David’s place. Did Anca say anything?’

‘She got angry when I suggested it, said I was imagining things.’

‘So this is all your instinct – your gut feeling?’

He shrugs. ‘Yes.’ Then he frowns. ‘No – there are rumours among some of the migrant pickers on the other farms.’

‘And you’ve been up there – gone to see for yourself?’

He gives a short laugh. ‘I have. Many times. There’s too much security. I can’t get past it.’

I think of David’s house, how easy it was for me to get in through the gate, and how I wandered around, looking into the stables, going towards the farm buildings and caravans. I didn’t see anything that made me suspicious. Just people working, packing fruit.

Luca has found a radio programme with rock music. He's nodding to the beat, staring out through the window into the rain with an intensity that makes me think he's longing to get away, to tramp outside into the weather. His fingers curl and uncurl at his sides.

I allow myself the luxury of switching on the heating for the first time this year. The boiler roars and I hold my breath, hoping it's going to stay alight. Luca goes from room to room, bleeding the radiators, happy to have a task. There's nothing more to do while it's still raining.

Luca sits on the sofa with his German novel. He's taken his boots off, and I notice that he's darned his sock with the same green cotton he used to mend his rucksack. The shape of his toes is strangely intimate and I look away. I take a seat opposite and pick up my book. But the text slips past my gaze in a blur, because this is how Will and I used to sit, either side of the fireplace, and I keep glancing up at Luca, seeing his angular, flinty face instead of Will's kind, ruddy one. I snatch another glance at Luca and find that he's staring at me in his fixed hawk-like way. I blink, clearing my throat. David's gaudy flowers are lying limp and abandoned on the sideboard.

'I should do something with those.'

I pick them up and go into the kitchen, open the bin and shove the flowers inside, putting the lid back with a clatter.

The rain doesn't let up. Puddles become small ponds. The lawn is sodden. A crack of thunder makes me pull on my coat and wellingtons and run outside to check on the animals. Luca follows me, slipping across the muddy surface, his jacket over his head. He ducks into the pen to shut the hens into their hut, while I open the gate to the paddock and find that Nutmeg and Gilbert are already in the stable, Nutmeg with her rump to the driving rain outside, and the goose standing under her stomach looking sorry for himself. He perks up when he sees me and opens his beak to hiss. I close the door before he can attack, take some handfuls of straw from the lean-to and scatter them onto the floor, so that they can bed down for the night. Luca fills a bucket with water and leaves that too.

'Coals to Newcastle,' I say.

He frowns, not understanding, his hair dripping into his eyes.

'A joke,' I explain. 'Not a very good one.'

We make a dash back to the house as lightning flashes through the darkening sky, picking out the silhouettes of trees in silver. He doesn't take my hand. Inside, we stand apart, shaking the wet from our clothes. His leather jacket reeks of animal.

'I think I'll get an early night,' I say awkwardly.

I can't meet his eyes. I don't want him to try to interpret something that I don't understand myself.

I'm cleaning my teeth when I hear Luca shouting.

I spit into the sink, staring at my face in the mirror, listening. He shouts again. He's calling my name. I wipe my mouth, dropping the toothbrush.

He's on the landing, a bucket in his hand, tilting his head to stare up at the ceiling. A darkening flower spreads across the surface, rippling out from the dangling light flex. Paper bulges and leaks. Water has begun to drip and splatter onto the floor. Luca places the bucket at his feet and immediately there's a metallic drum beat, the drops setting up an escalating rhythm.

'Damn.' I wipe a dribble of toothpaste from my chin. 'There must be a tile loose or something.'

'Where's the hatch? I'll go up and take a look.'

I find the metal stick that unhooks the latch, letting the door down, releasing the sliding ladder. Luca puts a torch in his mouth and shins up the rungs, disappearing into blackness.

Downstairs, I open cupboards, pulling out three saucepans, then dash back to put them down on the landing floor, trying to position them under the worst of the drips. I can hear muffled scrabbling and occasional thumps as Luca moves about over my head. The water is getting worse, cascading into the bucket and pans, filling them quickly. The carpet squelches under my bare toes. I pick up the bucket and stagger to the bathroom, tipping dirty water over the edge of the bath.

Luca reappears with his hair wild over his eyes, and his shoulders dark with wet. He has that look that men get when they're in control of a crisis, a little self-important, distracted from everything else.

'I'm going to need some tools. There's a hole in the roof.'

He insists there's nothing I can do to help. He won't let me climb the ladder. I end up in the kitchen boiling the kettle for something to do. I look into brown, swirling liquid and blow into the steamy heat, and push it away. If Will had been here instead of Luca, it would have been me up in the attic. I was always more practical than my husband.

When Luca finds me, he says that it's all patched up. 'I'll look at it again when it's light,' he says, 'and the rain has stopped.'

'Thank you.' I hear the edge to my voice.

'Are you all right?'

My mouth twitches. 'Yes. It's just that . . .'

I want to explain what I'm feeling, but I don't have the words. There's a ball of frustration gathering inside. It's not the roof. It's not that he took over. It's more than that. It's my own desire eating me up, and the terrible knowledge that he doesn't feel the same.

I turn away. 'Nothing. Just tired.'

His fingers are on my arm. They curl around my bicep and tighten. 'Look at me.'

My heart kicks in my chest. I glance up at his stern expression, his black eyes. He leans closer. 'What is it?'

'Nothing.' My voice is sullen.

He won't let go of my arm. 'I'm going to leave soon,' he says quietly. 'I don't belong here. I don't know how long I'll stay. A week, or a month, or two. But I will go.'

'So?'

'So that's not fair on you.'

'Why do you get to decide what's fair for me?' I can hardly breathe.

'Because this is about me, too.' He places his fingers against my lips, tracing their shape, as if he's healing them.

I take hold of his hand and kiss his palm. 'I don't care about you going away. I only care that you're here now.'

He inhales as if he's in pain.

I let go of his hand and he curls it into a fist. We are almost touching. I smell the stale damp of the attic, the feral scent of his sweat. There's a gleam of silver around his neck, a chain sticking to his damp skin. I pluck at the links with one finger. 'I never noticed this.'

He doesn't blink. 'It belonged to my sister.'

Questions drift through my head, questions about his family and why he hasn't been home for so long; who he really is. But they don't seem to be important any more.

His arms are wrapped around me, pulling me against his chest, and there's a sharp contraction in my lower belly.

He drops his face to mine and we are kissing.

I take him into my bedroom. He watches while I find a candle in the drawer, coming over to click his lighter. He looks at me in the small flickering flame. We have to begin with the truth.

'I slept with David,' I tell him. 'We had a relationship. It was brief. But it happened.'

'I know,' he says quietly.

The candle burns down lower, throwing our joined shadows across the walls and ceiling. He pulls away, settling against the headboard; we've lost the pillow and half the covers somewhere on the floor. My head lies heavy on his shoulder. He runs a finger across my skin, round and round in looping circles.

'I didn't think you wanted me,' I murmur.

'I did the moment I saw you in the garden. But I was worried you'd be frightened of me. Then after I moved into the garage, I realised you and David were seeing each other.'

'You used to look at me sometimes . . . as if you didn't like me.'

'Never,' he says. 'It was never that. But I used to wonder . . . I didn't know how close you were to David, if you knew anything about his business.'

'So you didn't trust me?'

'I trusted you – I didn't trust the situation.'

He dips his head and licks the salt from my wrist. And it begins again. The kissing. The slow, deliberate exploration of each other's bodies. I am overwhelmed by his power, not just muscular strength, but the intensity of his passion, as if he wants to devour me. We slip against each other, sweating. Teeth and tongues and nails. This is the only thing that matters. This moment. And inside it, past and future collide. Luca has always been here with me. In the boat, all those years ago, it was his face against the moon, his body I was reaching for.

Outside the open bedroom door, drips are still falling into the bucket and saucepans. Slow, occasional drops. The uncertain, ringing sounds are like strange jazz percussion or a clock that's winding down, time losing its beat.

THIRTY-FOUR

When I wake the next morning, my body and mind are alert with remembering. I'm afraid to open my eyes, expecting an empty pillow. But he's lying on his hip beside me. He smiles, face crinkling, and pulls me against his warm chest, enveloping me in a hug, so that I'm inhaling the peppery scent of sleep-soaked skin.

'You were dreaming,' he says.

'Was I?' I mumble into his arm.

I struggle onto my elbow, pushing a hand through tangled clumps of my hair. My whole body feels raw and tingly. He sprawls beside me, one arm behind his head, loose limbed and relaxed as if we've been sleeping together for years. His chest hair is grey, his muscles have the thickened density that comes with age, but his skin is tight and supple as a young man's. I sigh, not wanting to move, but my shoulder is aching with pins and needles, and I need to pee.

I slip out of bed, holding the sheet, reaching for my dressing gown.

'Don't,' he says.

I turn, startled, holding the folds of my gown in front of me.

'Don't cover yourself. I want to see you.'

I drop the fabric and stand slowly, my fingers clenching at my sides. He looks at me, his expression soft.

'You're beautiful.'

I take a deep breath.

He pushes the covers aside and gets out, giving a languorous stretch, arms raised. 'It's stopped raining,' he says. 'I'm going to mend the roof.' Then he pulls me to him. We stand locked into each other, my head turned against his shoulder. I listen to his heart. Through the window, cloud shadows move across the field and orchard, darkening the woods, and David's land beyond.

Luca drinks a black tea and goes off into the damp garden to check on the animals and find things for the roof. His loping figure disappears behind the shed. And I remember him telling me, 'I will go away. One month. Or two. But I will go.'

Not yet. I think. He's not leaving yet.

I can't stay away from the tearoom for another day. I need to catch up on the baking. I get into the Fiat and drive to the village, enjoying the private space of my car. I don't want to listen to the radio, not even music. I need peace to absorb everything, to replay last night, going over the smell and feel and taste of it. I can't stop smiling.

I move my arm, changing down a gear, switching into neutral to stop at a crossroads, before indicating and turning left. As I pull out, I notice migrant workers hard at work in the field opposite. Their stooped forms have become part of this landscape. There they are, out in the open. Any one of them could simply walk if they wanted to. There are no gates or locks here. Luca must be wrong. Rumours mean nothing in a place like this.

In the village I see Mary; she waves at me.

'We'll be getting the weathervane soon.'

'Sorry?'

'We won. Didn't you hear?'

'Congratulations. And you get a weathervane as a prize?'

She nods, triumphant. 'Best Kept Village in Kent.' She comes closer. 'I was shocked to hear about this business with your lodger.' She lowers her voice. 'Nasty thing. Did you never feel in danger yourself?'

'No, because it's not true, Mary,' I tell her. 'Luca is a good person. He didn't do it.'

'He's gone back to Romania?'

I keep eye contact with her. 'With Anca and Luca both gone, I don't think there's much to talk about, do you? We should forget about it and get on with our lives.'

We have another quiet day at the tearoom. Kate asks me if she can have next week off to do her Beauty Therapy course.

'No problem,' I tell her. 'We're not exactly overrun with customers.'

The brigadier comes in and takes his usual table. I go over

with his scone and tea. He puts down his newspaper and looks up at me. 'I heard the news,' he says. 'But I did warn you.'

'Everyone warned me about Luca, but—'

'Not the foreign chap. David.'

'David? I don't understand . . .'

'The man has no class. He fooled Henrietta into marrying him. But he never fooled me.'

'He told me about his background. He didn't lie to me.'

The brigadier makes a harrumphing noise and glares at me under his hairy eyebrows. 'All this nonsense about the migrant girl. It wouldn't have happened when the Aiken-Browns owned the farm.'

'David and I . . .' I swallow. 'We're no longer together.'

The brigadier gives me a pitying glance and snaps his newspaper open.

THIRTY-FIVE

It's getting dark earlier, the nights drawing in. I leave the stable open for Nutmeg and Gilbert to take shelter when they want to. I'm spreading fresh straw, checking that the water bucket is full. There's no electric light out here, and I can hardly see beyond my outstretched hands. Both animals are in the field somewhere. As I straighten, picking stray bits of straw from my jumper, I catch a movement in the far corner.

My heart stops. Another hedgehog perhaps, or a rat. But there's a shape there, more solid than shadow, something dense, something bigger than a rat, much bigger. I hold my breath and quietly stretch my arm behind, feeling for the rake that I left leaning against the wall. Rustling is coming from the corner, and then a low grunt, an angry punch of sound.

I grasp the wooden pole, pulling it to me. Holding the metal head in front, I edge a little closer. 'I have a weapon. Stand up. Slowly.' I'm trying to sound confident, but I'm trembling.

The thing. The creature. It freezes. It doesn't stand up.

I want to shout for Luca, but the cottage seems far away and my throat has closed.

'Who are you?' I manage, voice scratchy with fear.

And then there is a lurching, an enlarging of the thing. It unfurls, rising up into distorted human shape. I gasp and step back, gripping the rake hard. It moans like a B-movie monster and staggers towards me, growing into something that looks like a woman. I flinch away from pale hands stretching out, hooked like claws.

'Please.' A hoarse voice comes through the darkness.

A spark of recognition flares. The rake falls from my grip. There's a panting sob and her face looms into visibility, caught in the wash of moonlight coming through the door. Her features are contorted in pain, mouth pinched and forehead furrowed. She comes close. My arms go around her. I can feel how big she is, her stomach a swollen balloon, her hands clutching the bulk. And I understand. She's in labour.

'Anca.'

She slumps onto me. My knees nearly buckle. She's a dead weight. I straighten my spine, bracing myself, supporting her across my shoulders, one hand holding her dangling wrist.

'Can you walk? Can you get to the house?'

Anca makes a brief nod and we stagger forward together like a badly paired team in a three-legged race. She's panting hard, and between the pants she groans. I'm scared. It sounds as though the baby is well on its way.

'Have your waters broken?'

She makes a noise that I think means yes. I glance up. The

cottage is painfully far. The windows are lit up. Where's Luca? She stumbles and her legs lock and drag behind her. My bones jar, pain shooting through my shoulder. I raise my head and yell.

The back door opens, letting out a shaft of light that falls across the darkness, making a path. Luca's tall shape bursts through the brilliance and he's there by my side, reaching for Anca, pulling her into his arms.

In the kitchen, my eyes play tricks in the electric glare, sprinkling dots of gold and black. When I blink them away, Anca has collapsed over the back of a chair. Luca's leaning over her, speaking in Romanian, and I can see that he's trying to persuade her to sit down. I put out my hand. 'No. She can't. She's in labour.'

Anca doesn't react. Her eyes are closed and her lips move silently as if she's praying. Her grey skin is slick with sweat; beads quiver on her top lip.

'I found her in the stable. We need to call a doctor. The hospital.'

'No.' Sound rips the air. 'No. Coming. Now.' She grasps the back of the chair, her face squeezing shut.

I throw a glance at Luca, frowning, and turn to Anca, my hand under her elbow. 'Can you move? Come into the living room.' I help her shuffle forward. 'Luca,' I call behind me. 'I'll need my sewing scissors. Fetch sheets. Lots of clean sheets. From the airing cupboard.'

Inside my head, I'm trying to remember what to do. I throw cushions onto the floor for her to kneel on. 'Better for you on your knees. But can you lie on the sofa for a moment? I need to see how far along you are.' She turns her head, and I see the whites of her eyes. 'I trained as a midwife.'

She eases onto the sofa and heaves onto her back, her stomach rising above her. 'I . . . I am . . . a nurse,' she pants between her words as I wrench off her underwear, hoist up her skirt.

'A nurse?'

A spasm crosses her face. She bites her lower lip, and a drop of blood oozes. My mind has gone blank. I can't let her know how scared I am. But there's no time to get her to hospital. She's right. My searching fingers have found the baby's head. A curve of bone, slippery and warm. It's crowning already. Anca is writhing in agony. She needs to bear down. She scrambles off the sofa onto her knees. The violence of her need roars through her. She'll tear.

'Wait,' I tell her. 'Wait. Don't push yet.'

But I don't think she can hear me; she's straining and moaning, and her shoulders tense with effort. With a yell like a war cry, her whole body convulses and the baby comes slithering into my waiting hands, waxy white and squirming. The weight of it shocks me, the human weight. It's moving, turning its head. I slip my fingers inside its mouth to check that it can breathe, touching a stub of tongue. The baby pushes against me, lips stretching wide to show a tiny arch of ribbed flesh and naked gums, and suddenly a desperate bleating tears the air. My belly clenches at the sound.

I crumple a corner of sheet and use it to wipe streaks of blood and vernix from blunt features, swollen eyes tightly shut. Gingerly, I balance the crying baby on my knees and examine the wrinkled skin, vivid torso, two arms and two legs. A boy.

The umbilical cord trails between Anca's bloodied thighs, a thick, rippled rope. She's crawled off the floor to lie flat on the sofa, exhausted. But the placenta has to come out. She can't go to sleep. 'Look.' I place the baby in the crook of her arm. 'Look. You have a son.'

She stares at me blankly and turns her head away. Her baby is rooting, making little mews of hunger and frustration. Her arm lies slack. It's as if she can't hear, can't feel. She must be in shock. The birth was too quick. She might need stitches.

I lean close and take her hand in mine. It lies inside my fingers, lifeless. 'Anca? I know you're tired. But we haven't finished yet. And you have a beautiful little boy. Don't you want to see him? He's hungry.'

She's crying. A slow tear rolls down her cheek. She doesn't make a sound.

I bite back my frustration, trying to think what to do. And I look down at her passive, unresponsive hand. Her palm is covered in blisters, raw, weeping wounds. I turn it in horror. A mottled red rash creeps up her forearms. The baby begins to scream.

I scoop him up, wrap him in a towel. He nestles into the curve of my neck like a kitten. His mouth turns towards my ear to nuzzle before he realises and begins to cry again. My heart swells with the need to feed him, soothe him. I can't go anywhere. He's still attached to the placenta.

'Luca!' I shout.

But he's in the room already, his face anxious. 'Is everything all right? The baby?'

'A boy,' I say. Then I step closer, whispering, 'I don't think she's going to feed him. Can you drive to Canterbury? Find a chemist that's still open. Get formula milk for newborns, bottles, nappies.' I press my forehead, thinking. 'And something for him to wear. Babygros if you can get them at this time of night.'

He touches the baby's hand. 'He's beautiful. You could give him a little sugar water on your finger, just to keep him calm for now. I'll make some before I go.'

I nod towards Anca's inert form. 'She's got these horrible marks on her hands.'

He kneels by her side, whispering in Romanian. She doesn't respond. He lifts her wrists and looks at her palms, examining the skin. He shakes his head, replacing her arms gently. He hesitates, bending close, and I think he's going to kiss her. Instead, he sighs and stands up.

'It's going to be all right,' he tells me. 'I'll get back as quickly as I can.'

What will happen if someone recognises him, or he gets stopped, or has an accident? He's not insured either. I close my eyes. This is an emergency. We don't have a choice.

Anca has turned towards the back of the sofa and wrapped her arms around herself. She doesn't respond when I talk to her. She's made herself absent. Her baby has given up and hiccups softly.

I dip my clean finger into the water and touch his tiny lips with a drop. He opens immediately and latches on, suckles for a moment, and then his face contorts. I quickly dip my finger again and replace it, slipping it inside his hungry mouth. He gets used to me breaking off and coming back. His hands flex in desperation, but he waits like a baby bird for me to return.

'I know it's not perfect,' I tell his scrunched face. 'You're hungry for proper food. But this will have to do for now. You'll have some milk soon, I promise.'

He twitches sparse eyebrows like an old man.

I lean close, inhaling the secret, raw scent of him. That long-lost smell. 'You're safe here,' I whisper. 'I'm going to keep you safe.'

Anca has managed to birth the placenta. Miraculously, she doesn't seem to have torn. I couldn't find any internal damage. There are bruises on her inner thighs, but I'm sure she didn't get them while she was in labour; they're green and fading. She won't look at her child. She has her eyes closed.

I'm not sure how much time has passed since Luca left – an hour, three hours? I've lost track of time. But it feels like he's been gone too long. I go to the window and draw back the curtain, peering out at the dark drive. Trees and bushes move against the sky. The wind has got up. I chew my nails, willing a pair of headlights to appear, twin beams shining towards the house. Behind me, the placenta lies on a bloodied towel, shockingly huge and exposed. The baby sleeps next to it, tethered to his mother. He's still hungry, but he's too exhausted to stay awake.

As I leave the window I hear a car turning into the drive, and my heart stops. There's the sound of feet crunching across to the front door. I dare to leave the baby for a minute to run into the hall. Luca stands there with his hands full of plastic shopping bags.

I want to hug him, but I'm already edging back to the doorway, scared to leave the baby on the sofa. 'I was getting worried.'

'Took a while to get everything,' he says. 'I'll make the formula. Has she taken any interest in the child?'

I shake my head, and he turns his mouth down in disappointment. I watch him disappearing into the kitchen, hear the click of the kettle going on, the muted clatter and rustle of things being unpacked. Relief settles like something weighted and true.

When I check the baby, the cord has stopped pulsing. It's white and limp, ready to cut. I call for Luca and ask him to sterilise the scissors. 'I need string too,' I tell him. 'Maybe my knitting yarn?'

'No.' He squats next to me. 'Look, it's ready to cut or burn off without ties or clamps.'

'How do you know?'

He shrugs. 'In the circus women never went into hospital to give birth. And I've seen many mother animals. Dogs, cat, lions, they all chew through the cord when it's ready.'

He's right. The cord doesn't need clamping. It cuts cleanly. Luca holds a candle to the end and it pops and sizzles, giving off an unsettling smell of burnt flesh. 'Best way to sterilise it,' he says.

The baby opened his eyes as we bent over him, but he's drifted back into sleep, cocooned on the sofa, wrapped in a towel next to Anca. She hasn't turned to him once. I stand up, rolling stiff shoulders, shaking out the cramp in my calves.

'I need to bath him and put a nappy on him. Give him a proper feed.' I rub my eyes. 'Anca needs a bath too, and I should dress the wounds on her hands.' I peer at the strange marks. 'How do you think she got them?'

He scratches the side of his nose. 'Maybe chemical burns. Or a bad reaction to something.'

Luca pulls me to him and kisses the top of my head. 'You did well,' he says quietly, and something inside me expands, an exhausted happiness, syrupy and golden.

THIRTY-SIX

Cradling the baby over my shoulder, I pause outside the spare room. I settled Anca in there in the early hours of the morning on clean sheets, gave her arnica for the bruising. I hope she got some sleep, but now the day is slipping past and she needs to meet her son. I raise my hand to knock, but I hear something – voices. I lean closer, listening to the low sounds of a disagreement.

I push open the door. Anca sits up in bed, wearing one of my nightdresses. Her skin is the colour of a greying vest against the white pillow. Luca is standing by the bed. He looks up at me with a frown. Then he wipes it away, giving me a cracked smile.

The room is tight with tension. I look from one to the other. Neither meets my eye.

'How are you feeling?' I sit on the side of the bed, cradling the baby on my lap, his sleeping head surprisingly heavy on my arm.

'OK.' She shrugs. 'Thank you . . . for last night.'

‘Won’t you hold him?’ I ask her. ‘Just for a moment.’

She looks at me with dull eyes.

Luca touches my elbow lightly. ‘I was asking Anca about the farm. About the migrant workers.’

He leans forward and talks to her in Romanian and I listen hard, as if I can understand through sheer concentration. Sounds slip between them. I watch Anca’s exhausted face as she answers; she speaks rapidly, but her expression stays defensive.

‘What?’ I’m impatient.

Luca stands up, and I hear his knees creak. ‘She says she’s been working at the farm illegally. She got the marks on her skin from chemicals on the fruit. David doesn’t let his pickers wear gloves.’

I remember her yellow rubber gloves. How she used to pull them on every time she walked through the door, covering her hands.

‘We have to go to the police.’ My words catch. ‘And she has to go to hospital. To check everything after the birth.’

‘No.’ Anca struggles to sit up. She’s shaking her head. ‘Please. No. I am illegal. They will deport me. Prison.’ She begins to push her legs out of the sheets.

‘All right,’ I tell her quickly, to stop her getting out of bed. ‘We won’t call anyone. Not yet. But what about your baby’s father . . . ’ I drop my voice.

I can see that she understands me. Her face is wary.

‘Who is he?’

She shakes her head.

‘David said you told him that it was a Romanian, another worker?’

She presses her lips together, her face closed. I glance at Luca, but he's looking out of the window, arms folded.

I use my spare hand to smooth her sheets down, patting them. 'We won't phone anyone now. But if David is using illegal migrants, it's him that will get into trouble. Not you.'

Anca looks unconvinced. The baby stirs, wrinkling his face, yawning to show the wet of his tongue.

'I'm going to bring you up something to eat. Chicken soup. Toast. Tell me if you'd like anything else?'

She shakes her head again.

'What shall we call your son? He doesn't have a name yet.' I hold him up, carefully supporting his head so that she can see his face, how the swelling is going down and how his slate eyes have opened, swallowing the world.

She raises her shoulders and lets them fall. She mutters something in Romanian, and I look at Luca.

'She says he isn't her son.'

We've left Anca to sleep after her meal. Luca leans against the wall, watching me on my bed feeding the baby, who's suckling from a bottle, his toes curling with pleasure. His fontanelle pulses under black hair. Every time I pick him up I'm afraid of hurting him. His head rolls terrifyingly.

'You were right to be suspicious,' I say. 'David should be prosecuted.'

He frowns. 'I think the police will be more interested in the migrants than David.'

I shoot him a questioning look.

'The workers may or may not be legal. But if David has taken their papers, then he's keeping them in debt bondage.' Luca's voice is hard. 'They'll have paid someone a lot of money for getting them into the country, and now for board and lodging too. They probably aren't making anything for themselves.'

'Debt bondage? But that's got to be against the law.'

'It's also against the law to be a migrant without papers. David is well-connected. His friend . . . the police inspector . . . he probably knows about this.' Luca raises his shoulders. 'Maybe he's cashing in on the profits.'

'What shall we do?'

'Nothing yet. Anca is our key to all this.' He rubs his nose. 'We need to get her to talk more. She's holding things back. She's frightened.'

'David told me she'd gone home to Romania.'

'She said she ran away from the farm. She's been surviving on her own somehow.'

A thought strikes me. 'With Anca here, we can prove you're innocent.'

'That's not the most important thing right now. Anca's scared. There's something she's not telling us. I want to get her trust. We need more time. Before David realises she's here.'

Anxiety clenches in my gut. I angle my shoulders away from him, bending over the baby. 'I'm sorry, but I want to call the police sooner. Tomorrow at the latest,' I say. 'We have to let the authorities know about all of this. We can't manage on our own.'

'And you trust them so much, these authorities?' He looks angry. 'You are very naive, Ellie.'

It's as if he's slapped my face. I can't look at him.

'This is my home, Luca.' I find his gaze. 'I'm not the one who's going to be moving on soon. I have to do what I think best – for everyone.'

He pushes his hands into his pockets. 'I'm going out.'

'Luca!'

He's gone. I drop my mouth onto the baby's head, humming an old nursery rhyme. His rapid, butterfly-wing breathing tells me he's asleep. I listen to the sound of his lungs, the flutter of his breath. Everything about him is delicate. He needs me. Just like my own baby did, my tiny lost son.

THIRTY-SEVEN

I'm using an emptied drawer as a cot, with a mattress from cushions and a folded sheet. The baby wakes every couple of hours. Time blurs into hallucinatory scenes, the room lit only by a night light, shadows leaping against walls. I'm scared – what if he stops breathing? When he sleeps, I force myself to stay awake. Sometimes I put my hand on his chest to check that his lungs are moving.

Throughout the night, I get up and change his nappy with stiff, automatic movements, stumbling downstairs in a daze to make more formula. The hours merge into each other. I start up in a panic, dragged out of a dim underworld by his yells. I'd dozed off with him sprawled across my chest. I manage to get him back to sleep and into the drawer without waking him.

The room is pale; a slab of daylight falls through the gap between the curtains, dissecting the floor. I must have slept. I sit up, looking around for Luca. He didn't come back. The realisation hollows me out. Then I stare at the makeshift cot, suddenly anxious.

There are little mews, sounds of stirring. I relax, rubbing my aching head. I can't believe that it's time to get up again – to make more formula, unload the dishwasher, take Anca her breakfast. I hope that Luca has done the hens this morning. I stumble out of bed, yawning, and bend over the makeshift cot, looking into expectant, no-colour eyes.

In the kitchen, as I measure spoons of powdered milk into bottles, spilling some across the counter, I know that this is what I missed all those years ago – everyday moments, the responsibility of looking after my baby. I was never alone with my son. The smell of the hospital surrounded us, nurses watching as I fed him, waiting to take him from me. I push my knotted hair behind my ears, then carefully pour out boiling water. My tired brain miscalculates and a splash falls on my wrist, scalding me. I curse and hold it under the cold tap, looking at the patch of red blooming under gushing water. I mustn't fantasise. I'll take him up to Anca. When he cries, I won't go in and pick him up. I'll leave them together. His crying will trigger some deep need inside her.

I pad up the stairs, the cooling bottle in my hand. He's moaning and fidgeting, hungry for breakfast. I push open the door to the spare room with my foot. The bed is empty, sheets flung back, blood smeared across the middle. The pillow is crumpled and I can see the indentation left by her head. She must be in the bathroom. I settle on the unmade bed and begin to feed the baby. He pulls at the teat, his hands moving to the rim of the bottle, fingers feeling and patting at the plastic.

Why doesn't she come back? I frown. Maybe she's collapsed, fainted in the bath? I look at the brownish stain, worrying that she has internal tearing that I missed. I hoist the baby onto my shoulder, noticing as I stand a slippery circle of fabric on the floor. I prod it with my toe: my nightdress. Then I realise, Anca's clothes aren't on the chair. I stand outside the bathroom, calling her name. The door isn't locked. The mirror above the sink reflects nothing but my startled face.

I hurry to check the rest of the cottage, calling her. She's not here, and there's no sign of Luca either. A gust of fear rocks me, and I go into Will's study, where Luca is keeping his stuff. The rucksack is on the floor. My shoulders unknot. But time slips past and he doesn't appear. I go out to the garage and put my head round the door. There's no trace of him. I shout his name into the garden. If he's gone, he'll need money. I run to the filing cabinet, turn the key and wrench the drawer open. The package with the five thousand is still there. I count it to make sure. Then I remember the cash he earned from fruit-picking. He keeps it in an envelope in the front pocket of his rucksack.

I pull everything out of the rucksack, clothes and books and tin cup and a pair of shoes. No money. I sit down heavily on the chair by the desk. The baby flops in my arms; he's drifting into sleep, unconcerned, satisfied. I wipe a dribble from his chin. I don't know what to do. I don't know what this means – whether to call the police or not. Should I call local hospitals? Maybe Anca's ill. Maybe she's been admitted somewhere? Maybe Luca took her?

*

Outside the cottage, there's the purr of a familiar engine, a swish of tyres through gravel. I know who it is. Blood hammers in my ears as I go into my room and carefully place the sleeping baby in the drawer, creeping out and closing the door, before stumbling down to undo the lock.

My movements are weighted with dread. Fingers clumsy. Quick, quick, a voice in my head shouts, let him in before he rings the bell.

'Hello.' I tug at my nightdress.

'Mary said the tearoom was closed. Thought I'd look in on you.' David steps past me into the hall. He looks different. And I realise that his shirt is creased, his hair rumpled and not shiny and clean as usual.

'I'm OK.' I raise my palms. 'I have a bug or something.' I wrap my arms around myself. 'I was in bed.'

'Flu?' He places cool fingers on my forehead as if he's checking my temperature. I try not to flinch. 'You're always ill. You don't look after yourself.'

I clear my throat, putting my hand to my mouth and giving a cough. I don't know if he'll notice the new-baby smell in the house, that bloody, milky scent mixed with a whiff of soiled nappies and detergent.

'Can I fetch you anything? You shouldn't be alone.' He hovers on the threshold.

'No thanks,' I tell him quickly. 'I just want to sleep it off.'

I know I look convincingly terrible, dark rings under my bloodshot eyes, greasy hair around my shoulders.

'Kate's not holding the fort then?'

'No. She's doing a course. I thought it was easier to close the tearoom for a while. Until I'm better. We haven't had many customers recently anyway.'

He hesitates and then begins to turn. He's leaving. Relief makes my legs weak. I put a hand against the wall. And then I hear it. A staggering cry.

David stops. My heart skips a beat. I begin to cough and splutter with desperate overacting, but it's too late – there's no covering up the yelling that rages from my bedroom.

David begins to go towards the stairs, head cocked to listen. He's got his foot on the first step. 'Is that a baby?'

He strides up, taking the stairs two at a time. I hurry behind. He makes for my bedroom, following the noise. He takes one look at the squalling baby, and around the room, and then he's out in the corridor, twisting the handles to the spare room, the bathroom and Will's study. Doors flap open on their hinges, emptiness pooling. 'Where is she?'

I pick up the child and shush him, patting his back, jiggling him up and down. There's no point in pretending. 'Anca's not here,' I call out. 'She left this morning. I don't know where she is.'

He comes back. 'Why on earth didn't you tell me she was here? You know I've been worried.' He stares at the baby. 'They're both all right?'

I raise my chin. 'She told me Luca isn't the father.'

David's eyes widen in surprise. He makes a low noise in his throat, rubbing a hand over his unshaven chin. 'But it sounded like Luca. Anca's obviously been telling us different stories.' He gives me a sharp look. 'Luca didn't go back to Romania, did he? He's been hiding here, waiting for her to show up. And you helped him—'

Shock makes me catch my breath. I stare down at my naked feet on the carpet.

'He's gone too?' He sighs and runs his fingers over his forehead. 'You are so innocent, Ellie. So trusting.' His voice softens. 'It's not your fault. It took me a while to understand. They're running a scam. They're traffickers. They must have been managing it right under our noses.'

'She told me it's you that's keeping illegal migrants.' I take a step away. 'I'm going to call the police.'

'I've already told Ian. The police are on the lookout for both of them.' He looks at the baby, and blinks. 'Abandoning her newborn child. Does it get much lower than that?'

'How did you know that Anca would come here?'

'I didn't. I came to see if you were OK.' He nods. 'But now of course, I can see that it makes sense. She's the sort of person who will turn kindness to her advantage. I think she was here to recruit contacts.' He's pacing up and down. 'I have a lot of migrants at my site, and most will know people back home who are looking for a chance to come to the UK for work. Desperate people are easily tricked. Once they've got them over here, those workers are worth a lot of money.'

I breathe in the clean, milky scent of the child in my arms.

'Bill told me that he'd spotted Anca and Luca whispering together. It only dawned on me after Anca ran off that she and Luca knew each other from before. Maybe he didn't rape her. That was just a sob story, to confuse us. Maybe they're lovers.'

'She had burns on her hands. From the chemicals. She said you don't let your workers wear gloves.'

'Of course they can wear gloves. I tell them all the time. But some of them choose not to. The more they pick, the more they earn. Gloves slow them down.'

My mind is twisting, trying to make sense of everything. Is that why Anca turned up in my stable – to see Luca, to be with the father of her child? I can't afford to lose my ground, to be pushed off balance. I mustn't argue, or disagree.

'I see,' I murmur.

He gets hold of my chin and looks into my eyes.

'I wish you wouldn't pretend, Ellie.' He drops his hand. 'I know you don't believe me.' He frowns. 'The thing is, you are out of your depth. You don't know what these people are like.'

THIRTY-EIGHT

As soon as David leaves, I dial the number of the local police station. My fingers are shaking. A receptionist's voice answers, asking me who I want to speak to, what department. My throat closes.

'Hello?' The voice repeats several times. 'Hello?'

I hang up quickly. I touch the phone again. I should let social services know about Anca's baby. But they'll take him away and put him in care. I can look after him better. He knows me. I don't want him taken from one place to another, strange voices around him, prodded and held by unfamiliar hands.

I haven't named him. He's not mine to name.

The day passes. Feeding, changing nappies, dozing, making formula, waiting for Luca to call me. I wrap the baby up warmly and take him with me to do the hens. I need one of those things that allow you to strap a baby to your front. A pram would be useful, too. There's a whole list of things I want to get for him.

I do all my chores one-handed. Balancing him against me feels as natural as shifting my own body weight from one side to the other. When I check on Nutmeg and Gilbert, the donkey puts her nose over the fence and snuffles at this surprising scent, her muzzle wrinkling. And I let myself imagine how, in a couple of years' time, the baby could ride on Nutmeg's broad back, holding onto her stubby mane with his fat, toddler fingers.

I shut off the thought. This baby isn't mine. I'll give him up soon.

There are other thoughts waiting at the edge of my consciousness – David's words. How else to explain Luca and Anca's disappearance? I'm so tired, I can hardly stand up. I don't have the energy to eat anything, and I take the baby into the sitting room. It's dark now and the black glass makes me uncomfortable. I draw the curtains and slump on the sofa with his sweet, musty head under my chin.

'What are we going to do?' I ask softly. 'Everything is upside down and nothing makes sense.' I kiss his ear. 'Except you.'

I remember Luca's arms around me, his face above mine, our lips finding each other's cheeks and noses and eyes. The way he looked at me. I press my knuckles against my forehead until it hurts. First Will, and now Luca.

My arm is aching. The baby is asleep, his lips moving. I wonder if he's dreaming. I should put him down, but I don't want to. I shift so that I can flex my elbow, trying to get rid of pins and needles. I place my lips on his cheek. I love the way his head fits into the gap between my jaw and shoulder, the way he clings to my finger when he's feeding, staring into my eyes, telling me things, searching my soul. I checked his belly when I last changed his nappy. The shrivelled twist of cord will fall off in a week or so, like a lamb's tail.

I caught him when he came into the world. I cut his cord. But he's not mine.

I'm dozing off when the sound of a car door slamming jerks me upright. My arm is dead under the weight of the baby's sleeping head. Could it be David again? The police? Luca? I hush the waking child, manoeuvring him against my chest, so that I can heave onto my feet and go to the window to lift the curtain and peer out.

The night is dark as molasses. A sharp rap at the door makes me start. I creep towards the sound and stand with my fingers on the handle, listening. Someone on the other side clears their throat, shuffles their feet. Then another knock, louder this time. I bite my lip, afraid that the baby will begin to cry.

'Ellie?'

I fumble with the latch, turn the key. Kate stands on my doorstep, lit by the porch light. I beckon quickly and lock the door behind her.

She's staring at me. At the baby. 'What's going on?' Her eyes widen. 'Who does that belong to?'

'It's a long story. Come through. Do you want a drink or anything?'

'Alcohol please – don't mind what.' She fiddles with her hair. She looks better than the last time I saw her. She's in full make-up, bright lips and glittery eye-shadow; silver hoops dangle from her ears.

She sits down while I root in the fridge and find an opened

half bottle of white wine. No idea how long it's been there. I slosh it into her glass, the baby folded over my arm. She takes a large gulp and watches me lift the child to smell his nappy.

'I need to change him in a minute,' I tell her.

'Who does he belong to?'

'Anca.'

She's just taken another large swig, and she splutters. 'Anca? The one that was ... Oh my God, the whole village has been talking about it.'

'Luca didn't ... he's not ... he's not even the father. Anyway, she had the baby here, and now she's gone.' I reach across and touch Kate's hand. 'Don't say anything to anyone. Please. It's complicated.'

'She had the baby here?' Her eyes are round. 'No doctor or anything?'

'I trained as a midwife. A long time ago.'

'What will you do with him?' She leans close to him. 'He's so tiny. What's his name?'

'He doesn't have one yet. I think it's up to Anca to choose it.' I rock him back and forth to stop him grumbling. 'I know I should contact social services. But I wanted to see if Anca was going to call me first or come back. I thought I should give her a few days. She is his mother.'

She clicks her tongue at the baby. 'How could she leave you, poor little mite? Look at you. You're gorgeous, aren't you?' She turns to me. 'Where's she gone, anyway?'

'That's the thing, I have no idea. I went to her room this morning, and she wasn't there. No note or anything.' It's a relief to be able to talk about it.

'How weird. Do you think she's all right? Maybe she's got . . . what's it called? Postnatal depression?'

I remember Anca's dull eyes, her refusal to feed the baby. 'Maybe. She was in shock, I think, and unhappy. Not bonding with her baby. But now she's gone and I have no way of contacting her.'

'Should you report her as a missing person?'

I bury my face in my wine glass. 'I will,' I murmur. 'If she's not back soon.'

'Well, she's lucky you're being so good about it. You seem really natural with him.' Kate pushes her hair back. 'So that's why you don't have any paraphernalia.' She watches me juggle baby and wine. 'Not even one of those baby bouncers.'

She puts her hand to her temples. 'Oh my God, I'm an idiot! This is why you've shut the tearoom! I feel terrible now, going off to do my course and abandoning you.'

I shake my head. 'Don't be silly. It's OK to close it for a couple of weeks. How's your course going?'

'Fine.' She glances away, and down at her lap. 'But I need to talk to you about something,' she says. 'It's been nagging and nagging at me. Only I don't want you to hate me.'

'That sounds serious.' I can feel damp under my hand. 'Let me change this one, and then you can tell me. Pour yourself another glass if you like.'

When I come back into the room, she's nibbling at her nails. I begin to worry.

'I didn't say anything before,' she says. 'He told me not to. He said it should be our secret. And I was so . . . infatuated. I would have done anything he said.'

'Who?' I sit very still.

'Adam,' she whispers. 'You know how I felt . . . I couldn't believe he was interested in me. He started to meet me after work.'

'In The Old Dairy?'

She nods. 'He was lovely. Funny and flirtatious.' She swallows. 'He said he was fed up with his father, that it was getting heavy at home. We hung out together. Nothing happened. But I was sure he was going to kiss me.'

'Well, you shouldn't really have used the premises without asking me.' I stroke the baby's downy hair. 'But it's not the end of the world.'

'That's not the worst part.' Her shoulders slump. 'I'm sure he was responsible for all the weird things that went wrong. It had to be him.'

I clasp a hand over my mouth. 'Are you still seeing him?'

She shakes her head. 'I haven't seen him since the night before the dead rat appeared. I told him how much I liked him. I tried to kiss him. Then he said he was in love with someone else. I cried and pleaded with him.' She shudders. 'It was pathetic. He told me that he'd never thought of me like that. He already had a girlfriend.' She raises her hands. 'I mean, what the fuck! The next morning, the dead rat was in The Old Dairy. It was then that I knew . . . he'd been using me to get into the kitchen, tamper with things when no one was around.'

'Did he think it was a joke? He could have got us shut down.' I remember his smile as he asked *How's it going at the tearoom*? I shiver. Was he behind the bad reviews, too?

She begins to cry, small shaky sobs, her mascara running in

navy dribbles. She takes a tissue from her handbag and tries to dab at the damage.

I put my hand on her shoulder. 'I'm not angry.'

Panic is squeezing my ribs, making it hard to breathe. Perhaps Adam found out about Will and Henrietta, and he's taking it out on me? I go upstairs and put the drowsy baby in his drawer, leaving my bedroom door open.

In the kitchen, Kate is blowing her nose and taking deep, steadying breaths. I hand her some tissues. 'Did Adam ever mention me?'

Kate shakes her head. 'He talked about Henrietta a lot. And David. He hero-worships him.'

'What about his birth mother?'

She leans her chin on her hand. 'He only told me that once. And he was a bit drunk. He seemed really angry, you know, about his birth mother deserting him. He said all women are weak.'

'Did he . . . ever talk about William?'

She shakes her head, looking surprised. 'They didn't really know each other, did they?'

'No,' I agree. I get up and walk around the kitchen, drumming my fingers on the backs of chairs. And I think about Adam meeting the woman in the cafe. They had some sort of contract together. What had David said? *It's part of the deal.* I frown; what day had it been? A Tuesday. Eleven o'clock. If they meet at The Tarot Pack at the same time, then I can find her again.

Kate pushes her hands into her jacket, does it up and reaches out to hug me. She's tentative at first, but when my arms go around her, she squeezes hard, and I feel her tremble.

‘Thanks for being so understanding,’ she says when we break apart, her eyes suddenly shiny. ‘What will you do – I mean, about Adam?’

‘Nothing. We have no real proof. I’m more interested in finding out why he did it.’

‘What about the baby? And the tearoom?’

‘I’ll give Anca a couple of days to come back. Then I’ll call social services. And the tearoom can wait another week. I can manage for money. I had a small windfall a little while ago.’

Kate blinks back tears and rubs the end of her nose. ‘If I can help, call me.’

I watch her hurrying over to her car in the glow of the porch light, impractical wedges twisting under her ankles, bright red handbag swinging. She turns and waves.

I didn’t tell her the whole story. I couldn’t talk about Luca. She knows me too well. She would have seen my feelings in my face.

THIRTY-NINE

Early on Tuesday morning I phone Kate to ask if she can borrow a baby seat from her sister on my behalf. Kate comes over half an hour later to drop it off.

'It's a bit stained, I'm afraid.' She rubs at the chair as she hoists it out of her car, brushing off crumbs. 'Her youngest one's grown out of it.'

I take it from her, puzzling over the straps and fastenings.

'So Anca hasn't come back then?'

'Not yet.' My voice is muffled as I bend over, leaning into the back seat trying to work out how to attach it to the Fiat.

Kate pushes me gently out of the way, grabs the belt and threads it through the plastic shell of the baby carrier, pulls, and then snaps it into place. '*Voilà!*' She raises her hands. 'But why don't you let me look after him – you don't have to take him everywhere with you.'

I know she's right. But I can't leave him behind. It feels as though he's joined to me by an invisible cord. The idea of being away from him makes me panic.

'Maybe I will, next time.'

'So where are you off to? Shopping?'

I'm longing to share my plan with her. But I don't trust her not to gossip. She can't help herself. I've already told her too much. I have to hope that she won't talk about Anca and the baby.

I nod. 'Just a short trip.'

I've packed a couple of bottles of formula milk, nappies, wipes and cloths. I'm only going into Canterbury.

I get to The Tarot Pack before eleven. Adam's Defender is nowhere in sight. Last time, he got there late. I'm hoping it will be the same today. The baby is sleeping, his head slumped at an uncomfortable-looking angle, dribble on his chin. I decide to risk taking him out of the seat. It's too heavy to lug around and too difficult to put back in the car.

He stirs and whimpers, but I hold him against my shoulder and jig him up and down and he settles again. In the cafe, my eyes blink in the gloom. It smells of coffee, and under that there's the whiff of damp. Paper stars hang from the ceiling. There's a table of students chatting loudly and an old man at a window table, staring into space, a dog at his feet. At first I don't think she's here, but then I see her. She's slouched at a table right at the back. She has a beret on over her bright hair, and her huge sunglasses fixed in place.

She keeps her head down until I'm standing right beside her. Then she glances up and I see her features for the first time. Shock makes me gasp. She turns her back. I frown, beginning to doubt myself. But under the strange new hair and behind those glasses I recognise the slender nose, high cheekbones, the neat mouth. 'Henrietta.' I hold the baby tighter, my heart beating fast. 'It's you . . . isn't it?'

She shrinks in her seat. 'You've made a mistake.' Her voice is gruff.

The baby mutters and coughs against my neck. His warm presence gives me confidence. I slip into the chair opposite. 'It *is* you.'

She doesn't answer, looking obstinately in the other direction, shielding her forehead with her hand.

'I don't understand . . . I went to your memorial.' The cafe is reeling around me. 'You were dead.'

She turns her face, the glasses making her look like an insect. I clutch the table, remembering that odd argument between David and Adam. I gasp. 'David knows? He knows you're alive?'

She flinches as if I've slapped her. Then she leans over the table and grabs my fingers, her long nails digging in. 'Shut up,' she hisses. She begins to stand, looking around her nervously. 'We can't do this here.'

She's dropped my hand, and she's moving swiftly towards the staff entrance. I follow as she goes through a swing door into a small kitchen. There's a jumble of pots and pans, an overflowing bin. A radio plays a pop song. A boy leans against a sink smoking a joint. He gazes at us as we squeeze past and out through the back door.

She faces me in the daylight, between black bins. There's a pungent smell of rubbish. She pats at her shirt with uncertain fingers. 'How . . . how did you find me?'

'I followed Adam.' I can't stop staring at her. 'I wanted to find out who he was meeting—'

'Don't tell anyone.' She takes her glasses off, gazing at me intently. Her voice is full of desperation. 'Please?'

Daylight shows up details. I notice a nervous tic in her jaw. Her bleached hair drains her skin of colour. 'Why do you want people to think you're dead?' I ask quietly. 'Were you really ill – or was that a lie too?'

She licks her lips. 'I can't tell you – you just have to believe it's for the best.'

'Best?' The baby snuffles against my cheek. 'For who?'

Henrietta rubs her eyes. 'I can't tell you. I can't talk about it.'

'You slept with William. My husband.' My voice rises. 'And now you want me to keep your secret?'

She looks confused. 'Nothing happened between me and William.'

'But your clothes were hidden in our house. I found them. And the money. William took money out of our account for you.' I lift my eyebrows. 'You returned it, didn't you?'

'Yes,' she admits. 'I wanted you to have it back. I got Adam to drop it off. I can see why you might have been confused by the clothes. But . . . but it wasn't like that.'

'Then maybe you should tell me what it *was* like.'

'We have to be quick.' She glances behind her. 'David and I married despite my parents' disapproval. I was in love with him.'

'I know . . . and some of the locals disapproved of him.'

She shakes her head impatiently. 'David changed. He'd always been possessive, but it got worse. He was paranoid and controlling. He was disappointed that I couldn't have children.' Her voice trembles. 'I . . . I couldn't seem to do anything right after that. The things about me that he'd found attractive at first, he began to hate – he seemed to want to punish me.' She wraps her arms around herself. 'It spiralled out of control after my parents died and David took over the farm. The bruises were usually under my clothes. If they weren't, then we agreed on a story.'

I feel cold. I remember David holding my wrists as we made love, pinning me down. The way he'd hurt me, gripping too hard, when I told him I was leaving. I remember Henrietta in a plaster cast. David helping her tenderly.

'That time . . . you broke your arm . . . ' I falter. 'And your ankle?'

She looks at me and nods.

'Why didn't you leave? Or throw him out?'

'Do you think I didn't want to?' She gives a short, bitter laugh. 'He would always apologise, say it wouldn't happen again. I wanted to believe him. There were weeks, sometimes even months when he didn't touch me, and I thought . . . this is it, it'll be different now. But eventually something would set him off again. When I told him I wanted a divorce, he said it would ruin his life, his reputation. He said he'd never let me go. He would never give up the farm.'

'Surely he couldn't stop you from leaving?'

She gives me a sad half-smile. 'Difficult to believe, isn't it? I was terrified of him. And by then we'd adopted the children. I had to protect them, too. When the children were grown up, David still wouldn't accept a divorce. My only hope was to run away, start divorce proceedings from a safe distance.' She shakes her head. 'But he had control of our money. He watched me all the time. He used to check the mileage on my car. He didn't let me see friends – he was jealous of every man. Except William. I suppose he believed that William was safe. But Will saw one of my bruises and he made me tell him the truth. The first time I'd told anyone . . . I felt so ashamed. But he said he'd help me. He kept a bag of clothes ready—'

Bright sparks of clarity are bursting in my head. Relief making me weak. 'William was helping you escape from David? You didn't have an affair?'

She moves her head. 'I can't believe you thought that.'

'What did Will do?'

'He lent me money. He was going to collect me in secret, take me to a train station with my bag. But then I discovered that David was sleeping with one of the migrants. I told him that I'd tell everyone what he'd been doing if he didn't let me go. He went crazy. I thought he'd kill me. What he was really afraid of was the scandal – the loss of face. I told him that I wouldn't publicise his affair if he let me walk away. He could tell everyone I was dead as far as I was concerned.' She looks at me. 'All I cared about was that I'd still see my son and that I got my share of my money. I couldn't spend another moment . . . with him . . . in that house.'

My head is spinning. 'David told the whole village you were dead, to save his pride – his position? And you let him?'

Her mouth pulls down. 'You have no idea how important it is for him – being the Lord of the Manor. Having everyone look up to him.'

'And what about you – you went along with it?'

'You don't know who the real David is. But he can't hurt me

now; I know too much.' She nods. 'He likes to behave as if he's a big man – but he's in financial trouble. I've told him to sell the farm. Otherwise he can't give me my share of the money. Only he's stubborn. He won't sell. But I've got something over him . . . I've told him, all he needs to do is put the farm on the market, and pay me what I'm owed. I don't want revenge, to go to court, to have all of that raked over again. It would be a scandal and it would damage my children. This is better. A clean break.' She gives a small smile.

'Didn't Adam and Rachel know what David was doing to you?'

Her smile fades. 'When they were little they thought I was accident prone, clumsy. All the violence happened behind closed doors. Dr Waller saw to any injuries. When they were older, they might have guessed that something wasn't right. But we never talked about it.' She rummages in her bag for a tissue and blows her nose. 'Slowly, I'm picking up the pieces, learning to be myself again. I lived inside that small community my whole life. It was like being in a fish bowl, having to keep up appearances, having to be this perfect person. Everyone discussing your every move.'

'Do any of them know that you're alive?' I have a sudden thought. 'Does Rachel know?'

'The only people who know are Adam, David, Dr Waller and Rachel. My daughter's a daddy's girl.' Her face drops. 'She hasn't even tried to see me since I left.'

'You pretended you had cancer?'

'I've always had headaches. We went to a specialist about them. That gave me the idea.'

'But didn't someone need to witness your body?'

'David has Peter Waller in his pocket. He paid him to sign a death certificate. The cremation was a fake. Haven't you noticed that David likes to have useful people on his side – Ian, Peter? David bribes and blackmails people when he needs to. He always gets his own way – you don't know him.'

I feel a blush spreading across my cheeks.

She looks at me closely. 'Don't . . . don't get involved with David.' She seems to see the baby for the first time. 'He's very small to be without his mother.'

'He belongs to Anca. She's gone. I'm looking after him.'

'Anca.' Henrietta steps back, makes a noise in her throat. 'David's son.'

'What?'

'It was Anca that he was seeing.' Her forehead crumples. 'He was obsessed. I couldn't help her.' Her voice trembles. 'I couldn't stop it.' She looks at the cafe. 'I have to go. Adam will be waiting for me.'

My stomach gives a queasy lurch. 'You mean David forced Anca to sleep with him?'

'If Anca's got away from him, I'm glad.' She puts her glasses on with shaking fingers.

I blink in the sunshine, feeling chilled. 'What's going on at the farm?' I put my hand on her arm. 'Is he doing it to anyone else?'

She moves away from my touch. 'No . . . and there's nothing else going on.' She shrugs dismissively. 'Maybe some of the workers don't have the right papers. It's no different from anywhere else. Don't get involved, Ellie. And stay away. Stay clear of David.' She turns towards the cafe door, looking back over her shoulder. 'Have you ever experienced abuse? You think it must be your fault. You lose all your power, all your self-belief.'

So many questions are running through my mind. 'Wait – why do you and Adam meet here? Why doesn't he come to your home, if you're afraid of being seen?'

She takes a deep breath. 'I can't risk David finding out where I live. It was simpler like this. Safer. But now . . . I'll find a new place to meet my son. Goodbye, Ellie. We won't see each other again.'

She's gone. I can hardly believe that she was here. The things she told me have the sickly, slipping feel of a nightmare remembered in the morning. The baby squirms in my arms, his mouth beginning to quiver. His eyes are open. Slate grey. David's son. He looks around him, blinking at the light. He's hungry. I bend to kiss him. His innocence makes me want to weep.

I walk to the end of the alley, past more dustbins, along back gardens. Over the fences I glimpse washing flapping from lines, a black cat, a woman sweeping. Then I turn a corner and I'm on the main street, walking past the front of the cafe. The Defender is parked outside. I imagine mother and son reunited inside. The baby is crying in earnest, howling for his milk. I hush him, holding him close. But there's one thing I need to do before I feed him.

I drive slowly along the kerb, checking parked cars, looking for the Mini. When I see it, I pause to scribble down the number plate.

FORTY

The answer phone is flashing.

'Ellie? It's me. I'm sorry I had to leave like that. I'll be back tomorrow and I'll explain everything. Just stay put. Don't talk to anyone. Especially not David or Adam. Anca is with me. So don't worry about her either. Stay safe.'

Luca. I missed the call. He must have been ringing from a phone box. He has no mobile. It's so frustrating. There's no number to call back. I replay the message several times just to hear his voice. He hasn't abandoned me.

I go upstairs and take a long shower. I scrub my skin until it stings, rubbing at every area of flesh that David's hands touched. Why didn't I see any signs, read any clues? The hidden part of him must have surfaced sometimes. I remember the argument I half saw once, the way his hands had balled into fists, the way he and Henrietta had ironed out their expressions for my benefit.

They fooled everyone into thinking that they were the perfect couple, always immaculate, charming, but cool, untouchable.

I tip my head back under the deluge of water. Let the needles of heat fall over my skull, splatter my closed eyes and flood my open mouth.

Henrietta looked different with her new hair and clothes. But she was scared. She'd escaped David. But she was still hiding. Why does she want people to think she's dead? I'm sure she didn't tell me the whole truth. Her story doesn't quite add up. The bit about David hitting her and William planning to help her rang true. But why would David suddenly agree to let her go just because he'd slept with Anca? Going to the effort of pretending she was dead was extreme. There had to be more to it. And she was very quick to answer when I asked about the farm. She didn't seem surprised by the question.

I get out of the shower. I've been in so long the water has run cold and the ends of my fingers are quilted and pale. I wrap myself in a towel, shivering.

I'm sure there are things she was keeping back, things she wasn't revealing. I frown, calculating the time that's lapsed since Henrietta's memorial. Anca couldn't have been pregnant then – it was over a year ago – which means that David has been sleeping with her all this time. Forcing her. That's what Henrietta said.

The baby sleeps in his makeshift cot. I pace the floor, feeling confined, anxious. Guilty. I'd thought the worst of my husband, when all the time he was innocent, trying to help an abused woman. Being a knight in shining armour.

I'm sorry, Will.

I should have known. Over twenty years of friendship and of faithful and steady love. He deserved better.

I've taken every single photograph of him down, bundled them into the dark, out of sight; I've given away his clothes and wiped the cottage free of any sign of him. My body is cold at the thought. I've betrayed him, not the other way around. I get down onto my knees and rustle around in the chest at the bottom of the bed, and find a framed photo of us together. We're at a history faculty reception, standing arm in arm in our smart clothes, smiling, heads touching. It's the most recent picture of him, and I put it back in pride of place on the mantelpiece in our bedroom.

William stares out at me, clear blue eyes meeting mine. I drop my gaze, shuddering, feeling sick again at what I've done, the thought of David touching me. I want to strip off and have another shower. I don't know if I'll ever feel clean again.

I can't do as Luca asks. I can't just stay here and wait, twiddling my fingers. I want to know what's really going on at the farm. If I can poke around in the barns, have a look at the caravans, then I might find out whatever it is that Henrietta wasn't telling me. Luca couldn't get access because he's a stranger. He'd be spotted in a moment and turned off the land. But if I'm discovered, I can pretend I'm visiting David. He doesn't know that I've met Henrietta. There's no reason for him to suspect me. I don't want to see him – not ever. The thought of being near him turns my stomach. But if I have to bluff my way through a meeting, then I'll do it.

It's getting dark as I park the Fiat outside Kate's house, the hot engine ticking in the cool of the evening. I lean into the back to take the baby seat out, leaving him sleeping inside; he's too small for it, and he crumples up, the belts crossing above his shoulders, his head crooked to the side. But he's bigger than yesterday. He seems to grow hour by hour. The seat is heavy. My fingers grip the handle. Kate's mother answers the door.

'Mrs Rathmell?' Her eyebrows startle across her forehead. 'This is a nice surprise. Kate didn't tell us you were coming.' She pats at a loose strand of hair, her eyes sliding towards the baby.

'Hello, Mrs Smith. I'm afraid I'm springing this on her. Is she in?'

I keep my voice light, stepping inside the cramped, hot hall. I can smell cooking. Lamb chops. Boiled potatoes. Kate appears from the living room; the sound of a TV blares behind her, canned laughter and clapping. It fades as she shuts the door. She raises her eyebrows in an exact copy of her mother's expression.

'You know you said you'd babysit? Well, if you could take him, just for an hour or two . . . Something's come up.'

Kate frowns, but she says, 'Of course.'

I give her a grateful smile.

'Kate, you never said that Mrs Rathmell had a new baby.' Mrs Smith's voice is dripping with double meaning as she bends to take the car seat from me, her face softening as she coos, 'Just look at the little mite.' She places the seat on the carpet with exaggerated care.

'He's not mine.' I slip the changing bag with the bottles and nappies inside off my shoulder. 'I'm not his birth mother.'

'Oh, adopted is he?' she whispers over the baby's head, eyes out on stalks. I can imagine the grilling Kate will get after I've gone.

'Thanks for looking after him.' I look down at his face. Dribble leaks from the corner of his mouth, and I squat to wipe it away. 'I won't be long.'

I leave the car in the lane, parked as far off road as possible, and walk the rest of the way on the verge, stumbling every now and then on a tuft of grass or a drainage channel. To my relief, there's no traffic. The road is deserted. The tall gates are closed. I look left and right to make sure there's nothing coming, nobody in sight. Then I begin to scramble over. But as my hand grasps the top bar, I'm electrocuted. My arm stiffens, my body jerks. White pain shooting through bones and flesh. My fingers snap open like scissors. I'm falling. Stars flying past. I hit the ground hard. The world is red, spinning. I gasp for air, staring up at the moon looming over me like an eye. I whimper and roll onto my side. When I can, I struggle to my feet, rubbing the ache in my arm.

My mind stumbles around the problem. I have to open the gates. There's a code. Last time I was in David's house, when I'd retreated to the front door mat, I'd stood for a moment facing the intercom. There had been a number typed beside it. I concentrate, trying to will the memory of the figures up out of my subconscious. I've always been able to memorise the phone numbers from every place I've lived at.

With shaking fingers, I tap digits into the intercom. I hold my breath. On the second try, the gates swing open.

I stay on the grass next to the drive to avoid making any noise. My ears are alert for baying, for the sound of swift paws tearing up the ground. Max and Moro. I don't want to meet them on my own in the dark.

I pass the sweeping branches of a horse chestnut tree, and the house looms out of the dusk. There are windows lit on the ground and first floors. The second- and third-floor windows are dark. I edge around the side, feet on turned earth, keeping to the bushes, rose thorns scratching. I know there's a security light that will come on if I step too close to the house. When I get to the kitchen windows, I push the waxy leaves of a laurel bush out of the way and squeeze underneath, crouching on damp earth. I'm praying that the dogs are locked up. I wait, wondering what to do next, how to get to the field of caravans without being intercepted.

There's movement behind the glass. The blind on the kitchen window is up and, with a lurch, I see Adam. He's carrying a bottle of wine. My heart stops. Constanta appears. He seems to be speaking to her. She goes to the sink. Adam comes up close behind her, presses his lips into her neck. She closes her eyes. Adam moves out of sight. I watch her as she puts things under the tap, dries plates and bowls. Then she is taking off her apron. I can't see her any more. I understand now. Her accent. The way she seemed uncertain when we met. Constanta is a migrant; she works for them. She's taken Anca's place in the kitchen. I wonder if she lives at the caravan site.

The back door opens. Constanta comes down the steps lugging a black bin bag of rubbish and heaves it into the dustbin. She wraps her coat tighter and begins to walk towards the farm buildings, towards the site, moving quickly through the shadows.

I glance at the bright window. Nobody is looking. Adam's disappeared. I push my way through leaves, breaking cover, and hurry after Constanta. When I touch her shoulder, she spins round with a cry. I wince at the noise, and put my finger to my lips. We both stare at each other.

'What are you doing?' She glances behind her nervously. 'Go away.'

'Anca sent me,' I say.

'Anca?' She steps closer.

I swallow, and nod. 'She's safe.'

She opens her eyes wide. 'She's free?'

'Yes.'

Constanta's face crumples and she pushes her hands over her eyes. 'She had the baby?'

'A boy.'

Her face is stretched tight with relief. 'Did she pass a message – for me?'

My mind scrambles in panic. I need to get this right. 'She wanted me to see the caravan site.'

Constanta looks surprised. 'No message for her sister?'

'Her sister?' I frown.

'Me.'

'Only to say that she's safe. And the baby.'

'We can't stay here.' Constanta looks into the darkness. 'Adam's going out. But the others will find you.'

She sets off at a rapid pace, head down, hands in her pockets, and I follow, stubbing my toe on a loose slab of concrete, glancing into open doorways and black windows as we go through the deserted yard. A bird calls in a long, whistling shriek. Something scurries in the darkness. My hands are clammy.

She stops, puts out a hand to halt me and frowns up at the barn wall. 'Camera. Up there. Put my coat on.'

She slips off her anorak and I put it on, pulling the hood over my face.

'Quickly.' She hurries to the gate, takes a key from her pocket, undoes the padlock, metal clanking, and ushers me inside. We're in a huge, rough field lined with ragged trees, a tall fence. Caravans make pale rectangular shapes. Constanta hurries to the nearest one and pushes open the door.

The space is airless. I can hear breathing. Constanta flicks a lighter and a small gas lamp casts shadows under her sharp face, turning her mouth into a sneer. My skin prickles with the sense of being watched. I'm surrounded by eyes. Pale, expressionless faces peer at me from the floor and from bunks against the wall. There must be eight or ten women. One of them says something in a foreign language, and Constanta answers in a hushed undertone.

'Gangmaster will be here soon,' she tells me. 'You want to see inside?' She nods her head, looking around.

I clench my hands. 'So many of you . . . you all sleep in here?'

She shrugs. 'Same in other caravans.'

'You can't leave?'

'No papers. No money.' Constanta's voice is harsh.

'No money? You don't get paid?' I remember Luca's words.

She frowns, her lips moving as she listens and translates. 'Some. But we owe money. Much money.'

'But why don't you run away?'

She lifts her shoulders again. 'No place to go. Police will get us. We are not legal.' She gestures at the door. 'We're locked in at night.'

'But you're not locked in now.' I stare around the cramped

room. The women are muttering among themselves. 'And you have a key to the gate?'

'Because I work at the house.' She looks at me with something close to pity. 'But at night they take the key. If we complain, they beat us.'

'You will help?' A nasal voice comes from one of the bunks.

Constanta grabs my arm. 'Go now. Men coming.'

Another woman has got out of her blankets, an older woman with grey-streaked hair and a worn face. She stumbles to her knees in front of me, cupped palms raised. She begins to wail, a long, low keening. I look down at her pleading hands. In the hissing light of the gas flame, I see that her skin weeps, mottled and raw. The other women are sitting up, talking amongst themselves, agitated voices flying across each other.

Constanta looks terrified. 'Go!' She hisses.

But it's too late. There's the rattle of the caravan door opening. Someone below me grabs my wrist, pulls me down, jerking me onto a bunk. A body rolls across me. I struggle to breathe. The women are silent.

'Let's be having the key,' a voice says. 'Lights off. You know the rules.'

None of the women answer. There's a hard laugh and the door slams. I hear a key turning. The scrape of a chain.

I try to sit up in the darkness and bang my head. My heart is thundering. I reach into my pocket for my mobile, searching into the corners. I struggle out of the bunk and shove my hand into all my pockets. But my phone isn't here, and neither are my keys. I think of my fall from the gate, the hard slap of the ground.

The women are murmuring together quietly; someone strikes a match. I see Constanta's face lit up for a moment. She stares at me. 'We give you clothes. Put them on. When they come for us, you follow. Then I'll make a fuss, get their attention. Then you must run. Understand?'

'Come for us?' I repeat.

I see her impatient nod before the match goes out.

Darkness. There are words. Foreign words. Hands fumble around me, touching my face. I jerk away. Then I realise they're pressing items of clothing into my fingers. I feel for the openings, pull on a fusty jumper, a jacket. Someone reaches for my head and covers it with a scarf.

'Lie down. We have to sleep.'

'I thought you were Adam's girlfriend?'

There's no reply, and I think she hasn't heard me. Then a bleak voice comes through the dark. 'He wants . . . not possible. Sex. Not love. I can't love – not a man who does this.'

I lie in the bunk, my body pressed up against a stranger's, her hip jutting into mine. Her breath on my face. The stench of unwashed skin makes me sip air through my mouth. Why didn't I tell Kate where I was going? Nobody knows where I am. Panic bubbles in my chest. I can't fill my lungs. I'm suffocating.

I lie right on the edge of the bunk, my arm trapped beneath me, pins and needles prickling, and stare into the dark, wide awake. All around me I hear coughing, muttering, snoring. Outside the thin walls of the caravan, a fox screams. A mile away the village sleeps.

I must have dozed off. There's a pounding on the door.

The woman next to me is pushing my shoulder. I see a tangle

of legs emerging from bunks, sleepy faces in the half-light, anxious eyes gleaming.

'Get up,' Constanta's voice hisses. 'Follow us. Don't talk. Run when you can.'

The door swings open, bringing a gust of fresh morning air, cold and dewy. A tall man stands outside. 'Hurry up. Get a move on.'

The women huddle together and begin to leave, filing out of the stuffy van, down the steps into the field. I pull the scarf over my face, bow my head, and I'm caught up in the middle of the group, bodies closing around me, shielding me.

We shuffle through long, wet grass. The dawn is breaking. Red streaks slash a grey sky. Shifting layers of mist hang across the ground. There is another group walking from a caravan further across the field. A motley collection of shambling figures. I see that this other group are men.

'No talking,' says the tall man.

There are other men – the men in black jackets that I saw before – standing near the gate. Several are smoking. They push some of the migrants as we file through into the yard, slamming palms into shoulders, shoving them on the back so that they stumble. I tug at the scarf on my hair, pulling it lower over my face as I walk past, keeping my chin tucked in, my eyes down. The back of my neck prickles. There's an old bus parked on the concrete of the yard. The door is open. A driver sits at the wheel. The women form a line and begin to climb the steps, weary and stooped. Nobody says anything.

Fear is scratching at my chest. I can't get in. I'll never escape.

Then I hear a movement, a protest. Constanta is shouting. 'I need to use toilet!'

'You can piss in a bag. Get inside.'

She's flailing her arms, screaming. 'No. No. I am not an animal!'

The men in black move towards her.

'Go!' A voice hisses in my ear.

I hear the thwack of bone on flesh. Constanta's scream.

FORTY-ONE

I take a sharp left and dive through the entrance to a shed. I take a step and a body swings against me, heavy, fleshy. I bite back a yell. Hands up by my face, fur under my fingers.

I move away, eyes adjusting to the dim light that comes through a small, barred window. It's a creature hanging head down. The carcass of a deer. I smell blood. Something jabs at my leg and I look down. An antler. There are boxes all over the floor, full of animal parts.

I squat in the corner, heart thundering. Did anyone see me leave the group? My stomach writhes with fear. I retch. Constanta. I imagine her lying broken and limp on the ground outside. I bite my thumb, remembering Luca's black eye, his bruises. He said he'd tried to get into the farm, but there'd been too much security – I understand now.

I can hear the shuffle of feet outside. A man counting. 'Right. They're all here. Get going.'

A rumble of engine turning over. The cough of exhaust. The bus is moving away. There's movement outside the shed. Someone laughs.

'That bitch had it coming.'

I can smell cigarette smoke. I wait until I can't hear anything and the air is clean again. I know I have to leave, even though the thought of it terrifies me. I creep outside the entrance, looking right and left. My feet are heavy. The sky is brightening. I move from one patch of shadows to the next. A security light clicks on. I stop, holding my breath, scanning roofs and posts for cameras.

There are sounds coming from the big barn. People are working in there, packing fruit. I listen to the low muttering of movement and voices. The whir of a machine. I hesitate, wondering whether to run inside, to beg for help. But I don't know who will be there, who to trust, who would help me. I have to keep moving. I've reached empty buildings, open doorways gaping on either side. A parked tractor. A heap of long plastic pipes. Two figures are talking at the other side of the yard. I throw myself into the barn. I can hear their feet coming closer. I don't know if they saw me.

My knee makes contact with something hard. Something thin and slippery moves under my touch. Under the loose fabric is a metal surface. A low-slung car. I get down onto the ground, pushing my way under the trailing tarpaulin and roll underneath. The smell of oil and rubber is thick. The hair on my neck rises at the sound of stealthy footsteps. One of them is in the barn. There's a muttered swearing and a clatter as some object falls to the floor. I hold my breath.

My straining ears magnify the tiniest sound. I track the click and slide of his footsteps as they pass close to my head, moving further into the barn and back again. With a thrum of hope, I realise that he's leaving. I can hear the rustle of his clothes as he walks past.

I roll out and get to my knees, standing up, blinking. The dawn has become the morning. There's nowhere to hide. I jog past the rest of the outbuildings, push through bushes past the side of the house, and stumble down the drive, terrified that it's a trick, and that the dogs will come pounding after me. I glance at the thick, impenetrable shrubs that line the drive. Leaves rustle and move.

At the gate, I stand panting while I jab at the numbers on the intercom, remembering the code. The gates swing open and shut behind me. Relief makes me weak, makes me sob. But I need my car keys. I go to where I fell and squat, searching, scrabbling through gravel and dirt. I see a glimmer of silver. My fingers grasp the bundle of keys attached to a heart-shaped leather tag. My mobile lies nearby. It's scratched. When I press the button nothing happens. It's dead.

Before I can move, a car pulls up outside the gate. The Defender. Adam winds down his window. 'Ellie, what are you doing here?'

There's the thunder of barking. I see the dogs at the window, mouths open, teeth flashing, lips pulled back, hot breath on glass.

I scrub my sleeve across my face. 'I was just going to see your dad.' I hope my voice doesn't give me away. My legs are trembling.

‘A bit early, isn’t it?’

‘I couldn’t sleep. We had a row. I wanted to talk to him.’

‘Where’s your car?’

‘I wanted to walk – give myself time to think.’ I put my hand to my hair, find the tatty scarf, pull it off.

He gets out. ‘You should go home. It’s not safe for you here.’

‘Not safe?’

He gets hold of my arm and squeezes, leaning in close. ‘Mum told me how you followed me. How you questioned her.’

I take a sharp breath and stare up at him, my mind a blank.

‘She told you about him. You know he’s dangerous. So why are you really here?’

My mouth is dry. I lick my lips. ‘I’ve been inside one of the caravans.’

‘You’ve been—’ He breaks off, mouth curving down. ‘Fuck!’ He lets me go with a jerk and walks away, rubbing his face. I wonder if I could run. He stands still, and then he shakes himself, as if he’s made a decision. ‘I’ve been waiting for this to happen. I knew it was a bad idea, letting you inside the house, letting you nose around.’ He gives a short laugh. ‘And the thing is, I’m glad you know. Dad’s out of control. He won’t listen to anyone. It’s gone too far.’

‘Did he . . . did he force you into this?’

He runs his fingers through his hair. ‘It’s a family business. I’m in it up to my neck.’ He stares at the ground, then he looks at me. ‘My father was like a god when I was little,’ he says quietly. ‘He was the one I looked up to. He was dynamic, powerful, he made things happen. Then one day I heard noises behind closed doors. Saw things I wasn’t supposed to. When I realised what he was doing to my mother . . . I was afraid, confused. But it was all I knew. It was how I grew up. I was a child. I copied him, behaved like him. I know it's not an excuse.'

'If I go to the police, Adam, you'll go to prison.'

He nods wearily. 'It's my mother who can't accept it.'

'Why did you do all those things . . . in the tearoom? The fake reviews? I know it was you. Were you trying to put me out of business?'

'Stupid, I know.' He scrubs his hands over his face. 'I thought if the tearoom failed, you'd leave the village. I was trying to warn you off. You didn't understand that you'd got yourself into a bad situation.' He sucks in air. 'You thought my mother was dead. You thought we were an ordinary family. But I knew you'd find something out . . . and then he'd hurt you too.'

'You were trying to protect me?'

'I just wanted you to go away.' He glares at me. 'You don't know what you're involved in. What we've done.'

'My hen.' I swallow. 'Clover. You killed her.'

'I came to your house. I was going to tell you about Dad, to make you understand—' He breaks off. 'I thought I could . . . I don't know. Confess.' He makes a strange choked noise. 'Then I saw the Range Rover in your drive, and I knew he was in there. I was desperate. I had to do something to make you afraid. To shock you into leaving.' He grabs my arms. 'My mother says you've got something that belongs to her – something that will force Dad into paying up. Your husband was keeping it safe for her.'

'What? What have I got?'

'An envelope. Information.'

'But I've searched the whole house. There's nothing . . .'

He swings away, impatiently. 'Then it's up to you now. You need to stop him. Go to the police. But not Ian Brooks. My father thinks he can do what he likes. He's ruthless. I'm worried about Constanta.'

'What do you mean?'

His voice quavers. 'I've seen the way he looks at her. If he can't have her, he'll sell her to a pimp.'

'Adam,' I shake my head. 'It was Constanta who helped me get away. They beat her—'

His face contorts and he lets go of me, backing towards the Land Rover. 'Make the call.'

He gets in, slams the door and starts the engine. The car skids through the opening gates, the dogs barking.

When I get to the car, my hands are shaking so much that I can hardly turn the key. I lock the doors, skidding as I reverse over wet grass, grinding the gears, staring in my rear-view mirror.

FORTY-TWO

Parked outside Kate's house, I sit for a moment, pressing my knuckles to my temples, forcing myself to make my lungs work, to catch a rhythm, in and out. Adam's words spin in my head. He's part of it all – he's a criminal. I see Clover's body swinging from my door and shut my eyes. Then I think of that little boy glimpsing his father hitting his mother, and imagine his shock, his conflicting loyalties and confusion. I allow myself a flash of pity. But right now, Constanta and the others are in a bus being taken off to God-knows-where. I groan.

All that matters is that she's OK. That I can help. I glance at my watch. It's not a civilised hour to knock on their door. But I can't help it; I can't go home without the baby.

I hear the wailing before I reach the front path. Kate answers in her dressing gown, her hair sticking up in a halo. He is draped over her shoulder, his body rigid with pain and distress. My hands are already reaching for him.

'Where have you been? I've been worried sick.' Kate's voice is tight. 'You should have let me know where you were going. And the baby's been yelling since you left. Mum can't cope with him not having a name, either.'

'I couldn't contact you.' I hold him against me, rocking back and forth.

'What's going on?' she says. 'Where were you? Are you OK?'

'I was at David's. His migrants are like slaves.'

'What do you mean?'

'They're locked up, forced to work all the time.'

'But I see them every day in the open . . . in the fields . . . '

I step away from her, onto the front step. 'Tell your mum I'm sorry for the bother. I've got to go.'

'It's fine. She fusses.' Kate blinks and arranges her mouth in a smile.

I shift the baby into the crook of my arm, grab the changing bag from her and hurry back to the car. I need to get home. I hear Adam's voice in my head. *Make the call.*

Tilly appears out of the shadows, twisting her body around my legs, meowing for her breakfast. I shush her as I juggle the baby in one arm, stepping inside the kitchen.

He's there in front of me, waiting. He's taller than I remember, darker. He looks tired. We stare at each other, time slowing.

I've crossed the kitchen floor in two strides, and my hand flies up. I slap him once, hard across his cheek, my palm stinging. He doesn't move, doesn't try to stop me. I see finger prints on his skin.

'Where have you been? You bastard. You left me.' I'm sobbing and Luca's arms are round me and the baby, and my mouth is pressed into his shirt, his chest. His lips are in my hair. The baby wakes with a start and draws breath, begins to scream.

'I'm here now,' he says. 'I'm sorry.'

'Where's Anca?'

'Upstairs.' He glances towards the ceiling. 'She's asleep.'

'I need to call the police. Now. David's keeping his migrants like slaves . . . and Constanta . . . I think she's hurt . . . '

Luca holds my shoulders, steadying me. 'I've called them already. They know.'

I raise my eyebrows. 'You've called them?'

He nods.

My legs feel weak. I slump into a chair, one hand pressed to my mouth. He stoops to take the crying baby from me. I look up. 'Why did you go? Where have you been?'

'Anca left. I followed her.' He's murmuring to the baby, trying to quieten him. 'I saw her in the drive early that morning. I grabbed my money and went after her.'

'But why didn't you tell me?'

'You were asleep. There was no time to explain.'

The baby is still wailing. 'He needs his milk.' I take a deep breath, looking for the strength to stand.

Luca puts his hand on my shoulder. 'I'll do it.'

He puts a bottle to heat, makes me a cup of tea and places it on the table, leaving me to drink it while he feeds the baby and changes and settles him upstairs. The house is silent. The tea is hot and sweet. I curl my fingers around the warm ceramic sides of the mug.

'You look exhausted. You should go to bed,' he says, as he comes back into the room.

I shake my head. 'Not until you explain.'

He sits next to me, takes my hand. 'I'm sorry I disappeared, but I had to get Anca away from here. She was terrified David would find her. I promised she was safe with me, that I wouldn't tell anyone where we were going. We took a bus, then the train to Canterbury, booked into a small hotel. After a while, she began to talk.' Luca's mouth is hard. 'David is the father of her child.'

I fold my lips tight, holding back my own story, needing to hear his through to the end.

'David forced her to have sex with him. Months and months of it. He kept her quiet by promising to leave her sister alone.' Luca sounds empty. 'If Anca did what she was told, Constanta would be OK. Anca hasn't seen her little sister for weeks – they were kept apart. Then Adam picked her out, began to sleep with her. David threatened to sell Constanta into prostitution if Anca talked.' He stops, lets out a breath. 'She's terrified of the police. Thinks she'll be put in prison, that she'll never see her sister again.'

'Henrietta is alive,' I tell him quietly. 'I've seen her.'

'She's alive?' His eyes widen.

'He abused her too, for years.'

Luca drops his head into his hands. 'I could smell it on him. I should have acted quicker. Done something to stop him.'

'Luca, I went to the farm. I saw the workers in their caravans.'

I watch his face change as he understands what I'm saying.

'Constanta . . .' I force myself to go on. 'She helped me,

distracted them. I got away.' I begin to tremble. 'But I don't know what they did to her.' I lean forward, frightened again. 'When did you talk to the police? They need to go there now.'

'We were in London today. I went to the Metropolitan police to avoid David's inspector friend.' He nods. 'There'll be a raid at the farm. Maybe tonight. Even if David gets a tip-off, it's too late for them to cover things up.'

'I saw Adam. I think he's fallen in love with Constanta. He's sick of what's going on there. He wants it to end.'

'Then he'll get his wish.' Luca shuffles his chair closer and says quietly, 'I contacted Canterbury social services. Ellie, tomorrow, they're coming to collect Anca. She had the right papers. David lied. He confiscated them. And there's something else . . . '

I push my hands over my ears.

'They will take the baby, too.'

I collapse forward, crushed against his shoulder, and he's holding me tightly.

'I'm sorry,' he murmurs. 'It has to be.'

We get into bed, and I am so tired that I seem to be floating outside my body. Luca and I find each other under the sheet and press our bodies together, skin against skin. I can't cry any more. I know he is right. I have to let the baby go.

He's asleep in his drawer. Later I will watch them carry him away, like they carried my son away. I'm too wired to let go of consciousness. I don't want Luca to disappear again, not even into sleep.

'Will you leave now?'

He lies still. I listen to the soft rush of air in and out of his lungs. 'Do you want me to?' he asks.

'No.' My voice catches. 'Stay. With me.'

Luca finds my hand and squeezes.

'You knew about David,' I say quietly, 'because of your own father . . . what he did to your sister?'

Luca moves his head. 'David's smoother than my father. Cleverer. But the same. Sadistic, cruel. Weak. Like that kind of man always is.' His ribs rise and fall under me. 'He beat me and my mother – but it was Marisca who couldn't escape him. One day I knew I had to stop it. I was a tall boy. At fourteen I was nearly as big as him. I dragged him off her. We fought in the yard.' He's silent, and my heart begins to beat faster, because I know now why he never speaks of his family. 'I split his skull with a stone.' His voice is almost a whisper. 'A stone from the mountain.'

We hold each other tightly, my nose buried in his neck, his bristles rasping my skin. 'What did you do?'

'I ran. I ended up at a circus. They gave me work. A different name. When it was time, the circus people got me papers. They kept me safe.'

'But your sister and mother?'

'It must have been a struggle for them without a man. But they managed. My mother was a strong woman. I sent my wages home as soon as I was earning.'

'The necklace you wear . . .'

'Marisca took it from her neck and put it around mine before I left.' He pauses. 'I dragged my father out of the yard. Buried him. Then I opened the cage.'

'The cage?'

'The wolf. She ran, too.'

He bends his head and we kiss, slow and deep. It's how I tell him that I understand, that I know what it is to be betrayed. Through the dim early morning light the baby mutters in his bed on the floor.

'I know it will be hard to give him up,' Luca says. 'You're so good with him. I always wondered why you didn't have children.'

'I did,' I say softly. 'I had a son when I was very young. He was adopted. When he was eighteen I had the chance to make contact with him. I wrote a letter. He never replied. And—' I bite my lip. 'I think that he hates me for giving him away.'

'No.' Luca pulls me close. 'It must mean the opposite – that he's happy. If he resented you, he'd take the opportunity to get in touch to tell you exactly what he thinks of you. And if he was unhappy, he'd find you too, because he had nothing else. But if there's silence, then you must take it as a good sign. He's doing well in his life, he has a family, friends. Parents. He doesn't want to upset all of that.' He drops a kiss onto my shoulder. 'He doesn't hate you.'

I lie still, letting his words settle inside me.

Luca raises himself onto his elbows and reaches behind his neck. He finds my hand and pushes something into it. Warm metal coils inside my palm. 'I can't take this.'

'Yes. You can.'

He helps me put it on, fastening the silver chain, fingers fumbling at the catch while I hold up my hair. Sitting in bed, I see through the window – the curtains are open – and there's a glow on the horizon.

I startle forward, craning to see better. 'Luca. There's a fire over there.' The realisation falls through me. 'I think it's the farm.'

I get out of bed and stare at the smoky pall hanging across the fields. Black birds wheeling from the trees nearby. Luca is behind me, stumbling about, pushing his legs into his jeans, wrenching a jumper over his head.

'What are you doing?'

'It might be the caravans. The workers. I need to help.'

'I'm coming with you.'

'No.' He holds me by the arms. 'Adam and David could be burning evidence. I don't know if the police are there yet. Stay here with the baby.'

A sudden fear grips me. 'I don't want you to go.'

'I'll come back.' Luca takes my chin and looks into my face.

'You'll need the code,' I tell him. 'For the gate.'

I shout the numbers as he runs down the stairs. He stands at the bottom and repeats them back to me. He's memorised it exactly. I nod and he gives me a broad smile. And then he's gone.

FORTY-THREE

I shiver, watching the car disappear out of the drive. I turn to go in when I can no longer hear the engine, the fading roar as he accelerates around country lanes.

Upstairs, at the bedroom window, I stare towards the red glow where charcoal smudges pale air, and acrid black rises in waves, spreading out so that it covers the horizon. I hear a siren, far away, coming closer. It must be the police. Fire engines. I wonder what's happening, hoping that Luca is wrong, that it's not the caravans. All those workers are locked in. I chew my nails, frustrated by my ignorance, squinting towards the blaze.

In the bathroom, I fill the basin with cool water and splash my face, over and over. When I pat myself dry with a towel, my skin stings as if I've been flayed. I've never been so sleep-deprived in my life. My eyes are bloodshot, my complexion grey. But there's no way I can go back to bed now, not until Luca comes home. I may as well get dressed. The hens have been neglected. I'll go and do the animals as soon as the baby has woken and I've fed and changed him.

He is still sound asleep. He's shattered after the change in routine, the night of howling in a strange house. I crouch next to the drawer to look at him. His face is alive with movement: eyebrows dancing, forehead wrinkling, lips puckering. His dark hair is just a fuzz of fluff. I wonder if it will fall out and be replaced with a completely different colour. The knowledge that I won't be there is a sharp pain. I touch his plump cheek. 'You'll get used to being without me,' I tell him softly. 'But I won't get used to being without you.'

He was never mine, I knew that.

I pull on my clothes, and on my way downstairs I pause outside the spare room, listening. There's no sound. Anca must be asleep. It's hardly eight o'clock.

I pad into the kitchen and roll up my sleeves. The dishwasher needs emptying. Tilly is asking for food, and I fill her bowl. I turn the tap, water sloshing into the kettle, and flick the switch, get a mug from the cupboard, dropping a teabag inside. The bottles Luca made are standing ready in the fridge, and I take one out to warm. The baby will be waking any moment.

I wonder when the social services people will arrive – Luca didn't say. I don't put the radio on; I want to be able to hear him coming back. I'm listening for the noise of the Fiat's wheels rolling into the drive. My fingers go to my neck, touching the silver chain.

From the corner of my eye I catch a darkness, a slantwise movement across the kitchen window. It startles me, and my body jerks round. I am staring into David's face. A pane of glass between us. Shock pins me into stillness, and then my eyes slide to the back door, to the key left unturned in the lock.

I throw myself across, fingers reaching, but he's got there first and the handle is moving, the door opening. I shove my shoulder into wood, hard as I can, putting all my weight behind it, slamming it closed. My feet slip as I try to get more traction. He's pushing from the other side. I can't manage to turn the key. I gasp and pant, my muscles straining, but the door opens again, enough for his hand to slide through the gap. I cry out, using every bit of my strength. The door bangs against his wrist; his fingers flex. Then it flies free, throwing me backwards.

I blunder away, getting the table between us, grasping the back of a chair. David straightens, pulling his jacket into line. He's panting. There's mud on his shoes. He wipes them in an unhurried way on the back of his trousers, one at a time. He must have come across the fields.

My chest is tight. 'What . . . what do you want?'

'That's not much of a greeting, Ellie. I'm disappointed in you.'

'You should go . . . someone will come.' I'm struggling to speak. 'The police.'

He laughs. 'They're all a bit preoccupied. We've got time, Ellie. Plenty of time.'

I glance at the clock on the wall. When will Luca be back? It must be soon. I need to keep David talking. 'Henrietta's alive.' I take a deep breath. 'You lied to me. To everyone.'

He raises an eyebrow, moving towards the table, and places his hands flat on the surface. We stand opposite, facing each other over the fruit bowl and a half empty cup of cold coffee.

My muscles tense, ready to run. He's staring at me, and I can see the calculations he's making in his head, the distance I'd have to cover to get to the door before him. He knows he's got me trapped.

'Why . . . why did you ask me for dinner that time?' My voice quavers. 'What did you really want from me?'

He takes a couple of casual steps along the length of the table, running his fingers along the surface, and I shuffle back. He stops and smiles. 'You're different from the rest. You were a challenge. You didn't fall straight into my arms.'

'But then I left.' I swallow. 'And you didn't like that. Because you need to be in control, don't you?'

'Nobody makes a fool of me.' His eyes narrow, his voice hard.

'There's something here, isn't there?' I don't take my gaze from him. 'Something that you want.'

His cheek twitches. 'That's right.'

'You were the intruder.' My mouth is dry, remembering the figure at the top of the stairs.

'One of my men.'

'But he didn't find it. Anca didn't, either.'

He shrugs. 'We'll find it now. Together.'

'No.' I clench my hands.

He leans against the table. 'You went to the police. Friends aren't supposed to inform on each other.'

'Friends?' The knot of anger in my stomach tightens. 'You've been keeping your migrants locked up. Sending them to other farms. Beating them.'

'The farm was going bankrupt. I couldn't lose the business, the house. I couldn't fail.' He opens his fingers. 'You do see that, don't you? Failure isn't an option for me. It never has been.' He sees my face. 'Don't look like that, Ellie. I'm not the only one making money out of migrants. I'll do whatever it takes to survive. I thought you'd get that.'

He begins to move again, prowling slowly. I edge away, keeping a length of table between us. I must keep him talking. 'You told everyone that Luca raped Anca. But it was you. Her baby – he's your son.'

'Women lie.' He shakes his head. 'I took care of Anca, singled her out, gave her special food, nicer clothes. She wasn't grateful. Why is it that women are so difficult, so spoilt, they don't appreciate things the way they should?'

'That's why you beat your wife? Because she wasn't grateful?'

His mouth hardens. 'What happened between Henrietta and me is private.'

'No,' I tell him. 'It's not private. It's a crime.'

I snatch a look at the draining board with the rack of knives. Only he's between me and them. I'd never get there first. I can see a vein beating at his neck, the tensing of his shoulders.

From outside comes a sudden noise: Nutmeg's hiccupping bray. David lunges, hands reaching for me. I swivel the chair between us. But he knocks it to one side. He's got hold of my arm. Fingers digging in. I'm struggling, feet slipping beneath me. 'Someone's coming,' I gasp.

'I don't think so.' His eyes are cold. He's twisting my bicep.

I swing my free arm back, aiming at his face. He catches my wrist. His fist hits my jaw. Then another blow smashes into my cheek. Pain spins through my skull, splintering the world, sending everything red and then black. Dizzy silence.

A hammering in my brain. I'm reeling backwards, stumbling to the floor.

He's caught me. He's pulling my arms together with rough jerks behind my spine, twisting something around my wrists. Rope. I keep binder twine on the dresser. He must have seen it.

He's pushing me towards the hall. The knots bite into my flesh. We climb the stairs together, David shoving my shoulder, making me stagger.

'What – are – you – doing?' I can hardly speak. My cheek is on fire. My teeth are ringing with pain. A sound cuts into the atmosphere. A hiccupping cry. The baby. 'Don't,' I whisper. 'Please don't do this. That's your son—'

He drags me into the study and pushes me into the chair by the desk. He's kneeling at my feet, tying my ankles. I struggle, pulling my arms, twisting my hands. But the ropes won't budge. I close my eyes. Not wanting to see him.

'Open your eyes,' David's voice is saying. 'I want you to look at me. You're going to help me find the envelope that my wife gave your husband. It's somewhere in this house. I'm guessing in this room. We'll take the whole place apart if we need to.'

I clench my eyes tighter. I won't do anything he asks. I wait for the next blow. The next explosion of pain. Nothing comes. I hear a dull thump and a strange, slurred gulp. My lids snap open.

David is on his knees, a hand pressed to his head. Anca stands behind him, the cricket bat trailing from her grip. She's wearing my nightdress, her feet bare. She's panting, and she looks at me, her eyes glazed with fear. But David is already twisting around, staggering back onto his feet.

'Anca!'

He lunges for her, grabbing a handful of nightdress. She pulls back with a cry.

'Hit him!' I shriek.

She swings the bat and it cracks against his temple. He staggers to the left, and she strikes again, the wood thwacking hard onto the back of his head. Now he's on the floor on his hands and knees. I see dark red swelling through his hair. Anca stands over him, the bat raised. She hits him again. He tries to crawl away with fumbling, urgent movements on hands and knees. But the bat slams down on his neck and he slumps with a groan, lying flat. She lands another blow with a dull thud.

She looks over at me, spittle on her gaping lips. Her hands tremble around the handle of the bat and she lets it drop, fingers flaring wide. There's a slick of red on the wood, a splatter of blood on the hem of her nightdress.

David is stretched out on the floor. Liquid darkens the back of his head, trickles over his forehead. Anca lets out a cry and clasps both hands across her mouth.

'Anca. Quick. Untie me,' I gasp.

She crouches behind, panting, and her fingers scrabble. 'I can't—'

'Scissors. In the drawer.'

She finds them and saws at the ropes with sobs of frustration. Steel points scrape my skin. The strands of rope loosen and snap. My hands are free, and I'm rubbing the life back into them, bending over to untie my ankles.

David doesn't move.

'Is he dead?' I whisper.

Anca doesn't answer. Doesn't move. I squat beside him and

pick up his wrist. It's warm. There's a pulse. I drop his hand. 'He's alive.'

Anca's face contorts into a soundless wail. I go to her and put my hands on her shoulders. She slumps against me, limp and trembling. We hold each other. She stares down at David. 'I wish . . . I had killed him.' Her voice breaks.

The room spins. I'm trying to sort things into an order, trying to find a way to move on from this moment. But everything is blank. Then from across the landing, the sound of frantic screaming tears the air. The baby. He's hungry. I imagine his stretched mouth and red cheeks.

I make her look at me. 'Go to your son. He needs you.'

I kneel and loop the remaining rope around David's floppy wrists, knotting it tight. Anca is still staring at David, horror snagging her features.

'Your baby needs you,' I repeat in a loud voice. 'I'll come in a minute. I'll bring a bottle.'

It's as if she's snapping out of a trance; she looks around with wide eyes, and then starts towards the door.

I find my mobile, but as I dial the police, I hesitate and click off. What if Ian Brooks turns up? I can hear more sirens roaring towards the farm. I need to tell the police at Langshott that David's here. I double check that the rope around David's wrists and ankles is secure. His arms are hooked up behind his back, otherwise I've left him where he fell, belly down, his head twisted to the side. Sticky blood creeps across his cheek, dripping onto the rug. His eyelids twitch and flutter. He won't be able to get free of the knots. I turn the lock on the outside of the door.

The baby's cry is piercing. I hurry down to the kitchen and grab the warmed milk, running upstairs with the bottle. Anca is pacing around my bedroom, the baby in her arms. She's rocking him automatically with stiff arms. I hand her the bottle. She sits down, but doesn't seem to know what to do. I guide her hand so that she nudges the teat into his mouth. He begins to feed with greedy, desperate gulps.

'That's better,' I say quietly.

Anca looks into her son's face, and her features relax. She glances up at me and nods. Her eyes slide across, her attention caught by something behind me. 'That picture,' she nods towards the fireplace. 'Is he your husband?'

I turn towards the recently reinstated photo of William and nod. 'He was killed over a year ago, in a car crash.'

'I know about the crash,' she says. 'Your husband, he came to the Hall that night. I opened the door. He was kind to me.'

I frown. 'William came to see David?'

She moves her head. 'They went into the library with Adam.'

My head is reeling. Will was at Langshott that night with David and Adam? He must have got drunk there. Now I remember, he had been coming from the direction of the Hall when he passed me on the road. I squeeze my eyes shut. I can make no sense of it. Then the image of Luca's face swims up out of darkness, blotting everything else out. Why isn't he back? He should be home by now.

'Here's the key to the study,' I tell her. 'Don't go in there. I have to go to the farm. I'll tell the police to come here. The people from social services will take care of you and the baby. '

'Yes,' she says, but she's not looking at me any more. She's staring down at her baby, an expression of wonder on her face.

'Good luck, Anca,' I whisper. 'Goodbye, little one.'

I drop a kiss onto the small wrinkled forehead. He takes no notice either; he's concentrating on the last drops in the bottle, his eyes closed in bliss.

FORTY-FOUR

I stare about the drive helplessly, before I remember that Luca took the car. I dash into the apple-scented darkness of the garage and grab my bicycle. The sky has begun to spit, and I cycle, head down, pedalling as fast as I can. The wind is against me, and my legs are like lead. I grit my teeth, gasping as I stand up on the pedals, pushing down as hard as I can, my hands gripping the handlebars.

The lanes are deserted, and I cycle on past hop fields and oast houses, through the village and out on the road to the farm. It's raining harder, and drops sting my eyes, get into my open mouth. At least the water will help to put out the fire.

Now that I've got over the brow of the hill, I can see the rising smoke, a pitchy darkness scrubbing out the day. There is so much of it. Panic kicks in my chest. It might be faster to abandon the bike and cut across the field. I scramble over a stone wall and drop into the mud. It's thick and damp and clings to my boots.

I skid and slip onto my knees. Then I'm out of the field, clambering through a barbed wire fence, one of the prongs raking my spine. Another field, wet grass, rabbits scattering, white tails bobbing. Piles of hop poles on the ground. The smoke is in my mouth; I can taste the sour scorch of it, hear sirens, people shouting, a scream.

My heart is beating like a drum. And Luca's name is on my lips. I love him. I haven't told him yet, and I need to. It takes on a sharp and desperate importance. The need to find him and tell him.

There's a thick hedge between me and the farm. I push my way into it, struggling against thorns and stiff branches, rain-soaked leaves holding me back. I battle through, shoulder first, twigs catching, hooking and tearing at my clothes. I emerge on the other side, shaking, triumphant. But in front of me there's a fence. It's like a prison fence, tall, electrified, impenetrable. I see a notice telling me that this is private land. There are others. Red writing. No entry. Keep out. This is what Luca was talking about. A sob breaks in my throat. I have to double back, hobbling along the rough ground following the line of the fence. There's no way in. I have to go all the way to the road, to the main wrought iron electric gate. For once, it stands wide open. I sprint up the drive.

The Hall seems untouched by fire. The front door gapes. Several police cars are parked. A policeman is using a walkie-talkie. I run up to him, almost falling onto my knees, and he turns, surprised. 'David Mallory,' I pant. 'He escaped. He's at my house. He needs medical care.'

My chest is tight with impatience as I give him my address,

and repeat the news to a policewoman, who wants me to come into the house with her. I pull back. 'No. Please. My friend is here. I have to find him.'

I'm running again, following an ambulance as it goes towards the farm buildings. Its light is pulsing. I tag behind, not able to keep up, jogging past the barn, the stables.

The ambulance is rolling through the big mesh gate. The grass torn up, deep ruts gouging it, turning it to mud. There are other ambulances already there in the field. Three fire engines are parked between the caravans, engines running. I cough. The air is thick with the stink of smoke. It burns my throat. The ground is soaked. People are milling everywhere, some with blankets draped over their shoulders. Policemen with grim faces are helping workers away from the burning wrecks of caravans; two paramedics are lifting a man onto a stretcher. A group have gathered around the back of an ambulance. A girl sits with an oxygen mask on her face, bandages on her hands.

Several of the caravans are blackened carcasses, smoke pouring from the charred remains. Some are merely scorched, windows smashed, doors hanging open. One is still blazing, flames leaping from its roof and windows, and three firemen stand with a hose pointing, water rushing and hissing. The stench is unbearable: burnt plastic and metal, singed hair and wool and skin, dense, poisonous gases.

I begin to shout Luca's name, running across the broken grass. Nobody takes any notice of me. I see a familiar figure. Constanta. I stumble towards her, shouting. She doesn't seem to see me. She's rubbing her eyes. She's been crying and her tears have made tracks through her filthy face.

'Constanta.' I grab her arm. 'Are you all right?'

She stares at me wildly. 'So much fire.'

Both her eyes are swollen, her cheek is red and raw, her lip is split.

'They did this to you.'

She touches her face. 'It doesn't matter.'

I put my arms around her and she's hugging me hard. 'You'll be OK now. Your sister is at my house with the baby,' I tell her. 'Social services will make sure you're all together again.'

I pull back, staring across the field. 'Have you seen Luca?'

She looks confused, and I realise that she doesn't know him. I turn away in frustration, staring around me.

And then it occurs to me, Luca must be on his way home. I didn't see the Fiat. He wouldn't stay any longer than he had to, not now that the emergency services are here. Relief trickles inside, and I start to relax, to let go of my crushing terror. I turn for home, trudging back over the mud and grass, hearing snatches of foreign voices, the calm tones of paramedics, the crackle of radios from their vehicles. Roaring engines. It's over. The injustice of what's been going on here, the lies and the cover-ups, the cruelty. Despite my exhaustion, it's like a weight lifting. Beyond the swirls of smoke, the smuts rising into the sky, is the clarity of the day, waiting.

I need to get back. I walk faster. I want to see the baby one more time before they take him. I think of David lying on the study floor, his coagulating blood darkening the rug. I'm expecting my drive to be full of vehicles – police, ambulance, the social workers. But Luca will be there too. We can face it together.

Rain is falling steadily. Sheets of water through a grey sky, blurring trees and hedges into inky shapes, catching in the mesh of the fence, puddling inside the filthy remains of roofless caravans. I'm aware of the ache in my cheek and jaw. I move to the side to let a police van drive past, windscreen wipers going, wheels skidding in the mud. I can see a man with a camera at the gate, a policeman pushing him back. I wonder where Adam is, where the dogs are.

And then something makes me turn.

Luca is at the other side of the field. He towers above everyone else, taller and broader. He's standing with a group of others, paramedics, police. I begin to run, my feet stumbling over tussocks of rough grass, the breath coming hard in my lungs. 'Luca!'

I'm nearly there. Details spin into focus. The flames crackling at a caravan window behind him. A man on the ground; the texture of his greasy hair; the weave of the blanket around him. Luca bends down to speak to the man.

'Luca,' I call again.

He startles at the sound, standing for a moment, caught inside drifts of smoke. I see his tired, dirty face light up when he sees me. He raises a hand. Then someone screams, and he turns and begins to run towards the blazing van. A policeman puts out his arm to stop him. But Luca barges through.

A noise rips through the atmosphere – sharp, fierce – I see the outline of Luca's figure against a blaze of red and orange. Heat scalds my face.

The world has gone silent. I am on my knees in the mud. I look up, not understanding. My ears are ringing. I blink through dense black smog. Bits of litter are twirling around, scraps of paper. Grit falls from the sky. The caravan has gone. It's a shattered wreck. A shell of burning plastic.

I stagger to my feet. People are running towards the scorched ground. And then I see him, face up in the grass. Paramedics gathering around him. I push my way through. His shirt has been ripped from his chest, shrivelled fabric clinging to raw patches that I don't recognise. His face is charred, blackened. I smell burning sinew and skin. His open hands are red flesh.

Someone knocks into my shoulder as they push past. The impact unbalances me and I fall outside the ring of medics. Pain kicks through my shoulder, jarring my bones. They are rolling Luca onto a stretcher. Talking quickly. He's wrapped in a silver blanket. An ambulance arrives. I twist onto my knees, staggering to my feet to get to him, but the agony is overwhelming. The ground rocks beneath me, everything spinning. A door shuts. He is gone.

The world gathers in a roiling cloud of confusion and disappears into nothing, leaving me alone. I shiver, wracked with the breaking of lines that have been holding me steady, connecting my spirit with his, my body with his. Nausea wells up, and I kneel on the broken soil retching and retching. My fingers tangle in grass.

I close my eyes. But all I can see is the ruin of his body, his burnt empty face.

FORTY-FIVE

I seem to have been walking for miles down this green corridor. People pass me, looking equally lost. A man in a wheelchair rolls by, pushed by an orderly in white. There's the squeak of shoes on linoleum. The smell of disinfectant and plastic. I don't recognise anything, can't work out where I'm supposed to be going.

After the fire I was taken here in an ambulance. I was dizzy and weak, desperate to find Luca. It was chaotic. So many migrants had come in with burns and smoke inhalation. I refused to leave until they found Luca. He'd been in surgery – there was nothing I could do. A young doctor checked my right shoulder, my swollen cheek and jaw. She told me that I should go home and rest. They gave me painkillers, and the name of a ward. Thomas Becket. Luca would be taken there after his surgery. I waited for hours. But I couldn't talk to him even when I was eventually allowed to see him. He drifted in and out of consciousness. I sat by his bed, looking at his damaged face, until they told me to go home.

I got back to an empty cottage, and went upstairs to the study. The door was open and I stepped through it cautiously, almost expecting David to still be there, waiting for me. The scissors were open on the floor where Anca dropped them; coils of frayed rope lay next to the chair. There was a dark patch on the rug. Dried blood. The stain would never come out. I didn't want to touch it, to have any part of him in my home. I knelt and began to fold the rug back, rolling it up into a big, dusty tube.

As I heaved it into my arms, I staggered, my toe catching on something. I looked down. One of the floorboards didn't seem to be nailed down properly. I got back onto my hands and knees and felt around the splintery edges, getting my fingertips underneath to prize it up. My heart was hammering. Feeling inside the dark void beneath, my searching fingers touched paper wedged between joists: a large envelope. On the front it said: *In the event of my death – give to newspapers and police.* Henrietta's name was scrawled underneath. I ripped it open, shaking the contents out: papers and photographs shuffled out onto the desk. I picked up the photos and leafed through them – some were out of focus or at an angle, as if taken surreptitiously. And I recognised the caravans with locks on the outside; a group of dishevelled migrants getting out of a van; the bald man, Bill, pushing them into a huddle. There was a blurred picture of David raising his hand to Constanta.

Dr Waller was in one of the pictures, watching a group of migrants getting onto the bus. There were close-ups of parts of a woman's body: a wrist, ribs, thigh, all covered in green and purple bruises. I realised that it was Henrietta. She'd taken them herself. I found one of her battered face reflected in a mirror, and behind the image, her hand holding a camera. Each photo had a date on the back.

There were photocopies of documents, passports. The migrant papers. There was a list of names: I recognised Ian Brooks, Dr Waller. There were other names, too. All of David's contacts.

I remember Henrietta's words: *I've got something he wants.*

The hospital corridor is busy with people. I hear the ping of a lift arriving and follow the sound, hurrying around a corner, just in time to slip inside before the doors close. When I get out, a nurse points me in the right direction.

Now I know where I am. This is where I limped to, after the doctor sent me away. This is where they brought Luca after he came out of the operating room. My stomach flutters in anticipation.

Luca has a bed by the window. He's asleep. I approach quietly and sit in his visitor's chair. His hands are bandaged. I stare at his face. I was so afraid the first time I came. But the soot and dirt that covered him as he lay in the field has been wiped away, and the skin underneath isn't damaged, except for a jagged cut caused by flying debris. His eyebrows have been singed off. He's lost some of his hair, too. His chest took the main force when the gas canister exploded, and his hands, seared by the blast as he'd raised them to protect his face. His poor hands had already been burnt from his efforts at breaking doors down, and carrying people out of flaming caravans, before the police had arrived and taken over. But the impact of the explosion hadn't been as dangerous as the smoke inhalation he'd suffered.

He opens his eyes. I lean over and kiss his forehead, careful not to touch his cheek or his hands. 'How are you?'

'Good.' His voice croaks, still hoarse.

'I heard from Anca,' I tell him. 'She rang to let me know that she and her sister have decided to stay in England. She named the baby.' I pause. 'She's called him Luca.'

He smiles, as I'd hoped he would. But then his brow furrows. 'And you. Are you OK?'

'Yes. A bit sore, but—'

'That's not what I meant.'

'He's with his mother. It's how it should be.' I meet Luca's steady gaze. 'I'm not going to visit. Not for a while.'

'Any news of David and Adam?'

'The raid and their arrests have been all over the papers. Rachel's been arrested, too. I don't know how long it will be until the trial.' I lean forward, wishing I could hug him. 'Adam handed himself in, apparently. He's co-operating. The police are still at the farm. The whole area is cordoned off.' I widen my eyes. 'You can imagine the conversation in the village.'

He tries to speak, but his voice rasps. I pour him a glass of water and help him to drink through a straw. 'You did it,' I tell him softly. 'It's because of you.'

He moves his head on the pillow. 'No. It was Anca. You.

One thing leading to another.' His eyes fill with tears. 'There was someone in the caravan before it blew up. I heard them scream.'

'You saved so many people.'

I wish I had better words. I know he'll go on thinking of that one person – the one he didn't reach.

'Adam was there with me, before the police and fire engines arrived. He was helping people out of vans, too.'

'Adam?'

I think of him at the gates of Langshott. The way his expression softened when he talked about Constanta. And I remember that time I met him at the farm and how he seemed to want to tell me something, before Rachel came along.

Luca's face is slack with exhaustion. He raises a bandaged hand towards my face. 'Your cheek?'

'It's not fractured. I'm OK.'

'Good bruise.'

'You can talk.' I smile.

I tell him about the envelope, what was in it. 'The police have it now. Henrietta must have given it to William to keep it safe. I think she used it later to blackmail David.'

'But why wouldn't she just expose him – tell the police what he'd been doing? The abuse, Anca, the migrants?' Luca frowns.

'Because it wasn't just David that would have been caught and sent to prison. It was Adam, too. He's involved in everything. I found a letter in the envelope explaining what David's been doing, but also trying to play down Adam's role in it all. She paints him as a victim. She only intended to expose David as a last resort,' I say, 'because she feared she'd be condemning her son to jail at the same time.'

Luca makes a noise in his throat. 'The police must be looking for Henrietta, as well?'

'I gave them her number plate.' I touch my cheek. 'I feel sorry for her, knowing what she's been through. But she tried to save Adam, when he's guilty. And she did nothing to help the migrant workers, to protect Anca.'

'I suppose she was afraid. Even after David let her leave, she was probably scared of him.'

A nurse comes across. 'Visiting time is up, I'm afraid.'

'She's right,' I say. 'You need your rest.'

His eyes slide towards the poetry book, Rainer Maria Rilke, that I've brought in for him. 'Read to me before you go?'

My fingers flick through the pages. 'Any poem in particular?'

He shakes his head. 'I just want to hear your voice.'

I open the book at a well-thumbed page, clear my throat and begin to read. I carry on reading, although Luca's eyes have closed.

I shut the book and place it softly on the table beside him, remembering the moment that I stopped him on the road and asked him to work for me. Sometimes I wonder what made me trust him, and why I kept on trusting him, despite moments of doubt. It wasn't just that I'd seen his bravery inside the circus ring, or my gut feeling that he was a good man, it was also the need to prove to myself that trust doesn't have to be earned, that sometimes it can exist in the world like air, invisible and necessary.

*

The cottage is empty without Luca. And I miss the baby. Knowing that he is with Anca helps, because it's the right thing for both of them. But the lack of his gaze and milky smell is an ache. I'd become used to the physical warmth of him tucked into my neck, held against me. Without him I feel unbalanced.

Each time I fall asleep, I have nightmares about the field of burning caravans, the moment of the explosion coming back again and again. And I wake in a panic, afraid that David is outside the cottage, that I smell smoke, hear his voice, the dogs barking. But then I remember, and the first thing I see when I open my eyes is the picture of William and me on the mantelpiece opposite the bed. I stare at my husband's friendly face, his open smile.

David reappeared in my life a year after William died. Until then he'd thought he was safe – that all his secrets were safe. After Will's funeral he came to see me, to check that I didn't know anything. Then something changed. I think Henrietta got desperate. David wasn't paying her, or selling the farm. So she told him about the envelope to try and force his hand. He must have guessed that William had hidden it in our cottage. That was when he invited me to the circus. He had to develop a relationship with me as a way of getting into the cottage, to try and find the evidence and to keep an eye on me in case I found it first. I think it was him who took the missing page of William's letter. It had to be. The page would have explained what William was really doing, how he was helping Henrietta leave David. It might have told me the truth about the migrant workers.

And I remember what Anca said about letting Will into the Hall that night, and my insides clench. William would have wanted to do something to help the enslaved migrants. I think he went to see David to try to reason with him about them, about Henrietta. He didn't understand how dangerous David was. I imagine him turning up at Langshott Hall, Anca opening the door and taking his jacket, David, all smiles, ushering him into the library, Adam slipping in quietly behind and shutting the door. The first thing David would have done was to offer William a drink. As I play it out in my mind, a scene from *North by Northwest* pops into my head. It spools past my vision in black and white, James Mason and a couple of thugs forcing Cary Grant to drink a bottle of spirits. The drunken Grant being dragged outside and put into his car. I sit down, feeling sick. David chose that film for us.

And what did Henrietta say to me? 'David can't hurt me now; I know too much.' She was in the house when Will came to see David. She saw what happened that night, and she used her knowledge of William's murder to make David let her go. Her silence for her freedom and her son's safety. That was their uneasy contract.

At the police station in Canterbury, I have to wait for only a few minutes before I am shown into an office to see Chief Inspector Davies.

He gets up and shakes my hand, gesturing to the chair opposite. He's tall with thinning hair and tired eyes.

'I've taken over from Chief Inspector Brooks,' he says. 'I'm handling the Mallory inquiry.'

I know how busy this man is, so I don't waste his time. I clasp my hands in my lap. 'I think David Mallory had something to do with my husband's death; in fact I'm certain of it.'

A police officer comes in and puts two mugs of coffee on the table. The inspector spoons sugar into his cup and stirs. 'What makes you think so?'

'He went to see David at the Hall on the night of his death. And I can prove it, because Anca let him in. She'll confirm it. I think he was forced to drink alcohol. His death was arranged. I don't know how exactly – but Henrietta will, I'm sure of it. I believe it was William's murder that was the catalyst that finally made David let Henrietta go.'

He nods. 'We tracked Mrs Mallory down through the registration number you gave us. We're talking to her at the moment. I'll let you know if we get any further with this.'

'And Ian Brooks? David's friend? What happened to him?'

'He's suspended. Internal Affairs are involved. It's a separate investigation.'

'How long will it take for David and Adam to come to court?'

He shakes his head. 'It will take some time to gather all the evidence. The Mallory case is huge – several charges of statutory rape, false imprisonment, arson and criminal use of illegal migrants.'

'And now,' I say, 'William's death.'

He nods, his face grim.

They'll call me as a witness at the trial. And I'm prepared

to stand up in court, even though the thought of seeing David makes my stomach knot and my breath come fast and shallow as if I'm surfacing from a nightmare. It's the last thing I can do for William.

FORTY-SIX

Six months later

The block of flats towers over me. I shade my eyes, gazing up. Above its roof I see the disintegrating trail of an aeroplane. I ring the buzzer. Number thirty-three. A voice crackles through the intercom and I push at heavy steel doors, take the lift to the third floor. Inside the confined space, I stare into a smudged mirror and struggle to calm nervous lungs. There's the stink of fast food, someone else's perfume. Outside on the concrete walkway, graffiti makes a splurge of colour against the grey. I walk past kitchen windows, glimpsing unknown lives, inhaling cooking.

Anca opens the door. She is slim, bright eyed, dressed in jeans and a pink T-shirt. She invites me through to a little sitting room, clearly proud of her new home. Constanta comes in with a tray in her hands, and sets it on a low coffee table. She gives me a shy smile.

Over the clamour of my blood, I'm listening for the cries of the baby, knowing he'll sound different, that he'll be making noises. He's too small to speak, but he'll be trying out shapes in his mouth. I imagine him saying my name. But it's made up of difficult letters, requiring the exact positioning of lips and tongue against the roof of the mouth. D is an easy sound for babies. D for Da, Daddy, Dada, and then M for Ma, Mummy, Mama.

He will be sitting up, maybe even crawling. He'll be poking his fingers into things, plucking at different textures, wanting to taste and feel the world. I'm trying to keep my excitement under control, already feeling the warm weight of him in my arms. Will he recognise me? Perhaps he'll reconnect with my smell, the shape of my body against his. My eyes dart around the room. I'm aching for him. There are no toys, or bouncy chair; no cot or pram. I look at the neat furniture, the cheerful prints on the walls, the rag rug on the floor.

'We've been taking English lessons,' Anca tells me, smiling.

'That's good.' I nod at Constanta when she offers me milk for my tea. I don't want to upset them – they've been through so much – but I can't stop myself. 'Anca – where's your son? Where's Luca?'

She crosses her legs. 'With foster parents.'

'Foster . . . ' The room seems to empty of air. I can't breathe. I begin to pant, dragging in oxygen.

Constanta is leaning over me. 'Are you all right?'

A glass of water is pressed into my hands. I curl my fingers around the slippery cool of the glass. Automatically, I raise it and drink. Liquid enters me in hard, cold gulps.

'I don't understand.' I wipe my lips, staring around me. 'You didn't keep him?'

Anca's face closes. 'I couldn't.' She shakes her head. 'My sister and I, we have to find a way of living in this country.'

'But you'd get some support with childcare and—'

I see the sisters' blank expressions. I can't finish my sentence. My hand trembles as I place the glass on the table.

Constanta says something in Romanian, and Anca nods and replies. Then she turns to me. 'You were kind. The first person in this country to show me kindness. I want to thank you. And Luca . . . ' Her eyes brighten. 'He saved me.'

'He saved lots of people.'

I lean towards Anca, conviction searing through me. I can't let her make the same mistake as me. She will regret giving her son away. I know she will. I find her gaze. 'I never talk about this, but I want you to know something about me. When I was a girl I was raped . . . by a family friend.' The words stumble, and I swallow. 'I got pregnant.'

Anca is staring at me.

'Nobody believed me,' I go on. 'Or perhaps they did. I don't know. Maybe they just didn't want to believe it. My parents didn't support me and I was afraid. I gave my son away to be adopted. And now I have no way of tracing him.' I press my hands together. 'I've longed for him all my life.'

Anca's mouth is set in a line.

'I don't want the same thing to happen to you.' My voice cracks. I need her to hear me, to really hear me.

Anca settles her shoulders and gives me a steady look. 'Thank you. But I won't change my mind.'

'I don't think you understand . . . ' She's too calm. I want to shake her. 'He's your flesh and blood. He's not his father. He's an innocent baby. He needs his mother.'

Constanta puts her hand on my knee. 'Anca has suffered,' she says quietly.

Anca stands and walks over to the window, looking down on the roofs of Canterbury, the spire in the distance. 'We came to this country thinking we could make a life, a home. Instead we were tricked, kept like slaves. We had to work twelve-hour shifts, we were taken around the country in buses to work for other people for no pay. We weren't allowed to get off the bus to use the toilet. We weren't given any food. When we protested, we were beaten. At work, they push you harder and harder to meet the order. No rest. No drink of water. When you are treated like that – you lose your strength. Only fear exists.'

She turns to me. 'Then David began to single me out. He gave me better food. He brought me clothes to wear. He told me that he'd employ me as a cook, make my life easier, my sister's life easier. And in return he wanted me to sleep with him. At first I resisted. But I never had a choice. There was nowhere to go. He liked to give me bruises. He liked me to be afraid. My son is better off without me. There's a family who want to adopt him.' Her voice is sad and small. 'I understand what you are telling me. But when I look at my child, I see David.' She folds her arms across her chest. 'Me and Constanta want to forget. To start again.' Her voice is a whisper. 'I have nightmares. So does my sister.' She stops and presses her fist to her mouth. 'I tried. But the love won't come. It won't.'

My eyes fill with tears. I don't have the right to judge her.

'I think you love my son,' she says.

'Yes,' I manage.

Anca crouches by my chair, looking up at me. 'Then you should want him to find a family too – parents who can give him a good life.'

My head spins with confusion. My disappointment at not seeing him, at not seeing him ever again, rips away hope. I want to howl. The thought that I could adopt him presses into my head. But I am too old. Luca and I are too old to be considered.

'You know that this family . . .' I say, 'the family who want him . . . you know they're good people?'

She nods. 'They want a child badly. They have a nice home. They have love in their hearts.'

I take a deep breath. 'Then . . . it's for the best. I want that . . . I want the best for him.'

A choking noise comes out of me, and I crumple. She is holding me tight. We cling together. Her hair is a tangle over my face, and through it I'm telling her that it will be all right, and she's hugging me and whispering that our boy will be happy, will be strong and bright and loved.

I wipe my eyes. Anca takes my hand in hers. 'He'll carry you inside him. Deep down. You brought him into the world,' she says. 'The first person he saw.'

I squeeze her fingers. She has trust in people. After everything that's happened, she can have faith in strangers, believe that they will take care of her child, that they will love him. If she can believe it, then I must too.

'You lost your husband,' Anca says. 'Something bad happened that night at the Hall, didn't it? Before the crash?'

I nod, pressing my hands together. 'Henrietta told the police that William went to the farm to try to reason with David. David knew that William's next move would be to report him, so he offered him a whisky and pretended to consider what William was saying. Then David and Adam restrained him, forced him to drink a whole bottle of spirits. When Will was blind drunk, David put him in the car – he got the idea from one of his favourite films.'

'Film?' Anca looks confused. 'But … but they couldn't have known your husband would crash the car, even if he was drunk.'

'David told William to hurry home, that I'd had an accident. Adam had already gone ahead along the lane. He was waiting around a corner with his dogs. When he heard Will's car coming, he released them. They ran into the road and Will swerved and crashed. Adam was supposed to check that William was dead. But he couldn't, because I'd arrived on the scene.'

Anca shakes her head, puts her hand on my arm. 'I'm sorry.' Her voice is quiet. 'David beat his wife. He beat me. But Adam didn't hit Constanta – in the end he tried to protect her. I think he hated his father for what he did to his mother, but at the same time he wanted to be like him. It was as if there were two sides to him, his mother and his father – and he couldn't be true to both.'

'I got a letter from Adam,' Constanta says. 'From prison. He told me he was sorry for everything. He had a message for you.'

'Me?'

'He said he knows he can't ask forgiveness. And he said,' she frowns. 'I need to remember the words. He said he hopes his real mother – his birth mother – is as strong as you.'

I can't speak for a moment. I shiver, looking around at the bare and unassuming room, the bright daffodils in a vase, so different from the grandeur of Langshott Hall. 'You didn't want to go home?'

Constanta gestures around her. 'This is what we dreamt of when we first came. We want a new life, to work hard, send money to our family.'

'It's ironic – just as you're settling here, I'm leaving.'

'Leaving?' Anca and Constanta chorus together.

'I'm selling the tearoom,' I tell them. 'The cottage, too. Luca and I are going to move.'

'Where?'

'I don't know.' I smile. 'Just somewhere else. Luca once said that he could turn his hand to anything. Well, so can I. We can start again.'

'Your animals?'

'They'll come with us.'

The sisters stand at the door of their flat. Anca puts her arm around Constanta's waist. They wave goodbye, their smiles bruised and wise. The door closes.

My feet drag as I walk towards the lift. I stop and close my eyes, swaying. My palm presses against rough concrete. I hear the shuffle of feet; breathing. My eyes snap open. It's a young man, a hoodie over his face partly obscuring his features. He's standing too close, a chain swinging around his neck.

'You all right, love?'

I nod, standing upright. 'Yes.'

He hovers anxiously, watching me. 'Sure?'

I force a smile. 'Thank you.'

He wanders off, but I'm not looking at him any more. I'm imagining a couple taking a baby carefully into their arms, looking into his small face. I let them go, that couple and the boy cradled between them. A sadness inside me shifts; a lightness comes in its place.

I need to go. I'm too impatient to wait for the lift. I take the stairs, three flights, my feet clattering on concrete, and push through the doors, going out into the busy street, into the swell of midday traffic.

Luca will be in the garden, the cat trailing behind him, her tail in the air. Or he'll be in the orchard, under the apple trees and fading ribbons, a poetry book in his hand. He's waiting for me so that we can finish packing together, then we'll sit across from each other at the kitchen table, a map spread before us as we make our plans.

Walking towards my car, I break into a jog. The impulse to run takes over. My legs gather speed, so that I'm sprinting along the pavement, my bag flapping behind, my jacket slipping over my shoulders.

It's busy. Everyone out on their lunch breaks. I have to dodge between solitary walkers, shoppers, groups of meandering office workers clogging up the path with takeaway coffees and laughter and careless gossip. I weave and duck between them, calling out 'sorry' and 'excuse me', my breath catching in my throat. Frustration gathers like a knot as I have to slow, stumbling around bodies.

But one by one, they move. Startled strangers stepping out of my way, letting me past. It feels as though they are setting me free.

AUTHOR'S NOTE

I wanted to tell a story that had the plight of enslaved migrants at its heart, and my plan was to set it in the 1990s, around the time that the Chinese cockle pickers drowned. But I was writing my manuscript over the summer of 2015, and the biggest migration of refugees since the Second World War was happening. It was obvious to me that I had to make changes and set my novel in the present, so that I could include this unfolding tragedy. The radio and TV were full of stories covering the events, and like so many others I became a witness, an onlooker from the safety of my sitting room, as people risked their lives and their children's lives in flimsy boats, and trekked across countries only to be turned away at borders, put into makeshift shelters and kept there indefinitely. As I write this, the struggle of many to flee war and poverty and find new homes is still causing political battles, outrage and fear; it's also opened people's hearts and minds. Amongst the horror, the pictures of dead children on beaches, there are glimmers of hope, examples of kindness, stories of strangers helping strangers. And I wanted in some way to include that too in my novel.

Anca and her sister are fictional, but their story is one that is being enacted all over the world. Although the Trans-Atlantic slavery trade was abolished in the nineteenth century, the International Labour Organisation estimates that around twenty-one million men, women and children are still slaves all over the world. In the UK it's estimated that there are over ten thousand people in modern slavery, mainly in forced labour, domestic work, sex exploitation and criminal activities such as cannabis growing. Many work out in the open, in fields, in offices, in sight of ordinary people living ordinary lives. Unbelievable as it seems to us, they can't walk away. Most are migrants made vulnerable by being in a strange country where they don't speak the language fluently or understand the law. All are kept against their will through a mix of violence, physical restraint, mental and physical threat, financial debt, lies and fear.

Humanity is better than this, should be better than this. Nobody is born to be another's slave. No human, no creature, should ever be put in a cage. And a stranger is only a stranger until we hold out our hand in greeting.

The Stranger

Reading Guide

Reading Group Questions

1. What are the main themes in this story?
2. Do you agree that the stranger of the title could refer to a number of different characters?
3. Can you comment on Eleanor's backstory? Do you think backstories influence the ways in which a reader responds to a character?
4. Were you taken in by David's character? Did you trust him in the way that Eleanor seemed to?
5. What are your thoughts on the love triangle between Eleanor, David and Luca? Do you understand why Eleanor was drawn to Luca?
6. Can you discuss the way in which the villagers react to migrant workers in their community?
7. Are you sympathetic to the decisions Eleanor makes in regards to her husband, David and Luca?
8. Do you think you can ever truly *know* somebody?
9. Can you comment on Anca's role in the story?
10. How did the ending make you feel, in regards to David, Luca, Eleanor and Anca?

Author Q&A:

What inspired you to write The Stranger?

Several different things came together and began to bubble up into an idea for a novel – I was driving through a tiny, 'perfect' English village and I wondered what that façade might hide. Then I read about migrants kept prisoner on an English farm, and a little later, I watched the refugee crisis unfolding. I wanted to put these elements together, and thought it was the ideal time to experiment with a more overt thriller genre.

Do the themes explored in the story have any bearing on your own life experiences?

No, not really. This is a novel that has come largely from my imagination and less from my own experience. The motherhood theme is one I understand from the inside, as I have four children. So I could relate strongly to Ellie's grief at losing her baby, not being able to have another child, and her need to be a mother.

The plot is very carefully layered. Can you talk us through the writing process?

I wish I could tell you that I approached it with military precision and had wall charts cross-referencing everything. But it wasn't like that! I had a fairly tight synopsis, but found it had to change as I wrote my way into the story. Sometimes it felt as though I'd written myself into a dead end – but puzzling out solutions proved to be a creative process.

Did a lot of research go into writing the novel?

I read a lot about the refugee crisis and talked to charities like Walk Free about the plight of domestic slaves in the UK. It was a sobering experience. I had no idea of the extent of domestic slavery in this country, and it seemed incredible to think of slaves in 2016. I really hope that in some small way my novel might spread the word about this horrific, shameful reality.

The Stranger *can be considered a dark love story but it has definite thriller undertones. Do you enjoy experimenting with genre?*

I do enjoy experimenting with and mixing genres – I never set out to write a book based on genre, but rather on character and story.

A number of your novels have been set in Suffolk. Can you tell us why you chose to set this novel in Kent?

I chose Kent because it's known as the garden of England – it's full of fruit and soft fruit farms; these farms are often worked by migrant labourers.

What motivated you to write about migrant workers?

I read about the drowned Chinese cockle pickers with horror. Later, another story emerged in the press about migrants kept prisoner on an English farm. I was appalled by the way migrants and refugees were being written about by some journalists. The lack of humanity made me think about who these people really were, all these strangers that the press were depicting in terms of mere numbers were someone's mother, father, child, sibling, uncle, aunt.

In your mind, who is the 'stranger' of the title?

I suppose Luca is the obvious character to claim the title. But of course the novel is full of strangers – William becomes a stranger to Ellie after his death; Ellie thinks David is a particular kind of person, but he turns out to be someone else entirely. Her lost child is a stranger to her. The migrants are strangers to the villagers. There are two sides to the meaning of the title: the first refers to the fact that we can never really know anyone completely. But the flip side is that a stranger can become a friend once we've reached out a hand to them.

Can you tell us the part of the story that moves you the most? And that scares you the most?

The part of the story that moved the most, as I wrote it, is when Ellie accepts that Anca's baby is lost to her as well as her own child. But with that loss comes a greater kind of selfless love, and a trust in humanity. The part that scared me most is the part when David comes back and breaks into her kitchen to threaten her – I enjoyed writing that scene and scaring myself.

What are you working on now?

I'm writing a book called *The Wonderful* set on an American airbase in 1950s England in the midst of the Cold War. I've mixed up my genres again, with elements of family drama, love story and thriller. There's even a dash of science fiction!